TRY NOT TO DIE

At

Meadow Spire Mall

P.W. FEUTZ

VINCERE
P R E S S

Published by Vincere Press
65 Pine Ave., Ste 806
Long Beach, CA 90802

Try Not to Die: At Meadow Spire Mall

Printed in the United States of America
First Edition

ISBN: 9781961740266
Library of Congress Control Number: 2024921983

Front and back cover by Jun Ares
Interior illustration by Cat Scully
Edit by Mark Tullius and Horrorsmith Editing

This one's for J.L.

P.W.

A Note from the Publisher

Although I didn't play a part in writing this novel, I'm thrilled to release P.W.'s second title in the *Try Not to Die* series. Three years ago, I had the privilege of mentoring P.W. through the Horror Writers Association, and was immediately impressed by his talent. He did such a great job coauthoring *TNTD: Back at Grandma's House*, I was confident he'd kill it writing his own title.

This novel, the longest to grace the series, blew away my expectations. P.W. has done an incredible job transporting us back to 1998, creating characters and creatures you won't soon forget. So get ready to return to your high school days for a quick trip to the mall.

Make bad decisions. Live on the edge. Learn you're not immortal. And have fun trying not to die.

Mark Tullius

What's the name for air that's bound to earth?

Floating and flying and so close to touching

Grazing this port without accepting a berth

Above and aloof, caressing, takes nothing

Praise is given to the air that gives breath

By light and rain and rays of the sun

Which stays by our side, lays over our death

Its life-giving work moving on, never done

Unto us it bows, this partner in dance

Whose music makes steps we take at its will

Whose lyrics whisper earth into a trance

Before dropping our hand and giving our fill

And troubled earth tumbles down, far too shy

To stop its flight and cry, how I love you, oh, sky

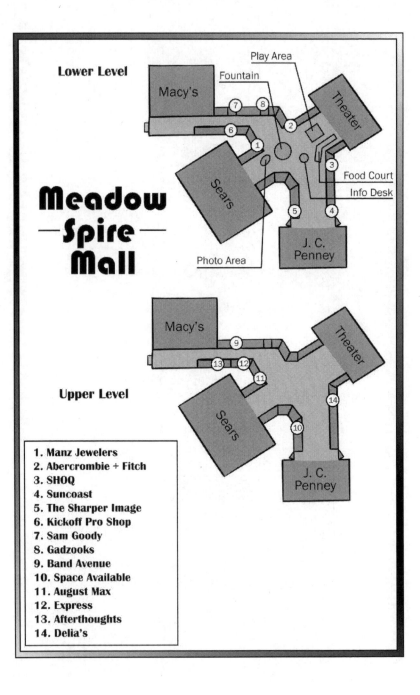

Lower Level

Play Area

Fountain

Macy's

Theater

7 8

6 2

1

Sears

3

Food Court

Info Desk

**Meadow
—Spire—
Mall**

5 4

Photo Area

J. C.
Penney

Upper Level

Macy's

Theater

9

13 12

11

Sears

14

10

J. C.
Penney

1. Manz Jewelers
2. Abercrombie + Fitch
3. SHOQ
4. Suncoast
5. The Sharper Image
6. Kickoff Pro Shop
7. Sam Goody
8. Gadzooks
9. Band Avenue
10. Space Available
11. August Max
12. Express
13. Afterthoughts
14. Delia's

TRY NOT TO DIE
At Meadow Spire Mall

Kill me now.

I don't have a lot of time left, so seriously, make it end.

Even from under the covers, where I've been cocooned in the same hot bubble since midnight, I sense the light creeping in, the drapes recovering their color, the blinds glowing brighter by the second. The February wind pushes at the panes. The night didn't last forever like I wished for—the *only* thing I can wish for after what happened yesterday.

My parents move around downstairs, perfectly predictable, guided by habit: front door for the Saturday paper, kitchen for the coffee maker, clanking of pans, and sizzle of the skillet. Soon will come creaking knees up the stairs, shuffling into the ensuite bathroom, running water and brushing teeth, closet doors clapping, rustling of bodies wrestling into clothes. Then the knock on my door. A singsong scolding.

C'mon, dear. Up and at 'em.

The routine might go faster this time. Less dawdling downstairs. Dad'll glance at Mom, who'll be chewing her fingernails to the quick while the steam from her coffee disappears and the liquid goes cold. He'll crease his brow, rush through the funnies—he *never* rushes through the funnies—fold the paper with a sigh, and find out what in the actual hell is wrong with his youngest daughter.

Crick, crick, crick.

Knock, knock, knock.

Quinn, you decent?

Spare me the chitchat. Take me now.

Everything I need is right here. I'm a pharaoh ready to shuttle off to the afterlife, brains scrambled for a canopic jar. Do it before they come looking, while I'm warm and cozy and barricaded from the rest of the world. I already know what's out there, what everyone's thinking, and there's nothing I can do about it.

Let's really give them something to think about. Me dying. How about that? Let everyone start out whispering and laughing and mocking and saying, "I'd die if that happened to me!" Let *that* be the truth.

Let the truth trickle in one phone call at a time. Let it spread from greasy lips across tables at Burger King, between tilted heads in the stands at the next basketball game. Let the headline appear after the gossip is subsumed by the rumor. Let the jeers of "Did you see her face?" be followed by "Shut up, dude. She died!"

Let that sink in.

Cheerleader Dead. Shouldn't Have Laughed, Folks.

And why not die like this? People would kill to go out in their pajamas, curled up in bed, head stuffed under a pillow.

Bridie's awake, moving down the hall. She won't look in on me, but if she's up, that confirms it's getting late.

The day is here, tapping its watch like, "Yeah, sorry. It's that time." Like the tiny-bladdered person at the movies getting up for the third trip to the bathroom, moving on tiptoes all sneaky and quiet, like you won't notice, but their butt's right in your face. You're ruining it, dude. Just admit it.

I don't think I can do it.

Yesterday, I barely managed, sleepwalking through class, marble-eyed and half grinning, pretending I was in on the joke. Raina kept her mouth shut and gave me space, but Kirsten didn't help, talking about tracking down the culprits, punishing every last one of them, threatening everyone in our vicinity. I tried to convince her I was fine, convince *myself* I was fine, pretend it was all a misunderstanding or an exaggeration of what really happened. Anyone who bothered to ask if I was okay went and did what I would've done if it had happened to them—they avoided me the rest of the day.

Please, give me the never-ending night like I asked for. I've been up the entire time anyway, counting heartbeats, chipping seconds out of the marble of eternity. Whenever I managed to doze off, I blinked awake in a flash of confused alertness, getting that falling-backward feeling of panic at the approaching day. Let me squeeze the night to my chest, and I'll never ask for anything ever again.

There's something about having so much stolen from you, the first thing that comes along that doesn't hurt you feels like it's saving you. The night's become my keepsake of a false salvation. It's the rope pulling me out of the ocean, and I want to hold onto it, even if it's like asking a surgeon to keep my tumor in a jar forever.

Seriously, what's taking so long? Don't make me face another day.

The night didn't last. It's like the inverse of the first time I heard *Ten* all the way through, when all the particles spread across the expanse of my life came together in a Big Bang, kneading together everything I wanted to scream. Then it burst, and every day after was another screw-you to that perfect suspension of my being, and I could never gather up those pieces again because they'd been blown so far apart.

I haven't had many eternities like that, not outside the odd album here, book there, or sleepover with Kirsten. But this eternity is one I'm happy to claim. Things can't get any worse. They can't get any better.

It's supposed to be terrible out today. They've been saying it since, like, Tuesday. Maybe Mom and Dad will leave me alone. Maybe they'll slow down, and I can stay curled up here a little longer. Maybe that means death can wait too. Keep it on speed dial, but don't call just yet.

My body's too stiff. I spread-eagle from the fetal position. Staying on my stomach, I splay my fingers and toes, enjoying the burn from the stretch, the coolness of the sheets on my ankles and wrists. A part of me wonders if I need more of this, moving around, shaking things off. Before the thought gains traction, I curl back into a ball and pull the pillow tighter to my head to block out the light.

So what if they come for me? I'll tell them to get lost.

They won't corner me into talking. I've never given them reason to—I'm a Good Girl, trademark, all rights restricted. The day's prospects improve. I can lay low and forget anyone knows who I am. Disappear. It's the best feeling I've had all morning.

I don't have to be dead. Instead, I can just be invisible, so unimportant I barely exist. I nuzzle my mattress just thinking of it, breathing in my own smell.

Yeah, I can get myself up if I have to, as long as everyone shuts their faces.

A sound reaches me through the walls.

Suddenly, I'm exposed more than if I'd been doing naked backflips at the intersection of University and Midvale, gaped at by an audience of University of Wisconsin students. My stomach tightens and my heart flutters. I go into a full body freeze.

It's a *burring* sound. We got new cordless phones around Christmas. They have this weird, muted ring, so it's like they're behind a wall, even if you're right next to them. Four receivers are spread around the house, ringing for my family to hear, which at this hour on a Saturday morning is highly unusual.

The sound stops. Someone's picked up.

I hope for a telemarketer or a wrong number. Or maybe it's an emergency. Maybe someone else has died! Maybe Great-Grandma bought it.

There are footsteps. Up the stairs. Coming for me.

There's no denying it. The night is ripped away from me, like a stuffed animal from a too-old child.

The door swings open, and the cold gust of reality billows through the comforter and over my back. Bridie mutters for me to pick up the damn phone if I know it's for me. Something hits my pillow, heavy enough the impact drills into my skull like a golf ball. Bridie shuts the door, ignoring what I've made of my room, as well as my grunt of protest.

Day is here. I'm forced back into the inevitable, with all the tricks and traps and theatrics I've known I can't hide from forever.

Throwing off my pillow, I kick the comforter away and twist onto my side, blindly grabbing for the phone Bridie lobbed at my head. My fingers knock it backward, almost pushing it off the bed. I lunge to get it and pull it up to my face. It presses hair into my mouth, and I spit out a strand, but that just makes things worse. My saliva sticks the hair in place. I look out at the devastation of my room.

Ugly gray light from a parchment-paper sky blasts through my windows. My cocoon has been shed, my body heat ballooning to the ceiling like a mushroom cloud. Goosebumps rise on my arms when cold air washes over me.

The room looks back in astonishment: the disheveled pink and purple bedding, the nightstand scratched by rings and earrings, dirty clothes on the dresser. Egg-yellow walls that normally smile sweetly add a question mark to their wake-up call. *Good...morning?* There's more to the mess today. Blank walls with putty marks, toppled trophies and flopping prize ribbons, streaks cut through the makeup dust on the broken vanity from when I swept away my photographs. Half the mirror is missing, and I don't see my miserable face in it from where I lie.

I couldn't take them all looking at me. The people in my room. People I know, people I admire or crush on...

No...not crush. Not anymore.

And troubled earth tumbles down, far too shy
To stop its flight and cry, how I love you, oh, sky

Traces of celebrities are left on the ripped corners of posters where the putty refused to quit. Skeet Ulrich, Matthew Sweet, Eddie Vedder, Susannah Hoffs, the chicks in Hole—they're eating carpet now. Magazines with wilted pages and obliterated spines are all under my bed. They can't see me like this. What if they're just as bad as everyone else? What if they laugh too?

Then there are the people who know me—my friends photographed at peak craziness and slipped into the inside frame of my vanity mirror, who watch me get ready every morning, crowded around my powdered cheeks. Now they're smiling at the ceiling or living in a drawer that was slammed shut so fast, it probably broke the track.

Why do I have to do this? Why can't I just die? Why, why, why?

Fine. Let them all laugh at me. Let them make a spectacle of me. In fact, I don't care anymore. I can die, or they can die, or we can all die together.

Get it over with. I hate everything.

Squinting until it burns, I grab my hair and squeeze to hurt my scalp, flatten my tongue so when I bite down, it's clamped between my molars. It removes some of the pain from my heart and spreads it around, enough to make me take the next step, even though it only leads to more heartache and humiliation.

Inhaling deeply, I lift myself onto my elbows and look at my room, which I don't want to leave. I consider putting on clothes I don't want to wear and speak the one word into the phone I don't want to say.

"Hello?"

A voice I don't want to recognize tells me the last thing I want to hear.

"Yo! Get your ass out of bed, slut! It's a girls' day today."

Tell her no and hang up. Turn to page 318.

Whatever. Get out of bed and deal with Kirsten when she comes over—because she's totally coming over. Turn to page 11.

A bloodstained guy leans out of Suncoast. His paunchy front and goatee are stained bright red. He looks close to my parents' age, a little more haggard, maybe a product of rougher living or harder partying. The man whispers and gestures again. I know I'm staring, working out what to make of him.

Kirsten asks, "What the hell's this now?"

Good question. It bounces around in my head too. How many people are in there with him? Is it safe? If so, do they know this place is about to fall down?

I mean, the door's right there.

So maybe they don't know...but I don't know something either. I scan the other darkened storefronts—ones we've passed, ones we haven't. How many more are hiding survivors instead of monsters? What if Bridie's in one of them and I never thought to check?

I approach tentatively, unable to shake the sense this guy looks like an ax murderer from any number of horror movies. He gets antsy, reaching for me at one point, only for someone to pull him back into Suncoast.

"Quinn, what're you doing?" Kirsten asks.

"Yeah, Quinn, we gotta go. I already tried—" Prairie starts, but Kirsten grabs my arm before she can finish.

I shake her off and call out to the man, as if he'd know the answer. "Who else is in there?"

"Get in! Come on!"

"But who's in there? Who do you have with you?"

I think back to our other encounters with people post-catastrophe. The panicked mob in the hardware department, Warren the security guard...Anyone could be with anyone. No one's in control. And no one's thinking straight.

"Just get in. Don't listen to that pink girl," urges the man.

"Bridie?" I call out. My heart's not in it. I don't say it loud enough for anyone beyond the entrance to hear.

But it gets the man's attention. He whispers something to the person behind him, who goes into the store.

I march up to him. The man shrinks away, beckoning still, pleased to see I'm coming. The girls are right on my tail.

"Quinn, this is insane."

"We can't help them."

"Quinn, I tried! They won't come with us," Prairie insists.

"Bridie isn't in there." Kirsten grabs my shoulder.

"Stop!" I shout.

None of them realize how much I need to know if Bridie is in there or not. It's like checking the most obvious place for your keys or sunglasses or whatever all over again, just to make sure you're not crazy and they're right where you always put them.

"I have to check."

Prairie says, "Quinn, don't you think I'd know if she was in there? Or that she'd know I was out here? They kept inviting me in, and I kept saying no."

"She could be hurt," I argue.

"Quinn, please. Do not go in there."

The man hangs back while I cross the threshold. A few more men materialize from around displays. They close in behind me, blocking the other girls. I don't let it bother me when arguments break out.

Other people huddle closer to the back, but it's too dark for me to see. People sit on the floor. Children whimper in their mothers' arms. They hunker down and nurse wounds. It's a triage center set in shadows, filled with groaning and weeping. To further confuse the scene, VHS tapes, coffee table books, and collectible figurines litter the floor.

"Bridie!" I call more loudly. We don't have much time.

Silence. But I feel better for checking. My stomach unknots itself, only to re-tangle when I realize she's still as lost as before.

The girls keep arguing with ax-murderer man. He wants them to come inside. They're attempting to fend him off, trying to reach me, confusing him, angering the other men. It grows louder.

"Bridie," I call once again, and this time, my own voice is absorbed by the walls, falling on deaf ears.

There's nothing hopeful about this place, no healing going on here. It reeks of something...An unpreparedness. When I don't get an answer, I know it's time to go. I can't leave the girls to the men out front, so I start inching away.

A head pops up from the new VHS release rack.

"Did you say Bridie?" asks a teenage boy.

My heart burns. Adrenaline, relief—I don't know what to call it— makes me go up to him.

"Yes! Bridie Carpenter. Is she here? Is she hurt?"

"I know the name. Like, I don't go to school with her, but I know it from track or something."

"Sure, but is she here? Is she okay?"

The boy scratches his head and looks over his shoulder. "Anyone here named Bridie Carpenter?"

I move deeper into the store again, scanning the silhouettes, looking for someone recognizable. The farther inside, the more the swampy odor of the concourse is replaced by the smell of blood, which only works my heart into another frenzy and makes me move faster, crouching to study faces. There's a taste on the tip of my tongue, a kind of bright spark. I realize now what that smell is...and what they mean by the smell of fear.

"Quinn," Raina shouts, "get outta there."

"Please, Quinn! Remember the store upstairs! Those sounds!"

A scuffle breaks out at the entrance. Prairie's warnings become more frantic.

A metallic shiver rends the air and sends the bodies around me into a frenzy of limbs scrambling over one another, startled into action. The security gate has been pulled down. The girls are left outside. They scream my name and rattle the mesh thrown down across the threshold.

"Quinn!" Prairie screams.

The piercing intensity of her voice prepares the way for a shriek of rending metal from the back of the store.

Remember the store upstairs.

What about it?

Something dashes past my feet, causing me to trip and fall into a stack of clamshell-cased kids' movies.

The screaming starts. Startled refugees begin to move.

Something with a spidery gait crawls over me, its legs pressing into my arms and legs. It ignores me in favor of those on the move.

I scramble backward, praying the girls are ready to open the gate and get me out of here, but one of the creatures decides I'm fair game. It dives straight into my stomach, fangs out.

The initial dual sting is followed by an icy cold sensation spreading through me, filling my legs, then rising with the flow of blood into my heart and my face. I bat away at the thing's relatively tiny head, but it pins me to a display case.

My arms fail me, and soon, my brain inflates with the anesthetic until I'm flying. Nothing about this store or Bridie or the girls bothers me anymore. The little water strider spider thing keeps me pinned until I fade away.

The correct choice was trying to convince these people to follow you.
Turn to page 192.

By the time I get downstairs, Kirsten is already inside. I hear her before I see her holding court at the kitchen table, back perfectly straight. She sits over a mug and a plate of buttered toast with the corners nibbled off, waving her hands while she talks. Kirsten's freshly made-up, hair straightened, wearing skintight jeans with a cream sweater. Ready to go out and be seen.

The clock says it's half past nine. An unseasonable housefly, apparently woken by the warm spell, trundles from the window above the sink and out into the hallway.

Mom bustles behind the counter, putting away the bread and peanut butter and jam jars, filling the dishwasher, twisting at the waist to face Kirsten and play the attentive host.

It doesn't register with either of them when I slump in the chair farthest from Kirsten, one of the chairs that sits empty for family dinners, reserved for guests only. Kirsten is in my normal spot. I'm wearing my oversized cheer hoodie, an XL I like to stuff my knees up into whenever we have a scary movie night, my hands shoved down the opposite sleeves to stay warm.

That's about the greatest length I've gone to make myself presentable. After I hung up with her, I lay back on the covers, knowing she was coming. Only after the front door opened and Dad's loud greeting filtered through the floor did I slip out of bed, pull my hair into a messy ponytail, and brush my teeth to eradicate the taste of plaque fuzz.

It's the pathetic card I have to play today. The worse I look, the more sluggish I am, the better. It only gives Kirsten more reason to insist on getting me out of the house, but I just can't summon the fakeness to pretend I'm fine. I mean, she'd see through that too, but it'd have been the preferable approach—insist she's come over for nothing, make an excuse about some prior plans, boot her out gently.

"Good morning, my fair lady."

Her address makes a chill run down my spine. I'd immersed myself in the cadence of her storytelling, whatever it was about, though I've hardly been paying attention. Cheer, friends, teachers, college—it's like background music. I'm content to be ignored.

Kirsten squints at me from across the table, her nose scrunched ever so slightly in a play-angry sneer. Her teeth chip off a toast corner, and she puts the slice down, looking virtually unchanged, but she chews as widely and loudly as if she'd stuffed a handful of Tostitos in her mouth. She brushes a blond bang back behind her ear. It glows white against her newly bronzed skin. Her spring break base tan, even though it's over a month away—as jarring to my Wisconsin-wintered eyes as blood on snow.

"You gonna make me eat for the two of us?"

Mom joins in. "What can I make for you, sweetie? You must be famished."

Kirsten's eyes dart to her. "Why do you say that?"

Before I reply, they're off to the races. Mom doesn't know what happened, and I don't want her to. It was the only thing that really got me out of bed: knowing Kirsten would sneak it into conversation while I was away.

"She didn't eat dinner last night. She just disappeared into her room."

"She didn't eat dinner?" Kirsten's gaze falls on me. "That's not a trend, is it? You know, Maura, that Whitney girl we went to grade school with? She got into modeling in, like, Milwaukee and Chicago. This is after she tried the whole beauty pageant thing, but there's no way she could answer all the world peace questions. Plus, you make more money modeling, and you don't have to win anything. Well, I heard she was anorexic, and if you're a model, apparently that's perfectly normal, and it's, like, what they expect you to do, but it's practically ripping her family apart. And no one wants to be her friend anymore, so what good is all that money if your life is destroyed? It's like it's contagious."

"That Whitney" used to be just "Whitney"—Whitney Malewski, one of our old homeroom friends from grade school, until she won a local pageant and devoted more weekends to the circuit. Kirsten never got over it.

She whispers "anorexic" like it's a curse. Her implication forces me to cock an eyebrow for Mom, the serial worrier, whose eyes flash on me to gauge my take on Kirsten's BS. We're not going to add fears of an eating disorder to the mix today, thank you very much.

Mom catches my reaction and reads the truth in a whipcrack of mother-daughter understanding. She continues tidying. If Mom lingered a millisecond longer, Kirsten might've gotten the wrong idea and thought Mom truly was worried about my eating. Gossip for centuries.

"That's awful," Mom murmurs.

"Oh my God, Maura. I swear I heard the girls track team was up to something like that last spring. They had these big dinners before meets because the coaches said they had to carb load or whatever. But then you know what? They didn't want to be fat, and they didn't think the pasta helped because they felt so bloated, so they'd go purge together. You know what that means?"

"I, uh...I'm not sure I follow." Mom's getting worried now. You hit her with too much crap, and it starts to stick. "Isn't that...?"

"Yeah. The big 'B'...Well...yeah, the big 'B' because the little 'B' would just be barfing, but same thing, right? We would never do that on cheer, Maura. Never. Especially if I make captain. I would shut that down immediately. None of my girls would get involved in that. Especially not Quinn."

"I should hope not." Mom finds what she needs to turn her back on Kirsten, though she refills the coffeemaker with anxious speed. Grounds patter onto the countertop while she scoops.

"*Especially* not my Quinny-girl. So, this means we can start with brunch, huh?" Kirsten takes a big bite of her toast and licks the butter from her fingers, staring at me the whole time.

Brunch, she says?

Dad walks in behind her, mug in one hand, paper in the other. "Quinn, you're up. Look at what magic you wrought, Kirsten."

"I take all the credit, Mr. Carpenter."

He joins Mom behind the counter and massages her shoulders. I sink into my seat, and Kirsten crinkles her face. It's gross, sure, but it's also strange getting swept up in everyone's normalcy after an entire prehistoric era spent in my room and lost in my head.

Dad pecks Mom's cheek and refills his coffee, but instead of leaving, he leans his hip into the counter. "So, ladies, what're the Valentine's Day plans? Not any hot dates to make a dad worry, I'm sure?"

Dad loves Kirsten, and it drives Mom insane. She and I recognize Kirsten for who she is. We live with it. Mom maybe less so. But I experience enough of the good to look past Kirsten's worst parts, or so I tell myself.

Dad, on the other hand, sees only what she puts out there: a chipper, glowing cheerleader at the height of her life, destroying the grade point average, photographed in the Sunday paper with pompoms high in a "V" above muddy football players, dragging boys attached to her ankle down the school halls, linked arm-in-arm with her sister-classmates but always a half-stride ahead. Sweet and mean and gracious and vicious, all at the same time—the epitome of the high school queen bee.

In Dad's eyes, Kirsten is the perfect companion to lead his younger daughter through the most eventful years of her suburban life, having all the fun and avoiding all the consequences. He's with Bridie and me too much to know we don't embody the same fantasy, so he lives vicariously through her.

Kirsten, meanwhile, takes pleasure in puncturing the fantasy every now and then to keep him on his toes.

"I could always have a hotter date," she purrs. Kirsten bats her eyelashes like a dragonfly beats its wings.

I nearly gag. Dad blanches, and it's a good thing he isn't sipping coffee. Spit Take City.

"But for real? It's actually the hottest date—with my girl Quinn. It's a mall day today. No boys whatsoever. We'll castrate whatever comes our way."

Dad recovers, his marriage in the balance. "Really? Even on Valentine's Day?"

"It's not Valentine's Day." Kirsten tilts forward in her chair and lowers her voice. She rests her chin on her hand and shoots me a dark, conspiratorial look, making me feel like she's thrown a blanket over us at a middle school sleepover. "It's *Anti*-Valentine's Day."

"There you go, making us worried fathers proud," Dad says, his attention drifting to the gurgling coffeemaker.

Mom swaps out the pot for his mug to speed him along. "Isn't the weather supposed to change today? I don't want you girls getting caught out in anything."

"Pfft, it's nothing. And even if it is, the whole way out to Meadow Spire will be salted and plowed. Where else is there to go around here?"

"I'd say it's already started," Dad mumbles.

A gust of wind sends snowy debris clacking against the front west-facing windows.

"Better decide fast, if you want to get any shopping in." He tucks the paper under his arm while Mom slides him his mug, then plants a kiss on top of my head before leaving.

It seems I don't have a say in the day's plans. I haven't said a damn thing. Mom might've noticed. Her worry lines are prominent.

"Have you decided on breakfast, sweetie?"

Before I tell her to load me up on enough eggs and sausage to give me heartburn, then agree the weather is horrible and I'm feeling flu-ish and I have too much homework to do, Kirsten butts in.

"You need a little more than breakfast to get you going." She says it suggestively, leaning over her plate and coming as close to me as the table allows.

My guts burn at her bringing up the bulimia thing again, anything to scare my mom until I say what's really bothering me. But remember Whitney? *That* Whitney? *Maura, it's so tragic. It happens to the people you'd least suspect.*

I glare at Kirsten. *That* Kirsten—the one Mom and I see under the polished exterior, the one who threatened to make yesterday worse than it already was. *Don't.* I bore it into her skull, and when she doesn't react, only holds my glare, I think she'll finally give me airtime.

Once again, I open my mouth to speak.

"I mean...after yesterday," she says.

Mom's head shoots up. She overfills her mug and scrambles to clean up the mess.

Dad reenters, hankering some cream for his coffee.

"Kirsten," I say through gritted teeth, "I'm not feeling so great."

"I wouldn't either after what happened."

I push back my chair with a loud scrape. "Let's hang in my room and watch the weather. Mom, I'll just have some cereal."

"We'll do brunch. My treat!"

"Food doesn't sound so good right now."

"Raina's gonna meet us there."

"Call her and cancel."

"She's already waiting for us."

"Is not."

"Is too."

Mom power-buffs the counter, triceps bulging, her brow pinched so tightly you could pop off a bottle cap with it. Dad hums and maneuvers around her, ears pricked by the change in atmosphere. Kirsten leans back with a vacuous look, holding my humiliation for ransom.

My nostrils won't flare any wider. "What if I don't feel like it?"

"Then I'll have to—" Kirsten stops. Her eyes widen, her pencil-lead pupils standing out from brilliant green irises.

Bridie enters the kitchen, hip-checking my chair out of her way. Her condescension drizzles over us like syrup. She picks up a banana from the bowl, snaps its stem like a chicken neck, and peels. Bridie knows what happened. How couldn't she? One grade above me, maybe not in the same hall when it happened, but in the same building. She totally knows.

My skin prickles in anticipation of an acidic comment.

Everyone looks at each other, wanting to explain or have it explained, all of us sensing an elephant in the room, half of us knowing its name. I don't want to talk about it, and on top of that, I don't want to fight with my best friend in front of my family.

The doorbell rings.

I'm saved. The tension redirects to this new mystery.

"Who on earth?" Mom asks.

"I'll get it." I jump from my seat and rush down the hall. Moving fast makes me realize how hollow my stomach really is, but I can't stand another second in that kitchen.

With any luck, Raina's at the door, meeting here instead of the mall. Kirsten would've told her I was cool to hang. I'll set them straight. Raina will see the truth in a heartbeat, and we'll shut down this sideshow once and for all.

A chill washes over me when I open the door. Standing on the porch is a short girl in a puffy pink coat, with a loaded backpack—most definitely *not* Raina. Who on earth indeed, Mom.

"Prairie?"

She pulls open the storm door, letting in a blast of arctic air. I turn aside and allow her to pass. Prairie stamps her feet on the rug and wags off her mittens, then tugs her scarf below her chin, exposing rosy cheeks and pouting lips, before taking off her hat. She'd have been severely overdressed just yesterday, but the weatherman got it right today.

"Hey, Quinn," she says.

"Hey...what's going on?"

Prairie collects her hat and mittens in one hand and runs her other through staticky, mousy hair. She looks in the family room, dining room, and down the hall, scoping out the place for my family, or Kirsten, whose Jeep is hard to miss out front. Her fidgeting doesn't cease, and she sniffs clear snot back into her long, thin nose.

The last time she and Kirsten were here together, in my house, was my eleventh birthday party, when mixing soccer friends and neighborhood besties seemed like a good idea. A wave of guilt washes over me. I mean, has she been over at all since that party?

"I wanted to see if you...forgot to bring anything home."

I don't know what to say. No beating around the bush. No prying or insinuations or manipulation. Is this what friendship is supposed to sound like? Like Mom but coming from someone who doesn't have any sort of control over me? I don't know how to respond, don't want to think about yesterday.

"It's just, I noticed how zoned out you were in math and bio...and I heard some stuff at lunch, so..."

Her words come quietly and quickly, but it won't help. Everyone's wondering who's here. The sudden silence will only increase their curiosity.

"Oh," I say, still at a loss. I mentally clocked out at about 7:55 a.m. yesterday and haven't checked back in. What was taught or assigned?

She can't meet my eyes. Regret is spelled on her face, like I've already told her off. "Sorry if it's not my place to say. It's just..."

"No, Prairie, it's cool. I, uh—"

"I don't want to keep you long. I just wanted to see if you need to borrow anything. Or y'know..."

"I mean, yeah, that'd probably be—"

"...copy anything."

We stumble over one another's words so much I barely register what could only be described as unheard of. I don't know which occurs first: my eyebrows rocketing off my head or her face blooming beet red.

"Prairie Hedlund, are you offering to help me cheat?"

"N-no! I mean, we could go over things together. Or you could use my work as a study guide. Or maybe, like...Okay, you know what? Forget it. Just take it." She slips off her backpack and unzips it, revealing what open-heart surgery would look like on a library.

"Prairie, no, I'm not doing that. You'd hate yourself. *I'd* hate myself. Can we just talk later? I'm not feeling great right now."

"Prairie!"

Dad is upon us, so fricking loud, everyone will know who's here now.

"What a morning! All my favorite ladies in one place. What brings you to this side of the road?"

She clenches her backpack and its suggestion of cheating to her chest, like a towel to hide her nakedness. Prairie greets Dad, turning her bird-like face into a luminous sun. Affirmation from authority figures is her manna.

"Are you taking part in Anti-Valentine's Day too?" he asks.

She stammers and halts, looks to me expectantly, and I realize I only have one way to go without coming off as a total heel. Kirsten's boxed me in.

I have to invite her. Prairie's seen Kirsten's Jeep. In the great cosmic Kirsten vs. Prairie battle, I know exactly who my family would choose. Kirsten's fine, as long as I'm her counterweight, but I can't become her. Prairie's unassailable. Tease her all you want, but spurn her at a time like this? That's a step too far.

At the same time, I can use Prairie. Only Kirsten will know I'm dragging her into this, and I could unmake all Kirsten's little schemes if Prairie plays along.

A chair scrapes along the kitchen floor, followed by hasty, heavy footsteps across tile and the hallway runner.

"Oh, hi, Prairie," Kirsten says from over my shoulder, as if she's only pulled up Prairie's name from some cobwebbed corner of her mind, watching my oldest friend and me through a gauzily vignetted fairytale frame.

Prairie leans over and offers a nervous smile and a meek hello.

Dad observes us all in clueless contentment. The housefly can't watch. It heads back into the kitchen.

Selfishness and diplomacy jostle back and forth in my head. Sometimes, they come together at once. Invite Prairie along to the mall? Insist we had a homework date when it's obvious we never did? Is anything the least cruel to her and the best for me?

Kirsten will sabotage any attempt I make to weasel out of her plans. I just don't know which will cost the most. There's no getting it right.

Fine, I'll do it, I want to scream, knowing I need to get Kirsten out of the house. It has to be the mall.

Prairie will back out anyway. No matter how crazy I come off, no matter how mean-spirited any of my options sound, it's up to Prairie now.

It's Prairie's choice in the end, okay?

It's Prairie's choice.

Invite Prairie to Meadow Spire Mall with Kirsten and you.
Turn to page 25.

Insist you have a homework date with Prairie.
Turn to page 313.

Skye Bodkin, out in the open. And at the mall. He's not here alone, no way. He's seen me. Skye's going to tell everyone—and I mean *everyone*—because they're all here, and they're going to come running. It'll be yesterday morning all over again, and my ride home just ran off.

With my other possible ride, dammit.

I feel myself falling backward. My head swells, and I break into a sweat. I clutch Prairie's leg instinctively to catch myself, making her leap and utter a startled cry.

"Quinn? What's wrong?"

"I—uh..."

"Oh my gosh, you're pale. Do you feel faint?"

Prairie tries to set me upright, getting herself wound in her own little tizzy. She turns to the crowd, then looks at me, assessing the extent of the emergency.

"I—Skye..."

"Aye-sky? What? Here, let's cool you down. Come on, lie down." Prairie presses me sideways on the fountain ledge. She drops her shopping bag to the floor.

I resist her, stabbed by the specter of more public humiliation, refusing to do what's necessary. Water splashes my face. I sputter and shake my head, batting away Prairie, who scoops water from the fountain to dribble on my forehead.

"Blechh!"

"Shoot, it's not even cold."

"What the hell, Prairie?"

I get up and rush away, inspired by her intentions but...No, absolutely *not* the way she's doing it. I race to the bathroom, praying I can outrun my faintness and avoid collapsing in the middle of the crowd.

"Wait, Quinn!" Prairie's a smidge less concerned about causing a scene than I am. "Let me come with you!"

She catches up halfway there, and since I'm wobbly on my feet and every step makes my head feel like it's orbiting the planet, I let her take my arm and hoist me.

When we reach the door, I put my hand on hers. "I'm good, Prairie, okay? Just...give me a second."

"But I can come in."

"No, I'm fine. I just need a second alone."

"No, I mean I *am* coming in. I have to watch you until you're back to normal, okay? If you do faint and you're alone, you could really hurt yourself."

"Prairie—" I start, but I don't want to argue.

Raina and Kirsten are nowhere in sight. I scan the crowd, fearful of seeing someone else I recognize. A classmate maybe, following in Skye's wake, as if he's the harbinger of drama when he's really nothing more than another victim of it, same as me. But what if Skye thinks I'm the cause of it? What if he blames yesterday on me and he's telling everyone exactly that right now?

Blood rushes to my head, my brain bails it back out again, and I sway into the wall.

"Okay, okay." Prairie takes me by my shoulders and nudges open the bathroom door. "C'mon, get some water on your face, okay? Oh, wow, this...smells terrible."

There's a woman standing in the middle of the bathroom, nose wrinkled, disgust on her face, who spins when we enter. I stumble into her, going straight for the sink.

She storms out saying, "This is unacceptable."

I fumble with the tap. When the water starts running, I paw it at my face, but the swampy odor coming from the drain negates any of its refreshing effects. Now I'm nauseous. My stomach roils, deciding pretty damn late I've had more breakfast than it can deal with. I leave the water running and head for the stalls.

"Quinn..." Prairie's voice quavers.

The odor fades, replaced by another strange scent, like how your hand smells after using the railing at a public park or something.

My nausea is so overpowering, I rush for the first stall, which overflows with water. Hadn't I just used it a few minutes ago? I move to the next, when my diaphragm contracts, nearly heaving then and there.

"Quinn...don't."

Inside the second stall, the third—overflowing toilets. I go to the last one, the handicapped one, which Kirsten apparently obliterated in her vandalism spree. The walls are red with ketchup, and when I knock against the stall's frame, the dangling door falls to the tile, revealing the source of the flooding.

Kirsten kicked the toilet loose from the floor, damaging the connection on its intake hose. It spits water at a steady rate, swirling the ketchup into a pink mess. She also bashed in the corner ceiling tile, leaving a gaping black hole.

Prairie's wet footsteps come up behind me. "Quinn," she calls again.

A loose toilet's better than an overflowing one. I bend over and throw up into the cockeyed bowl just as Prairie puts her hands on my shoulders.

Then she screams, and two hot sensations burn in my sides, directly under my rib cage. I'm lifted off the floor, and it's not Prairie who's holding me, but something sharp digging deep into my intestines. I'm brought higher, enduring a strangely painless sensation to a place so deep in my body, my nervous system has no way to register complaint there.

It hauls me into the ceiling, my body sandwiching backward at the waist, cracking my back.

The correct choice was to distract yourself with shopping.
Turn to page 63.

I know better than to think I can shake off Raina Harris. But she should know better too. I'm not that hard to read right now. My vision goes fuzzy at the edges, I'm so livid.

With one tug, I see if she'll yield, but she hangs on, so I turn on her.

"I will *scream*," I say.

"Go ahead."

My mouth drops open, but I keep myself from doing it. A couple of maintenance workers with extension cords turn to watch while their coworker wheels over a rickety metal floor fan to the wet area outside Manz Jewelers, where they knotted caution tape around some pylons. Other passersby are shooting us sideways glances.

I've been humiliated once this week, and now Raina's, like, going for round two? It's almost as if she said, *Go ahead. C'mon, Quinn. Cry, why don't you? Give us a show.*

How quickly my mind recategorizes her from a grumpier-than-normal Raina to a carbon copy of Kirsten. I pull away from her again, forcing Raina to lean in to keep her grip.

"Let *go*," I growl.

"Uh-uh. This is all your fault, apparently, so you're sticking around. My dad—"

I shove her this time. That's how to make Raina act like a normal human today. Her face opens in surprise.

"What the hell?"

"Whooaa," murmurs a maintenance worker, like he's witnessed a top-rope body slam on WWF. The end of his exclamation is consumed by the whir of the fan on the far side of the wet floor.

I shove Raina again. "*My* fault?"

She stands her ground and grabs my shoulders.

"My *fault?*" I repeat.

"What are you saying?" she sputters, grappling with my arms. "Kirsten said you—"

So much for avoiding the second humiliation.

Prairie and Kirsten scurry through the crowd right as I pull Raina closer, looking for a way to shake her off. She's expecting another push and is taken by surprise when I don't attack. And I don't want to. Just let me run away. Her defensive shove sends me off my feet.

The caution tape catches the back of my neck. The closest pylon to which it is tied whips over my body when I hit the floor, wrapping the tape over my throat. Water seeps through my pants and soaks into my hair. The pylon closest to the workers drops, too, pulling the fan's extension cord from one of their hands.

When the cord hits the wet floor, my body seizes. My palms are infiltrated with a tight heat that spreads into my arms and beyond.

"Shit!" The other worker rips the tape from the fallen pylon and kicks the cord away from the water.

By then, my heart feels like it's being squeezed for juice. My lungs press against my ribcage. I struggle to breathe.

The fan blows cool air over my face, and the fluttering end of the caution tape snakes through the air, then dives behind me. There's a strange mechanical wrenching sound when it leaves my sight. The tape tightens around my neck, cutting off my breath, just as my muscles begin returning control.

Raina towers over me, mouth agape, watching the workers to ensure it's safe for her to help.

"She's choking! Turn that off!" she shouts.

The tape pulls on me, but it turns out, I outweigh the fan.

It comes bounding forward on its rickety wheels, operating at full power and shaking loose its flimsy safety grill, which hardly has enough wire to prevent someone from sticking their hand inside in the first place.

My fault? I wonder, when the fan looms above me.

Raina grabs me in a late rescue attempt, but I seize again. She's accidentally kicked the extension cord back into the water.

My fault. How dare she.

The fan hits the cord and tips forward. A blade lodges deep into my face, chipping through bone, splitting my septum, and cutting a second diagonal mouth through my cheek.

The correct choice was to hear Raina out.
Turn to page 49.

We pile into Kirsten's salt-streaked, red Jeep Grand Cherokee, bound for Meadow Spire Mall, three girls without a clue how this is happening.

I sit shotgun, and Prairie takes the backseat, looking like a piggy bank in her puffy pink coat. Kirsten nearly snaps the teeth off her key, twisting it in the ignition. The engine kicks to life with a panther's roar.

At least we're out of the house. I won't feel this relieved until I'm back, alone in my room. But then it'll be that much closer to Monday...I can blame myself all I want for holing up in there, refusing to communicate, but Kirsten put the gun in my hand, and Prairie pulled the trigger. My intention was not to make today all about me. The best I can do is bring The Quinn Show on the road, even if our destination is the biggest high-schooler hangout this side of a varsity basketball game.

One small mercy: being accompanied by the most awkward pairing of girls imaginable. I can avoid talking about yesterday. It's actually kind of perfect, and it should cut this whole farce short.

None of this would be happening had Prairie said no. Under Dad's bemused gaze and Kirsten's eye-daggers, I asked if she wanted to come to the mall with us, *for a little bit,* and in the same span of time, with the same shifts in expression it would take her to mentally balance an honors-level chemical equation, she said, "Sure, that sounds fun."

I know why I want to go. And I know why Kirsten does—or *did*—too. But Prairie? What is she trying to prove? Or am I mistaking genuine camaraderie, clung to through years of dormancy, for pathetic do-gooding?

Prairie called her folks first, to explain why she'd be out longer. She didn't ask permission, didn't mention the mall or Kirsten, just kept it vague enough she could claim plausible deniability later. Dad smirked from over his paper when she hung up. It was another unique twist for the morning—seeing her utilize a decidedly Kirsten-like tactic. She's apparently learned some lessons toward governing her own life.

Mom issued a final warning about the weather, which I was ready to take to heart when I stepped outside. Shotgun pellets of sleet stung my cheeks. The wind clamped me in its maw and shook without letting go. Thirty seconds to get into the Cherokee and my teeth still chattered minutes later.

Five days ago, a massive storm dumped over a foot of fat, wet snow. The next day, it lost its sheen of wintry majesty and settled into a dense, austere coat of paint. Thursday afternoon, a warm spell hit and deflated the snow another half foot. Water ran down the curbs and flooded parking lots, gutters, street corners, and whole sections of low-lying roads.

Today is another about-face. A second cold front—bad enough I might get a couple of extra days before I have to worry about school.

The leftover ice-creamy snow is getting crusty on top, with water gushing underneath. Wind howls around the Cherokee, pushing us side to side. Kirsten white-knuckles through the neighborhood. I jolt forward in my seat when the front wheels plunge into puddles and kick up a wake which sprays past the sidewalk. We burst apart slush bubbles, maneuvering around plowed-in cars parked on the road.

Kirsten reverts to something like her normal self after blasting through a ridge of soupy snow getting out of the neighborhood. She interrupts my stilted discussion with Prairie about next Wednesday's bio quiz to yammer on about finding the perfect bathing suit for Spring Break in Jamaica, concentrating on me but icing out Prairie.

We get to Mineral Point Road and turn west, toward a brooding gray tsunami in the sky. On the ground, it looks like Moses parted a pigsty. Levees of blackened snow barricade roadside buildings from the drenched asphalt and its lines of mud-splattered, salt-encrusted vehicles. After the neighborhoods come razed fields and waterlogged plains boxed in by stands of scraggly trees.

Kirsten veers between lanes, staying out of tire grooves that have turned into hydroplane-causing runnels of snowmelt, swerving to avoid axle-killing potholes. The windshield mists over with a fine gunk of oily, grainy runoff kicked up by the car in front of us. The wipers fail to squeegee it away despite Kirsten spraying up to a gallon of bright blue washer fluid.

That describes our whole trip to Meadow Spire Mall.

The mall lies west of Madison by about ten miles. Hardly any development has gone up around it since I've been alive, but the place was built years ago on cheap swampland in the gaping maw between converging suburbs, with the expectation more stuff would close in around it. But nothing really has yet. It's all alone now—been there for years, a beacon in the boondocks, the one thing getting townies to spot a cow every so often on their way to the technicolor wonders and premium pricing of platter-served food and glitzy fashion.

We arrive at the country intersection where Meadow Spire resides, waiting on a freshly installed red traffic light. Meadow Spire is shaped like a big Celtic cross, its long shaft bent diagonally to run along Mineral Point. On our left, the brown block of the AMC theater juts out toward the intersection, marking the terminal point of Meadow Spire's stubbiest branch.

At this juncture, Kirsten and I would typically argue about the best approach into the parking lot, but I let her decision to go straight through the light instead of turning left go uncontested.

We pull into the driveway by Macy's, which anchors the cross's long arm, and venture into the massive parking lot spread across the meadow. The Cherokee rocks when we turn out of the wind.

"Ugh," Kirsten says.

The sections closest to the mall are coated in a thin sheet of water. Still, Kirsten was wise to take the north driveway. Around the west entrance, red and white pylons are set up to keep people from parking in deeper pools. And even though the place isn't busy yet, we have to park about ten rows back from the megalith of Sears.

"Ready?" I ask Prairie.

She murmurs, "Yes," and we scurry outside, hopping puddles, splashing through unavoidable ones. My boots keep me dry, and the wind's at our backs, but it bites through my coat, slipping under my armpits and into my collar.

Inside Sears, we stamp our feet and head for the concourse. The scent of water damage hits us immediately, and I hope it's only Sears. I won't be able to tolerate that all day. It smells like a cardboard box soaked in floor cleaner, then dried out in a root cellar.

We venture through hardware and into menswear, with its abysmal legion of grays, blacks, browns, and tans perked up by outbursts of safety oranges and neons.

The squeaks from our boots change with the shift from vinyl to tile when we hit the concourse. Kirsten stretches her arms, throws back her head, and breathes a relieved sigh.

I feel it too, that I'm in my element. It's one small step for teen, one giant leap for teen-kind. The things I want, I *can* get. Too-sugary sweets and too-salted pretzels, chance encounters with people I love and abhor. Ridiculous clothes I'll never afford but want to see how they fit. Time with friends out in the open, with pocket money to throw away, like candy from a parade float.

I'm suddenly not worried about what's waiting here for me but begin to fear the baggage I brought. My bedroom can take the drama. That's what bedrooms are for. What if I keep associating the mall with this terrible day? At this point, I have no choice. Maybe the Valentine's decorations splayed over the normal decor can bear the brunt of my misery.

Red and white tulle drapes run the length of the concourse ceiling, dipping and rising below the skylights. Ruffled bunting dresses the second-story balustrade. Strings of red and pink hearts—outlined, filled in, checkered, shiny, glittery, and polka-dotted—dangle from the rafters. Twinkle lights and bows garland the faux greenery near benches. Confetti litters the floor.

Window decals and promotional signs shout from shopfronts in red, white, silver, and gold: two for one deals, double discounts or rewards, half off for a second matching item, single-day price matching. Raffles and contests for couples, jokey consolation prizes for singles. Hell, raffles for everybody, single or attached.

Competing caricature artists are getting set up, showcasing some samples. Outside Kodak are cardboard stands of Hollywood icons, with cut-out faces for photo ops. Temporary kiosks have been arranged for vendors hawking sweets, treats, novelties, and jewelry. There's one right outside Victoria's Secret we've heard rumors about, designed like an Arabian harem tent—dark scarlet with fluffy white trim, with an actual bouncer checking who's allowed to view its racy wares.

We follow big red hearts adhered to the floor, directing visitors like bubbly, cherub-cheeked arrows toward the atrium. There, at the heart of Meadow Spire, its three-tiered fountain is lit by red, gold, and pink lights. Off to the side, red and white streamers snake across the children's play area.

We branch off from the heart path to visit the food court at the southeast corner. Continuing in the direction we were going would've led us to the red-velvet-roped queuing area for a very special photo op. The same place is used for Santa every Christmas, but on Valentine's Day, outside Madison, Wisconsin, it's Cupid.

The suckers this time around are the couples dorky enough to pay for a portrait with a local beefcake in a loincloth, who aims a toy bow and arrow at you. Different backdrops give couples the choice of chumming with Cupid in the clouds, letting him creep above you while you cuddle in a Venetian gondola, clink glasses on a good ole American picnic blanket, or offer your favor while wearing silly hats and wigs under an ivy-tangled Victorian trellis.

Foot traffic is relatively light, and besides a monotonous hum coming from one branch of the mall, it's easy to hear Sixpence None the Richer cooing "Kiss Me" overhead. There's no common theme among the current mall-goers: couples young and old, clumps of teens and twenty-somethings, families with kids, elderly mall walkers, solo shoppers speeding through their errands. It shouldn't take long for the massive crowds to materialize, weather be damned.

A trio of men in high-visibility vests, whose big black and green boots out-squeak our own, catch my eye. They carry hardhats, and one tucks a stack of yellow clapboard warning signs under his armpit.

The sound of their boots decreases. Then the sound of ours does too. I turn.

We've lost Prairie to the mall's many holiday wonders.

"Prairie, what's keeping you?"

She's gawking at the Cupid setup and jumps at my voice. "Sorry. I've just...never seen that before."

"Not surprised. It's only a Madison city institution," drones Kirsten.

At the food court, the open-air sauna of fried food aromas and umami temptations shoves away all other smells, which makes me realize the whole mall shares that ineffable funk from Sears. It's a heaviness or mugginess more than a scent.

Kirsten glares off to the side of the McDonald's counter while I order. Prairie goes next, feebly insisting to pay for herself. Kirsten, putting on a disconcerting cheerfulness, refuses. She follows up by forcing a coffee order out of us, which she picks up from the doughnut shop at the end of the food court.

Once I have my cinnamon roll, hash browns, orange juice, and machine-poured mocha, I'm almost close to content. I can even appreciate having Prairie along for the ride. She cups her hands around a decaf coffee and soaks in the milieu.

Kirsten slings her purse around the back of her chair and daintily sits down with a double caramel macchiato.

"So," she says, brushing back a particular lock of hair, which flourishes itself over her shoulder like a feather boa. "Prairie."

Oh, what's this?

"You missed the full conversation back at Quinn's. Do you have a hot date tonight? Got any guys after you?"

"Me?" Prairie slides her coffee to her chest.

Kirsten tilts her head and eyes her meaningfully.

"No. No way. I don't have any plans tonight. It's supposed to be so bad out anyway..."

"No? Good for you! Dating's overrated. Like, you think it's great having someone falling all over you and seeing them all the time, but then your nights become the same lame thing over and over. There's just another boring person to share it with."

I dig into my cinnamon roll, too hungry to butt in.

Prairie ventures a question. "So, I guess you don't have a date either?"

"Hell no. I'd rather spend Valentine's Day alone. It's so much better being single anyway. I mean, at our age. Look at all this. It's like still believing in Santa. You can imagine the perfect guy and not deal with the actual ones the world has to offer. I mean, the guys I've been with? They've tarnished this. I am, like, worse off because of them."

"Hence Anti-Valentine's Day?"

"Hence!"

Kirsten slings an arm over her chair and shakes her head.

Prairie sips her coffee, barely touching it to her lips. She grimaces after swallowing. Her parents would ground her for a month if they knew she tried it, even if it *is* decaf.

She clears her throat and quietly says, "So if you're saying Santa isn't real...what about Cupid?"

I stop chewing. The question floats in the air, so tiny and invisible as to be vapor.

Kirsten's head turns. Her gaze zooms in from a thousand yards to one, and she guffaws. "I got stone-cold evidence he's a fantasy, dead and buried."

Prairie smiles.

"I bet you do too," Kirsten continues. "Didn't you go to Snow Ball last week? You had a date, right? I mean, it was girls-ask-boys."

I catch her tone and open my mouth, but it's full of hash browns, and only a grunt comes out. Besides, Prairie gets the jump on me.

"Yeah, I went."

"Who'd you go with?" Kirsten settles into her chair, a Cheshire-cat-like smile on her face.

"Danny Valon, but we just went as friends. You know Danny? From U.S. History?"

"Oh, no, you didn't. Danny? The guy who won't shut up about war crimes during the American Revolution?"

"There *were* war crimes."

"And he did his whole report on that Lord Dormouse, or whoever, and almost gave Mr. Farmer a conniption?"

"Dor-*chester*, who helped evacuate a bunch of Loyalists and kept them from getting massacred?"

"Danny Valon...What a lobsterback." Kirsten wrinkles her nose.

A laugh bursts out of Prairie, completely involuntary. It's so unreal, I can't deal with it. I keep shoveling food into my face.

"I mean, seriously," Kirsten continues. "Where do his loyalties lie? And ugh, now I'm thinking seafood. Lobsters. Shellfish. Crawfish. Yuck. And French Canada, with their frog legs and everything. Ew, ew, ew."

"Yeah, I agree on the frog legs," Prairie says.

They both laugh. Prairie Hedlund and Kirsten Fortner, together, bonding over coffee. In fits and bursts, granted, but what in the living hell is this?

"I'm serious, though," says Kirsten. "Danny literally almost killed Mr. Farmer."

"Are you for real right now?"

They both freeze. Whatever vestiges of a laugh or a smile, any spark of a new remark, dies then and there. I bet Prairie appears wounded, but I'm all in on Kirsten, with her fake, dumbstruck, *who, me?* look on her face—the same one she goaded out of Prairie a moment ago.

I drink my orange juice and ask, "Where's Raina?"

"What?"

"You said Raina was waiting for us. Where is she?"

Kirsten's brow settles into steely contempt. "Doing breakfast with her dad or some crap. She'll be here."

"Are you going to ask me, or aren't you?"

I've caught her. She's too hungry for details to pretend any longer. Kirsten draws forward, like a cobra on its prey.

"I thought you didn't want to talk about it."

"I really don't. But why can't you admit that's why we're here?"

Kirsten and I are massive buildings tilting into one another, waiting to tip past the angle of repose, to enter free fall and smash together. Shrapnel, dust, a rumbling earthquake devastating everything in our vicinity. I'm nearly at that point, ready for the fireworks of a public fight, when she turns away, leaving me to face-plant into my own misery.

"Prairie, are you caught up on what happened yesterday?"

She's put back on the spot, an outsider to Kirsten's and my pairing once again, as if the last couple of minutes never happened. Prairie looks at me.

"Oh. I...heard the rumors. That you made Skye Bodkin a valentine and that he apparently didn't...like it?"

I explode. "What! No! I didn't make it!"

And troubled earth tumbles down, far too shy
To stop its flight and cry, how I love you, oh—

Just those two lines. They threw together some more, not even in iambic pentameter. I'd written a whole poem, but that's all they used...

Prairie blushes and turns to Kirsten, frankly the best person to go to after making that assumption.

Kirsten's on her game now, and with a raised finger, she stops me when I rise, ready to storm off. "Which! W*hich*...begs the question. Who *did* make it? Who pulled that *specific* prank? Why you? Why Skye? What's the connection there?"

"What do you think?"

"Well...do you even like him anymore?" Kirsten huddles over her drink.

Her phrasing and focus don't distract me. This isn't about finding the culprit, and it was never about comforting me either. She wants the gossip. Kirsten absolutely knows I had a crush on Skye Bodkin freshman year, which lingered into sophomore year, but I deliberately avoided the topic since we started class last fall. I told her I was over it. It was immature, ancient history, toxic waste buried in the desert.

Classic Kirsten.

How many times have I told myself that could be her mob name? *Klassic.* I could punch her right now. Break that little nose. Bite her ear and give her a full-on Holyfield.

"Here's what you need to know," I say. "I didn't do it. I don't know *who* did it. And I never asked for it. Thanks for making me feel better."

I stuff the rest of my hash brown and cinnamon roll in my mouth. Frosting and cinnamon smear around my lips and the tip of my nose. I take up my platter, march to the closest waste bin, and shove it in, platter and all. Orange juice spills, and my greasy wrapper flutters to the floor.

"Whoa there," a soft, familiar voice says.

Standing on the other side of the bin is Mr. Harris, with a giant coffee mug. Next to him is the one person who might possibly salvage this morning.

His daughter, Raina.

♥*♥*♥

Make small talk with Mr. Harris. Turn to page 40.

Storm off to the payphone. Turn to page 309.

The way those spindly fingers press the fret board...How he bites his lip in deep concentration...Yeah, I see it all. Skye summons his song from that guitar, depleting himself as utterly as some wizard in the throes of a spell meant to save a kingdom. God, he's probably doing that right now, rescuing a store full of wounded refugees, like the one we just ran from. They'll remember every chord, the swell of the bridge going into the chorus, the wet tip of his tongue sticking out of his—

"Oh my God, girl, don't even think about it."

I come to. Kirsten gives me the stare of death.

"We are right here," Raina says.

"It's him." It's all I can say. Bridie was with him. Bridie *is* with him. There's no being ashamed for recognizing his talent.

Raina slams her drill into the door, haggard and impatient, and stares at me from under a dark cloud. Kirsten scrunches up her face, like *who cares?* Prairie is fairer, wrinkling her brow in sympathy for my moral quandary, knowing what we risked to reach her, knowing I have to do it again.

The water laps against the doors, above the height of our knees. We would watch it rise inch by inch if we stayed here. Or we could go all the way to the other side of the mall. Or...

On a day like this, after everything Kirsten's done across a spree of petty mayhem and borderline—possibly *not* borderline—criminal mischief, I have to take my victories where I can find them. We got Prairie, and we're close to an exit, even if it isn't this one.

"Please tell me you're not going to go looking for him," Kirsten says.

"It's not him," mutters Raina. She smacks the glass with her drill. Its impact makes my heart flutter.

"No! I mean...yeah. We're here. Let's get Prairie out, like we said we would."

Kirsten balks. "Did I miss something? You think this was all about Prairie? We're *all* getting out of here, Quinn."

"That's what I'm saying!"

"Wait."

The challenge in Prairie's voice gives me pause. Even Raina stops her hammering. The railroad spike of anxiety that's been stabbing my heart repeatedly takes a break. It just lodges in there instead.

"I didn't ask you to come to me," Prairie says.

"I'm saying we made it all this way, and we should get you out like we planned."

"'You'? Like, just me?"

"Like, all you guys," I say.

Kirsten huffs. "You're seriously thinking of going back for him."

"Yes!"

My answer stuns them. They're clearly not thinking of Skye's guitar-playing. His eyes. His hair. His...

Right. I mean to go back for Bridie. For Skye, too, sure. For whoever's left.

"I'm not saying we abandon our plan." I have to cut this off.

"What is the plan, then? The door's screwed, and that one...Well..." Kirsten throws a feeble gesture at Raina, then another at the befogged mosquito beast across the way.

"Penney's," I say, and before they can object, "We made it through Sears. We know what to do, no matter what's in there. And the flooding won't be bad on that side."

Raina bites her lip, very Skye-like, and brushes wet hair from her face. Kirsten rolls her eyes, and Prairie struggles with my having pegged her as our damsel in distress. They just need to absorb it for a second.

Give them a few.

"Look," I continue, "I don't want to fail here. We got here, we found Prairie, and—"

With one barked word, the realization sinks in.

I've made a terrible mistake.

The railroad spike in my heart gains fifty pounds, and my thoughtlessness renders me speechless. Kirsten and Prairie stare at me, and the weight of their stares is anchored by the gravity of Raina's rage.

"You don't want to *what*?" she screams. The tendons on her hands swell like furrows in a field. Her teeth shine behind her sneer.

My vocal cords refuse to utter whatever fruitless explanation springs to mind.

"You don't want to fail?" she shrieks.

The drill smashes the glass.

Kirsten and Prairie flinch.

Raina hits the door again.

I didn't mean it. Not the way she's taken it. But I haven't been paying attention. I thought she'd recovered too quickly from her father's death.

Raina strikes the drill against the glass one more time, uttering a blubbering warning to watch out but giving none of us time to back away.

The door splinters. Thick glass shards drop from the top of the frame. The incoming water sends the lower pieces of the broken pane into our legs, followed by the deluge.

The weight behind all that backed-up water takes our feet out from under us, bowling us over and surfing us on a tsunami to the opposite set of doors. A pile of bodies travels with us.

My limbs scramble for purchase across the flooded tile. The corner where the concourse meets the hallway in front of J.C. Penney smashes my hip and whips me into the water, filling my mouth with a fetid taste.

Everything after is blur, but I come to a stop when I hit another pile of bodies. I struggle for breath, having already swallowed and aspirated a bunch of water. My feet can't seem to find purchase, and even if I could stand, the startled mosquito beast would make short work of me.

Its limbs stomp on my own, and its wings beat upon my body. With one final kick to my head, it knocks my face under the water, where I lose consciousness.

The correct choice was to fight to find Skye, and Bridie, since she might be with him. Turn to page 72.

I'm floating by the time Kirsten's blond hair bounces out of sight. Nothing else could have lifted my spirits so much. I'm in a tearing-things-down kind of mood, and she should have known that when she decided to crash my morning.

The other two keep their thoughts to themselves. Raina stares off in the distance. Prairie pouts and avoids my eyes, slightly hunched, like our fight gave her indigestion.

Since there's no such thing as maintaining a victory over Kirsten, I take charge immediately, careful not to squander this one small triumph.

"Prairie, you good to go?"

Her eyes light on mine and she nods.

"Let's get your dad, Raina."

"I told you he'll be doing his thing for hours."

"Then I'll tell him I'm deathly ill and I need to get outta here. Work for you?"

I march away before she can respond, and Prairie skitters after me, like I knew she would. Only once I'm past the cash registers does Raina respond.

A single word, sharp and sibilant.

Two syllables.

I turn on a dime, piquing the bored cashier's interest.

"*What* did you call me?"

Raina glares, then wanders to the back of the store, leaving me stunned.

Don't push it.

"Prairie, come on."

I stamp onto the concourse, where the swampy odor is unmasked by store associates' attempts to spray it away with perfumes and colognes. A fog has built up under the skylights, thick enough to cut.

A worker at the top of the main staircase wraps its corner post with caution tape. I blow past him down the steps, ignoring his gripes. He starts unspooling the roll across the gap to seal the whole staircase. At the bottom, the area is already cordoned off due to puddling. I pull the tape over my head and splash into the water. The only things on my mind are a warm pickup truck and a soft bed. Oblivion through Sunday night.

The first floor is densely crowded, so I head for the wall, aiming for Sears. I squeeze past bodies, keeping my head down to avoid anyone who knows me. Once I brush past a double stroller, I come to a stop and make a Prairie-like squeak.

Blocking my way is a handsome, fully-grown German shepherd looking at me with baleful eyes and a muttering jaw. It whimpers pathetically and scratches at the floor. The dog wears a specialized harness on its back, and its owner, a man in sunglasses, tilts his head, listening to the enthusiastic blathering of a janitor kneeling next to his work cart. He's inspecting an open vent by the floor.

"Big bastards in here," says the janitor. "You can tell, for it to shake a German like that. Good thing he's here. Best-trained dogs out there, 'specially for what you got it for, so I don't gotta tell you. Yeah, we killed ourselves a whole nest'a rats when winter kicked in, but today? Frickin' huge, from the sound of it. And don't tell my boss, but that's why we keep that surplus'a Gopher-Go. Illegal since '89, but Old Man Keith swore by it, rest his ass. Got the strychnine in it. Best way to deal with these sons'a bitches. One big serving of poison pie. Fit for vermin of all stripes."

The janitor slides a bowl of crushed pellets closer to the vent and starts scooping it in.

"Excuse me," I mutter, practically stepping over the dog's hindquarters and pushing past its owner.

Prairie chirps a scandalized warning at me, along with the dog, but I'm off, skirting the edge of the crowd, when the next obstacle appears.

A woman in her mid-twenties pushes a man into the wall. He throws up his arms. In her hand is a valentine.

"Who's *Prairie*, huh?" she demands loudly. "Does this explain all those Friday night plans? Does this filth say what you've been doing? Who is she, huh?"

I come to a stop.

Prairie bumps into me, settling her attention on the fighting couple. "*Huh?* What're they saying?"

Kirsten. Her madness is still at work.

"It's nothing," I tell her.

Before I can usher Prairie away, the man, looking any which way for a lifeline, locks his eyes on me.

"Her!" he cries, fending off his girlfriend's shoves. "Her and...that other girl!"

Having been seen riding the wake of Kirsten's mayhem earlier, my reputation precedes me.

"Back," I hiss to Prairie, who's still befuddled by hearing her name on a stranger's lips, then having it attributed to me.

"*You?*" snarls the girl, stomping closer. "*You* wrote this?"

"*Prai*-rie, go!" I push her backward, and she stumbles into the service dog, causing it to pull its owner forward and rattle the janitor's cart.

The janitor, crumbling more poison with bare hands and the butt end of a screwdriver, steadies his bowl. "Whoa!"

The German shepherd barks and leaps at Prairie. The owner reels back to restrain it, bumping into me. He loosens his grip and utters a cry. That alerts the dog, which turns and lunges for me. I cower to shield myself, catching a glimpse of the furious girlfriend storming up on us. She shoves me, cutting my cheek with Kirsten's valentine, right when the dog leaps on my back.

I spin away from both attacks and fall to the side, knocking the janitor's cart. The top edge digs into my back. When I hit the floor, the cart topples down behind me, and the janitor cries, "Schnikes!"

A bowl of floury brown Gopher-Go drops onto my face, into my open mouth, my eyes, my nose. It's already hard to breathe in this muggy air, and amid the combined attacks of a service dog and a scorned woman, the substance snakes its way into my sinuses. It's blinked deeper into my eyes. My mouth dampens its dryness, absorbing it into my gums. I swallow against my will.

It takes a few minutes for the muscle spasms to kick in, burning me and stretching me alive. Within fifteen minutes, my jaw dislocates, and my lungs and heart give out.

Besides pain, until the very end, I feel that damn valentine nicking my cheek, and I hear the janitor crying, "Shit! My boss! Oh, shit!"

♥*♥*♥

The correct choice was to track down Kirsten and make amends.
Turn to page 205.

Mr. Harris pulls Raina in under his shoulder. He's not so tall, but he's built like a rock. Mr. Harris likes saying he's the human hydraulic, that all he does at work is lift the cars and let the smart technicians do the repairs. Raina herself barely fits under his arm. She's just as brawny as him—the strongest base Holy Trinity's cheer team has seen in half a century.

"Found'em," he says, jostling his daughter.

His heartachingly sweet smile crumbles when he notices the state I'm in. My nerves are right on the surface, I'm sure. If I were his daughter, he'd have already swooped in for a hug. From what Raina's said, there's no problem too girly or immature for him to attend to, with the same intensity most fathers reserve for college football. Also according to Raina, his solutions to her problems are reliably, hilariously useless.

It appears he doesn't think it's his place to help, though. He ever so slightly nudges Raina forward, no doubt hoping she can handle whatever it is I'm dealing with. After all, he's taught her everything he knows.

"Quinn," he says, "it's been a while. How are you?"

"I...still got a roof over my head." I toss up my hands. The cliche comes out of nowhere and tastes bitter on my tongue.

"Is that Kirsten there? And who else is that?"

Raina doesn't rescue me from the small talk and doesn't meet my eye. She's made as much of an effort as I have today, wearing a stained sleeveless puffer jacket over her cheer hoodie. Her long braid snakes around to lie beneath her throat. The bottom of an oversized flannel sneaks out from under her jacket, draping her upper thighs. Everything about her says she wants no part of Kirsten's day.

I steam a little, resenting Kirsten for dragging her into this and resenting Raina for showing up.

"Is that...Prairie?" Mr. Harris asks, squinting and smiling at her.

I glance back as if to make sure myself. That old birthday party comes to mind, when Prairie last mingled with my soccer teammates, Raina included.

Mr. Harris can't have seen her since then, and no way does he know the Hedlunds from before—all the proof I need that he truly pays attention.

"Ah, yeah, that's Prairie." He looks down at Raina. "She gave you her party favor bag at Quinn's birthday, didn't she?"

My guilt strikes again, thinking of Prairie as an added appendage, a vestigial part of the old me. Maybe Cupid actually is out there, warming up by lobbing arrows of indiscriminate emotions, just to screw with people. Embarrassment. Shame. Regret. He's even got some fricking enhanced memory and clairvoyance in his quiver, just for Mr. Harris.

The movement of a bunch of red-shirted crew members draws my eye to the Cupid setup, where they place big boxy lights on twiggy black stands.

The mall is filling up, as if Raina's arrival opened the floodgates. The atrium swirls with the noise of bustling shoppers, the crowds so dense, people sidestep and squeeze past each other with purses and full department store bags. Half our class could be out there right now. I spot a cluster of freshman girls popping bubblegum and sauntering like divas.

Kirsten approaches, slurping her macchiato. "Wassup, Mr. Harris. You guys eat yet?"

Mr. Harris smacks his gut and exhales. "Did we. We hogged out at the buffet up the road. But I couldn't get this one to splurge on anything sweet."

At this, Raina nods and makes a face, a sure comment on her dad's gorging. He jostles her again, then frees her. She sticks close to him, sparing a glance for the swelling crowd, which now includes a troupe of guys I swear could be models—tall buzzcut brunettes and blond mop-tops, cut-glass cheeks standing out like diamonds in the rough.

"I got you covered, Mr. H. Rain, let's head to Starbucks and avoid this fast-food trash."

Mr. Harris tilts his head. "Kirsten, you don't gotta do that."

"But I do. We're date-free today. No boys allowed, which means no outside money is coming in. You can blame Quinn, if you like. It's all her fault."

The comment lands funny, and Mr. Harris's reticence is alleviated for a second by curiosity. He shakes it away. "You don't gotta pay Raina's way. If anything, I should be buying you girls something. All I ever think about is the rides you give her back from school and practice and...and football games. And you know something else? She's never laughing harder than when she's on the phone with one of you girls."

"Dad, it's okay if she wants to buy. And it doesn't matter. I don't want anything."

"All I'm saying is, they make you...glow, Raina. Can't a guy be pleased with his daughter's choice of friends?"

Kirsten rattles her drink. "You can't be the odd one out, Rain. Why you gotta be so special all the time?"

Raina sneers at Kirsten. I'm ready to sneak away and let them go at it, when Prairie sidles up next to me.

Mr. Harris observes the abomination of teenage emotions as if he's playing monkey in the middle and discovers the players on both ends have suddenly drawn guns.

I find myself blushing at his compliments. He sounds like my dad with Kirsten, and why? We barely see him. Kirsten and I make Raina *glow*? What the hell is happening today?

I'm so ready to be done with this, to restart the morning and push everyone away. Hardly any time has passed. How stupid my plan was in the first place. Having Raina here just makes it harder to get out, and I'm not going to placate Kirsten and use Prairie to retreat home early like I thought. I should have known not to underestimate Kirsten. She even turned Prairie's presence to her advantage.

With Raina in a mood, her dad steps out of the line of fire and laughs at Kirsten's dig.

"I'll let you two work it out. Spend whatever on whoever. And Prairie, maybe Raina can get you a little something, if there's no boys out there to do it for you."

"God. Dad, stop."

Prairie blinks, juggling his generosity with his unintended insult.

"I was just telling Raina how nice it was when you gave her your party favor at Quinn's birthday party. And I think you even snuck her an extra slice of cake, when I think about it."

"Dad!"

Prairie stammers. "Oh...that's nothing. And...I don't need anything. Raina doesn't have to get me something if she can't afford it." Her face grows redder, like textbook-drawing-of-the-circulatory-system red.

We freeze in horror while she turns into a human scandal barometer, dancing around the Harrises' finances.

My silent screams go unheeded.

Just stop, all of you.

Mr. Harris cuts in, and the awkwardness rounds the corner from anticipatory simmer to fading heartburn.

"As I said...as I said, you girls work it out. You're all grown up." Mr. Harris expels an exasperated chuckle and comments again on how much we've grown. He pulls up his sleeve and checks the scuffed face of a digital watch. "I should be moving. Raina, take all the time you need. I'll be in Sears, so pop by to let me know what your ride situation is. Even if I find everything I need, I'll be snooping around all the toys I'll never get to play with."

Raina grimaces at the order and nods.

Mr. Harris fixes each of us with a bright smile, squeezes Raina's shoulders, and enters the mix of mall-goers, walking funny with his bad back, vanishing from sight in seconds.

Raina crosses her arms, shrinking into herself now her crutch is gone. She squeaks her boots on the floor.

"It smells like shit in here."

"Yeah," I say, "I can tell you're *so* pleased to be with us today."

Might as well make enemies of everyone at this point. How else am I supposed to cut this short? By next weekend, we'll have forgotten everything—forgiveness is another story—as long as we keep a lid on our greatest hang-ups. I can't be the only one sitting on an arsenal of nukes ready for counterstrike, but in light of what happened to me yesterday, I don't think anyone's willing to start a new war.

Kirsten lights up, like Raina's only just arrived. "Rainy! Wow. Let's get a cup of coffee in you. And again, and without any argument, it's my treat because you're so stupidly important to me, okay?"

Raina takes a deep breath and shrugs. "Okay. Sure."

Maybe some liquid stimulation is what she needs. I, on the other hand, see how she and Kirsten now form a pair to oppose mine and Prairie's. Maybe I don't need to antagonize anyone else to blow things up. One phone call home and Prairie and I could be out of here.

Kirsten hops onto the half-wall and spins around, dropping to the floor next to Raina. Prairie inches past the trash bin, out of the food court seating area. The three of them now face me.

"You gonna sulk some more or get a new mocha to replace the one you chucked out?" Kirsten asks.

I am pissed about the coffee, but that's not the point. Now I have to contend with leaving Prairie to Kirsten's mercy, if she's naive enough to stick around. If only I can figure out what Raina's deal is. If she's on my side, then I can abort the whole outing without being the number one dick. But why do I care if I am?

My outburst should've made it clear to Kirsten not to try me again. In my book, that means for the rest of the day. In reality, it probably buys me half an hour. And that's about as long as I expected to stay here, right? I warned her once. Let her pester me again, then bail. Maybe the plan's back on track after all...

"I can sulk and walk," I say. I grab my coat and hop over the wall.

Kirsten leads us, strutting like one of those freshmen. I never took to the line-abreast formation Kirsten asserts is our right to maintain in public, barreling through the normal ugly people in our way. I don't think of myself the way she does.

"It's good you're coming. Otherwise, you wouldn't get to hear my theories," she calls over the crowd.

"Kirsten," I say, warning in my voice. I try to catch up to her, but a janitor has cordoned off a wet swath of floor outside Manz Jewelers. "Stop it. No one wants to talk about it."

"God, this place is so gross."

"Well, they had to drain this land years ago, when it was a waterfowl product area, but that doesn't change its elevation..." Prairie says.

Kirsten ignores her. "It was totally the seniors. You may not know because they won't talk about it at practice, but they've apparently been getting real creative with the hazing this year."

Prairie shoots me a worried look at the mention of hazing.

I jog ahead to speak into Kirsten's ear.

"Just shut up," I growl.

"My main theory? I think maybe Valerie or some other asshole from cheer wanted to screw with you, and she didn't want anything to lead back to her..."

"Will you shut the hell up already?"

I punch her arm. Not hard. Not really. Enough to make her know I'm serious.

Kirsten stops dead in her tracks. She looks down. Her macchiato dribbles along the back of her hand. Brown droplets soak into the white cuff of her jacket. Our eyes meet, and I struggle not to apologize. She takes on the expression of a wise old woman. Nothing pisses me off more than when she gets all maternal on me.

"Raina, can we get a referee over here?" she asks, her tone bored.

Raina stops a few feet ahead of us. She turns a slow circle, hands in her pockets. Exhaustion drags at her whole body.

"Can you tell Quinn she's being hugely immature about this whole thing? Wouldn't you rather work this thing out before Monday?"

"Work what out?" Raina mumbles.

Kirsten screws up her face. "Uh, hello? Yesterday? The prank? Are we just going to let Quinn suffer like this?"

I chime in. "Raina, can you tell Kirsten that I don't need this right now and that I'd rather, y'know, cool down and collect myself before I talk about it with anyone?"

C'mon, Rain. Tell her to lay off. Make her miserable so she'll want to leave.

Raina stares at us. I start to sweat. No, I'm already sweating. The mall is summertime muggy. The size of the crowd doesn't help either.

She keeps considering. Great. She isn't on my side. Raina thinks Kirsten is right, that I should rip the band-aid off, move past it so we can have some fun. Maybe that's what's stuck up her butt.

She shakes her head and shrugs, spreading her hands from inside her unzipped puffer jacket pockets so she looks like a flying squirrel. "I don't know what the hell you're talking about."

Raina turns and moves towards Kirsten's promised Starbucks.

Kirsten and I are stunned into inaction, united for once this morning.

Prairie observes us uneasily.

I actually punched Kirsten in public. That counts as a second outburst. I don't want to wait for a third.

There's a phone bank behind me, past Manz Jewelers, near the bathrooms and baby-changing area. Mom or Dad can pick me up. Prairie can come if she wants.

I turn and start marching through the crowd, but I don't make it far past the information desk. A hand grips my bicep and holds fast.

Raina. Again.

♥*♥*♥

Shake her off and call for a ride home. Turn to page 23.

Hear her out. Turn to page 49.

Raina squeezes my gashed arm. Blinding pain ricochets through me, and I go senseless. The fight leaves my body, and she hauls me under the chunky letters of J.C. Penney. A wall of fetid, body-strewn water rushes out of the fog, and my jacket rips free from Kirsten's grip.

The water hits the store entrance and fans inward. We fall to the floor.

Outside, Kirsten and Prairie hold each other. The hand Kirsten had on me stays open, like an action figure's. Her mouth gapes, eyes bulge. She inhales the horror of what's to come, turning only once the wave takes out her legs. Kirsten falls into it with Prairie, whose pink jacket disappears under a grimy mudslide.

The mosquito beast tumbles after them. Then the whole mess of bodies and beast crashes into the doors, leading to the roar of a new flood. More water comes inside Penney's and spreads down the concourse.

Raina splashes into the eddying waters, stopping just short of the spot where the current is strong. Her shoulders collapse at the impossibility of what's placed before her. The others are gone. In a flash, we've been halved, and the reason we came down here has been taken away.

We've failed twice over. Raina's dad. Prairie. And without a chance to rue our misfortune, our defeat comes back to taunt us in the form of an old opponent. The floor shakes, and the sprinkling of already-shattered glass and felled metal pylons ushers in the second mosquito beast.

My instincts kick in, and I scramble away.

"Raina!" I shout, but it comes out a hoarse gasp.

She does a slow turn, her whole being dragged by exhaustion. The mosquito beast bears down on her, and she greets it with nothing greater than annoyance. I flinch when a red line opens across Raina's torso—a diagonal cut from just above her right hip to her left breast. Her arms flail, and she disappears into the flood. The mosquito beast kicks up water and retreats before it's caught in the current.

A cacophony of clacking, scratching claws cause me to turn around. An army of pale, dog-sized water skimmers, arachnid-like things with vicious jaws and a desperate desire for water, have been attracted by the signs of a hospitable environment.

I get to my feet with nowhere left to go. They're coming from all directions, surrounding me in a semicircle, a flood and a mosquito beast at my back.

I step away from these smaller monsters but closer to the idiotic malformation of the mosquito beast. When I turn around, its proboscis sways left and right across my path, aiming for me.

Maybe I'd stand a chance if I had my hedge trimmer. Maybe. But whether it's a mosquito beast, a pack of spiders, or a giant centipede, death has come to Meadow Spire Mall today.

Still...I try.

I attempt to dodge past the mosquito beast, clinging to a dream of near-death, of a close call, nothing so optimistic as unharmed survival. My toes dig in, and I dart for the entrance.

The mosquito beast's proboscis, thick as a flagpole, pierces my side. It wags its head, knowing it's caught something. I hear the suction of its proboscis trying to drink blood from the air behind me. If I pulled the thing out, it would slurp pints of blood and maybe something solid. An organ or two. A length of intestine.

It wags again, the knobbly bits tearing through my skin. My gut is exposed, and I clap my hands to keep everything from falling out.

The proboscis cracks me across the cheek, flaying my skin down to the bone. The whiplash stings the whole of my spine. I collapse to the floor, my head swimming in the whiteness of fore-death. Brown water tickles my face and laps inside my stomach wound.

I pass out when the joyful water striders leap into the flood over my body.

The correct choice was to jump for the mall. Turn to page 212.

There's no shaking off that hand. It's hefted me up and held me six feet in the air countless times in practice and during football games. My vision narrows, and my rage increases. A nice long scream would feel good about now, but I have to remember who else might be here, hidden in the fray of shoppers or perched on the second-floor balcony, watching me have a public meltdown.

I speak through clenched teeth. "Let me go. I'm done with Kirsten. You can do what you want, but I'm done."

"Yeah, I don't think so." Raina lets go and slips her hands back in her pockets. "My dad'll be at Sears for at least three hours, whether I bother him or not. So no, I *can't* actually do what I want. The only thing I *can* do is listen to Kirsten piss and moan about whatever's going on between you. So, come on. Keep me sane, and I'll try to do the same for Prairie."

Up ahead, Kirsten awaits us, looking pristine except for the coffee on her wrist. She stares disbelievingly at a rumpled napkin offered to her by Prairie.

"How did this even come together?" I wonder aloud.

Raina sighs, like she's being squeezed flat and expending the last shred of her very being. "I couldn't care less right now." The hollowness in her eyes tells me it's true...and to drop the subject—immediately.

Compared to Kirsten, it's always been easier with Raina. I wouldn't say our friendship is shallower by any means. There's an imaginary journal entry ripped out, crisply folded, and stowed under the floorboards of my mind that asks: is Raina my real best friend? I probably wrote it sometime in the last couple of years, after a random blowup with Kirsten, when I realized I've never caught Raina in a lie or pinned her down for pursuing an ulterior motive.

Simply put, she's never broken my trust.

Not like Kirsten and I, who nibble at each other, testing for reactions. Raina and I don't do that. She keeps things close to her chest, and I don't push her to open up. On the flip side, I lay it all out there, and she never tells me to shut up, despite countless instances of my blowing past the conventional threshold for oversharing.

Maybe I only wish she was my best friend, and I fear if she felt the same, all would be ruined. Like a crush. A huge part of the attraction lies not in how easily you believe you could attain that special someone, but how easily they'd reciprocate your obsession. It's a fantasy, with no eventuality to wait on, no trying to win anything, but it always stays far away. To investigate a crush is to destroy it and maybe even yourself, if you're unlucky enough.

What's the name for air that's bound to earth?
Floating and flying and so close to touching

I remember more lines, like so much junky poetry I jotted over the years. Daydreams put to verse. Why didn't they use all of it? Is there any point in finding out?

Damn, what *haven't* I learned about the problems caused by crushes in the last day alone?

So, I bury the sentiment deep, pretending I've never thought it. But it's there, part of us—the striker on a matchbook, ready to light us up and burn us down.

Her levelheadedness gets to me too. Sure, Raina doesn't have any skin in this game, but she's the mature one here. Given another moment, I think through the consequences of storming off: more drama, grumbled apologies, faked forgiveness.

Raina seems satisfied with her work. She turns her back on me before I indicate I'll play along. When we return to the other two, she takes Prairie's arm and pulls her forward.

"We'll be at Sam Goody," Raina calls over her shoulder, leaving me with Kirsten, who has a dripping paper cup in one hand and a smeared napkin pinched between her fingers.

It's my turn to sigh. I snatch the napkin from Kirsten, grip her wrist, and dry the coffee from her well-moisturized skin.

"I'll shut up about Skye," she says. "This isn't what Anti-Valentine's Day is supposed to be about." She crouches and tries to catch my eye. "Okay? Forgive me? Let's try on a ton of clothes, get more coffee and slushies, and burn off the sugar mocking weirdos from the upstairs lounge."

I tug her hand closer for a more thorough clean. "Because that's what you really want to do today, right?"

"Yes, that's why we're here. We're celebrating being single bitches and sticking it in everyone's faces."

"That's the truth?"

I give her hand a final, rough rubdown, twisting the napkin around each finger. Kirsten inspects my work and, with a flourish marking her return to a state of perfection, dazzles her red nails in my face.

"Follow me."

She spins. The scent of her conditioner caresses my face and plants a soft kiss on my nose, masking the mall's mulchy odor for one heavenly second.

I follow her. For Raina. And Prairie. I'll try one more time. One *last* time.

If only I knew what Kirsten had in mind.

A normal trip to the mall entails a long discussion of its itinerary, the two most important parts being where to start and where to end. After that, it's about what you're looking for, betting on the kinds of impulse buys at checkout and what the girls at school will have bought—and thus, what to avoid—plus who has the deals, what'll be in stock and out of stock.

It comes down to the mood you're going for. In a rut? Go to the Gap for a pair of sweats. Itching to turn some heads in Holy Trinity's hallways? Express for a pair of butt-huggers.

These deliberations are thrown out the window on Anti-Valentine's Day.

We head down the mall's longest wing, which culminates in its grandest entrance, with a dangling chandelier and a naturally lit common area. In the summer, golden sunsets drop straight down the center line of its western windows. On a winter day like today, the sunset, if there is one, would be off-center, casting a pale glow that ricochets off the floor, onto the walls, and into storefronts to blind the cashiers.

At the end of the wing, one side is dominated by two stories of gauzy Macy's goodness. Whether you're an inch or a mile away, glancing at its jewelry and perfume department is like looking through eyes brimming with tears. Opposite Macy's is a two-story glass facade illuminating a seating area. Starting halfway down the length of Macy's is a string of skinny gourmet food stalls full of baked goods, coffee, confectionery, popcorn, ice cream, and fudge, next to stores featuring the edgiest in teen fashion. Delectable scents puff out and pile atop one another, drawing deep-pocketed shoppers into the mall's bowels.

Kirsten shoves me into The Limited. Before I know it, I'm drowning in on-sale winter tops—chosen by me—and definitely not on-sale exclusive spring maxi dresses and short skirts draped over my arms by Kirsten.

With the dressing room door locked—closed in by scuffed cream-colored walls, carpeted pincushion panels, and two full-length mirrors and sealed in from above by the muffled sound of overplayed pop music—I'm finally free, in a middle-class teen's version of a sensory deprivation tank. I sit on the bench, close my eyes, and lean against the wall.

For the first time since being in bed, I slow down. I wonder if this makes it all worth it—venturing out after yesterday's prank into the abrasive Valentine's decorations and bumbling crowds. Just me in a tiny box, with clothes I'll try on and never buy. I'm hibernating, metabolizing the excess, every second passing like a century in a bubble bath whose temperature never wavers.

My time alone doesn't last long. When I get around to slipping out of my jacket and trying on the first top, a rapid-fire knock comes at the door, and the handle rattles.

"Quinn, open up."

"What is it?" I ask, unlocking the door.

Kirsten forces herself inside, squishing me against the bench, and shuts the door. Before I can whine for her to make space, she doodles a big heart on the door with a Sharpie.

"Oh, that's nice."

"Wait for it." She adds wiggly black lines to the heart's two lobes and draws a shaft extending down from its pointed bottom.

"Yeah, nice, Kirsten."

She bisects the heart-penis with an arrow and signs it, "pin him down B4 QF does," then caps her pen, whips the door open, and bolts for the entrance. I get dressed and follow as quickly as I can, taking no time to see what else she's done or if anyone's noticed.

Outside by the coin-operated massage chairs, Kirsten pulls down the collar of my jacket, seeing if I'm wearing my own shirt.

"No taste for misdemeanor theft, Mrs. Fortner?"

I smile and shake my head at the inside joke—that we're getting married after graduation and I'm taking her last name. "You're an idiot."

She accepts the compliment and rushes toward the next store, pulling a vial of red glitter—likely stolen from an impulse buy bin—from her inside pocket and sprinkling it over unsuspecting shoppers' bags. Then, without checking to see who's watching, she empties it into an occupied baby stroller while the mother's eyes are averted.

I chase after her, stifling laughs and admonishments, insensible with terror and glee, drunk on her moronity.

She's only warming up. Kirsten bows, beckons me forward, and ushers me ahead with an outstretched arm. I take the lead, cutting the path for her to level everything behind me. We're partners in this. I'm dancing—just like Whitney Houston overhead sings about doing—with somebody who loves me. And though I'm not sure I love that someone back just now, it's a start.

Store by store, sign by sign, the pristine faces of models grow mustaches, devil horns, and huge Cindy Crawford beauty spots. They gain scars, lose eyes and teeth, make friends with even more penises, and speak horrible things to one another in hastily drawn word bubbles.

We pass like ships in the night. I find her work everywhere I go. Mannequins grope one another or reach out from clothes racks in despair. I check out the discount section at the back of Gadzooks, and a legion of balloons pop up front. On my way out of Crate and Barrel, I catch her racing through the doors. Butter knives are arranged on the polished oak dinner table given pride of place at the store's entrance. "ASS," spells one set. "SHIT," says another.

Heart decorations, wherever they are, get defaced or shredded. Oh, how much blood would pour from them if they were real.

I shut her out, try things on, window-shop to my heart's content. She appears out of nowhere and tells me I'll never guess what she's done. I say she's right, I won't, and she tells me anyway. Shoppers will find hateful notes in the pockets of newly bought clothes. Condiment dispensers have been switched up at the food court. I act like I hate it, but deep down, where maybe-best-friend Raina is chained in the dungeon, there's another secret. I *do* love it, and it feels like it's all for me.

After an hour, we've covered the mall's longest wing, backtracked, refilled on coffee, woven around all the "Danger: Wet Floor" signs, and checked out Delia's, Wet Seal, and Spencer's by the movie theater. It's not long before I have to pee and we head for the atrium, where Kirsten sits on the fountain's ledge to wait for me.

I'm shocked to find evidence of her menace has already reached the bathroom. The door to the farthest stall hangs by a hinge. A pool of red-tinged water encircles it, with soppy, crimson-stained toilet paper strewn about. A single red handprint marks the wall. It's a particularly rich tableau and another good use of condiments.

Has she hit the men's room too, with a bottle of barbecue sauce perhaps? The scene is nearly enough to make me head for the upstairs bathroom, but the place is empty, and I can take the first stall. I sit, the lights flicker, and violent rattling from the plumbing travels through the walls. My God, how far has she gone?

A rank stench drifts up from the sink drain when I wash my hands, reminding me Kirsten isn't the only force of nature at work. I've never thought that hard about how they keep this place from flooding on a normal day, but the sump pump's getting a hell of a workout from this weather. When I go to leave, I catch a faint whiff of another odor, something less decayed but still...organic.

The red puddle ripples, confirming a tremor I'd dismissed as either a product of my imagination or the result of heavy equipment running behind the scenes, like the plumbing or heating system. A fresh blast of mildewy air coughs up from the drains and sends me rushing out the door.

Kirsten has switched to the other side of the fountain, and I sit next to her.

"Nice job in the bathroom. That was some next-level stuff."

She ignores me, dangling her legs and biting her lip, looking like a queen gazing upon a kingdom she doesn't recognize anymore.

"Something wrong?" I look around for security guards, if only to snuff out a flash of paranoia.

While Kirsten was wreaking havoc, plenty of shoppers saw her, did double-takes, grinned if they thought it was funny, and glared if they didn't. No one tried to stop her, though. They know who the mall belongs to. We may not have the spending power, but we're the top of the food chain, as long as we act like it. Besides, the flooding keeps the mall staff well occupied.

"Wonder if they'll close early because of this," I say.

Kirsten remains silent.

"Hey, is something wrong?"

She blinks. "No, nothing. Just wondering how to put the finishing touch on my masterpiece."

A voice calls out. "I saw your handiwork, Kirsten."

Raina and Prairie come from the other side of the fountain.

"You gotta save me from this girl," says Raina. "Boston I can take, but Jars of Clay? No thanks."

"I told you, the Boston is for my dad...not that I can give it to him right away."

Raina stops in front of me and sticks a teddy bear with a red bow and sunglasses in my face. "Happy Valentine's Day. Freebie from Suncoast."

Kirsten snatches it out of her hands. "Five-finger discount, right, Raina? Come on, I gotta show you something." She stands, grabs Raina by the arm, and leads her away.

I get up to follow.

"No, stay there!"

"What? Why?"

"Just stay! Both of you!"

I don't know what she means, but I also feel like I don't *want* to know. More chaos, surely. It wouldn't be so bad to keep my distance, sober up from our last adventure, and remind myself I'd be best off at home right now.

This does, however, put me in another awkward situation, one I hadn't anticipated happening in a million years.

Prairie sits down. It's just the two of us now. The dorky, straight-A, all-around sweetie next to me—Holy Trinity's latest pariah and worst old friend in the world. I try to meet her eyes, but she's already distracted herself with people-watching.

"Hey," I say after clearing my throat.

She smiles warily.

"CDs?" I nod at her shopping bag. "Did you lift those yourself, or did Raina help?"

Prairie goes white. "What? Oh, no. I...well...Your dad gave me some shopping money on the way out."

I jerk my head in a spasm of surprise and blink rapidly. "Oh."

Until now, I hadn't realized she doesn't have a bag with her, probably no wallet or ID or anything.

"I'll pay him back. I just think he didn't want me to miss out on any of the fun. He refused to let me leave without it."

"Oh. Like how much?" My face goes hot. I'm not astonished, exactly. Just ashamed, feeling my dad's generosity paper over my lack of the same. I wave the question away. "Shit. Crap. No, actually, no. That was stupid. Don't worry about it. You're cool."

There. Take *that*, Dad.

After a moment of silence, I search for Kirsten and Raina, but they've disappeared behind the guest services desk. When I look back at Prairie, she's watching a couple laughing idiotically at the Cupid photoshoot. My eyes inevitably hunt down the Cupid model with his bared abs, then widen in surprise.

"Oh my effing gosh." I giggle. "Is that Joe? Monica's brother?"

Prairie turns to me, her cheeks red.

I point across her face, guiding her to look. "That's totally Joe Molson playing Cupid."

This counts as a small miracle, a slice of nostalgia to tide us over until the others get back. Joe Molson graduated from Holy Trinity a couple of years ago, when we were freshmen. Popular guy, the best wide receiver in years. All State. Responsible for more than half the touchdowns in every season he played. His family belongs to the same parish as Prairie's and mine, so we used to see him all the time before he went to college. Now he's here, back in Madison, shirtless and tanner than Kirsten, flexing and mugging for photos with ridiculous couples and at least a few slap-happy hen parties we've seen walking around.

"We can't let Monica forget this," I say. "We should get a picture, you and me."

Prairie laughs, and so do I. Photos with Cupid-Joe. Torturing Monica. We've never pulled those kinds of hijinks. But could we? Should we?

Eventually, our rowboat of pleasantry hits the bank. Prairie looks at me like she expects me to shove us off with the oar. I don't. I just smile, trying not to make it feel fake.

After a moment, she says, "We can go home if you want."

I guess I've zoned out because it takes a few seconds for her words to register. "What?"

"Do you want to go home? I mean, you've done everything Kirsten wanted, and Raina told me her dad won't spend all day at Sears if we ask for a ride. So, if you want to go..."

"No. I'm good." It comes out brashly, sounding dishonest, which means it is.

Am I that caught up in Kirsten's nonsense? Her steamrolling approach to repressing bad memories is doing the trick. She's made me feel like I could get over the prank for the first time since it happened.

"Are you sure?"

I swing my legs and shrug. "I'm fine with whatever...But I know your parents don't know you're here. You and Raina can bail."

And I don't need her to be my little protector. If anything, I should be hers. Her parents would flip their lids if they knew where she is. If it isn't church or school, it's the devil's business.

Prairie looks at her boots. "I should be okay, as long as it's not too late."

"Raina's dad'll take you. Just tell him to drop you off at my house. You left your stuff there anyway."

"We didn't get a chance to go over homework. Do you still want to do that today?"

Still want to, like we made a plan in the first place.

"Maybe tomorrow?"

Prairie slips off the fountain. "Before I go, can you tell me one thing?"

"You don't *have* to go."

Prairie's on the verge of tears. She isn't caved in on herself like normal. Her chest is puffed out.

She breathes in deep through her nose. "Can you tell me what happened yesterday?"

More amazing than her asking is how comfortable I am telling. There are a couple of reasons, I think. First, she brings it up so bluntly, like she's truly worried about me, without a hungry look in her eye for gossip. And secondly, I can see how much it's eating her up inside, not knowing what's wrong with me. I'm withholding from her the same thing Raina's always giving me.

Trust.

I clap my hands on my thighs and let her have it. She doesn't give me much choice, standing there, looking for all the world like Cindy Lou Who asking why I'm stealing Christmas. Besides, she's so far removed from my life at this point, I can act like it's no big deal. I want to test it out, in fact, to see how it feels.

"Okay, so, newsflash. I had a crush on Skye Bodkin the last couple years. I wrote about him in my diary and asked about him all the time to the girls on cheer. It's old news at this point. It faded by the end of last year, and when school started last fall, I told myself it was a dumb obsession and got over it.

"It just so happens that this year, Skye's locker is across the hall from mine. At first, it felt weird, but it's been fine. We don't really talk because we don't have any classes together, and there's always other people to talk to in the halls. So we've, like, smiled or said hi a couple times, but it hasn't felt odd. It's just fine. Then yesterday morning, his locker is covered with Valentine's Day streamers and stickers and paper hearts, and when he opens it up, this giant card and all this candy fall out. It's before first hour, and a ton of us were watching because it was so crazy. Everyone thought it was his friends playing a joke or, like, a really good friend who wanted to surprise him.

"So, everyone's laughing and trying to get a closer look, when he opens this card, and he's, like, half laughing, half confused, and everyone's telling him to read it out loud, so he does. It's this very cheesy poem, and people are trying to rip the card out of his hands, but it looks like he's trying to figure out who it's from. Before they can take it, he holds out the card for everyone to read. They stop laughing and stare at me because suddenly it's way too awkward. It's signed 'Love, Quinn C.'

"Long story short, it was a prank. And Kirsten's right, it was probably the seniors on cheer. It's a tradition for them to mess with the juniors, and Kirsten wonders if Bridie convinced them to do it. Or maybe one of them really doesn't like me, which is fine because I don't like some of them, but...of all the things they could've done, this was pretty fricking weird and embarrassing."

Saying it out loud makes me feel better. I *am* the victim after all. Yet I can't help but think that I got myself into this whole situation. I don't mention I recognized the poetry as my own and am still struggling to remember where I wrote it.

"That's really stupid," Prairie says. "I'm sorry they did that to you."

"Thanks..." Some of her emotion rubs off on me, and my voice trembles. I take a deep breath, quelling the impulse to cry, and offer her a hopeless grin.

She sits back down next to me, and her closeness makes everything seem the tiniest bit better.

I'm so caught up in the delirium of my explanation and Kirsten's mall rampage, not to mention the spectacle of grownups posing with a half-nude man-baby archer, I forget why I didn't want to come here in the first place.

Zipping around the mall like a housefly waking up accidentally in the middle of winter, going from room to room, bonking off windows, marveling at the lack of predators—no spiders or frogs or anything like that. Then I see a bit of greenery and I think, *That looks nice, that looks like summer*, and I land on it. But I landed on something only offering the illusion of welcome, a false sense of comfort. A Venus flytrap. And in a split second, the walls close in, and I'm squished, immobile, and suffocating.

The blissful sensation of anonymity granted by the massive crowds is ruined by the appearance of Skye Bodkin. He materializes from behind a screen of shoppers, lanky legs steering him through, long dark hair brushing his pronounced cheeks, torn jacket unzipped and swaying with his movement.

I catch his eye, and even though time has slowed long enough for me to write an essay on this particular form of agony, he recognizes me.

Given a century to react, by my reckoning, he only manages to purse his lips and offer a curt nod before moving on: universal body language for forced politeness, a knee-jerk coolness. Absolute dismissiveness.

Uh yeah...hey, is what it says.

And there it is again. The desire to die.

Go to the bathroom to cool down. Turn to page 20.

Distract yourself with shopping. Turn to page 63.

I flinch away from the scene below, pulling back from the railing and out of Bridie's and Skye's sight. My heart pounds against my chest, and my ears burn red hot. The seniors' riot of noise explodes across the mall, leveling everyone's Valentine's Day mirth into shocked silence.

The group saw me. They'll think I did it.

I gawk at Kirsten, a prisoner to her machinations. But I'm a victim too. I don't have to be covered in gunk for this to be the worst possible outcome for myself on a day like this. They'll blame me, even if Kirsten pulled the trigger.

She takes one last look at her masterpiece, her jovial, feral expression giving away the slightest hint of terror. For once, she might've gone too far.

And so what if she has? She's Kirsten Fortner. Invincible. Kirsten has never had skin in any game. She's gotten away with everything her whole life, even—*especially*—when she's been caught red-handed. I mean, she's practically made a career out of it.

That isn't me. I'm the one suffering under the haze of rumor right now. I'm the vulnerable one. She's ruined my life.

"Come on!"

Kirsten tries to bolt, grabbing my arm. That's not happening anymore. I clench the railing with one hand and hold her in place.

Her grip on me fails. She would never really tie her survival to my own, but I keep her glued to the spot.

"Quinn! Come on!"

Raina has already taken hold of Prairie and sprinted away, only to turn back and watch, given our delay.

I don't have any words for Kirsten. What I do possess is the will to separate myself from her, in my eyes and the eyes of everyone who's just been harmed. To do that, I have to hold on tight.

"What are you—" Kirsten tries pulling away, digging her nails under my fingers.

I haul her onto the couch. Shouts are lobbed up at us from soaked seniors. Their target is right here, and I grab her anew, fending off her nails and discovering a strength I didn't know I had. I find my words too—I'll need them for the seniors.

"You're staying right here, Kirsten," I growl.

"I...am...not!"

I climb on top of the couch. Trent and Gabe are pointing and swearing up a storm. They don't matter to me as much as the others, despite the damage their gossip alone could do.

"Bridie!" I shout. I want to yell Skye's name, but wouldn't that only make it look worse? "Bridie!"

"Quinn, get off me, you psycho!" Kirsten says.

My feet sink into the cushions, and I pull her forward, nearly knocking her head against the railing in my effort to force her to answer for her idiocy. She'll be caught this time. I'm going to make it happen. She won't destroy me like this. As awkward as it is, I keep dragging her upward, closer and closer for the seniors to see. She's the catch of the day.

Kirsten tries to pry me off one more time, and I adjust my grip, using my knee as a lever to break her hold.

I should have never doubted her resolve to beat back anything holding her prisoner, me included.

Kirsten pushes me, and Raina screams.

The backs of my thighs press into the railing. My grip on her slips, my hands hunting for a better hold elsewhere, and my spine bends backward. My legs go out from under me, uppercutting Kirsten's jaw. She makes one desperate grab for my boots.

Beneath me, Bridie and Skye reach in a futile gesture to break my fall.

The tile floor greets the crown of my head with a punch, and my vision goes bone white. It's immediately followed by a scissor snip straight across my neck.

♥*♥*♥

The correct choice was to run. Turn to page 80.

My face goes tingly hot, my heart clenches, my lungs swell, and every part of my body rubbernecks toward the brain to see what the heck it's going to do.

Skye's gone, but I still feel his gaze and can sense the whole mall staring and whispering. I'm utterly exposed, and I can't stay here anymore. If you want to get lost in a crowd, this is the perfect place to be. If you want to get lost to the world, it's the worst. Every storefront sheds its superficial attraction and turns into a bunker for me to hide in while the horde of shoppers passes me by.

With the preliminary decision made—run, just run—I slip off the fountain, surprised to find the floor beneath my feet, and make a beeline for the nearest shop.

I get under an awning, with its lit white letters for Arora Jewelers, main competitor of Manz, and step onto its sound-absorbing red carpet. The first display case holds a bunch of thin silver bracelets and necklaces adorned with tiny, tasteful charms.

"Hello, miss. Happy Valentine's Day."

A middle-aged man with thinning black hair offers a tiny smile. He's dressed to the nines, hands clasped behind his back. He bows forward to match my height. My evident discomfort does nothing to deter him.

"Are we waiting on a gentleman, or may I guide you through a selection of our finest charms?"

My eyes bulge. I squeak in his face.

He scrunches his brow, and his eyes flit behind me.

"Quinn, what's wrong?" Prairie asks, a hand on my shoulder.

I shake her off and wind through display cases, going into the next store on the right. A candle shop. I burst through its wall of scents, like a heavy beaded curtain, and scan the shelves. Colors. Fragrance. It hooks into the basest instincts, soothes me before I even know it. Skye becomes a shadow in the back of my mind—the outline of its hair and its bearing familiar, but the face is blank. My legs have followed where my brain needed me to go. The mall's still doing its magic, deeper work than before, acting as a narcotic right when I need it.

When Prairie and a sales rep descend on me at the same time, the illusion wavers. They hem me in. I shrink into myself, with nowhere to go.

"We're just looking. Thanks," Prairie says.

The rep smiles and spins on her heel.

I uncap and inhale deeply from a nearby sample-size candle—a pungent lavender that wrinkles my nose and which succeeds in bringing me back to earth.

"Quinn? I'm kinda freaking out here."

"I'm sorry," I say, taking another whiff. I could go for something else. Something stronger and fast-acting. Now that I'm down to earth, I want off it again. "That's literally the exact opposite of what I wanted to happen today. And I knew it. I just *knew* it would happen. There's nothing worse that could happen today."

"What happened?"

I raise my arm feebly in the direction of the fountain. "Skye walked by. He saw me."

"Oh."

I could just die, I want to say, but it's too dramatic. And it'll worry Prairie. Why complicate my time with her more than it already is? I don't want to cry on her shoulder; I can't afford to. It's just not who we are at this point, and it'd only open all sorts of other possibilities in her mind, or in mine, that we're far beyond.

Her face contorts with sympathy, and I can see her cycling through her options. Kind words? Encouragement? Pity? Should she go in for a hug?

Before it gets any more awkward, I take another deep whiff of lavender, then cap the candle, stuff it in my pocket, and square my shoulders with Prairie's.

"I want to go...try some more clothes on. And not because it's Kirsten's idea. I want to do it."

"But what about Raina? Do you want her dad to give us a ride home? If you don't want to see Skye again, or—"

"Raina can come find me. Believe me, if we go find them, we'll end up wasting just as much time dawdling around at Sears, waiting for him. I'd rather do what I came here to do."

It's a dangerous decision. The mall has eyes. It's seen me. Who knows who else is with Skye? Or what he'll tell them? A part of me says I should track him down and...apologize...clear the air or something. I hardly know what to make of the situation myself. How could it be affecting him?

Prairie seems to be thinking along the same lines.

"Do you want to find Skye? He's gotta know it was a prank, right? Based on what you said? He's always seemed like a nice guy to me. And he's the one at the center of it all, so maybe you can explain it to him."

I want to say yes, but it hardly matters. Does he know about my crush on him? And how much about it?

I replay my reaction to the prank, beat for beat, in slow-mo. Picture everyone's faces. See *his* face. Wonder what my expression looked like. There's more to it than I want to share with Prairie. Or with anyone. When Skye read that poem, there was more of me in there than anyone standing by his locker would've realized. I've only told Kirsten I recognized it.

"Quinn." Prairie says my name more forcefully than she's ever done before. "Don't you see him, like, a bunch at school? Just tell him. It's better than dealing with the gossip, isn't it? Get him on your side."

"No, I don't. Not really. We don't have any classes together, and I've barely said a word to him."

"But your lockers are right across from each other?"

"Yeah."

I realize how pathetic that makes me sound. Yeah, I've smiled at him or murmured hello. But I swear at some point I've made eye contact or exchanged greetings at least once with every person in the immediate vicinity of my locker, even the goth kids, the total nerds, the jocks who are too jocky, too mean-spirited. Have I actually avoided Skye more than that, based on my crush?

Prairie exhales and throws out her arms. "Aren't you in the same clique as him? I thought all of you guys hung out together."

My voice turns cold. "Who's 'you guys,' Prairie?"

"Well, like, he hangs out with some of the cool kids, and you're on the cheer team with a bunch of popular people and..."

"What do you think, that the *cool* kids are just one big group you're not part of and we all get together all the time and go do stuff together?"

"No, that's not what I'm saying."

"Because that's not how it works. It's not like there's a big popular group and a big loser group and the popular people get along all the time and make a point of keeping the losers out. It's broken up into little groups, like anything else, and everyone competes with each other. And half the time, we hate each other, and half of the people we don't even like anyway. And it all feeds into the drama. It's all high school, Prairie. You can only count on yourself and your closest friends, and even they'll screw you over at some point."

I'm not sure where the rant comes from, but it speaks to a massive sense of betrayal, like I've worked my way into the great big middle of everyone since grade school, trying to insulate myself from attacks on any side. That's what being cool is. It's not about having everyone looking at you; it's having everyone look away. Because in high school, if they're looking, they're attacking. That's come crashing down, thanks to yesterday.

Prairie looks half the size she was a second ago. "I thought it was worth asking. I really thought you two might be friends."

I take a deep breath and watch my words. "We're not, okay? I'm not trying to be rude or anything. I'm just...angry."

"Okay."

Prairie nods rapidly, keeping her eyes down.

I tell her I'm going to go try on some clothes and that she can follow me if she wants.

She does.

Abercrombie is closest, but it's too much of a classmate magnet. I speed by, using my peripheral vision to check out the shirtless models hanging out by the entrance. The same guys I saw earlier.

Models. I was right after all.

We slip into Express, and I mindlessly grab clothes off the rack. In the changing room, my mood shifts with the jackets I model, and I wonder if I should make things up somehow to Prairie, who idles around the women's section, looking for nothing in particular. When I start to feel too bad, I try something else on. It focuses me, reminding me how correct Kirsten was in distracting myself.

We move between stores, heading upstairs. There are nothing but blank faces in the crowd along the way. At one point, a loud crack sounds through the mall, and instead of rubbernecking with the rest of the people, I take it as an opportunity to plow through them unnoticed.

More piles of clothes. More dressing rooms. I end up in August Max. Slipping out of my jacket, I try on the first in a whole lineup of items.

The floor quakes with a rumble intense enough to give me pause. It's followed by a trickling or skittering overhead, as of water through pipes or pebbles thrown onto a sidewalk. It's like the rumble chased it across the ceiling. The fluorescent light directly above me vibrates when the trickling passes over it. I scowl, inspect my stack of clothes, and continue with my marathon.

I'm onto my last coat when a hand pounds on one of the changing room doors.

"Hello! Quinn!"

The hand knocks on another door, then keeps down the line, getting closer.

A flustered woman pipes up from the room beside mine. "Excuse me! Occupied!"

"Kirsten?" I ask.

Knuckles pound on my door despite my speaking up.

"Carpenter, where you been? I've been looking everywhere."

I shed the jacket, grab my own, and pull open the door, coming face-to-face with Kirsten. She has a wild look in her eye.

"You got your marker ready?" I ask.

"There's no time for that."

I step out, leaving a pile of clothes inside, and cross my arms, with my jacket in front of me. "Where's my teddy bear?"

"Floating in the fountain. She stabbed it with a fork and covered it in ketchup," Raina murmurs, checking out some blazers tagged with red sales stickers.

"It's where?" Prairie exclaims, coming up next to Raina.

"Everyone, shut up!"

Kirsten's expression shifts from beaming enthusiasm to outrage. She loops her arm under mine and pulls me to the back of the store.

"Quinn, you'll never guess who we just saw. And I have the best idea ever."

Prairie's face has gone white for—I don't know—the hundredth time today. There's disappointment there too. I've ignored her advice, and Kirsten has swooped in to reassume control. No better time like the present to make Prairie a little proud of me, to remind her and myself I'm not at Kirsten's beck and call. Not to mention, I do not like that Kirsten has resorted to manhandling me.

I resist her pulling. "I'm not interested, Kirsten."

She moves behind me and pushes.

"Hey!" I plant myself, and with a shriek of my boots on tile, I bring her to a stop and turn on her. "Knock it off! You're not dragging me into any more of your crap. I already got plenty of weird looks, being around you today."

"You haven't even heard me out yet."

She tries pushing me again. I step back and bat down her arms.

"I don't want to hear you out. Look, I saw him, okay? And he saw me, and it was totally cool. Nothing weird happened, and nothing weird *has* to happen. At this point, I'm just ready to go home, and the others are too."

Kirsten goes for another push but stops herself. "Huh? Saw who?"

I lower my guard. "What?"

"Who'd you see?"

"Who did *I* see?" I ask. "Who did *you* see?"

"I never said I saw—" Kirsten's eyes light up. Her mouth uncoils into a beautifully demented grin it's hard to believe hasn't been there all day. "You saw *Skye*," she says, as if she's caught me sneaking downstairs at a house party two minutes behind him.

"Yeah? Yeah, I did. But...did you—"

"Oh my God..." Her eyes flit back and forth, her brain computing and forming new circuits. "Oh. My. God."

"Kirsten, what *is* it?"

Lightbulb on, Kirsten pivots her eyes back onto mine. "Bridie is here!"

My sister's name renders me speechless. But not because I forged the same connection Kirsten seems to think I have. It's just the last name I expect. Bridie, here? Today? Kirsten could've said Keanu Reeves or Ryder Strong and I'd have been equally dumfounded.

Saying Bridie's name out loud seems to strengthen Kirsten's conviction in her new conspiracy. She bites her lips, imagination working overtime. "She was with Nicole Rylance...and Nicole hangs out with...Wait, where was Skye coming from?"

"I guess he was coming from Sears, so he must've just got here. Everyone has to park over there because of the flooding. Haven't you noticed half the entrances are taped off?"

I may as well have handed her the final unremarkable piece of a jigsaw puzzle, a monochrome hunk of junk pulling together the whole picture. She grips my wrists. I recoil, refusing to be drawn into any clandestine gossip sessions.

"Bridie *helped*," she whispers. Her face darkens, devious glee morphing into manufactured hatred. "Oh, that *bitch*."

None of this comes as a surprise. All yesterday, Kirsten prowled the halls of Holy Trinity, eavesdropping, gathering evidence and collecting hearsay, then barnstorming past my locker between classes to impart the latest developments in the story. She pledged to get to the bottom of things, and I did nothing to stop her. Nothing to goad her on either.

And after all that work...Bridie's her prime suspect? My own sister? I couldn't be less convinced. Bridie and I aren't best friends exactly, but neither of us would pull something like this. It's the so-obvious nature of the insinuation that makes it the least believable.

Nonetheless, I can't help but follow the thread, to see what kind of sense it makes. After all, the specific targeting of Skye and the wording of the poem—which I guarantee is in one of my diaries—these are intimate things existing in physical form and which should be tucked away in my bedroom, safe from prying eyes.

But Bridie wouldn't have stooped so low as to go looking for them, breaking that sacred boundary. Once, when I was ten and she was eleven or so, we traded bedroom incursions, one night after another. She read excerpts from my diary at the dinner table. I paid her back the next day, and it led to such a horrible, bloody conflict, we were grounded for two weeks straight. The war's never gone hot since. Nothing in recent memory makes me think Bridie did this.

I flash back to the present, listening while Kirsten thinks out loud.

"—makes so much sense. You see? She probably traded secrets about you with Gina and Valerie so they could prank you and she could get intel on someone else. You know *all* the seniors prank *any* underclassmen, and they're always looking to outdo the last year's class. Dang, I wonder who Bridie's going after, to give the girls something that personal about you? But...No! Stop, stop, stop. Quinn, we can get them back! Right now! Come on, we need to go quick and see where they're at before it's too late."

She tugs on my arm, but I don't budge. Her snake's nest of a theory is doing nothing to make the situation better. It doesn't add up. She's just looking to inflict more mayhem on the mall. It's all for fun.

"What's the problem?"

The other two appear at her sides—Raina looking like pure boredom, Prairie a shuddering mess.

"No," I say. "Go ahead. Have fun. But I'm done."

"What do you mean, you're done? You can get revenge right this second. Gina and Valerie are *here*. You want to know who I saw? That's who. I guarantee *they* pulled this crap."

Crossing my arms, I look to Raina. I have to draw her into this. Her dead expression can become part of my argument, advocating for me with its unfathomable chillness. It does help to deflate Kirsten the tiniest bit, exactly as I knew it would. I'm not playing around.

"Go make your crowning achievement or whatever. Your prank to end all pranks." I twiddle my fingers toward the store entrance. "Collect your gold coins or whatever it is you get out of it. But whatever you're cooking up comes down to you. I know it's not for my sake. Otherwise, you'd leave it the hell alone. It's just for you to screw around."

Kirsten's jaw sets. "You don't care that Bridie helped humiliate you in front of the whole school?"

"You have no proof that she did."

She backs up, looking at me from down her nose. "You used to tell me I was more of a sister than she was."

I've never said anything like that to Raina or Prairie, and I feel my embarrassment showing. It hurts because most of the time it's true. Kirsten's like my sister—fighting like cats and dogs, then going right back to loving each other.

Right now? It's not a loving kind of time. Hearing her wield my own words against me makes it that much easier to do what I do next.

"Then I think Bridie gets to reclaim her title today."

Kirsten's tanned skin goes red, like she's bursting out in a rash. Her eyes glitter with tears. Angry ones, which threaten to brim over and fall on her trembling lips. Without another word or signal, she storms out of the store.

Track down Kirsten and make amends. Turn to page 205.

Go find Mr. Harris for a ride home. Turn to page 37.

The guitar solo belts out across the mall's devastated concourse and drops on the girls' confused faces. Had I not recognized it within the first three seconds, I'd be acting the same way.

Do I really know it's Skye? Or do I just think I know? Is it simply my former obsession welling up again, all mental roads leading to the dream of a lovestruck eternity with the one guy who doesn't know I exist?

No. It's totally him. And it doesn't help my burning embarrassment that on the one day I've had to insist, without a doubt, my crush on that super hunky, guitar-toting, shaggy-haired, leanly muscled heartthrob is finished, I have to trot out the sort of Skye-specific trivia which proves the extent of my culpability. But that's him, strumming a guitar across the hellacious swamp, the monster-stricken wasteland formerly known as Meadow Spire Mall.

So, before they can ask the questions bobbling around in their heads, I give them the real answer.

"That's the song he played in the talent show when we were freshmen."

Raina wrinkles her face. "What's that? Pearl Jam? Every guy probably learned how to play that song. Not like it mat—"

"No, it's Soundgarden," Kirsten says. "You're thinking of mumbly guy. This is warbly guy."

"No, it's not them," I reply forcefully. "Or...kinda. It's Temple of the Dog, and Eddie Vedder sings on that one song everyone knows but...whatever. Never mind. Skye didn't just play it at the show. He used to hum it all the time. He hums a lot when he's either, like, really focusing on stuff or spacing out."

I picture the back of his head in class while he doodles on brown paper bag book covers or flounces down the sidewalk, past the outdoor cafeteria seating, squinting into the autumn sun. Humming all the while the song he insisted on playing so well, then afterward, the song he'd play to perfection. It must be the first thing he thinks of when he picks up a guitar, something which magically flows from his fingers. Otherwise, he'd be playing something else.

Kirsten wrinkles her nose, runs her hands down her face, and shakes her head, like she's trying to rid herself of my secret knowledge.

"But...what does that mean?" Raina asks.

"It means he's alive and he's out there," I say, like this changes any of our math.

We haven't discussed Skye in the least, but it can't be lost on everyone. I need to get Bridie, and we remember who she was with.

"Yeah, okay, so he's across the mall at Band Avenue. Are you forgetting what we just went through?"

At that, the mosquito beast causes a fresh ruckus inside J.C. Penney. No human screams accompany it. Just the barreling sounds of a mosquito beast. Or two. Some other big thing is in there with it. Then it trundles out of the store, sliding into the jewelry kiosk and shifting it out of place.

We duck closer to our pile of lukewarm corpses for cover.

The beast's proboscis points to the opposite doors, which is where it goes, back to feed on its old supply of bodies.

"Ugh." Kirsten squats over a man's corpse, trying to maintain her balance without touching it, suddenly appalled for some reason.

"Case in point," murmurs Raina, nodding toward the mosquito beast. She turns to the doors, drill raised, readying for another assault on the glass. Her cockiness leaves nothing else to say. But she pauses, looking out into the darkness, and lowers the drill to her side along with her gaze. Her shoulders sag while she studies the water level, which has risen to the height of our mid-thighs.

I can't argue against what we've endured, but Raina can't debate Prairie's rationale. She wants to. I do too. But there are no guarantees once we're outside, especially if none of us has any keys.

"Look, my dad is *dead*," Raina suddenly blurts. "I have to get out of here. If I die, my mom will die. It will kill her. And my brother will have nothing. I already know how bad it's going to be for him not to have a dad. I can just see it."

Raina squeezes her eyes shut and curls her lips, swallowing back more points she wants to make. She looks as haggard as an old woman, nothing like the teenager she is, not even the sullen version of her from this morning.

I search for something to say, as if there's anything that would help, but Kirsten saves me the trouble. She pulls me away from Raina, her mouth close to my ear.

"Quinn, look what happened last time someone ran away to save someone. She split us up, and her dad still died. We can't get out of these freaking doors, *apparently*, but that doesn't mean we should haul ass across the mall."

"We'll freeze if we go outside here, Kirsten. We're soaking wet."

"We're at the mall, Quinny. Go shopping for some dry clothes before we leave."

Raina sniffs loudly and backs away from the door, brushing the glass with her hand. "Yeah, okay. This way is screwed. I'm thinking we go through Penney's. Who's with me?"

"Yes, that's all we can do." Kirsten's hand slips from my shoulder.

I'm suddenly left out of the planning, our last idea spoiled by floodwaters with a subzero windchill skating across their surface.

But the girls' idea doesn't sit well with me. They're only thinking one step ahead.

Skye *is* there. Bridie *is* alive. And the floodwaters...there's a reason *everyone* had to park by Sears. No matter where we get out, we'll freeze. We need the guarantee of a vehicle.

Kirsten and Raina scan the J.C. Penney entrance. They can't be relishing the idea of facing another mosquito beast, or whatever is in there. Within seconds, their backs are to me. They've become a two-person team.

"Or do we wait," Kirsten says, nodding to the opposite doors, "for that thing to go back into Penney's?"

"Could," Raina replies. "There's something else in Penney's. But if there are bodies by that door, it's either been locked or iced in."

"Crap."

"Guys," I say. "No."

"Quinn, we decided back at Sears that we'd get out of here first thing." Raina uses her monotone boss voice on me.

Suddenly, I'm the unreasonable one. I lean into it. "That was then, and this is now. Skye is playing music over there, and there has to be a reason for it."

"We wanted to find Prairie, and we have. All four of us can get out of here. If we want to come back for Bridie—"

"*If?* I'm going to find her!"

Raina opens her mouth, then shuts it.

What're you going to say? Huh?

I flash my eyes at her and shrug with exaggeration, goading her into saying it. That I should just leave if I want? Go out on my own?

The mosquito beast rummages through its slop pile, banging against the doorframe and sending rattling tremors down the hall.

"We're checking Penney's," Raina says softly, making a placating tamping-down gesture with her hands, which only pisses me off more.

"Roger that," agrees Kirsten.

"So, it is down to me. I have to look for Bridie on my own," I say. "If that's what I got to do, I will. This is only the second time you've broken the same promise to me today. So that's just fine. And what about you, K? Are you too scared...or just too embarrassed to see those guys after what you did to them? Is that it?"

They don't even bother to look at me.

"We gotta go," Raina says.

"Yeah, we're done with this, Quinn. Let's get ready."

She and Kirsten stand, argued out, bracing to run into J.C. Penney before the mosquito beast gets bored of its current catch and comes our way.

Only, a peeping sound makes them stop. Raina and Kirsten look at Prairie, their expressions easy to decipher.

Prairie clears her throat. "You know, something else that's changed is that I wasn't at Sears to hash out our plans. And I get a say."

The mutineers exchange a look.

"Why're they playing music? Think about it. They're in the same boat we're in. Skye and...Bridie and whoever else is left. He could be playing music to get our attention. Maybe they need help."

"Yeah? They ever heard of screaming?" Kirsten nudges Raina, and they start walking tentatively into the open.

"Or," Prairie says, "he's playing to cause a diversion."

Maybe she's only talking to me at this point, that it's just us, my meek little friend who's preaching to the choir and expects me to amplify her message. But she hasn't given up on them. She speed-walks to catch up with Kirsten and Raina.

Raina can't help but stop. I swear she almost smirks in response, ready to turn down whatever Prairie has to say.

"Why'd Skye be causing a diversion?"

"Because they're fighting back."

The corners of Raina's mouth turn down. She stares more coldly at Prairie.

"Why else do you cause a diversion? They're either fighting back or trying to escape."

I jump in. "And Bridie will be there!"

Prairie stutters, looks back at me with a nod, and continues. "And look, if they're trying to cause diversions with these kinds of animals, it's probably not going to work. Maybe the big ones, but not with the ambush predators. They're already holed up and ready to pounce, so if they're trying to get into stores and rescue people or, like, draw animals into the open, it's not going to happen. They're going to get more people killed and—"

"Prairie."

"We have to warn them."

Kirsten looks disgusted, her sneer hooked onto an eyebrow that nearly reaches her hairline. "Dude, two things. One, it's too late to warn them. And two, we've been over this. We got to help ourselves before we can help anyone else. And Raina's right. She should get out of here too. The people over there, whoever it is, they aren't the only ones depending on us."

Another riot of noise comes from the mosquito beast, this time culminating in a loud crack. Following it is a noisy, continuous hiss. From out of the fog arcs a wave of water. Another booming bang and the wheeze changes pitch. The fog itself is disrupted by an influx of cold air, revealing the bulky shadow of the mosquito beast bounding between the walls.

The wave reaches us and spills over our boots. The hiss changes pitch again, and a fraying blast of water shoots out into the middle of the concourse—half of its droplets evaporating into steam, the rest drizzling into the standing swamp. It's all the evidence we need to know water is piled against the opposite doors. At any moment, it may crack open and send the full force of the outside flood against us. That and a desperate, bumbling giant mosquito.

Raina yells something and bolts with Kirsten right on her heels. They high step through the deeper, colder water.

"Would somebody *please* listen to me today!" Prairie screams, rushing after them. She grabs Kirsten's jacket, and when Kirsten shrieks and tries to pull herself away, Raina stops too.

Raina rounds on Prairie, more than willing to stand up to anyone she has to. I rush to Prairie's defense and put myself in front of her, expecting it to get physical.

Prairie doesn't mind. She just shouts right past me. Prairie raises her arm and points it across my chest, at the gated entrance to Suncoast.

"*They* didn't listen to me! *Quinn* didn't listen to me! No one has, and look where it's got everyone!"

"In this case, it's bullshit, Prairie. Penney's is our ticket out of here," Raina says.

"No! You didn't even let me finish. All these animals down this wing? They're locked in now. They've eaten. They're satisfied. And the other side of the mall is far less flooded than over here. Or didn't you notice that when you got here? Because we had to park way out by Sears because it was the only spot that wasn't underwater. And no one here has their keys."

Raina's eyes gleam with fire.

Prairie presses. "You have no way to escape the cold, and you're underestimating just how bad it is out there. I get that you have a plan that you're so close to finishing and you don't want to change it, but you *have* to. And you know it. So this is what I say. I'm going with Quinn because she's the only one who's got her head on straight right now. And she's the only one of you who's shown any faith in me, today or ever. It just so happens it's the right thing to do, too, because we can help those people. And they can help us too."

A steady current of water pushes at our feet now. The mosquito beast hops half-heartedly around the other entrance, sending rumbles through the floor and ripples across the water.

Raina's scowl shows she isn't convinced. My surprise comes from Kirsten, who almost looks like she's been won over. That or she's marveling at Prairie's second sudden righteous fury.

Prairie backs away from Raina. She looks at me and then off toward the atrium, where it's nothing but fog-shrouded darkness and watery devastation. Hands hang lifelessly from storefront security gates. The surrounding water is thick and soupy with blood. And from under the burbling sounds of an impending deluge are the shredded strands of a messy guitar solo.

My God, what have I signed myself up for?

Prairie hasn't exactly relied on wild guesses to reach her decision, but there are no guarantees for that number of assumptions. She's reasoned it out the best she could, if only to support me. I almost hate it because J.C. Penney really is *right* here. But I also like the feeling of a plan, if only to see it laid out like a nice long carpet.

We'd have to cross a lot of ground to get where we're going. I wish it didn't feel like the right thing to do. And I don't really think I'll be able to save everyone when I get there. We've endured more monstrous things today than anyone could sanely expect to witness in a lifetime, and our luck is bound to run out.

J.C. Penney is right here. We survived Sears. What could be inside here that we wouldn't encounter in the mall itself?

This is it. Our team may have come to an end, right as it's finally come together. I'll be ruining the headlines if Prairie and I don't make it.

Cheer Team Starlets Survive Mall Massacre.

Lucky Teens Escape Fearsome Freaks to Keep on Cheering.

Kirsten recognizes the decision in my eyes and starts looking worried, as if she wonders who she's going to steal heat from when she succumbs to hypothermia and I'm not there. Raina looks like she could take our heads off.

I turn to Prairie. I need to. It's come down to her determination. She says I'm thinking straight, but I'm not. I know how ridiculous it is to go back to where we came from. She hasn't seen what we have.

The opposite doors pop. Fog billows into our faces, and a vacuous non-sound, like the whistle of a bomb, accompanies an incoming tidal wave of water and the frantic hulking figure of a mosquito beast.

Time is up.

Raina grabs my arm. I grab Kirsten. She grabs Prairie. For the first time, our whole team is braced together, and I have no idea which way I'm going to let myself be pulled.

♥*♥*♥

Jump for the mall. Turn to page 212.

Jump for J.C. Penney. Turn to page 47.

I lock eyes with Skye. His face is rearranged by disbelief, eyes squinting, mouth sneering, looking completely...uncollected.

How could I ever explain what Kirsten's just done? How? We've detonated a bomb. I'm party to assault. There's no kidding around, no calling no tap backs. Nothing can or ever will fix this.

My eyes laser into Skye's, cycling through forms and variations of diplomacy, wordlessly screaming anything and everything that frees me from responsibility: it's not my fault, I'm sorry, it wasn't me, it was all her, I didn't know this would happen, it was an accident, a horrible accident, there was a second thrower, why didn't you duck, *ha ha ha*, got ya this time, we'll be laughing about this Monday, funny, y'know, I actually had a crush on you!

And man, do people notice when you're chucking ten-pound buckets at people's heads. The mall's collective attention, already jumbled about by the flooding, focuses on the raging seniors. Clusters of teenagers, couples on dates, mothers with kids, cashiers and associates, maintenance workers, security staff—you name it. Everyone seeks to uncover who wrought this havoc.

While I lean over the railing, making my mental amends, Kirsten slips out from under me and twists me around. I slide down the smooshed faux leather cushions and land on the floor, cracking my head against the couch's hard deck. Hands grip my jacket and pull me forward. I groan. Kirsten kneels in front of me, her coffee breath mingling with her conditioner. She looks more serious than I've ever seen her and utters one word.

"*Run.*"

The walls come crashing down. I scramble to my feet, and they carry me away. Whatever I've tried to communicate to Skye is ruined for good.

We head for the atrium, back to Sears—our fastest way out of here. Raina's no fool. She grabs Prairie and hauls her like a kite in a weak wind.

Witnesses laugh and catcall. A few snide old fogies point us out to security, and even though I'm in complete agreement about Kirsten's monumental idiocy, good Lord, are they the whiniest voices I've ever heard in my life. Threats of revenge float up to us from the seniors.

Splashing, running footsteps, and bellowed commands come from a handful of red-lapeled, navy-blue security guards on the first floor. They're more organized than usual, already wrangling crowds around the flooding, and now they're turning to us.

Kirsten's Cherokee is all I think about: piling in, screaming at her to step on it, engine kicking up, rooster-tailing out of the floodwaters while pudgy guards burst from Sears, out of steam from their first sprint since eighth-grade gym class, too tired to wave their fists in anger. We barrel out of the parking lot, laughing the whole way. We made it, I'd say. I can't believe we made it.

We *can* make it. Every footfall fills me with a thrill. A sick part of me records every second of our escape for posterity. I'm not just running toward freedom; I'm running toward the only version of this story I can tell at a party and sound like I came out on top. The underdog juniors versus evil seniors. They took their shot, we took ours, and we won.

No one bears a grudge when the dust settles. No, I've earned their respect—*everyone's* respect—and I'm not running scared. I'm stealing victory from the jaws of oppression. It's against the rules, it's ragtag, and no matter what happens next, whether we get arrested or beat up or whatever, we'll have won. This is *our* mall. Our day. I steal Kirsten's cockiness and put on Raina's coolness, cheering myself for making Prairie's life exciting. It'll all work out.

We come to the atrium stairwell, where the Macy's wing meets up with Sears. Kirsten has the most speed. She'll lead us into Sears, down the escalator, and out the door scot-free.

The fantasy falters when her boots shriek on the floor and she slides to a stop. Blocking the way are two security guards holding walkie-talkies. One puts his walkie to his mouth, and points us out to his partner.

Kirsten turns and darts for the stairwell.

"Guys, guys!" Prairie squeals. What could she be protesting? Doesn't she know how adults work? Or teenagers? Our classmates? She's guilty. Doesn't matter if it's only by association. Every one of us is dead meat.

We can still make it. Just have to take a detour. I still have my wind. We're in good shape. But the second time Kirsten's boots screech, I begin to worry.

Her feet slip out from under her at the top of the stairwell, and she grabs the railing to keep from falling. The area at the bottom is blocked off by a web of caution tape stretching between pylons and half a dozen "Wet Floor" signs. Tape is wrapped between the railings up and down the stairwell too.

The taped-off area is fair enough. The water's so high, we'd be high stepping out of there like toddlers in a kiddie pool. The flooding looks worse than even the J.C. Penney wing. The sight is accompanied by a billowing cloud of steam and a chewy stench, whose source I'd rather not contemplate. The bathrooms are nearby, and I remember what I saw in there...

"Screw it," says Kirsten. She descends, snapping the first band of caution tape across her stomach like a race champion.

We slip and slide after her, using the rails to keep from falling. Our squealing boots announce us to the crowd below, followed by the avalanche of shouts from the seniors and security.

When we make it past the landing, three little security goons break from the crowd and slosh through the water, faces red with excitement. This is what they dream of—something real and crazy happening in their very own mall. Whether it's teenage girls or do-it-yourself bombers in unmarked vans, they finally get to play the hero. Crashing into them could turn into an all-out brawl. We might escape, but not with our self-respect intact.

My victory story starts to unravel. I won't be telling this at a party. Everyone else will be.

The two guards up top descend the stairwell while the other three close in. Kirsten stops, and I can't help but look to her, waiting for her next call, when a seed of rage grows inside me.

With one look, I know exactly what she's thinking. She can't afford to get caught. Nor can she risk a physical altercation, especially with the likes of mall security. There are no other options. At least, not for all four of us. I can tell she knows it too, and she's considering another option. There are only three guards to the four of us. She's got the keys, she's fast, and she knows she can make it. Just without us.

I grab her sleeve. Kirsten flashes me a furious look.

"Don't even think about it," I hiss.

The seniors storm into view: Trent, Gabe, Gina, and Valerie. Fists clenched, drenched in muck, one with soggy toilet paper draping his shoulders, their faces red as raw steak. More security guards corral them in a loose cage, making floundering attempts to halt their progress.

Gabe throws a Coke can that ricochets off the railing and sprays us with soda.

"Fortner, you total *psycho!*" Valerie shrieks.

"Kirsten! What the *hell*, you bitch!"

Gasps and laughter rise from the crowd, like they're a movie audience at the moment the plot's central mystery comes to light.

Gabe shoves a security guard. Two others yank on Gina's coat to keep her from advancing. The rest of the guards change their calculus. Rather than boxing us in, the three guards at the bottom of the stairwell close in and shoo us upstairs. My grip on Kirsten strengthens, and I pull her back. Raina, cursing under her breath, does the same with Prairie.

The crowd groans, robbed of the spectacle of a gaggle of teenage girls ripping each other to shreds.

Kirsten's calculations change too. She gives the seniors a pouty smile, making them explode in another fit of rage. A smug perp walk is her only way out of this.

Prairie looks petrified, literally shaking in her boots, while Raina maintains her brooding, resigned expression, only darker than before. I tell myself I can get them out of this. There are plenty of witnesses who can attest to Kirsten's guilt. And mine...

"Where we taking them?" calls down one of the guards.

"The office is totally underwater," says one below.

"There's that store under renovation by Penney's that's wide open," replies another.

"Perfect."

Guards grab each of us by the arm and guide us across the skywalk. Our passage is marked by hoots and hollers. One of the guards, a woman who's all chest and ponytail, outpaces the group and unlocks the rolling gate of a darkened store between an optometrist and a handbag outlet.

"In you go," she says.

The place is gutted. It's clammy and dusty all at the same time. Scratched and punctured drywall lines its walls. Vents are visible above the exposed drop ceiling grid. The floor is stripped down to cement and littered with rolls of ripped-up carpeting and random buckets.

The guards consult among themselves, determine we're not going to kill each other, then file out of the store, one by one. Their ostensible leader mutters that they need to hurry up and close the mall early, leaving behind Ponytail with one other man.

"Y'all turn out your bags now." She pulls over a rolling utility cart. "C'mon, I'm not telling you again."

Her partner stands with hands on hips, glaring at us from outside the door. This has to be the first time they've apprehended anyone in their lives.

Kirsten and I drop our purses on the cart, then our shopping bags, before milling around in the dark.

The seniors are out of sight. The crowd's attention has returned to the flooding. It's just the four of us again. I wonder what my parents will make of this. Or Prairie's and Raina's.

Still, on top of it all, seared into my brain, is the expression on Skye's face.

"We could've made it."

Skye's face disappears. My head ticks upward, and I sense Raina and Prairie looking at me. The dank, dark air goes still, and all outside noise goes on pause. The voice that just spoke, every syllable of its every simpering word, ignites a fresh blaze inside me.

I turn to see Kirsten with arms folded across her chest, staring wistfully into the distance.

"What did you say?" I ask through clenched teeth.

Her gaze snaps back to me. "We could've made it if you didn't grab me and freeze up like that."

I don't respond. Instead, I shove her.

She's ready for it, planting her feet so I basically do a pushup against her chest.

"Why did you do that?" I yell, going to push her again.

Kirsten slaps my hands down.

"Do what? Stand up for you? Give those a-holes exactly what they deserved? Because that's what I did. I gave them *exactly* what they deserved."

"I never asked you for anything! Did you even see who was there? Did you see what you *did* to them?"

"It's payback, Quinn! You know it was Gina and Valerie, and you know Bridie helped, and there was nothing silly about it. Do you even remember yesterday? Do you know what it did to you? You were like a shell of yourself. I thought you were going to kill yourself last night, I swear to God."

"You thought this would make it better? Dumping shit on people's heads?"

"You won't stand up for yourself, Quinn. At no point would you have tried to get back at them. I had to do it on my own. Otherwise, nothing would've happened. You're too scared. That's who you are."

"You call that standing up for me? I don't want you to help me! Not now or ever! That was *Bridie* down there! And—and—"

"Oh, and who? Who was there? Skye? A bunch of seniors we can't wait to scribble out of the team photo?"

"That's not what matters! You *humiliated* me!"

"*They* humiliated you! And at first, I wanted to help you get over it. I thought you could come out to the mall, head held high, and show the world you didn't care. But you didn't want that. You've been shuffling around all day, like you think you're worthless, and you dragged along Prairie, of all people, to be your security blanket, like I'm the bad guy for suggesting you cut loose. So when I saw all of those jerks laughing it up like nothing happened, like they didn't hurt you—the one person who matters more to me than the whole world— I had to act, Quinn. I *had* to."

"Oh my God, Kirsten. Prairie's the only one who's been anything resembling good to me today."

"She's not even supposed to be here."

"Hey, knock it off!"

Our glares whip toward the male guard, whose partner has wisely kept her head down while she pokes through our possessions. He steps into the store, as timid as the boom he tried to put in his command.

"*Can it, blueberry!*" Kirsten hollers.

"So Prairie's your only friend today, huh?" Raina's voice is cold, and it should leave me stricken, but under the current circumstances, I wheel on her.

"Rain, you didn't ask once how I was doing yesterday, did you? I was the talk of the whole school, and you were nowhere to be found. Even at lunch and in Lit, even when Jimmy Laplante asked if I was okay, you didn't check to see how I was doing."

"You want to get into that? What do you think I told Kirsten when she pulled me aside earlier? I told her to let you go."

"You never take my side when Kirsten does crap like this. Any time we fight, you go inside your shell and pretend like nothing's happening. I was hurt more than I've ever been hurt in my life yesterday, and you couldn't even look at me."

"Because it's all so freaking stupid!" Raina shouts. "Call me when someone asks to see your dad's scalp collection or Indian-whoops at you from across a parking lot! How can you not see that Kirsten loves pushing your buttons? And I'm not saying she doesn't do it to everyone, but you let her get away with it. Even now, you're dancing around like she's your puppet master. Do you seriously think she dumped that crap on their heads for you? No, dude, you're just her excuse. You should've freaking ran."

"Why didn't *you* just run, then?" Kirsten asks. "With your precious little cake buddy, Prairie?"

"Prairie's only cool to me because Quinn told her I'm poor."

"And besides, I do, too, care about Quinn and you. You're the one throwing me under the bus and saying she should've ran."

I leap back in. "Uh, says the person who literally chucked herself under the bus? You know what I've noticed, Kirsten? You back away from every confrontation unless you got a crowd at your back."

"Uhh, uh—did you see what I just did back there, all on my own, without anyone to back me up? And all on your behalf?"

"Yeah, you did it when you had us to share the blame. And earlier, you were sulking and bitching because I didn't want to leave my house. Raina's right. You make everything about yourself, and apparently, I let myself get pulled into it. Thanks to you, we're in, like, a literal dungeon, on the worst day of the year, with a freaking snow hurricane coming in, and the ground is—I don't know—*sinking* under our feet. We are *literally* in hell."

"Then why'd you come?" Kirsten cocks her hip and dangles her hands by her side. She's over it. Or she's acting like she is. "C'mon, huh?" she prods. "Why'd you come with me?"

"When?" I demand, insisting on clarity, wanting to be sure of a precise comeback. "When you ran away just now or like this morning, coming to the mall?"

"You tell me."

"Oh, so you've run out of excuses, is what you're saying. You're saying everything that's gone wrong is my fault because I...what? Made the horrible mistake of thinking of you as a friend? Of trusting you to show me a good time on *Anti-Valentine's Day*?"

"Yes. Say that that's your big mistake. That you see me as a friend."

She's so good at this, leading you to the cliff's edge, putting the loaded gun in your hand to kill her off. I've fallen for it so many times, reached the point at which I balk and chuff and throw up my arms, leaving her acting like she's somehow taken the high road.

But it's not going to work today. I lean into her and say what she thinks she knows, which is the actual truth. "You're the biggest mistake of my life."

Here come the tears. She wells up, nods, and wanders into the corner of the cored-out store.

My stomach twists. I've uttered universe-shifting words. The roiling sensation spreads to my limbs, and I wonder if my boiling emotions will settle themselves into an ultimate triumph or regret.

I don't get to find out right away. Next thing I know, the store's windowpanes rattle, and vibrations work their way from the soles of my boots up through my legs. I widen my stance to keep from falling while the utility cart slowly rolls past Ponytail, whose gaze darts up. She pulls a funny pose to keep from falling.

Outside the store, the air goes foggier. The shaking culminates in a booming crack and a shocked cry from the direction of the atrium.

♥*♥*♥

Stay put since you're detained and don't know what's going on.
Turn to page 245.

Keep attacking Kirsten.
Turn to page 227.

Use the distraction to get Prairie and Raina out of there.
Turn to page 166.

When Kirsten finishes, Joe curls his lip and stares into the distance.

"Wha...Ugh. Say that again?"

Kirsten looks crestfallen for a second—like if her point hasn't been taken immediately, it's hopeless. Joe has proved to be pretty obstinate. He's on the same mission as us, has people to protect—same as us—and pride that won't let him do otherwise. But I can't help but crave more company to fight our way out of here.

I nod at Kirsten, urging her to keep it up with this guy. "Go on, K. Tell it again."

"Okay, so these things didn't just spring out of the ground today. They've been around for, like, ever, right? And they've never had humans to chase around. They probably don't even know what we are, when you think about it. They say sharks don't attack people because they want to eat us, but because they think we're seals or something. When these things came into the mall, there was a ton of us walking around, so either they freaked out or they figured we were a ton of food and went to town. And...Okay, that sounds bad.

"What I'm trying to say is that all these monsters that are attacking us? They're *used to* eating each other. So, what if we make them remember? What if we can make it so that, uh..."

Kirsten wheels her wrists, looking to regain her train of thought. I never put it past her to keep rambling in any other scenario, for better or worse. Usually worse. But she's trying right now. Hard.

It's a good thing Prairie is there to pick up the thread because Joe and the moppy-haired models scowl, so far unimpressed.

"You're talking about a diversion, right?"

"Yes! Thank you, Hedlund. A *diversion*. We could try a diversion, by like..."

"Making them hunt each other instead of us."

"Yes, exactly!" Kirsten practically jumps at hearing it put so simply.

The guys don't exactly jump onboard.

There are lots of averted gazes while they contemplate this new strategy, which would put us all near to the creatures. Actually, it *really* depends on our close proximity to them.

As the boys think, another deep rumble causes the mall to shake. Plastic awnings, the cash registers, and kitchen equipment rattle around us. The food court seats, bolted to the floor, dance a little jig.

To top it off, a giant burp of water comes from across the atrium, where Joe says the crack opened.

"Come on. Think about it," Kirsten insists. "We're making them do what they've always been doing. If there's anything I know about nature and shit, it's that you can't take that instinct out of an animal. We want to give these sharks a real seal to eat. Not us." She punches Prairie's shoulder enthusiastically, as if Prairie's said everything Kirsten wants to hear.

Prairie rubs where she was hit, looking troubled by the metaphor. "It makes the most sense," she says slowly. "They've clearly existed in a functioning ecosystem with an established food chain well before the, uh, sinkhole or whatever brought them up here. We've seen it for ourselves. There are predators and prey, harmless animals and bigger, more dangerous ones. We're the aberration. They don't really know where we fit in. I agree that *maybe, if* we get them to turn on each other, we could avoid their attention and slip past them."

"Hell yeah. Get them to eat each other. Pit them against each other, like the animals they are," Kirsten says, now positively radiant, playing to her strengths and eager to be pulling strings.

For once, I can appreciate her turning her basest instincts—which I think are her *only* instincts—to good use. The strangest aspect of it all is the fact Prairie Hedlund has become her second-in-command.

Still, it's Joe who needs convincing. He has a platoon of models at his beck and call, and it seems they won't do anything without his say-so. But he's made it clear he's done taking risks.

"Look, I get it," he says. "It makes sense—on paper, you know. But it's not like we've been watching these things for long enough to know how they work. We've only seen them one fight at a time, so how would we know how to make them fight each other? Besides that roly-poly over there, I don't think I've seen any of these things go after another. It might've been an accident. That little guy might've been the surfer dude, and we're supposed to be the seals, you know what I mean? So, really, how would we do it?"

The brother-models look agitated. Joe's wheels are spinning, and they're aware they might be forced out into the open again. One after another, they slip back into the kitchen. If we don't get Joe completely on our side, a full rebellion will burst through that swinging door and shut this down. They'll meet their ends at J.C. Penney, and we'll be on our own again.

When I hear a raised voice echo from the kitchen, the answer comes to me.

"Improvise."

Joe turns to me. Kirsten and Prairie clam up and give me the floor.

"We don't know exactly, okay?" I say. "No one does. But...look, we're in a food court, surrounded by food. We could haul it with us and throw it around. See if vegetables and lettuce and stuff draw out the prey and see if *they* draw out the predators. We could even throw meat around to see if the predators like that."

Raina comes up behind me, her arms crossed. "You haven't tried that yet, have you?" Her voice is low, still full of disappointment. But she must feel some glimmer of hope, to start engaging with us.

Joe shakes his head, and my heart lifts. "No, we haven't. That's an idea, though. Do you have any proof it'll work?"

Prairie raises her head, then lowers it. She knows she has to lie, but she can't make herself do it. Not if things went wrong. I almost don't care. We're so desperate, I'd say I saw it happen with my own eyes. But we don't know, do we? And if people get killed, it's on us. She can't lie because it's Joe Molson from church, who she's known and admired from a distance her whole life.

Kirsten doesn't say anything either, though I don't understand what stops her. Maybe she thinks her part is done. Maybe her project of empowering Prairie rests on her to win over Joe.

In the end, the three of us don't do anything else to keep the argument going. It's Raina, in her grim monotone.

"I do," she says. "The pretzel and cotton candy kiosk down by Penney's was ripped apart. Monster slobber everywhere. I didn't think anything of it at the time, but that's what I saw when we were on our way down to find Prairie."

"Oh!" Prairie says. "Yeah, that's even better. Sugar and salt. Lots of it. That should get any of these things' attention."

Her excitement builds so rapidly, I don't think I'll ever have the heart to tell her Raina's lying. If we live long enough.

"Sugar and salt," Joe murmurs.

"You couldn't be in a better place for that," Kirsten adds.

The mall shudders again. Sounds of cracking plastic, crumbling masonry, and shattering glass suggest the place is twisting and bending more than we realize. But it's past time we ignore our suspicions that the water rises infinitesimally with every new tremor. We're sinking. It's now-or-never time. If Joe and the boys don't sign up, we'll be on our own. There's no going backward.

Just then, the kitchen door swings open in tandem with a growled declaration of defiance. The wounded buzzcut model comes out, staring hard at us, like he's trying to figure out which of us is causing all the trouble. He marches up to Joe.

Hello, I think, looking at our own *Lord of the Flies* Jack facing off with his Ralph.

Behind him come the brother-models. Stool pigeons. More guys appear at the door.

Let the rebellion begin.

Before Jacky-boy says anything, Joe begins, "Alex. Good timing. I just ran an idea past the girls. They got proof it'll work."

The brothers look at each other. Joe fixes on them.

"Sam. Tim. Get the others out here."

"What's going on?" Alex demands. "I thought we were heading to Penney's."

Joe rubs his hands together like he's warming them. "Weapons ready, Alex."

His fatigue has disappeared. He's back in charge, turning it on like a faucet. Joe can't be feeling great about this, but if he doesn't act, Alex will be running the show. People will get killed. And no matter what, Joe will blame himself.

I can hardly believe it. He's thrown his lot in with us, and we can't say how he took our idea as his own.

"We're going on a treasure hunt," he tells Alex.

While Alex sputters, Joe calls out the troops. Everyone comes out, obedient and eager for action.

There's thirteen of us total, and we break into four work parties to start the food raids. I go with mop-haired Sam and Tim, plus the tall and dark five-o'-clock-shadowed Brian. Prairie joins Joe and Alex, Raina tags along with the gawky Omri and slender Tremaine, and Kirsten goes with the Chicagoans, muscular Tomi and shorter Ramon.

Each team clears out a kitchen—if it's safe to enter, at least. Raina's group retreats from the shadow of a multi-legged menace at the back of McDonald's. They block off the swinging door before sneaking over to Sarah Andigan's Doughnut Shoppe at the end of the line. My team starts next door in Sbarro. It's loaded with jugs of salt and packs of flour, its fridge stocked with cheese and pepperoni, its freezer full of sausage, vegetables, and mushrooms.

We move fast, and aside from a few gripes from the models, we get things done. Before I know it, we've stacked four bus carts full of food: savory items like frozen burger patties and chicken nuggets, Chinese food, Italian noodles and sauce, premixed bread dough, ground beef, cheese, lettuce, peppers, and tomatoes; sweet treats like ice cream, coffee grounds, sweeteners and creamers. And sugar and salt. Lots and lots...and *lots*...of sugar and salt.

Joe orders the guys to devise some more weapons and torches, leading two of the teams to break off and scout the area while another goes back into Calgary Kitchen to prep some torch heads. Raina helps improvise weapons, and Kirsten recommends a slightly risky trip along the wall to Shoq, the perfumery right around the corner of the J.C. Penney wing.

"What for?" Joe asks.

She shrugs and flashes him a smirk. "Chemical weapons."

He nods and returns her grin. "Right. Tomi? Ramon? Get on it."

"Come along, beefcakes," Kirsten calls.

Joe acts as an extra lookout as they leave.

When Joe returns from his post, he sighs and tosses aside his broomstick sword. He looks at the gathered foodstuffs, then to Prairie and me, who are the only two left at the counter. Prairie, who came across a first aid station in the Chinese restaurant, takes off my original cobbled-together bandage, wanting to sanitize and rewrap it.

"Is that from the lizard?" Joe asks.

"No, it was a giant, uh, mosquito thing at Sears. They were running the show until the frogs and centipedes showed up."

"Dang." He shakes his head and looks out into the swirling mist, like a porch-sitter reflecting on what his life has become, having aged fifty years in the space of an afternoon.

My arm breathes with relief when Prairie peels off the layer of shirt I wrapped over my wound. As welcome as the relatively cool freedom is, it looks bad. The cut is shallow, but it's jagged, and my skin at the edges is scraped apart—road rash, courtesy of the bug's bristly leg.

I look away, my head going swimmy. Now's not the best time to figure out if I'm a fainter. I just let my arm bathe in the open air—no one could call it fresh—before Prairie applies whatever stinging antiseptic she's scrounged up.

She goes to the sink behind the counter and starts washing her hands. While her back is turned, Prairie clears her throat and says, "Thank you for helping us, Joe. We wouldn't have made it out of that if you weren't there."

I think Joe's still lost in his own little world, his leg fidgeting, eyes glazed. After a moment, though, his lips pout and his gaze refocuses, and with it shifts his train of thought.

"It was nothing. Really. But I'm glad you're safe."

Joe looks at me before glancing down, frowning at what I think is disappointment from their failure to escape. He's tied his fate to us now and still doesn't know what to make of it.

Prairie flicks water from her hands and dries them with napkins plucked from a dispenser on the front counter. She clears her throat again. "How'd you end up by the playground if you were going to Penney's?"

Joe squeezes his arms into his sides and hooks his thumbs into his loincloth, finding no pockets to hide them. He shrinks into himself, despite Prairie barely prying. Joe's trying to hide from her question. I don't know what makes him so suddenly uncomfortable. He hasn't looked this uneasy before.

"I mean, we heard you screaming right when we were leaving."

"There's been lots of screaming today," I say.

Prairie applies some liquid antiseptic to a wad of gauze and readies herself at my arm. I nod for her to proceed, and without hesitation, she rubs it against my wound from top to bottom, making me hiss and jump. The second time she does it, it stings less. In fact, it almost feels good, like mint chocolate chip ice cream left on my tongue.

"Yeah," Prairie says, "there's been more screaming today than I ever want to hear again. I figure, if you wanted to get to Penney's, you would've stuck to the wall, like Kirsten just did."

She finishes up with the gauze and drops it in a metal bowl—instead of just tossing it into the trash swamp circulating through what can only be described as the former Meadow Spire Mall. I follow her movements, and when she catches my smirk, she removes a pair of plastic tweezers from a sealed plastic bag.

"Babysitter training. Have you never?"

"No. No, I never...had to."

Prairie has babysat all the little kids in our neighborhood, even the ones right across the street from me. I guess I could have done it if I wanted to. Could have made a few bucks, learned responsibility and put it on a resume, blah, blah, blah. But it never crossed my mind.

Maybe as a younger sister, the nurturing instinct never took hold. It's not like it did for Bridie either, though. Prairie's territorial overreach just makes me feel weird for having never done it, like I was neglecting my duty. Or perhaps knowing she was often so close by after we stopped talking is what bothers me.

She starts tweezing away the fibers stuck to my torn skin, and I wince at the worst pinpricks of pain. For as much dwelling as I do on the wrongs I feel like I've done to Prairie, her thoughts seem elsewhere. With every thread she deposits in her bowl, she glances at Joe—all shriveled up like a dead bug but with nowhere to hide his tanned, muscular body.

Talking out into the atrium, he says, "I think you can tell how important it is that I get these guys out of here."

"I know," Prairie says, a hint of a challenge in her voice, which makes me forget the pain in my arm for a second. "I'm sorry we messed up your plans."

"No, that's not it," replies Joe. "When this all started, I found myself fighting off one thing after another, just running for cover. Lizards were bulldozing people, using their claws and their snouts. That is, if they weren't just eating them. I had to get to cover. I ran to Manz, then from one kiosk to the next. Then I was by the fountain and the info desk. I don't know where I was going. I was just running. I saw these guys holding their own and sorta gravitated to them, but you know, I had to pass the play area to get close to them."

Prairie stops tweezing and soundlessly places them back in the bag. She goes for more antiseptic and gauze.

Joe continues. "It was full of kids, and...well, I guess, some parents too. The ones who hadn't been picked off already. They were hunkering down, just shrieking and bawling. And this big centipede and these silverfish-looking things went in there and took them apart. Parents tried to scramble over the walls and got pulled back in. Kids tried to run out the entrances and got yanked out of sight. I honestly didn't see too much. I was moving so close and staying so low. But the screaming. The screaming got louder and louder, and then it got less and less. Because no matter how hard those kids were screaming, there were fewer of them left to scream. I just ran for the guys. They were my target. But those kids...I didn't do a thing."

A new hot dagger carves into my arm, and I slap Prairie's hand. Her fingernail is digging into my wound, and I mouth, *ow!* at her. She doesn't pay attention, pulls away the gauze, disposes of it, then gets out a tube of Neosporin.

"I don't think anyone would know what to do in that kind of situation," she says.

He shrugs robotically, his arms remaining tensed against his sides. His fingers dig at his loincloth for pockets, like woodpeckers hunting for grubs. He begins pacing, still addressing the fog and the things lurking inside it.

"I wish I did. But then I teamed up with these guys, and for as strong as they are, they're scared as hell. None of them are from around here. Everyone's from Milwaukee but Tomi and Ramon, and they're from Chicago. Their families don't know what's happening. Somehow, every one of them made it this far. So, you know, they're the ones I'm supposed to help today. I have to, if I couldn't help those kids. I have to make up for that, even if I shouldn't look at it like that."

Prairie squiggles lines of Neosporin along my arm, then peels open two large bandages. From each one, she rips off an adhesive edge so they don't pull on the wound, then squeezes more goop on them and applies one at a time. Next, she wraps it snugly with gauze and clips it in place.

I rotate my shoulder and inspect her work. As much poking and prodding as she's done, it feels better already. Just...cleaner. Nicer.

"I think that's what you should do," Prairie says. "You can't help that you were taken by surprise. I don't think there's anything else you could do."

Joe exhales through his nose and shakes his head. His arms loosen, though, and he looks more comfortable with himself, having said it out loud, having been understood by someone else and spared the judgment and shame he's heaping on himself.

"It's not just the boys anymore. It's you. That's why I hope you're right about Macy's. I think it's a good idea, no matter what the guys think. I'm just not sure about anything anymore. And now I have the four of you."

"No, that's not right," Prairie says.

"What isn't right?" Joe asks, finally looking at us and casting a skeptical look at Prairie.

She glances at me, as if she needs my permission to speak further, but there's no secret she can be holding. Not from today, at least. This is Prairie Hedlund we're talking about, after all.

"All I've been doing today is running away. When we faced off with our first lizard, my friends went one way. I went the other. I just ran away."

"Prairie..." I object, remembering how her quick thinking led to Boston's *Third Stage* smashing into the lizard's schnoz, baffling it for long enough that we made it out alive.

"No, Quinn. I ran. And I kept running until I was safe in that kiosk. And I was ready to run out the doors. All these people ran past me to do the same thing. All the same people we found dead in front of those doors. The only thing that stopped me was seeing that guard's walkie-talkie. And then, I...instead of going to you guys— instead of that—I made you all come to me."

"That's not fair," I say.

"I *told* you I had a way out. And I really thought I did. That wasn't a lie. But I didn't really make sure. I could've saved you from the danger of finding me if I only poked my head out for, like, ten seconds and checked. And it turned out I was wrong. And then, after that, when all those people were locked up in the stores, getting attacked from inside, I did nothing. I knew they were there all along. They knew I was hiding in the kiosk. They were whispering for me to come to them, but I didn't trust them. I knew the stores weren't safe, but I didn't tell them that enough. And then I watched as they were all slaughtered. So, I didn't do a thing either."

She stops and bites her lip, having confessed this all to the mall, just like Joe did.

His eyes are fixed on her with a mixture of curiosity and gravity. I might even call it admiration.

Prairie swallows. "If you say you have four more to look out for, I have nine more. Ever since the girls came to find me, every idea, every decision I made, has been to get us out of here alive. I wouldn't say we should go to Macy's if I wasn't absolutely sure it was the best chance we have."

Prairie has stood up to Kirsten's swagger and Raina's natural aura of authority. She's never done anything like this in her life. Not as far as I've ever seen. I'm witnessing a new side of her, a strength no person or situation has ever allowed to shine before now. And I believe what she says.

Joe must too. He puts on a real, genuine smile. "It sounds like I have your word on that."

"You do," she says. Then she squeezes my good arm in a way that would normally make me bristle, thinking of Kirsten doing it in one of her insincere maternal moments. But Prairie's words are a pledge, and her gesture is meant to convey the love and trust that goes with it.

I cover her hand with mine and stand with Joe—the three Holy Eucharist Church Elementary kids, ready to take on the underworld.

And on that note, Joe twitches his head in recognition of our shared background. He rifles through the folds of his loincloth, scandalizing Prairie and me for the briefest second, until he reveals a silver flask and sloshes it around. A little eucharist before we get on our way.

"If the boys knew about this, it'd already be gone. Come on, a toast to us getting out of here. To the Meadow Spire Thirteen."

"Fourteen," I say.

He looks at me, and his smile fades into seriousness. "Yes. To Bridie too. Make it the Meadow Spire Fourteen."

He takes a swig and, at my direction, passes it to Prairie. She's suddenly timid, but I squeeze her hand, which I'm still holding by my side. Prairie puts it to her mouth, turns it upside down, and grimaces at the effects of whatever cheap liquid fire Joe brought for his lunch break. She swallows with difficulty, stifles a cough, and passes it to me.

Dear God, do I grimace at this sorry excuse for gasoline too.

Joe stashes the liquor in time for Kirsten, Tomi, and Ramon to sneak back in from the fog with three shopping bags full of loot. Soon after, the rest of the guys filter out of the kitchen with Raina. Given the newer weapons in their hands and a moment to rest, they look more confident and relaxed.

While Kirsten and her beefcakes create some pheromone-drenched rags, Joe lines up the guys. "We move. Five-meter spread. No sound," he says, his Schwarzenegger impression only recognizable as the actor because it's so wrong. "Seriously, though, tactical teams in close proximity. Same as before. But we have the girls now, so who's going with who? Same teams, or no?"

Heads turn. Ideas are floated.

The mall creaks again. More glass cracks and metal wrenches. Waves lap at our ankles. Meadow Spire Mall is going down, and we have no time to waste.

♥*♥*♥

Mix it up with the boys. Turn to page 163.

Stick with the girls. Turn to page 252.

Is that really her? Prairie? I can't be the only one who thinks so.

Raina practically dives across the guard, dumped into the trench coats, to snatch his walkie-talkie. Her action snaps me back to the present.

How is Prairie alive? And where is she?

It's hard to picture any place in the mall not infested with mutant swamp monsters. A chill runs through me, just thinking about any of us going out there.

The guard slashes his way through the trench coats. He takes hold of Raina's arm, yanking the walkie-talkie away from her mouth when she's about to speak. She holds tight, pulling him toward her until they're nose to nose.

"Stop!" he hisses. "You'll draw more of those things in!"

Kirsten moves in, puts her hand on the walkie-talkie, and gives Raina a stern look.

It's too much for me. I swat her hand away and yank the walkie-talkie for myself. Raina fans out her arms to keep the other two back while I get up and move to the end of the carousel. But she faces me, annoyed by my having jumped into the fray.

I fumble with the walkie-talkie, get the right grip on it, and press the most obvious button on its side. "Prairie? Is that you? This is Quinn. We're in Sears. Where are—"

Raina's barrier fails, and I'm shoved into the trench coats. The guard goes under Raina's arm and claws at me. His fingernails dig into the tender spot on my side, where the mosquito beast got me. He shushes me when I scream. So does Kirsten. They interrupt a response over the walkie-talkie.

My face is hot, and I kick at the guard, catching him in the shoulder and on his head. They're vicious kicks, but I'm seeing red, and I don't stop until Raina yells.

"Jesus, Quinn! Knock it off!" She holds Kirsten in an armlock.

"Everyone, shut up! Listen to this guy!" Kirsten squirms to free herself.

"No," I say. "I'm not listening to another word from either of you. Prairie's alive. We need to figure out how to reach her."

"Are you mental?"

The guard growls. "Everyone, please!"

I loom over him. He flinches away, his panicked expression shifting to rage.

"Okay, you know what?" I say. "You can find a new hiding spot because we're working this out with Prairie. Me and Raina."

"Screw you. Find your own new spot," replies the guard.

"Dude, shut up," Kirsten says. "Quinn, be quiet, all right? Everyone's gotta chill and take a deep breath."

She's followed by a crackling radio. *"Quinn? Is that you? Are you safe? Over."*

I back away from the guard, look at the walkie-talkie, and punch the speaker button. "Yeah. Hey, Prairie. It's Quinn. We're in Sears. Where are you?"

The guard grabs my leg, but I kick him away. He gets to his feet and reaches for the radio again.

"Stop this. You can't even think about going out there."

"Get off of me, goddammit!" I shout.

If the mall were a normal place today, my shouting would have stopped him in his tracks—a girl screaming at a guy in the middle of a mall to quit touching her. Instead, the guard's eyes go wide. He enters a new frenzy and is on me again, shoving me through the coats.

Raina and Kirsten come to my defense and haul him off. But this time, I've lost patience. If the little bull wants the corral to himself, he can have it.

"Screw this. Raina, I'm outta here. Help me find another spot."

I thrash my way out of the trench coats and stomp into the aisle, one ear on the hardware section. The mosquito beasts are making a fuss. Toward the mall, more indiscernible chaos. Raina follows me out of the carousel, telling me to wait. Inside the carousel, Kirsten is berating the guard.

I creep around, checking the aisle leading to the mall, then look past the carousel for someplace deeper in the store to hide.

Something stares straight back at me.

I freeze in place.

It looks like one of those plastic animals kids can climb on in the atrium play area. A big green frog. Its tongue lashes out before I can move and catches me under my chin. Its gummy grip takes hold of my jacket, then it retracts, pulling me through the store.

My body slaps hangers when I swish through clothes racks. The blood rushes from my head. When I reach the frog's lipless mouth, my spine bends backward and cracks. The heels of my boots bounce up behind my shoulders.

The frog's tongue pulls once more, and I'm clamped inside its mouth.

Not dead yet.

Shock comes first. I go cold all over, and my vision narrows. My legs will not move, nor will my arms. By the time my face is pressed against the slimy roof of its mouth, I'm nearly gone.

The correct choice was to interrogate the security guard.
Turn to page 135.

The lizard thing rears back and swings its head between Kirsten and me, bleary white eyes staring into space. It falls onto its fat tail and slashes its claws at us—new targets who haven't acted like normal and run from it.

Just the boost I need. Even this thing thinks I'm weird.

And yet I'm suddenly filled with confidence coming face-to-face with it. My focus narrows. This I can see. This I can react to. It shows me a death leaving nothing to the imagination. That's self-preservation for you. Taking a Polaroid of a precise kind of death and slingshotting yourself away before the film develops. Whatever counts for this lizard thing's brain is going to connect the dots any second and make that death a reality.

I put away all confusing nonsense filling up my head and move, my instinctual slingshot stretched taut.

The heels of my hands slide out from under me when I scramble backward. I sprawl and crack my neck against a step—same place where the couch got me. My boots don't grip the floor. I scramble desperately, getting nowhere, and turn on my side in a frantic bid to gain a purchase, taking my eyes off the lizard thing. Something grabs my arm and squeezes. I spin around, horrified by the thought of unlatching myself from the lizard thing's maw.

It's Kirsten. She has me in a death grip, eyes bulging, frozen in the face of the monster.

I dig my fingers into her palm to pry her off. She won't let go, and I can't make her. My attention keeps going back to the lizard thing. Its glistening white teeth disappear behind thin lips. Its filmy eyes center on me, and its claws spread open with the measured patience of a flower coming under sunlight.

The final strand of restraint quivers at its back, the only thing keeping it from lunging. It's figured us out. We're fair game. Food.

Kirsten's hand holds me in place. She's actually going to be the death of me. Kirsten freaking Fortner. And instead of prying, I clamp down and hold her back. My breath is shallow and fast, and the lizard thing draws out its threat of attack, getting the spacing and timing just right.

I might not even feel it when it comes. And I hope I don't.

A blocky white missile flies over our heads and pelts the lizard thing smack dab on its snub nose. It reels back onto its tail again and stumbles, sloshing through water and dropping to all fours.

The missile drops. It's a department store bag, and it sheds its contents, which clatter onto the steps and splash into the water. The emptied bag takes a cursive descent through the fog and lands on Kirsten's face.

I let go of her and reach for one of the scattered items. It's a CD case. With a photo of space on it, like from one of the moon missions or something. Except...is that spaceship a guitar?

From above us, someone goes, "Whoop!"

Then comes the *thud-thud-thud-thud-thud* of someone tumbling down the stairs.

A pink-clad body falls between us, breaking Kirsten's grip on me. Boston. *Third Stage*. Huh.

"Ow," says Prairie.

The lizard-thing scampers off, if something that size can be said to scamper. It's bigger than an alligator but more limber, and its movement reverberates through the floor. It stops, a silhouette in the fog, studying us for any new surprises.

"Q-Quinn?"

I get to my feet and pull Kirsten to hers.

Our bottom halves are drenched with warm water, and I feel a burning sense of shame. I gave up on myself. And on Kirsten. She froze, she held me in place, and I didn't fight.

Shadowy creatures buzz through the fog. Slithering tails, skittering appendages, the blur of iridescent wings. They come from the direction of the Macy's wing, from the direction of the sloshing water.

The lizard thing draws nearer.

"She went to Sears, right?" Prairie asks, masking pain in her voice.

I nod. "Yeah, and—"

"The Jeep," Kirsten finishes.

The lizard thing stands in our way—that and who knows what else.

"Back," I say.

We go up the stairs. Either we wind our way through Sears's second floor, or we take the other mall stairwell back down.

Without another second to think through our options or voice them aloud, I look at the top of the stairwell and scream. A man is on the highest step, struggling with something attached to his back like a robe. Only instead of having a fluffy white hem, this robe has dozens of sharp spindly legs clasping around the man's entire torso.

The man manages one scream before the mutant centipede catches his neck between two pincers as big as hedge clippers. With one messy chomp, it bites off his head, which tumbles down the steps and hits Kirsten square in the chest.

The bloody neck stamps her with a neat circle of blood. She gasps, as if she's stared straight through the gates of Hell. It's not so far off. The head rolls to a stop, and I recognize its face. The rest of the security guard's body falls under the centipede.

We spin back around. Fewer legs, no pincers for us, thank you very much.

The lizard thing closes in, raising its head, listening, testing our defenses.

"Come on!" Kirsten screams out of nowhere. "Come on!"

The lizard thing does as it's told, skittering another few yards toward us, close enough we couldn't make it to the landing even if we wanted to.

"Okay, okay, now what!" Prairie cries.

Something comes out of the fog, flies in front of the lizard thing's face, and lands at our feet. A heavy bar with a wide base—a rope stanchion, probably from where the line was set up for the Cupid photoshoot. The lizard throws its neck to the side and hisses. Another stanchion comes careening through the air, end over end. It clips the lizard thing on the nose. A man's voice roars. The lizard thing turns around, ignoring us and bracing against an unseen threat in the fog.

I catch the vague outline of our rescuer, but there's no more time to stand around.

"Come on!" I shout, grabbing Kirsten and Prairie by the sleeves.

I don't know what we can do to help that lone man. It isn't our battle, I tell myself. We have to find Raina.

And *Bridie*. Bridie, Bridie, Bridie. Where the hell is she?

The fog thickens in pockets, clearing up without warning and showing us more glimpses of creatures borne from the very pits of Hell into the mall. The water gets deeper as we go and faster flowing. The current pushes us closer to the walls.

People are still scattered all over the main floor. Some are alive. They cower in places with minimal cover and stumble in every direction, unsure of where to go. Some are in the midst of fighting.

Another lizard thing zips into a storefront ahead of us. The round humps of some creatures crowd together like livestock and bumble their way off to our right. Arachnoid monsters with threatening spear-like appendages trail them, slinking without making any noise.

Human screams become the only noise I focus on, despite the sloshing water and skittering creatures. At any second, a beast will appear from under the water, a snake or a worm or some horrible thing, and coil itself around me or Kirsten or Prairie.

I force myself to keep going, keep leading. Raina's the one I should worry about. The next corpse we encounter may very well have her face, wear her clothes, spread-eagled in bloodstained water.

And Bridie. Where is Bridie?

I shake my head to rattle away the indecision. *Raina.* She's closer, and I know where she's going.

I don't realize I've slowed down until Kirsten loops her arm under mine and pulls me forward. My limbs have gone wobbly, resisting the urgency of the crisis. I know what I have to do, but my body fails. It happened to me once before. Stage fright. Seventh grade—the only time I ever tried to act. I was a supporting actor on the edge of the stage, but I felt like I was remote controlling someone else's body and the batteries were dead. Who the hell knows how I cheer? Maybe it's the synchronicity, the athleticism needed to pull it off. I could use more steam now.

Kirsten helps me through until I'm fully under my own power again. We charge into the chaos, using it as cover. The monsters and people around us are too preoccupied with their own conflicts to see us.

The chunky letters of Sears beam through the fog like a discount version of the pearly gates. Every last step comes with paranoid fear of getting caught at the last second. Some beast will swoop in and pin me to the floor. The lizard thing will remember us, sprint out of the dark, and chomp my whole torso.

Kirsten makes it first, getting as far as the jewelry counter.

Shattered glass and gold jewelry cover the floor. I kick Valentine's gift boxes and stray chocolates out of my way.

"Tools, tools!" I say.

We turn toward the hardware department. The water thins out the closer we get. Soon enough, the tiles are dry.

We shout for them.

"Raina!"

"Mr. Harris!"

The store is filled with screams, with squeaky shoes. Display racks shudder with the movement of panicked shoppers and assaulting beasts. Tadpole-pale appendages and mica-shiny beetle armor flash from among hanging clothes.

We run down the main aisles and zigzag around fallen racks, toppled shoes, hats, and jackets. We pass into the hardware department, shouting for Raina.

Then we see them.

Raina is in the main aisle, flanked by tall displays for gas-powered yard tools. Her jacket's torn. She wields a wiry metal rake, the kind that can really take out an eye. I'm surprised they even make them anymore. But it's the dad section at Sears, and dads like old stuff.

A running hedge trimmer putters and vibrates on the floor near her. It's covered in blood.

I get close enough to see what Raina's fighting from behind the nearest display rack.

Towering as high as I do when Raina holds me during a routine is the most repulsive thing I've ever seen in my life, worse than anything I've glimpsed today. The creature looks like a huge mosquito but...incomplete, in a tortured kind of way. It has a bulbous, half-larval thorax, pierced and oozing white gooey blood, and a shiny, fingernail-hard abdomen. Its six legs each have one too many segments, so it struggles to move with any sort of finesse. Streamers of saliva leak from a proboscis split like frayed wood, and the beast leers at us with fishy domed eyes, suggesting its compound vision has deteriorated over generations of disuse.

The mosquito beast lashes out at Raina, but she deftly deflects its blows with her rake. She's sluggish, though. Raina's been fighting hard, and she's hurt. There's a strong chance she wouldn't last much longer if we hadn't shown up, assuming we're of any help.

Kirsten arms herself with a rake from the barrel nearby and starts taking vacuum-packed products from the shelves to throw at the mosquito beast.

I run for the hedge trimmer and heft it up. Its chainsaw-like grip fills me with power. If I had this in front of the lizard thing, I would have killed that son of a bitch and saved the whole mall. When I squeeze the trigger, the hedge trimmer chatters to life, sawfish teeth opening and closing, forming a double row of tiny, devastating guillotines.

Raina groans, losing energy. Her swings weaken. Kirsten stops throwing things at the beast and takes up a spot next to her.

I rush past Raina, up to the beast's gangly legs. First, I hold the hedge trimmer straight, then swing it back and forth until I make contact with a leg. The teeth bounce off, and I swing again, until I start taking out chunks, pushing harder every time it lands on flesh. The beast recoils. It flails its proboscis at me, and I meet it with the trimmer. The tool's teeth carve into it with ease. I'm splashed by saliva, and the thing exudes a monstrous squeal, batting its leg in my direction.

Pain radiates my side where its knobby limb got me, and I fall over. The mosquito beast retreats. Raina advances. Kirsten stops and runs past me.

"Hey!" she yells, just as I'm getting to my knees. She holds an armful of hatchets. "*Move!*"

The light glints off a hatchet blade when she winds up. I fall to the floor. She throws, and there's a heavy *thwack* of it lodging into the beast's body. Kirsten chucks hatchet after hatchet. Some hit the beast with the butts of their heads or their handle. Some land blade-first and dig into the soft flesh of its thorax.

When she runs out, I get back up and charge past Raina, slashing wildly with the hedge trimmer. Hatchets litter the floor.

The beast is covered in open wounds, its milky blood weeping from everywhere. Its legs splay out, and it falls to the floor, still retreating.

I close in on the beast with my trimmer, aiming for the proboscis. My weapon cuts jaggedly, screaming with the impact, splattering everyone with saliva, until the monster falls to its side like a dry stick. The thing can no longer do us any harm. I back away, my arms burning and my side complaining. Kirsten picks up a stray hatchet and steps on the ends of the beast's legs. She starts hacking away, diligently chopping apart its legs segment by segment, reducing the thing to a lump of a body. Kirsten keeps her distance to avoid splashing blood.

Raina pushes past me. She holds two hatchets. Her breathing is heavy. One at a time, she destroys its eyes, these pathetic eyes. This creature was not meant to be here. It was not meant to exist. And it definitely did not want to be in the Sears hardware department any more than a bunch of cheerleaders did.

When Raina finishes, the beast's head resembles something like a bowling ball, its eyes cored out, turned into juicy, shredded finger holes.

"Nice one, Rain—" Kirsten sighs.

Raina drops her hatchets and runs away.

"Oh, what the hell?"

"Raina, wait!" I run after her.

She leaves the main aisle and cuts between display racks. I can barely keep up. How can she move like this after all that?

Screams rend the air. Shoppers pop up, running in all directions, chased by pale shapes made blurry by their speed. Raina leaves hardware and enters men's workwear, where the flooding has started to spread. I bounce off racks of coats and security vests she leaves waving in her wake. She takes another turn toward the boots and hardhats and drops out of sight.

I round the corner and stop to watch her.

Kirsten's feet clap against the thin layer of floodwater.

"Rain! Quinn, what is she doing?"

She comes up behind me. I throw out my arm and catch her in the chest to stop her. Kirsten opens her mouth, about to whine, when I shoot her a look. She stops and glances down.

Raina is hunched over on her knees, looking at her father. His legs stick out straight, his jeans blackened by blood. The toes of his work boots are splayed outward. She moves her hands up and down his torso with unsure anxiety. He reaches to touch her arm, but his hand is so bloody, the fingers practically stick together. Mr. Harris holds her gently, and Raina's frantic movements stop. She falls onto his chest, and he lets out a heaving breath.

Kirsten races around a clothes carousel and comes up on the other side of Raina's father. She crouches next to them. I kneel behind Raina and touch her back.

She lifts her head and looks at her father.

Mr. Harris is in bad shape. His face is scratched up, and blood seeps from the corners of his mouth. He coughs and looks at Kirsten, his eyes creasing in friendly recognition. His head lolls toward me, and he smiles at me too. I don't know what face I make at him, but I want to return his smile. That's what you do when someone kind smiles at you, but I'm too shocked, too horrified by what's happened to him.

He doesn't seem to expect me to. Mr. Harris knows it's not in me right now, that even against the greatest efforts of my conscience, of my sympathy, I'm simply too sad to do it.

He turns his attention back to his daughter.

"This was coming," he says in a whispery voice, trying to hold back more coughs.

Raina sobs, her back shaking under my hand.

"I was going to break your heart, you know," he says.

Raina sniffs. "You *are* breaking my heart."

"I had something better in mind."

"No," Raina manages between sniffles.

"You have to be brave. Not in six months. Not twelve."

"No. You can't go. I love you, Dad."

I glance at Kirsten. She looks to the side, shying away from the intimacy. I see her wondering how this has all come to pass, imagining this same scene playing out between her and her own parents one day.

"I'm glad they're here. And you're here for them."

Mr. Harris couldn't appear more serene.

Raina snorts back heaps of snot, whimpers sputtering from trembling lips. I spread my fingers along her back, feeling every shudder, trying to press as much of my love into her as I can.

"You're good girls," he says.

"Dad..."

Mr. Harris coughs weakly, then he regathers himself and sets those peaceful eyes on her again. He whispers with a smooth, deep voice, just like normal, like he's telling her goodnight.

"Gizaagi'in, Raina."

"Gizaagi'in, nindede."

His eyes glaze over, and his body stills. Raina collapses onto him and cries.

Kirsten and I look at each other. This isn't the end. Not by a long shot. We have to get out of here, or we'll all end up in the same spot, as cold and calculating as it is to admit.

I'll have to tell that to Raina, and while I try to figure out what words to say, Kirsten squints in consternation. She searches the area behind me, then stands up and scans the whole store. Kirsten doesn't tell me what she's thinking, but her confusion sparks a new fear in me. I think through everything that's happened since we left that empty store.

My hand slips from Raina's back, and I get up too. I search the store fruitlessly and end up looking Kirsten dead in the eye. We both ask each other the same question.

"Where is Prairie?"

♥*♥*♥

Backtrack immediately for Prairie. Turn to page 115.

Hear Kirsten out and look for an escape first. Turn to page 118.

A loud pop punches through the fog when Skye plugs in his guitar. It fills me with confidence—one tiny indication at least *one* thing works in our favor. A loud holler and the scuttling sounds of the beefcakes cancels it out.

Of the millions of things going through my mind, I need to see Skye strum that guitar. I need proof it's going to work. The beefcakes can handle one more bug.

Kirsten is rooted in place. The others remain in Band Avenue. Skye's ears twitch at the beefcakes' commotion. He settles the guitar in his lap, presses his fingers in an instinctive pattern on the strings, and strums. An acoustic trill mumbles from the guitar's body. Skye's face falls, which is like seeing the sun go out.

He tries again, then again with the same result. Skye switches the amp on and off and unplugs and plugs the guitar cable from both ends, each action more frenzied than the next. Strums again. Nothing.

The beefcakes' shouting turns to grunts and thuds when they enter pitched battle. Kirsten tiptoes to the balcony for a look.

"Skye, come on. What is it?" I ask.

"I don't know!" He twists knobs and checks the power cord, switches the amp on and off again.

Prairie comes out of Band Avenue, but she disappears from my peripheral vision immediately. One second, she's there; the next, she's not. Except she hasn't gone anywhere. Her filthy pink coat glows in the dark. The lights in Band Avenue have gone out, obscuring her silhouette and joining the outlets robbing Skye's amp of its power.

"Shit." I scan the other stores. Directly across the concourse, lights cut through the fog. "Prairie! Unplug it. We're going across."

Skye looks up, pale as bone, breathing hard and fast. I snatch his guitar, pull the strap from his neck, and furl its cord.

"Grab the amp." If I can cut Kirsten down to size, I can order my former crush on what to do.

Luckily, no one needs much telling right now. Skye sprints inside Band Avenue to unplug the amp and commands everyone to get out.

I jog across the balcony, followed by Kirsten and Skye with the amp. Our pattering footsteps come as one movement, one team. We sweep along the balcony, toward the glowing store with its much-needed electricity.

At the top of the stairs, I slow down and squint, my vision cutting through the fog like flame through cotton. Three beefcakes are on the landing, heads down, arms around shoulders. The center one's head droops. His front is dark with blood, and his feet drag. The other two heft him up one step at a time. He helps by planting his feet as best he can.

The strain causes him to jolt upright. Brian's features are clenched, wracked with pain. His body is cross-hatched by gashes drizzling a zigzag path of blood, staining his jeans a shiny vinyl black.

Their slow progress holds up the other beefcakes.

The unmistakable buzz of a mosquito beast loudens. The rearmost beefcakes raise weapons, like hackles from a cat's back.

Joe, lost in the crowd and unable to see what we're doing, yells, "Start the music!"

I pull myself away and run ahead of the upstairs team, straight into the accessories store, where I hunt for outlets. My faith in our teamwork cracks. What if the amp worked a minute ago? Would Brian be okay?

A neon sign hovers above a display of sterling silver jewelry to my right. Juice. I'll take it. Skye is still coming.

I trip on a rolled-up rug lying across an aisle. The guitar hits the floor and releases a faint, pained twang.

The rug presses up against me when I try to kick away from it. It's softer than it should be and squishes against my boots. It's the color and texture of a soaked toilet paper roll, and it rises from the floor.

A mouth opens at the end of the roll, exposing rows of inward-hooked teeth.

Skye runs into the store. His surprise at the giant worm thing's appearance makes him freeze. His feet slide out from under him, and he hits the floor, the amp landing on his lap.

The worm looms over me, its mouth coming closer and closer. I scramble back, but the store is too tightly packed. When I bump into shelving, I can't retreat any more, so I put up an arm to fend the thing off. It twitches and adjusts its aim in response to my contact with its outer lip.

A tingling sensation envelops my hand and my wrist. The thing swallows inch by inch, its teeth barely registering. The compression is what terrifies me, like an arm-length blood pressure sleeve pumped to the max.

I scream for Skye. He rolls the amp off his lap, grimacing. The rest of the seniors come in behind him, stunned by what they see.

They can help. The seniors can hack this thing apart, cleave it in two, and get my arm out.

The thing's mouth reaches my shoulders. It expands, allowing its lip to slither up past my neck, disturbingly warm. Its tiny nettle-teeth climb my cheeks and scrape past my eyeball until it has enveloped my head.

The sting of its teeth coats me like a full body rug burn. I start to suffocate from the pressure. My team comes up on me, scrambling around my legs and beating the thing from every direction, sometimes thumping me in the process.

I want to believe they can help me, but shock kicks in. Asphyxiation steals my concentration. The horror of my predicament continues unabated. They may get me out, long before this thing starts to digest me, but there won't be any air left inside my lungs.

They need to remain a team. I'm just one more casualty on the way out the door.

The worm squishes me into oblivion. Blackness overtakes me.

♥*♥*♥

The correct choice was to rejoin the beefcakes.
Turn to page 286.

Prairie's Boston CD is still in my pocket. I pull it out, picturing the blush on her cheeks when Raina teased her. Boston for her dad, Jars of Clay for her. Will Prairie hear them ever again? Am I supposed to, like, give this to her dad? My stomach knots, and then the knot burns like a fire poker. All hope burns into ash and blows away.

Raina collapses onto her father's body. I want to hug her, but it wouldn't be right. It's prohibited, like I'd be running my finger over the *Mona Lisa* to sense the bumps and curves of the brushstrokes.

The only thing is, I don't know that Prairie is dead. Nor Bridie. If there's some way I can make up for this loss of life, to prove there is still a chance, it's for me to save them. Raina's dad hasn't died in vain. We haven't just destroyed a mutated mosquito beast for nothing. Hope cannot die.

Kirsten is in the midst of collapse. She paces, yanking at hair she really can't afford to screw up. Think of Spring Break, K. I place my hands on her shoulders but keep her at arm's length. She gazes at me, mouthing words without voicing them.

"Kirsten, look at me."

Her lips stop moving. Her eyes lock on mine.

Prairie's my responsibility. She's only here because of me.

"Stay with Raina. Don't move. I'll be right back."

"Wh-what?" Kirsten makes a feeble grab for me.

"I'm getting Prairie."

She can't be far. We ran out of that store together and made it down the stairs. She saved us from the lizard thing. All I have to do is retrace my steps. She'll be right along the path.

I catch a final glimpse of Raina's back. It shudders with sobs. When she's ready for my support, I'll be back.

I walk into the aisle and venture a glance at the hardware section. Does Prairie lie by the mosquito beast's corpse, a casualty of battle? I don't remember seeing her. And there's no way she ran past us.

A group of people sprint down the intersecting aisle by the jewelry department. A blur of something low to the ground gives chase—purplish-white and slimy, like a salamander. It makes me miss my hedge trimmer.

I start jogging, calling Prairie's name. At the intersecting aisle, I scan the destroyed jewelry department, partially flooded and smeared with mutant slime. Through the fog, more people scatter, more shadows in pursuit. At the first shattered glass counter, a worm as thick as a rolled-up sleeping bag writhes behind a clothes rack.

I get to the mall entrance and shout, "Prairie!"

Bodies lie face down in shallow water stained red by blood, giving the swampy odor a tinge of copper. Before I venture into the mall, I glance over my shoulder. A webbed foot disappears down an aisle in the men's casual wear section.

Shouts and screams assault me from all directions. Twice, people pass so close, I catch their eye. They look at me like I'm insane, traversing a landscape of dropped shopping bags and toppled mall decor all by myself. I stick close to the walls, under the overhang of the balcony, with raised half-walls and faux greenery to shield me from what roams in the open. Once I'm close to the stairs where we last saw her, I take a risk and step out into the open.

"Prairie!" I shout, waiting for her head to pop up from a hiding place, for her to call my name.

Instead, something like a crane swings through the fog in my direction.

The snout of a lizard thing.

I stumble backward. My hip hits a half-wall, and something jabs my shoulder. When green leaves fall over my head, I shriek and bat at them until a fake tree flops over in front of me. I retreat behind the wall.

The lizard thing investigates my position, nostrils flaring, head tilting, before it grows bored and leaves.

I wait a couple of minutes before getting to my feet, which is when I notice the added weight on my back. Something white and slimy is attached to me.

I scream and smash into the wall. It cushions my impact, but I ram it again and again, grinding it against the wall. I fall to the floor and shove my shoulder back, battering the thing until something slips out from under my scapula, a strange sensation followed immediately by an intense itching.

The thing curls up on itself. The mouth on its underside seals shut before it's covered by its own rolled-up body. Under its translucent skin, a digestive tract of sorts gleams a vivid red. I back away and slip, not on swamp water, but my own blood pouring from the hole the mutant leech gouged in my back.

My hands can't reach. I hardly know where to press down anyway because there is no pain.

"Prairie!" I shout, desperate now for her assistance. "Prairie!"

The itch spreads and intensifies. My blood pressure drops. The water around me grows a dark crimson. The heavy dose of mutant anesthetic spreads, and I become nauseous and cold. My hands turn white, my cheeks tingle, and my eyes feel like they'll fall out of their sockets.

The fog closes in.

I collapse in a pool of my own blood. I'm no longer there for anyone. To save them. To be saved *by* them. I leave the mall's atrium for a giant lobby of white light, and every entrance on its concourse leads to a black hole.

The correct choice was to hear Kirsten out and look for an escape.
Turn to page 118.

From my jacket pocket, I take out the Boston CD I hardly remember taking. I wonder if it's the last piece of Prairie I'll ever see, if it's as good as mine now, instead of going under her bed for months before it's giftwrapped for Father's Day. Prairie was given a wad of cash to spend on a secret mall outing, and she spent it on someone who'd be furious if he knew how she got it.

I don't know what I'm supposed to do with this thing.

I don't think we're going to find her.

My gut twists itself into knots. Mr. Harris. Prairie. Bridie...How many more people I know are inside the mall? Are they safe? Are they thinking about me? Do I wait for help or go to help them? I try to read minds, try to envision where they are and what state they're in, try to predict what they'll do.

Raina rocks over her dad's body. Her mother and her brother join the cast of characters in my head. A sing-songy taunt prances around them in circles. I know something you don't know.

Kirsten pulls at her hair and paces on the other side of Raina. When a new scream rends the air, she flinches and looks for its source, her view over the clothes racks no doubt as obstructed as mine. Our position is the safest it's going to get, but one of us needs to make a call. I'd try, but the wheel of fortune keeps spinning in my head. And I can't bring myself to interrupt Raina.

The self-torture doesn't last too long. Kirsten comes back around the carousel and beside me. She alternates between flexing her fingers and clenching her fists. Her body shivers under her soaked white coat. Her hair is in disarray.

She mutters, "Okay, okay, okay..."

I nearly blurt out something, anything, I don't know what. We need to find Prairie. Bridie's out there. I'm wracked with guilt, unable to land on the right words, wanting instructions, when Kirsten grabs my jacket.

"We need to get the hell out of here," she whispers.

"I...Well, yeah..."

She holds her finger to her lips and glances back at Raina.

"We saw what just happened, right? And this, like, sucks. But we can't sit here. We gotta go. Right. Now." Kirsten stomps to the last two words.

She pushes past me and pulls on my sleeve, for what reason I don't know because she doesn't pull Raina along. Assuming, that is, she wants Raina to join us.

I shake her off and scowl. "But Raina...and...and Prairie."

"Huh?"

"Prairie!"

Her face twists in incomprehension. "She ran."

"What! Did you see her?"

Kirsten pauses. "She ran straight out of th-the hardware section. We could've done the same thing. We can *now*."

My mouth hangs open. I search my memory—the short-term stuff. No, I couldn't have missed that. "Then why'd you ask where—"

"Hey, look. It's nothing against her. I don't think she saw what was going on. She ran straight for the exit like we planned, like she was wearing blinders. Any one of us could've done the same thing. I didn't have time to say anything."

She's lying. I know it so hard. Even after all this, she's on top of her game, twisting logic, rearranging the past to stay ahead of any objection. But as much as I hate it, I have to admit, neither of us has faced an absolute life-or-death situation like this. It's hard to draw out the argument when there is no certainty, when your surroundings have broken everything in existence you took for granted, when you're not equipped to help anyone in any way whatsoever.

I feel a lot smaller without my hedge trimmer. And knowing Prairie isn't ahead of us, contemplating backtracking to find her...I'm not sure a horse-sized lizard would be as vulnerable as that pitiful abomination we left behind, with a dozen hatchets sticking out of it.

Screams and sounds of battle continue. We're nowhere near out of this mess.

I stammer in reply. "But I...I didn't see—"

"Yeah, you were kinda busy. So was I. She ran straight past us, I swear to God."

Kirsten's desperate, for her own sake, but there is a sheer coldness toward Prairie on her face. Thoughts swirl in my mind. Condemnations and insults. But there's so much, just *so* much, and it ends up coming out so...poorly.

"But...Bridie." I feel like I've made my sister small, using her as nothing more than an excuse to find my friend.

"Dude...Bridie? She's fine. She got out by Macy's or something. I guarantee she's outside in the parking lot. But we gotta split right now. Do you hear me?"

Kirsten tugs at me again, but I plant myself to the squishy wet carpet. I'm not in the right frame of mind to be bullied. Raina mourns over the literal corpse of her father, who was so unnaturally nice to us, and Prairie disappeared, but maybe she escaped? And Bridie. Where the hell is Bridie?

"Dude, are you mental? We gotta go!" Kirsten drops my arm and jogs away a few feet. She looks back expectantly and stutter steps, like I'm her dog and she's goading me into chasing her.

I swallow back a ton of phlegm. "You're sure you saw Prairie leave?"

She guffaws and throws up her arms. "It's *Prairie*."

No. That's not Prairie. I don't know what happened to her, but she's not outside.

"She wouldn't leave us like that. And besides—"

Kirsten scrunches her face and slashes her arms in an "X" motion, crossing out what she said. "It's every man for himself, Quinn. Prairie's just smarter than us, okay? There, I said it. She only did exactly what we were gonna do. She's waiting for us."

Raina sighs heavily. It's the sound of a thousand tiny wounds exiting her mouth. She stands up, pulls a denim jacket off its hanger, and drapes it over her father's face and torso. I catch a glimpse of the gaping wound slashed down from Mr. Harris's chest to his stomach, the pie filling held in place by his gory hand, before it's covered up. Raina rubs her eyes with the inside of her sweatshirt and surveys our surroundings.

The fog is rolling in. I swear, every breath smells more foul than the last. Water is coming in waves down the main aisle. Running feet and otherworldly screeches fill the air, and a low rumble underscores it all.

"You want to leave, Kirsten?" Raina says. "Fine. Leave. The doors are right there."

Kirsten blinks. "Are you coming?"

"Prairie was with us. I don't know how you lost her, but she must be back in the mall."

"Hey, *I* didn't leave her behind. It's not like that."

"I'm not accusing you of anything. I'm saying you can get out of here. I'm not holding you to anything, and neither is Quinn. No one's gotta be a hero."

"But you're talking like *you* gotta be. And...But...I'm not going without you guys."

Raina looks at me. "Quinn, what do you think?"

I hear them both, and I want to have it both ways. Want to be safe, want to be brave.

"I don't know."

Just then, a piercing scream comes from somewhere near the mall entrance. Splashing water, the sounds of a death struggle, and the horrified cries and moans of those too helpless to make it stop.

"*Guys*," Kirsten pleads, shrinking into herself, backing closer to the hardware department. She shakes her fists, looking ready to curl up in a ball and cry.

"I just don't know."

Raina puts her hand on my shoulder, recognizing my decision in my eyes. "We get Kirsten out first. Then Prairie."

One step at a time, putting things in the right order. Prairie's surely the closest. And as much as I'm worried about Bridie, she came of her own accord. She has other people. Prairie's alone, and she's here because of me.

I put the Boston CD back in my pocket. It's my ticket to find her. It has to make its way back to Prairie.

I nod.

"And then?"

"Bridie."

Kirsten makes no objection.

We scan the rest of Sears, listen for ominous sounds, and head back to the hardware section toward freedom. Raina leads the way, keeping us off the main aisle, zigzagging between racks and shelves. I wonder how it'll go at the door, when Kirsten has one final shot at convincing us to leave. But I tell myself I'll turn her down.

We pass by our battlefield with the mosquito beast, and I'm tortured by the wild thought that it's not dead, that it'll spring to life and kill us all. My fear is redirected at the sound of something crashing through shelves deeper in the hardware section, by the back wall. It moves with a flapping of wings, pushing things over.

Clattering wood and clinking metal tools fall to the floor. I picture its size, realizing it's another mosquito beast.

We run.

From the clothing department come more screams getting closer. Raina leads us onto the main aisle, forgoing secrecy for speed.

The exit is straight ahead. We tromp in our boots on the wet floor, lifting our legs high for one final sprint, and make it to the doors. Not a single obstruction blocks our way. The gray darkness of the blizzard is just one vestibule, just a pair of glass doors, away.

"Yes!" Kirsten gasps. She shoves the horizontal crossbar on the inside door and swings it open.

The air in the vestibule is twenty degrees colder and nips at my nose. Kirsten digs her boots into the sopping wet entrance rug, rushes into the exterior door, shoves the crossbar, and has all her weight smash into the heavy glass pane. Her head bonks the door frame, the door shudders, and she crumples to the floor.

"No!" she screams.

I try next, pushing in the crossbar. It unlatches, it's unlocked, but it doesn't budge.

Kirsten scrambles to her feet and tries the next door over. Raina rushes between us and checks the top and bottom corners of both doors, making absolutely sure the bolt locks aren't slotted into place. No such luck. What is the problem?

I look down at the ground outside—the world we're one step away from—and I see what we're facing. My eyes trace the problem upward.

"No."

Raina tries pushing to no avail. Kirsten pushes and complains.

"Guys, look."

The gaps between the doors are coated in solid ice thick as a skating rink. Top to bottom. It's worse at ground level, where the doors are abutted by a rounded levee of ice thicker than any rolling pin I've ever seen.

"The flooding," I say.

"The wind," Raina murmurs. "Goddammit." She runs back into the store.

"Where are you going?"

"We're breaking through. You're getting out of here."

It's my turn to be stunned. "Wait, what? I'm not going anywhere!"

"Wait, what? Yes, you *are*," Kirsten cries.

Raina spins in the middle of the aisle, looking for the right tool. The sounds of the new mosquito beast's movements become louder, closer. So do the sounds of an approaching group, whose presence is confirmed within seconds.

A dozen people or so slip and slide around the corner, racing straight for us.

Their pursuer comes into view too. A globular mass with hairy appendages—another mosquito beast—going too fast to maintain control. It slides down the aisle and crashes into a display case, causing circular saws to fall to the floor.

"Over here!" Kirsten screams, though I don't know why.

I guarantee the guy leading the way is a Sears member. And I bet he thought he knew the best way out of here. Except he doesn't. And he doesn't know it. None of them do. None of them know the doors are frozen shut and they'll need a sledgehammer to escape.

They barrel toward us, eyes wild, completely oblivious to our presence. Raina steps in front of Sears Guy, belting out a warning, but he clips her shoulder, and she spins and falls to her knees. The mosquito beast recovers from its tumble and comes after them. Raina flashes me a terrified look before she slips between racks to stay out of its line of sight.

Kirsten kicks at the outer door to no avail. I pose like a mannequin, stuck between shouting my own warning and helping Kirsten.

The group refuses to process what's going on and barrels toward us. That's when Raina's terror becomes mine.

"Kirsten, get out of there!" I yank her back.

She digs in.

Sears Guy has a mad glee in his eyes. Our presence doesn't register. He thinks he's saved, thinks he's going to get out. The man is going to crash right into us, and his people are going to crush us— easy pickings for another disgruntled mega-sized mutant.

"What are you doing?" Kirsten screams. She clutches the cross bar.

"We need to go!" I wrap myself around her waist, press my foot into the door, and pull.

She isn't prepared for the power I put into it. I yank her away, and we fall to the watery floor.

"*Quinn!*"

I scramble to my feet and lift Kirsten onto hers.

Boots smack into water, the same water we're in, the puddle encompassing the vestibule. Sears Guy is right on top of us. There's a flash of confusion while he considers too late what's going on. Why aren't these random girls opening the doors and leaving?

Then I'm shoved from behind and go sprawling into the puddle outside the vestibule. Kirsten falls on top of me. Raina races up, kicking water into my face. I army crawl to the side, and Raina reaches over me, helping guide Kirsten, who jumps over and splashes me again. My feet barely manage not to get stomped by passing boots. I stagger to the closest shelf, out of the entryway and the main aisle, and come up alongside Raina and Kirsten, who back away in horror.

The group rushes the vestibule, and I watch a replay of our failed escape. They press their shoulders into the doors, sure they'll give. But they don't. And there's more of them. They smash into one another, chests pressed into backs until no one can move. Faces turn to grimaces. The pitch in their voices rises when they realize they're trapped. Their panic prevents any coordination or communication, and none of them think to look back.

The mosquito beast drives itself into them, followed by another one—the one we heard smashing around the back of the hardware section. The entryway turns red, and my ears ring with the sound of bloodcurdling screams.

"Move, move!" Raina cries. She leads us down the row until we reach the wall, then takes us deeper into Sears, back where we came.

We approach the entrance to the clothing department, but the blurred shapes of rushing creatures pour through it, following the scents and sounds of a fresh kill to be fought over.

Raina skids to a stop outside the entrance and peeks around the corner. My pulse rises, expecting a claw or something to wrap itself around her face. Instead, something grips my shoulder.

I scream.

Kirsten and Raina jump, and we look back to see a security guard—a heavyset guy with a full beard—who managed to escape the melee at the vestibule.

"Oh God, didn't I...Aren't you?" he says between breaths. "The girls that—"

"Come on," Raina growls.

We creep through the hardware section entryway and immediately hide among clothes racks when the scraping and sliding sounds of more mutant monsters approach from the mall.

Raina takes us to a long oval-shaped clothes carousel and parts a gap between trench coats to let us all sneak inside. We huddle back-to-back and take a breather.

Each of us is a mess, and it stands out in such close quarters. Heavy and wet with smelly water, covered in mosquito goo, sweating through our winter wear. Our hair frizzes out, and our foundation smudges on our faces.

Raina's brow creases in thought—or at least I hope so—to devise our next strategy. Somehow, her head is screwed on tighter than Kirsten's and mine.

Or is it?

I mean, her dad did just die in her arms, and she did just try to chuck us outside before going on the hunt, alone, for *my* childhood friend. Not to mention—and without trying to brag—that mosquito beast would've killed her if we hadn't shown up. I may admire her single-mindedness, but it may not be accurate to say she's thinking straight.

Kirsten, on the other hand, sports a thousand-yard stare. Her chest heaves up and down, and she gulps the fetid air. She should know how to navigate us through this mess, more than any of us. The mall is her second home. But unless she can hold herself together, she's a liability.

Then there's the security guard. He sits between Kirsten and Raina, exhausted and shivering, but still scrunching his brows while he makes sense of the situation. He should know the layout of the mall too. More than the layout, in fact. Now that I'm thinking more sharply, I wonder what kind of back-access hallways are here for, like, janitors and maintenance people.

This guy should know. He better.

I catch my own breath. This is the most rest we can expect to get. And it's not like anyone else is rushing faster than me to go out there again.

Prairie. Bridie. Gone. Disappeared.

"Hey. You," I say.

The guard looks at me, speaks through a clogged throat. "What?"

Then he jumps. And I jump. All of us jump at the crackling noise emanating from his body.

A tinny voice calls out from his walkie-talkie.

"Hello? Is anyone there? Anyone from security? Over."

The volume is set at its highest, and the voice bounces off the ceiling. The security guard clamors at his belt, pressing buttons and missing in his panic.

"I repeat—"

He pulls the walkie-talkie free, juggles it in his hands, and muzzles the speaker with his palm before turning down the volume.

"Is anyone there?" asks the voice, now set to a whisper. *"Looking for assistance. Ov—"*

The security guard snaps off the radio, then sighs with a trembling breath.

"Wait!" Raina cries, holding out her hand to the guard.

"Yeah..." Kirsten murmurs. "Was that not just me?"

"No. It isn't," I say. I heard it too. "Hey, man, turn that back on."

"No! Everyone just shut up, okay?"

Kirsten yanks the radio out of his hand. He lunges, but Raina keeps him back while Kirsten finagles with the buttons. She turns it on, increases the volume to a loud hiss, and presses the speaker button.

"Hey, who's this?" she asks.

The security guard gets to his knees and throws all his weight behind another lunge. Raina falls into Kirsten, and the walkie-talkie flies from Kirsten's hand, landing between the guard's shoes.

Raina gets out from under him and pins him in place. He wriggles to get free.

Kirsten and I lean in and stare at the rectangular piece of black plastic. It keeps crackling before it comes to a stop.

"My name is Prairie. What's yours? Over."

Interrogate the security guard. Turn to page 135.

Formulate your own plan with Raina. Turn to page 100.

Idea? We've had lots of ideas today. Under the boys' gaze, on the wrong side of so many bad plans and decisions, I don't want to hear any more. There's one thing we have to do, and at this point, I can only do it out of brute force.

Macy's or bust. That's the only idea there is.

"Quinn? You know what I mean?"

Kirsten leans into me to squeeze out my support. When I don't respond, she looks to the other girls. Raina casts her eyes down, and Prairie's mouth parts, like she's ready to speak, but she defers to me.

I *do* know what Kirsten means. A long shot of an idea which would involve a lot of logistics and a hell of a lot of luck, both of which have been in short supply. It seems to me stealth and a sharp weapon are the only things that serve us well, and we should stick to it.

I look at her, at Joe—two thermometers simultaneously telling me I'm boiling and freezing. Kirsten juts her head forward, like *do you get me or don't you?*

And if I do? What then? The boys will take over. We'll lose control. Even if they do entrust themselves to us, we're three times as liable for whatever happens, three times more likely to goof things up.

I shake my head. "I gotta think." I cross my arms and wander into the food court.

"Quinn, careful," warns Joe.

"Quinn, come on," says Kirsten. "You know what I'm saying, right? Prairie, I know you do. Tell him what I mean."

I continue walking along the counter, not intending to go any farther into the seating area or enter any kitchens, just needing to be alone. This is the greatest crossroads we've encountered all day. Whatever we decide next could break us. If I had a second for my thoughts to unspool without anyone else around to screw with them, I could figure out the best decision. My head is too full, the house inside flooded. Bridie, Prairie, Raina, Skye, Kirsten...They're all banging on the ceiling, crying out for rescue.

"Quinn, what the hell?"

Kirsten. She can't leave me alone.

I walk past Sbarro and stop in front of McDonald's, where we started our morning. My body tells me I should eat. I'm craving something sweet and carby from Sarah Andigan's Doughnut Shoppe at the end of the counter. A doughnut doubled in size by its frosting, coated with sprinkles thicker than rice, pinker than a Barbie house.

By stopping, I prevent Kirsten from touching me, which would be too much. I will sock her if she tries to spin me around one more time and make me listen to her version of rationality. So, I let her try without fighting, having had all the alone time I can hope for.

Kirsten looks terrible. Her hair is wet, flat, and stringy. Her cheeks are so red and there's so much dried blood scabbed over her perfect skin, her base tan has disappeared, and she's back to a shade of midwinter mink.

"You need to sell him on this, Quinn. You know him. We *need* his help."

"No."

"No what? We can't do this on our own."

"We're not going to convince them to come with us."

"Yeah, well, we know more than them, and this guy'll listen to you. If we got more firepower, we'll make it out of here. If they go their own way, we can't help them, but at least we tried, right?"

It's the most diplomatic she's sounded all day.

"Yeah, I know," I sputter, "but...I don't know."

"What is it? Do you need something? Can I do something?"

Yeah, a double mocha and a box of doughnuts...with a quart of deer trax ice cream, now that I think of it. Where was this hospitality last night, my friend?

"Come on, tell me what you need."

"Are you serious?"

Am I asking if she for real wants to get me something? If that's my problem? Or am I asking if she's serious about this whole thing, convincing Joe Molson and his crew of beefcakes to accompany us to the end of the world?

She decides for herself. "Hey, come on. We're at McDonald's. It's a girl's day out. Let's get you a pop or something." Kirsten sits on the counter, spins around, and hunts for cups.

The soda machine sits behind her.

Prairie's voice rises from the fog, telling Kirsten's idea. I tune it out, not wanting to hear her fail.

Back in the McDonald's booth, Kirsten gasps. A plastic bag full of nested paper cups goes flying. The soda machine wobbles, taunting me with its contents. Kirsten is no longer there. Instead come sloshing sounds.

I peep over the counter. The floor is moving.

The tile has transformed into an opal carapace slinking into the back of the kitchen like a conveyor belt, dragging Kirsten by her ankle. She clenches her teeth, grabbing at table legs and metal drawers.

"Kirsten!"

I dive over the counter and land on the creature's back. It looks like a smaller cousin of the Sears centipede—a nimbler, sneakier relation.

Kirsten falls behind, and the segments of the carapace travel under me, not unlike the escalator steps thudding beneath me during our earlier escape.

The segments end, and my face scrapes against the pair of pincers that had been holding Kirsten.

She screams. The patter of footsteps from the rest of the gang come from two restaurants down.

By the time Joe reaches over the counter for me, the pincers have latched around my neck. I grab them futilely while they squeeze inward, pressing into my skin, breaking it, puncturing every kind of tube inside. Arteries and veins, esophagus, trachea...All that stands between the pincers' union is my spinal column, and when they find an easy path through a soft disc between vertebrae, they close completely.

♥*♥*♥

The correct choice was to try to convince Joe with Kirsten's crazy idea. Turn to page 89.

Kirsten's base tan drains away, leaving her a midwestern midwinter pasty, five shades lighter than she was a minute ago. My eyes flash to the lifeless hand attached to her severed arm.

"Raina! Joe! Anybody!" I scream.

I look around, pull a corpse over, and strip its coat off.

"Quinn?" Kirsten murmurs my name as part of a litany of flighty, thoughtless mumbling.

I wad up the coat and stuff it against the gaping wound below her shoulder. She winces. I struggle to keep her in place, to keep a tight compress on the wound.

Raina and Skye appear before I try anything else. Together, we apply pressure and elevate Kirsten's shoulder, doing the bare minimum. Raina cries out for a belt to tie off the nub left over. A buckle swats my cheek when Alex throws his, which is taken by Raina and deftly wrapped around the wound.

Three of us in attendance and I know this won't save her. Kirsten is on death's doorstep. Firecrackers go off in my head just looking at her, knowing it's already come to pass. We need better people, better treatment, and...and...

"Where's Prairie?"

"She can't help," Skye tells me.

"What?"

He doesn't answer. I throw a wild glance toward Prairie on the balcony, moving slowly and covered in blood. I step away from Kirsten while Raina remains in position, pressing with all her might. Skye keeps Kirsten tilted on her side.

They don't need me anymore. But this isn't enough. It's time to finish what we started.

Help is right outside, just beyond view. It has to be.

Well, it better be because without it, Kirsten will be gone. I find the dumbbell Kirsten brought to the door and tell Raina and Skye I'm going for help.

I nearly twist my ankle twice climbing through the bodies in the vestibule before I get to the doors, where I kick away corpses leaning against them. With my sleeve pulled down over my hand, I hit the glass with the dumbbell. The door rattles. I strike again, making spiderwebs. After a third, the glass breaks and falls away, letting freezing air cannon inside. For one bracing second, I revel in victory and bathe in the dry cold, loving it now while it still feels good.

I use the dumbbell to clear the full doorway of glass before dropping the weight on a corpse's head and taking my first step outside.

An ice dam against the door is coated in shimmering, gritty snow, but it's slippery as ice, and I do an accidental split—my left leg out, my right leg inside the vestibule. I lift my trailing leg and slide myself forward. On level ground, I try getting to my knees, but my butt breaks through the snow into several inches of water. I gasp from the shock. My backside is soaked through, and without any leverage to get out of the hole, I clumsily flip onto my knees like I'd planned, which dunks the rest of my lower half.

Help is right around the corner.

My hands break through next and burn with the shocking cold. I growl, but nothing more than another gasp comes out. Ice forms on me, seizing my body and stopping me from moving. I get up, and one step at a time, I trudge through the snow-crusted floodwaters.

Off to my left is an empty parking lot, a giant field of snow. Taking a right will lead me up to the road, and from there, I can signal for help. Or I can follow the road around to the other entrance and find emergency vehicles there. Distance-wise, neither way is better than the other, but if no one is already at these doors, then getting to the road is my best shot at spotting help.

If only I could see someone or something *now*—a vehicle, blinking lights.

Kirsten can't wait. I keep that in mind and clutch my arms to myself, tucking my head into my jacket. The wind tries to throw me over. My boots' insulation begins to fail against the water, but I keep pushing.

It's all her fault. If Kirsten hadn't rushed for the doors, I wouldn't be doing this.

I can't stop myself from blaming Kirsten. She's made everything today about her. It was supposed to be *my* day. She told me so. I knew not to buy it, but I never had a choice. Unlike now. I *do* have a choice. I could stay behind, could wait for someone to find us. But I know what the consequences would be.

Only one choice will let me live with myself—the one in which I sacrifice everything for her.

I traverse the rest of the parking lot and reach the berm rising to the road. Plowed snow stands in front of me, and I use my claw-like hands, turned red by water and wind, to clamor up it. My knuckles tighten. Uncontrollable shivers wrack me. I barely make it to the top of the plow pile, and once I do, my body is rigid enough for a coffin, and I tumble down the other side. My body bounces on icy boulders plowed up when the snow was fat and wet.

I keep going up the hill, my bleary eyes searching the road above me. The snow cover here is just as deceptive as it was in the parking lot, with a thin, crunchy crust dropping me into a slushy under-layer. And now I'm doing it uphill.

Halfway, I see it.

A flicker of red and blue lights cuts through the night and coats the snow on the other side of the mall, beyond the theater. What is inside that theater is something so terrifying, Joe wouldn't even consider going through it and making for the emergency exits. I'm half satisfied to see them drifted up with snow.

But I'm not able to think much anymore. My chest goes hot, and my legs lose sensation. I refuse to look down because, for one thing, I can't even concentrate enough on doing so and, for another, I have to trust I can stay upright.

The pressure of the snow crust breaks against my legs while I move diagonally up the hill, aiming for the road, trying to cut the distance between me and the emergency vehicles. I wish I could scream. Wish they could hear me if I did...

At a dip in the snow, my leg crashes through the crust and keeps going, until I fall forward into a down-sloping stream of water. It originates from the culvert up by the road, draining runoff to a retention pond behind the theater. My entire body sinks beneath the level of the surface, and water rushes over my head, soaking my whole body.

I can't move. Even though I try, nothing responds. My body slips farther down toward the pond, carried by the rushing water.

With the iciness sapping my heat, the wind buffeting me from above, my core goes hotter and hotter. I'm alone. All thanks to Kirsten. Finally alone, tucked away and fading into darkness.

Fireworks go off again. My vision splits and goes kaleidoscopic. My mind retreats from the front seat of my head, toward the back of the theater. Everything comes at me through a tunnel.

I don't really want to thank Kirsten, and I don't think to either, sarcastically or not. In fact, I don't focus at all. Instead, I fade into death, freezing in a deluge of water, left to myself because I tried to save my friend. She won't make it either. I guarantee it.

If only I could tell her to her face, really stick it to her. Thanks to her, we're both dead. She wouldn't have it any other way.

The correct choice was to get Kirsten out of there.

Turn to page 321.

The sound of Prairie's voice makes me grunt with instinctual ape-like excitement. Raina reels backward over the security guard's body and launches herself at the walkie-talkie.

Prairie is alive. She has to be close, but in my mind, the path to her becomes a chasm. Since our sprint through the fog, the mall has taken on a new geography.

The guard sits up, his arms fanning an opening through trench coats to clear the way for his head. He claws at Raina, getting up to her until they're nose to nose.

"Stop!" he hisses. "You'll draw more of those things in!"

"Yeah, can I agree with him there?" Kirsten places her hand on the contested walkie-talkie like she's blessing the worst marriage in the world. "We need to figure this out, but we need to be quiet."

Raina grimaces. "Oh, I'm being too loud for you? I got Prairie, and you want out, but now you want to figure this out as a team?"

"Look, let's stay here and wait for those things to go back to the mall," says the guard. "Then we run back out and smash our way through. Otherwise, they'll kill us all."

The radio crackles. Prairie's voice comes lower. *"Are you there? Over."*

Raina wrenches away the walkie-talkie, but before she responds, I place my hand on hers.

"Hold on a second," I say to the guard. "What makes you say that?"

"Say what? That we should wait? That they'll kill us all?"

"Quinn, we don't have time for this." Raina shakes me off and clicks the speaker. "Prairie, it's Raina. We got this security guard who...Hey, what's your name?"

"Uh, I'm...It's Warren."

"Prairie, say hi to Warren. We're in Sears. We're safe. But don't come here. I repeat. Do. Not. Come. Here. Are you safe where you are? Over." She releases the button and looks at Warren. "Okay, what can you tell us? What'd you see?"

"Yeah, how do we get outta here?" I ask.

Warren wipes his sleeve over his eyes and shakes his head. "Ah, man, you see what's happened."

"You were with that group," Raina says. "What'd they say? Where'd they come from?"

The radio crackles. *"Okay...Hi, Warren. Hey, guys. Over."*

"I didn't know them. They came charging, and that one guy led the way, and he seemed to know what he was doing, so I just followed them." As if we're ashamed of him, the security guard wags his hands like he's shaking a couple of cocktails. "Look, it's not like we're trained to handle this...mutant kinda crap!"

Crackling radio: *"I'm safe where I am, but I gotta be quiet. Over."*

"At least not non-human mutants, right?" Kirsten says. "But I second staying here. In here, we know what we're dealing with. And there's gotta be fewer people in here to start with, which means fewer of those things creeping in. I mean, come on. It's Sears. On Valentine's Day. Who's shopping in Sears?"

Raina stares daggers at her. I jump in before things get ugly.

"Warren, you're saying you have no reason to believe any other place is better or worse than here. So, where'd they come from? How do we get out of here, assuming all the Sears exits are frozen shut?"

"Dude," says Kirsten, "which way won't be filled with mutants? We need to wait and see if those mosquito things go back to where they came from."

Raina shoves Kirsten. "Knock it off. Stop pretending you're taking control when you're just playing the victim again."

"I am not!"

"She isn't wrong," I say.

"Shut up, Carpenter!"

"No, *you* shut up," Raina scolds. "If we weren't stuck in this clothes rack with you, we'd be solving actual problems, not shooting down every idea until you decide to play the damsel in distress and wait for help to arrive. Then you'll act all grateful to whomever finds us, if they ever *do* find us—"

"*Then,*" I continue, "you'll act like you were the one holding us all together and be all like, 'We didn't actually need to be rescued!'"

"Quinn!"

The radio crackles again. *"Guys, are you okay? Over."*

Raina punches the speaker. "Hold on a second. Over."

"Let me know what you decide. I might have an idea. Over."

Kirsten goes onto her knees, rising a couple of inches higher than us. "You don't have to be a-holes about this. We're safe where we are.

Why can't Prairie come to us? Find out where she is. I guarantee she's, like, ten feet away and she can just sneak over here."

"Would you sneak ten feet over to her if her spot is safer?" I ask.

"She's right." Warren nods at Kirsten. "We're safe here, and there's more of us."

"Oh my God," Raina mutters. She thumbs down the speaker. "Prairie, Raina here. Where are you, over?"

While we wait, with two of us still pursuing another way out of here, Kirsten juts out her jaw and Warren deflates. Prairie's going to be the tiebreaker. That is, if Warren counts. I guess he should. In the great battle between humans and mutant swamp monsters, he's on our side.

Crackle. *I'm hiding in a wristwatch kiosk outside The Sharper Image. Over.*

I scrunch my brow. "That's...by Penney's. How's she over there? She backtracked that whole way?"

"Backtracked? Dude, she's practically *in* Penney's," Kirsten says.

"It's a straight shot," notes Raina.

"Yeah, duh, it's a straight shot! It's a mall! Everything's a straight shot. And that means it's not hard for her to come here."

Prairie comes on. *Did you say you're at Sears? Do you have a way out? Because I...uh, I could come to you. Over.*

There's hesitation in her voice—the same old Prairie caving to expectations. It takes the knot already in my stomach and presses it into a hardened pit. Not just because I hate seeing her taken advantage of, but because I'm side by side with the people doing it. A part of me wants Prairie to come to us. It'd be one less thing to worry about with Bridie out there. But then, couldn't Bridie come to us too? The knotted pit in my gut solidifies, its mass multiplying and sinking to the floor.

Raina groans at Prairie's offer. "Yeah, hold on, Prairie. We're discussing—"

Before she can finish and release the speaker, Kirsten lunges and says, "Yes! Prairie, it's safer here. Start coming to us."

Warren nods vigorously. He and Kirsten look awash with relief, like they've put the argument to rest. Prairie has offered; we've accepted. A nasty fight breaks out in my gut. One side struggles for relief, having the decision taken out of my hands. The other grapples for disgust, for having done nothing to stop this. It reminds me of the times I've won arguments at home out of sheer volume and obnoxiousness or silent-treated Mom or Bridie into submission.

Raina pulls the radio away. "Prairie. Raina. Don't move, okay? I repeat, don't move. Our exit is blocked. We're iced in. We're safe where we are, but there's no way out."

"No, that's not right," hisses Kirsten. "We can break through the doors."

"After we get past those monsters?" I ask.

Kirsten swipes my argument down. "You think Prairie's alone? There's gotta be more people to help her. The mall is packed. We have an exit. We just saw it."

"People like the ones who helped Warren? The ones lying in pools of their blood?" I ask.

"Watch it," Raina snaps. Her patience, which has accompanied her relatively coolheaded leadership, is starting to wear thin.

If I'm not careful, I'll find myself on the wrong side of her, with Kirsten and Warren. Her flaring temper shuts up Kirsten, who watches for a blowup.

Warren studies us, trying to read the situation, not knowing our history.

Shut down, I wait to hear Kirsten's new angle. If she wants to talk, she will. She's dragged us this far, coercing me to come here, humiliating me in front of the seniors. Now this.

Raina has the best case for standing up to her. She's just shown it. I need to be there for Raina, and I'm sick of Kirsten getting her way.

Crackling radio. *"Are you guys there? Over."*

Raina thumbs the speaker like a detonator. "We're thinking. One second." She drops her hand, then lifts it again. "Over."

Kirsten settles back on her haunches. Her breathing smooths out, and I can tell we're in for one of her matronly acts of maintaining order. She'll run her hands over her thighs, like she's smoothing out an apron, then she'll clear her throat in a high, dainty pitch. The instant she opens her mouth, her voice will drip with condescending pleas to remain calm.

And then I'll lose it on her.

Kirsten rubs her thighs and wets her lips with her tongue. Her throat clears. *Hem-hem.* Her lips part.

The act lights a match under my heart, and my heart's covered in lighter fluid.

Prairie: *"Okay, but I think I have a way out. Over."*

Kirsten's mouth snaps shut. Raina and I exchange a look.

"Say again? Over," Raina says.

"I think I have a way out. Over."

Kirsten chuffs and looks for support in Warren, who shrinks into himself, knowing he has no real pull with any of us.

"Uh, where? Over."

"One of the exits outside J.C. Penney. It's pretty quiet over there, and the floodwaters aren't too high. But we shouldn't wait long. Over."

Raina looks to me, and I nod. I can picture it, getting to Prairie and breaking her out. The mission takes shape. She is my responsibility. But there's still the matter of finding Bridie, and I suddenly wonder if we should tell Prairie to do the unthinkable and save herself.

Kirsten reads my mind, telling which way I'm leaning.

"No way," she says. "That's all the way across the mall. And besides, what about Bridie? Are we going to leave her out there?"

"Since when do *you* care about Bridie?" I ask.

"Why doesn't Prairie just leave if she has a way out? She can't do anything for us! She's wasting time sitting there. Tell her to get out!"

"She might not make it. What if the doors are blocked or frozen shut? The mall is surrounded by water, and the storm is only making it worse. And on top of that, it seems like the whole place is caving in on itself. Or haven't you noticed?"

On my cue, another low rumble strikes. Hangers clatter on the rack. Trench coats sway to the soft music of the mall's structure failing.

"I'm sick of this!" Kirsten cries. "Tell Prairie to get her ass out that door *now*. Is that not in her best interest? Am I not sticking up for her by saying that? Then we can stay here and wait for those things to leave."

It almost makes sense. Prairie could make a break for it. She might be the safest of us all. Raina stares off, stony-faced, holding her objections close to her chest. I'm ready to change sides. It just might be the right way to go.

Then Kirsten does it.

She rubs her thighs, spreads her fingers in a pacifying motion, clears her throat—*hem-hem*—and starts in with her most schoolmarmish voice. "Girls, we are going to keep our heads on straight. This just makes the most sense."

I rise. "Oh, *screw you*, Kirsten!"

Warren raises his hand to my mouth, a wild fear in his eyes. I bat him down and wheel on Kirsten.

"You're forgetting one thing, aren't you? Bridie! You're fine letting Prairie fend for herself? You're good staying put? What about my sister? You don't care if she gets out of here, do you? You want to be cheer captain so damn bad, start acting like one! Or next season, you'll march into the gym for our first practice to see Raina's cut you from your own squad!"

Warren tries butting in. "Hey, can we please—"

"You wouldn't've come to Sears in the first place if Raina hadn't come here first. You just followed her because you had no clue what was going on!"

"Yeah?" Kirsten gets to her feet, and so do I. We close in on each other, our exhalations mingling. "And look at the good it's done us. We're split up, Raina's dad is dead, and we're fighting because of what she got us into."

I almost don't move fast enough—and my strength is hardly adequate to make a difference—but I stop Raina's hand from connecting with Kirsten's cheek, turning a full-palmed slap into a fingernails-only smack. It digs furrows through Kirsten's skin, leaving ragged white scratches on her perfect face. Her eyes double in size, and as I move between them, Kirsten pounces on my back.

We bounce off trench coats, squishing our waterlogged jackets against one another. I could almost say this is where the day was going to lead us to anyway. The mutant swamp monsters just made it happen faster. It almost feels good to wrestle it all out.

We end up in a pile in the middle of the carousel, breathing hard, our limbs spasming with feeble attacks and defenses. Warren bellyflops us all to the floor. Our brawl collapses, my face smooshes the wet carpet, and the three of us groan under his weight.

He slips off our squirming pile and shouts, "I can't take this anymore! If you're going to go, get out of here! And if you're going to stay, just shut up! Please! Shut! Up!"

"No one's talking to you, Warren!" Kirsten yells.

Warren struggles to catch his breath and brushes his combover back in place. "Yeah, so go find your own hiding spot! Please, just...stop!"

Kirsten pulls her leg free from under Raina. "We're staying right here, so if you want out, *you* go."

Raina says, "No, we're going to Prairie."

"God, *Raina!*"

"This is insane," Warren mutters. He goes to one of the carousel's ends and parts the trench coats. The security guard squeezes a clump of coats on one side of the opening and throws it to the floor, then does the same to a few on the other side, opening a huge gap. "Get out!" he cries.

Just seeing more of the store makes me break into a cold sweat.

Raina and Kirsten scramble to their feet. Any hint of precision, mental or physical, is gone, and Warren isn't helping us get it back. I admit, we lost control. But I can't help restore order when I'm petrified by the specter of some new monster creeping toward me. Some clumsy, gelatinous thing so clear in my mind, I can picture it at the edge of the jewelry department near the escalators.

Maybe Kirsten and Raina see the same thing. Maybe that's why they freak out and back away from Warren.

The fascinating thing is, the monster doesn't disappear into the smoke and mirrors of my imagination. It leaps closer, making the floor shudder when it lands, then it jumps again.

Warren moves to the side of the gap and wheels his arm for us to leave. He looks outside, probably stricken by our terror, noticing the danger he's put himself in. The security guard must see the monster, if only out of the corner of his eye, right before a pale pink mass as thick as a tree trunk adheres to his chest and grips him firmly with gummy jaws, like a slimy sock puppet.

The wind gets knocked out of him in a *whoosh*, and then he's not there anymore. In the blink of an eye, he's yards away, midair, and in another, he's nothing but a crumpled bundle of limbs protruding from the lipless gulch of a giant frog creature's mouth. Its limbs are as slender as its body is corpulent, its pale eyes staring unseeing in all directions. The monster rears its head and opens its mouth, swallowing its prey and making Warren disappear for good.

We stand in a stunned silence until Kirsten rushes forward and pulls the trench coats shut like window blinds. The omnipresent mixture of human screams and inhuman invaders fade farther into white noise. We might be safe if we stay quiet and don't move. The thing can't see us anymore, right?

A slight tremor travels through the floor. Then another and another, stronger each time.

Raina's brain fires up. She pulls a trench coat from her side and hands it to me, gives one to Kirsten, and keeps one for herself. Raina stuffs the walkie-talkie into her jacket. "On the count of three. On go."

Another tremor.

"One."

I get ready to part another opening between coats.

"Two."

Kirsten raises her coat like a crusader's shield.

"Three."

Raina digs in her heels.

"Go."

I rip open the trench coats, and Raina bursts out, followed by Kirsten and me. She zigzags between racks, going toward seasonal decor. An elephant trunk of pale pink tongue rockets out between me and Kirsten, snagging a mannequin and yanking it through an array of hanging clothes.

Raina aims for the exit in the women's department, making Prairie and Bridie flash through my mind. But we don't get close enough for me to re-face my moral quandary. Close to the far wall, vaulting over women's shoes, is another mosquito beast.

We veer left. There's only one other spot for us to go, no matter how dumb it seems. Raina steers us to the escalator, back toward the frog. I hold my coat in front of me, just barely keeping sight of Kirsten's bobbing blond hair. So when she's punched out of line as swiftly as Warren was snatched, I scream. She's there one second, gone the next, like a giant finger has flicked her off the picnic table of life.

But it's *not* a giant finger. It's a tongue stretched out taut in front of me. I trip over it, land hard on my hip, and roll over, yelling Kirsten's name.

The tongue's grippy nodule retreats, clutching a wad of brown cloth and leaving behind Kirsten, her eyes facing impending death, hands held out like claws, as though her trench coat still shields her.

Raina comes back. And we get Kirsten to her feet.

The frog spits out the coat and homes back in on us. We rush onward, virtually unshielded, and since we don't get a real say in the matter, we double-time it up the downward escalator.

Kirsten snaps back to herself and pushes Raina, who slips and misses a step, causing all of us to slide down and lose precious seconds. At least we have walls on both sides. The ceiling comes closer, with no threat from above.

I check behind us. The frog appears around the corner, its head tilting, pointing a gauzy, bobbling eye at us.

"Go!" I scream. I can't take the sensation of the stairs fighting my every step, the floor falling out from under me, the rubber handrail sliding me down to the frog's killing zone.

My lungs deplete while we climb. I catch up to Kirsten and shove her butt, not wanting to use the guardrails or scramble with my hands on the metal steps, just wanting to be higher and higher.

A wet slap sounds behind me. The tongue paws at the edge of a step two beneath mine.

Raina and then Kirsten clear the top and race on. With a final burst of energy, I pump my legs up the last set of downward-moving steps. My coordination fails. I'm going so fast, I end up stepping on air and fall forward. My chin strikes the flat conveyor at the top of the escalator. My body reverses motion, back down to the frog. I have to find the energy again, but the aches of our mad dash and more blare through my body.

It's over for me. I can feel the clapping wet oven mitts of the frog's prehensile tongue closing on my calf and pulling me toward its gullet to join Warren. Prairie and Bridie are on their own. Kirsten and Raina will have to work as a team.

Lucky for me, the whole teamwork thing comes naturally to them. At least when it most matters.

A hand grips my collar, and my motion stops. Escalator steps thud against my whole body.

I grab ahold of Kirsten's sleeve, and she pulls me up.

Raina snatches Kirsten's jacket and jerks her back.

We collapse on the floor and watch. Up in the air, arcing in a wriggling line over the escalator, a pale pink tongue grasps for prey. It falls out of sight, like an obscene bit of silly string.

Take a breather. Turn to page 148.

Keep going. Get out of Sears. Turn to page 295.

The mall gives Prairie's proposal a thundering endorsement. Skylight glass drops to the floor of the atrium, and the haunted roar of the incoming storm races down the concourse to us. I break into goosebumps. Everyone tenses up. In the wake of this urgent reminder to get out of here, I say Prairie's name, like she's forgetting something.

Yeah. My sister.

She looks at me. I don't follow up. There's nothing she can do at this point and no chance to argue. Our time is up, rocketing my concern for Bridie to the front of the line, but there's nothing to be done.

"Quinn, what is it?" Kirsten asks, her features having collapsed along with her mall.

I open my mouth, but I can't stop Prairie in her tracks. She and Joe can take this home.

Prairie gives me an odd look, then announces, "That wind is only going to send more things this way."

Joe clears his throat. "She's right. This is the way out. Macy's."

And like that, they're off, dividing the group into teams and assigning tasks. We have to smash a ton of glass. The group needs bodyguards, weapons, and a distraction. I keep my mouth shut and struggle to listen, pushing Bridie down where she can't get in the way of my own survival. If I can do that, I'll be good and will be able to help. All I have to do is step back because Prairie's got this. Our salvation lies with her and Joe.

Skye's name pricks my interest. He's going to blast more music to freak out the monsters. Prairie says she'll help. Raina and Kirsten will get them set up.

"Quinn."

"Huh?"

Joe looks at me, flanked on one side by his beefcakes, Gabe and Trent on the other.

"Follow me. We're grabbing weapons from Kickoff."

Stuck among them, I wend my way through the fog from inside their protective shell, avoiding shadows, until we arrive at the darkened storefront. Joe peeks inside, checks his corners, and guides us in.

"Weights are in the back right," he whispers.

I keep to the middle of the pack, still troubled by Bridie and struggling to work up the will to operate independently. I just need to be a part of the team. I owe it to them. My insistence on finding Bridie brought us here. Was that leadership I was trying on? I don't know. But I don't think so, and they don't need more of it.

The beefcakes lead us deeper into Kickoff Pro Shop, the formal wear giving way to casual, which fades into athletic gear. Past a display of socks and sweatbands appear baseball bats and tennis rackets, helmets and basketballs, running shoes and free weights.

"Let's load up." Alex finds me in the fog and points me out. "You, Joe's girl. Grab some backpacks."

My gut burns at the command. I nearly tell him to screw himself, but the boys are already hefting bats and inspecting free weights. I remind myself Alex was just beaten into submission by Joe. Literally, beaten. I march past him without breaking my stride or looking him in the eye, pretending I was going to do what he commanded all along. If I'm the butt of his teensy power trip, I'll accept it.

The sporting goods transition to hiking and camping gear. A smattering of backpacks dangle on the wall. Another pile lies on the floor—some unzipped, mouths open, advertising their capaciousness.

I bend down to grab a couple of open packs when I notice one in the middle of the pile. It continues past the point where it should stop. A tail curls around the other packs, and when I close in, it shifts.

I follow the tail up to a mouth open like a backpack-shaped decoy. Instead of a zipper, its rim is lined with tiny razor-teeth. Where a binder pocket should be, a tongue protrudes from the base of a filmy mouth bed. The mottled gray backpack raises by millimeters, and from its sides, it sprouts dripping fans of blue tendrils. It doesn't make a sound, and neither do I.

The mudpuppy opens its maw, and before I can speak or move, it lunges with legs I don't see, giving up its hiding spot. Its snout hits me in the solar plexus and knocks the wind out of me, making me fall. The creature lunges again, its jaws finding purchase around my midsection. It shakes its head, tearing my skin, leaking my blood, shredding my nerves.

It was only a backpack a minute ago. Why couldn't it stay that way? Why couldn't it keep hiding?

I wrestle with the thing, but despite its corpulent mutations, it's too strong. My life force shrinks to a kernel of heat in my chest, my brain too rattled to think straight.

The correct choice was to back up Prairie and take the lead.
Turn to page 263.

The last time I was on the second floor of Sears, Mom grounded Bridie and me. She carted us up here to get new sets of sheets after Bridie got a bigger bed and I complained about inheriting her Rainbow Brite ones. It just wasn't my thing.

After getting tired of Mom feigning enthusiasm over an assortment of solid pastels and cooing when she came across some cartoon ones I hated even more than the Rainbow Brites, Bridie and I started jumping on mattresses. And they were the good ones. That's why they're on display. Poofy and bouncy—pretty much trampolines. We stretched our fingers to the ceiling. My ponytail slapped my back when I landed.

And I can still picture how red Mom's face was with embarrassment and rage. What followed was the longest grounding I've ever had. We'd screwed around like that all the time at home, to make no mention of our fights, but Mom didn't like our misbehaving in public.

I don't figure she'd approve of me now either, collapsing on an out-of-this-world poofy, pearly white comforter. It's perfectly fluffed on top of the king size bed in the first bedroom diorama next to the escalator.

I lie on my back, pressing mosquito beast blood and swamp water into its 500-thread-count linens. Raina takes a seat next to me, and Kirsten spins in all directions, watching for another incoming threat. I gaze up at the drop-tile ceiling and the bland fluorescent tube lighting and wonder how this sterile showroom ended up being the place where hell was unleashed. The roof creaks from the pummeling winds just overhead.

I'm back to where I started this morning, where I wanted to stay—tucked away in a soft, cushy bubble far away from anyone and everything. If only I could strip out of these clothes, roll over and pull the comforter over me, turn off these ugly lights, and tell everyone to leave me alone.

But that's not going to happen. Not while we're stuck here. Not while Prairie is left alone and Bridie is who the hell knows where.

"Prairie, you still there? Over." Raina speaks into the radio with a tired voice.

I should be on watch, same as Kirsten. There's got to be some other monster creeping around. Yet just by coming up the escalator,

I feel infinitely safer. But we can't stay forever. There's a second-floor entrance. The escalators aren't the only way to get up here, among the bedroom sets and home furnishings.

Crackling radio: *"Yes, I'm okay. Over."*

Raina sighs. "Guys..."

I know what she's gonna say. And yeah, what else are we supposed to do? While I'm thinking of a counterargument, a rumbling vibration passes through the floor. The tube lights wiggle ever so slightly.

Raina stands up. I stay where I am, in bed, where I wanted to be all along. Before Kirsten called. Before I dragged Prairie into this.

No, Prairie volunteered to come.

Dammit, I know it's my fault she's in this mess, but I don't want to admit it. What makes it all the stranger is she seems to be safer than us. She can get out, and she should.

The rumbling continues, and from the mall come the sounds of rending metal, glass cracking and shattering, and electrical pops of cords and electronics contacting the water.

"I don't think we can wait for rescue." Raina sounds far off, preoccupied.

To her credit, Kirsten doesn't argue the point.

"Prairie's still safe?" I ask, trying to regulate my breathing.

"Apparently."

"You're saying we got to move."

"You feel that? You hear it? The mall's falling apart. It's sinking into whatever underground void they built it on top of, whatever void these fricking monsters came from. The fricking wetlands."

"Huh?" Kirsten makes her first noise since coming up here.

Let's give her a prize. *Huh.* A genius contribution.

"Don't you remember what I...?" Raina begins. "Oh, wait, no, you weren't there. You stormed off to dump mop water on some idiots' heads. They built this place on a big ass swamp. Fought off the protestors, drained the place, drove off whatever was left of the wildlife, bulldozed, and made it into a giant steel and concrete block, with a parking lot attached to it that's been sinking into the ground for years."

"They didn't drive off *all* the wildlife," I say.

"How do you know about that?" Kirsten asks.

"For one thing, everyone should know it," Raina continues. "My mom protested it. That's how I know. She fought for years to keep developments from gouging out more of the countryside. It all started with the army base up here, spilling industrial waste into the watershed. That's what got her attention, right after Vietnam. And that's how she met my dad.

"He was patrolling the fences during one of their demonstrations, and he laid eyes on her and fell head over heels in love, served out his enlistment, and stayed out of the army for her instead of going for officer. He probably wouldn't have made it, but that's not the point. That's how they tell the story anyway. But what I'm really saying is that we need to move. The mall's like a wide-open hand closing into a fist, and we're in the middle of its palm. If the monsters don't get us, we're going to get sucked right down into the swamp."

"Then why don't we go back downstairs and head straight for the doors?" Kirsten demands. "We just got past more of those things, and the Jeep is right outside. We know what we're facing now. We can take it."

"*Prairie*," Raina reminds her. "It's Prairie. I'm not having this conversation again."

I pipe up since Kirsten's playing the same old hits. "Then why don't we have a new one? You two find Prairie, and I'll go look for Bridie."

"That's the dumbest thing I've heard all day," Raina says. "You have no clue where she is."

"I know that. But—and I know how stupid this sounds—she's my sister."

Kirsten scoffs. "Yeah, but it's not like you're the reason she's here. Not like with Prairie. Look at her, right?"

She went there. I sit up and glower at her, projecting every dark thought that's been in my head since I first met her, since I first learned what a nightmare she could be. And I'm reminded, for all the missiles I expended on her in that empty storefront, I barely let out any of the rancor that's built up over the years.

"No. *You* look. *You're* the reason she's here. *You're* the reason any of us are here. Because you insisted on it."

"And now we're repeating another conversation..." Raina starts walking away. She inches over to the escalator. Raina peeks down it to see if the frog or something is following and walks away, unconcerned.

"Can I be clear on something here, without either of you interrupting me?" Kirsten asks. "And I know how hard that can be because it seems like all our conversations are just a ton of comebacks piled on top of each other. For the record, I'm trying to be rational. I say that Prairie should book it out the nearest door—which she says she can do—and run around the outside of the mall to get back to the Jeep. Then I say the three of us get some weapons—like some bars or pipes or, I don't know...like the stuff we used on the globby mosquito thing—then sneak back down to the same exit we just came from and bash our way out. Then, that way, we can see who else made it outside, find someone with a car phone or a flip phone or whatever—because someone around here's gotta have one. And that way, you can see if Bridie's okay before you charge back in here to look for her."

I let her finish, but I'm already shaking my head before she gets to the part about us sneaking back downstairs. Prairie can't be left on her own. Not if there's a chance she'd encounter anything like we have. I think of Raina versus the mosquito beast, on the brink of exhaustion, almost succumbing to defeat...The fact her father, Mr. Human Hydraulic himself, was felled by it...The doors that were flash frozen by a roll of ice thicker than the ten-year buildup in our garage freezer.

"You're not listening," I tell Kirsten. "I'm not betting that Prairie can get out alone. That's why I'm saying we should split up. So you two can hook up with her while I get Bridie."

"Oh my *God!* Why do you want to rescue Bridie?"

Kirsten's explosion is so abrupt and so shocking, my comeback comes nowhere near close to piling onto hers. It sputters out and makes my mouth hang open.

I mean, she's my sister, Kirsten. What else do you want?

"You realize who we saw her with, right? You realize she probably helped plan that prank. She's got a reason to screw with you. She's got access to your diary. The poetry in the valentine that you recognized? How else would the girls know about that? It was Bridie reading your diary, just like you thought. And now you want to help her.

"If there's anyone to blame for any of us being here, it's her. She had to get one over on you because she's an asshole. Face it, Quinn. Your sister is just a big jerk. She always has been; she always will be. How many times have you called me bawling because of something she said or did to you? How many times has she embarrassed you in front of boys or talked crap behind your back? How many of her friends pick on you because she tells them to? She's never been a friend to you, and I'm not saying that means she deserves something horrible happening to her. I'm saying you don't owe her anything. And that you shouldn't feel responsible for her being here today.

"And I mean, *she's* the big sister. *She* should be coming for *you*. But it doesn't look like it, does it? Where is she? So, if you want to know what I think—which you never do—she's here on her own, and I guarantee you can draw a direct line between what happened yesterday and why she's here today. That's it. She's made her bed."

Even Raina has turned to watch, and from the look on her face, though she's as appalled as I am, it'd be a weight off her chest not to have to go looking for Bridie on top of Prairie.

But that's exactly what I've told them they don't have to do. I'm asking to be free of them, as crazy, as selfish, as that sounds. I'm not trying to abandon Prairie. The endless back and forth is ripping me in half. Kirsten pointing out my bad blood with Bridie isn't helping. She's compressing an entire sisterhood's worth of life into one takedown rant. I've never found Bridie to be any better or worse than anyone else's sisters I've seen out there.

And yet, even though it shouldn't even factor into any decision at this point...did Bridie take part in the prank? And if she did, why? She has no reason to get involved in the cheerleader hazing, and if she's going to prank underclassmen, she'd do best to avoid blowing up our household by targeting me. It would be better for her to pick some random kid and get away scot-free, blending into the gauntlet of chortling seniors, all throwing up their hands and pulling stupid faces when the accusations start flying, bent on protecting their own.

And troubled earth tumbles down, far too shy
To stop its flight and cry, how I love you, oh, sky

Bridie wouldn't have. And even if she did, would she really have hunted through a stack of diaries to find the single most incriminating verse? Wouldn't any crappy poetry have done the job? Or did whoever actually pulled the prank need to see the recognition in my eyes?

None of it can make me forgive Kirsten, with her smug face and pathetic desperation. But I'm tearing up, the iron heats in my gut, and if I start screaming at her, I'll be left stumbling over my words and blubbering.

And there's everything else to consider. We're no freer of the noises from the collapsing mall and monsters running amok, all of it like a constant stream of music piped in through the hidden ceiling speakers—which, funny enough, keep belting out soft adult contemporary love ballads from ten years ago. Is that Duran Duran?

"Sorry, Prairie, we're discussing options. Over." Raina releases the speaker and sighs again, the whole world on her shoulders. She talks to Kirsten and me softly. "Look, that's an interesting twist and all with Bridie, but we got to make a decision fast. Frankly, Quinn, you're going to hate me for this, but I agree with Kirsten."

"Thank you!"

"It makes the most sense for us to join up with Prairie first, get out to the Jeep, where it's warm, and do some recon for Bridie out there, see if anyone else is outside. I know that sounds like a lot of time, but if we move now, we'll be out of here before you know it. We're beat already, you don't know where she is, and besides, she had a whole group of people with her. It stands to reason that they've either made it out or hunkered down. You just don't have enough information to run after her the way you are."

"Wait, what!" Kirsten cries out. She wheels on Raina, who drops her hands and stares straight at her, unamused. "That's not agreeing with me at all! I said Prairie's on her own. We have to make for the exit down below. If she was so damn smart, she'd be calling us from the outside! She'd already have *made* it out!"

"I am agreeing that we should reconnoiter at the Jeep. Get to safety first. Get the engine running to warm up. But we can't guarantee the exits aren't frozen over."

"Reco—? God! Prairie can find someone else to help! We're not it! I am sick and tired of all this Prairie shit today. Like, why is she here? Why did she come when she's not even friends with us? She's not even supposed to be here. I wanted to bring Quinn out with her *real* friends, to have a good time and forgot all the shit that happened yesterday, not to have her wimpy, Jesus freak, cling-on, little elementary school pity pal from the neighborhood, who she was forced to hang out with, tag along to bum us all out and make us feel awkward and dress like a freaking baby-child coconut-flavored doughnut that no one would ever eat.

"And now look what she's got herself into. Quinn dragged her along because she felt too sorry not to or because she wanted a human shield to deflect from me because Quinn is too afraid of her own feelings to talk to me like a big girl. So, there you go. She's always the more important thing, just because you make yourself responsible for something smaller than you that you can control. Prairie the human shield, right? Well, you know what, she's still fulfilling her purpose then, isn't she, Quinn? Have her scream her head off and run through the mall and attract all those damn things, and maybe we'll make it out of here alive."

Spittle flies from Kirsten's lips while she rants, and she's very nearly purple in the face by the end. Her lung capacity has never been better. She takes a great gawping breath when she's done.

I have nothing left in me to defend against her. Not to mention, it'd all be wasted energy, and I can't spare any. I understand she's as scared as I am, but I don't want to hear it. My tears won't be held back anymore, not after listening to my affection for my sister and my oldest friend torn to shreds—in fact, doubted with such certainty in the first place, as if my feelings aren't even real. Kirsten has taken every dark thought out into the open, and my only response is to weep, fall onto the bedspread, and wait for someone to scream that another monster is coming, that I have to run.

Just tell me what to do. I'm all out of ideas.

The sounds of chaos go on and on, and our bubble of safety is deflating. I cry and wipe my eyes and my nose on the new comforter, fully expecting something to sniff its way to us or for another group of shoppers to run into us, trailing some new beast.

There's a clicking sound near my head, and I flinch. I expect Raina wants to share some news with Prairie or put her off another minute with a quick update since we're getting nowhere here. But Raina doesn't speak. She holds her tongue while Kirsten recovers herself. Then comes the soft crackling of an open radio channel.

"Um, so, do you want me to try to get out on my own? Over?"

The crackling stops.

I stop crying, and I'm on my feet before Kirsten scurries up beside me, her head down like a bull, aimed at Raina, who stares into the distance, entirely nonplussed.

Oh my God.

Raina was holding the speaker down the whole time. She only released it when Kirsten was done. How much did Prairie hear?

I look at Kirsten, whose words should anger me more than Raina's trickery. She's trembling and whiter than any of the sheets on demo beds around us. The knowledge her vitriol was heard by its target has left her shell-shocked, and I'm as surprised to see such an effect on her. Even Raina raises an eyebrow, like this is not the reaction she was expecting.

"You...bitch," Kirsten says, as if she's putting it out there as an idea, practically talking to herself.

When I think about it, you want your friends to uphold whatever mask you wear in front of them, the one you put out there for others to see. That's what makes a friend your friend. You can say what you want about what makes a good friend versus a bad one, about how important it is or not to call you out on your crap or make you better, but a friend knows what you want to be. They get it. Raina has betrayed Kirsten worse than she's probably ever betrayed anyone in her life. I bet it nearly killed her to do it, for as cool as she plays it.

Still, Raina's face relaxes. She bites her lip and nods. "Yeah. That's me." She presses the speaker. "Prairie. Stay where you're at. We're coming to you. ETA ten minutes, barring any issues with swamp monsters. Over." She releases the speaker. "And that's it. Let's get moving."

Raina fixes the walkie-talkie to her pocket and scopes out the area. It makes me home in on the obvious for the first time: no one else is up here. Whoever was up here—if anyone, when the mall started shaking—they're gone now. It'd almost be an ideal place to wait things out, but like Raina said, it'd be suicide to stay.

After a moment, Kirsten asks, "How could you do that to her?"

Raina whips around, stony-faced, then snorts, shaking her head, before falling back into her haggard grief.

The radio static comes back on. *"Guys, I'm moving closer to the exit. Meet me near the jewelry kiosk outside J.C. Penney. There's something closing in on me. Over."*

Raina yanks the walkie-talkie from her pocket. "Prairie, you okay? What's going on? Over."

"I'm fine. But before you go too far, think about what these things are. It's a lot of insects and amphibians, right? They don't like being out in the open. A lot of them are hiding in stores and stuff, and if they want to get you, they're going to ambush you, so be careful when you're going past any openings. Over."

Raina levels the radio in front of her mouth. "Are you sure? Between the giant mosquitos and frogs, they're pretty comfortable chasing us out in the open. Over."

"I'm sure. Over," Prairie answers, her voice the deathly monotone of someone who's seen too much.

The channel goes silent, and Prairie's answer is punctuated by a loud splash echoing from the mall, followed by a loud scream.

Sloshing footsteps, another loud splash.

Then nothing.

The white noise of mall music, swirling water, and creaking walls.

Kirsten massages her temples. Raina's shoulders fall, and she looks down, mustering the energy to head toward the sounds of chaos. She's made the decision I couldn't make. I can barely forgive her for letting Prairie hear what Kirsten said, but it's not the time to hold it against her. Besides Mr. Harris, I haven't lost anyone today. I don't want someone else to die.

So, I step up to Raina and say, "Ambush predators, huh? Any ideas?"

Raina exhales a long breath through her nose and rubs her chin. She's a complete mess, covered in sticky blood and insect goo. Her hair is falling out of her braid, her jacket and jeans are torn, and she's soaked all the way through. "Well—"

"Oh my God!"

We turn to see Kirsten pointing a finger in the direction leading back into the mall. I only catch a glimpse of the tail end of something before it escapes out of sight. It disappears behind rows of ivory washing machines and dryers. Farther down the line of appliances, it moves across another aisle, and I catch a better view. It's the same color as the appliances, half their height, and after an unnervingly long time for its body to cross the aisle without ending, it vanishes with a flash of brown-tipped machete-long pincers.

We're no longer alone.

Raina and I retreat and scour the floor ahead.

Kirsten is already by the escalator. She looks down and shrieks, "Oh God!" and backs away, almost falling into us.

"Easy!" I hiss, but the frog's giant tongue flops through the air behind her, like a streamer, falling harmlessly out of sight once again.

Ambush predators, right?

This thing is probably going to stick close to the appliances. We'll just have to stay alert when we pass by.

I'm about to tell the girls what I think when, from the far side of the appliances, a pimple-colored cranium emerges, sporting a pair of probing feelers longer than car radio antennae and fore-pincers bigger and more vicious than my mosquito-killing hedge trimmer. The creature barrels toward us on infinite sets of clicking, impossibly synchronized talon-feet, its mouth emitting a hideous screeching sound, like the tape getting ripped out of a VHS cassette.

I scream, "The beds!"

We launch ourselves onto the nearest one, just as the nightmare centipede bears down on us. It turns, taking the aisle going along the foot of our bed, swaying its feelers and pincers up onto the comforter, and reflecting its mean little khaki-button eyes on the fluorescent lights.

"Jump!" I scream.

One after another, we leap to the next bed, then to the next. The centipede tracks us, moves fast down the aisle, and cuts into a row one bed ahead of us, bucking its head to block our passage. But we can't stop.

Raina and Kirsten clear it. I jump last and clip its pincer. Its head arcs after me, and the pincers close with a bony clap but miss. To cut off any possible paths along the floor, I start to knock down lamps and kick over nightstands, pushing over tall bookshelf-style headboards.

We get to the end of the beds in our row, scramble over the final headboard, and leap over to the next row, then go bed-hopping in the opposite direction.

I gotta say, they're making beds cushier and cushier. There's nothing better than a bed you can't afford, and we're launching ourselves between mattresses as fine as Olympic trampolines, leaving blood and slime and grime while a centipede trails us with its wet, glistening body.

Raina lands on the floor, nearly right back where we started by the escalator. She's about to rush down it when Kirsten stops her by grabbing her hoodie.

"No! Frog!"

I leap onto their backs when the centipede comes charging, zigzagging between downed lamps and furniture, insistent on finding out what we are and how well we digest.

"This way," Raina commands.

She leads us along the interior wall housing the elevator and utility closets until we're in the children's clothing section, near where the upward-climbing escalator is located. We'll have to go back downstairs with the same urgent and ridiculous rhythm with which we came upstairs.

"Are you serious?" Kirsten cries.

I yell, "What other choice—" right as the centipede rounds the corner, pivots on its walking bristles, and heads straight for us.

Raina shoves us, and without any time to argue, we descend the upward-moving steps.

I try jumping two at a time. Kirsten complains she'll break an ankle, but Raina pushes her harder. She screams when she falls, and while I'm trying to make sure I don't do the same, I misaim a landing and pitch forward, my leg going stiff under me and shooting pain into my hip. My arms break my fall, but throbbing radiates through me when I hit the steps. I push myself back up and turn around to see what progress the others are making.

Kirsten is grimacing, steadying herself in the same position I'm in, when her eyes go wide, staring in horror at something on the ground floor. My attention is next caught by the centipede at the top of the escalator, rearing its body and flashing its terrible pincers, screeching, readying itself to chase us down.

Kirsten's mouth opens, and she flecks me with spittle. "*Frog!*"

When a pink streamer darts through the air above me, I follow its trajectory and watch it adhere, with a glove-like grip, to the centipede's undercarriage. Then it retracts, hauling the centipede down atop us in all its chittering, slimy glory.

I scream as it slides down the escalator, its legs skating along the rubber handrail. Its bus-length belly skims within inches of my face and fills my nostrils with a revolting, swampy odor.

When the centipede passes, I spin back around and watch a pale frog wrestling to swallow its giant wriggling prey. I lie on my back, and my heart races. The escalator lifts me back to the second floor, and I bump into the stunned, prone forms of Kirsten and Raina.

The walkie-talkie crackles.

"*Hey, do you guys have any other questions? Over.*"

Take the upstairs path. Turn to page 230.

Take the downstairs path. Turn to page 169.

The beefcakes' swinging makes the chandelier's hanging jewels stand out straight against gravity when it nears the windows. Within minutes, they should make contact. We'll bring the storm in, and the doors will be just as blocked as they are now.

But what if the windows broken by the chandelier are enough? We won't need to clear the way if the mutants are already scared off.

Omri and Tremaine itch for something to do, fidgeting with their bats and checking on the other beefcakes' progress. Next to me, Kirsten watches the weight-throwing with nervous excitement, waiting, like me, to see what happens next.

I can't hesitate. Precious seconds are already being wasted. If we're all itching, someone has to scratch. I rush to the balcony by the chandelier team and look at the main floor. How bad is the drop, really? I've been here a million times, just never thought of jumping.

My stomach drops when I concentrate on it. It's high. And the floor is hard down there, where it's covered by a murky film of water and a battlefield's worth of corpses. I'm not thinking of literally jumping, but we can't afford to get the descent wrong. A broken leg would be a death sentence if the mutants aren't put off by the cold.

Macy's might not be a bad option. We have backup, and we know what could be in there. Just as I think to enlist Omri and Tremaine's help, Omri rushes past me and joins the weight-throwers. He rifles through Joe's backpack, uncoiling a rope and tying a weight to it. Tremaine is all that's left of our rearguard, looking disappointed. Left out. Just like Kirsten and me.

"Kirsten!" I call.

She jumps at her name.

"We need to get down there now. Through Macy's."

I tell Tremaine next. He casts a wary glance at the store, from which he had only just beat back some new creature. But there's no time to explain. We got to this point on speed and disorientation. And we'll do the same through Macy's. Whatever comes our way, we'll throw everything we've got at it and run.

Kirsten objects, sputtering out a litany of "buts" without any real focus. Just trying to get out of it. We won't have anyone watching our backs.

"Joe!"

He looks at me.

"We're going down! Send someone when you get a chance."

He nods and goes back to heaving on the chandelier.

I grab Omri's bat from the floor and toss it to Kirsten. For myself, I take a tennis racket from a backpack. With a deep breath, I lead us through Macy's.

The store is in disarray. Display cases are smashed. Racks and stands have been knocked down. Human remains leave a thin scrim of gore on the tile from which scattered jewelry twinkles. Paths from low-bellied creatures smear their way through the blood, which tells me which directions to avoid.

When we come to the first aisle intersection, the spiny tail of a centipede dawdles around some clothes racks to my right. I run the other way and bring us to the escalators. With some perilous skidding on blood, slipping on pearls and cubic zirconia, we get there.

"Oh...shit."

A pile of bodies—and body parts—clogs the escalator, which has stopped moving, either because its power unit has died or the bodies have forced it to.

"Not what I had in mind..." I murmur, but we have to start where we can.

The other escalator is also stalled and littered with bodies at its bottom since it's the descending one. There are fewer here, so it would be easier to leap over them, but I have to consider the centipedes and things roaming around.

It's going to be this one.

"Watch my back, guys."

There's only room for one of us to work. I drop my tennis racket and start sliding bodies off the top of the pile. Each corpse I haul makes others tumble toward me.

"Quinn, hurry up, please." Kirsten fails to put a sarcastic drawl in her voice.

I steal a glance at the nearby centipede, whose rear end turns in a wide circle, like a semi-truck.

"Yeah, I'm working on it."

I grab a pink jacket, my mind flashing to Prairie, whose music I can barely hear anymore. This one is smaller than hers. A child's. The body is face down, and I lift it like a bag of birdseed, moving it mechanically out of the way.

I spread my fingers to dig into clothing and grip the next corpse, but they wrap around something hard and covered in slime. Something as cool as a corpse but not a corpse.

A yellowish pearlescent beak points up at me. Two angry-set eyes, blearily white with the tiniest of black pupils, stare up at me. They come closer. The beak opens, pushed forward by a protruding neck.

"Quinn, come on!" Kirsten yells, no doubt watching the centipede. She turns and gasps.

The turtle creeps from its hiding place in the bodies.

It lunges, collecting my face in its mouth. Its bottom jaw pierces the skin behind my jawbone. Its top jaw knifes into my skull.

It applies enough pressure to nearly bite down completely, ruining my face and spreading my eyes. My last glimpse of the world is walleyed, with one eye on a horrified Kirsten and one on an incoming centipede.

The correct choice was to rappel to the first floor.
Turn to page 298.

"Same teams. Girls together. Guys together."

Joe gives Kirsten a stern look that says he isn't about to take her word over anyone else's. I don't blame him. We came up with a plan, and we need to put our weight behind it. If we cling to each other now, it looks like we're not part of the new team.

"I want Prairie up front with me. She knows what to do," he says.

Prairie makes a face like a goldfish giving its last breath on a tabletop. It's not often the idea woman is called upon to be in the middle of the action.

She says, "It's not rocket science..."

I raise my hand and cut her off. "You get me, Joe. I've been pushing to go that way. I should be up there."

He waits for Prairie to argue the point. I give her a look telling her not to. Her goldfish mouth shuts.

"Can I...? I can go behind you," she offers, which I accept on everyone's behalf.

Joe softens, leaving the hard-ass act behind with a glance at the beefcakes. There's more to it than that. A forlorn twitch of his lips suggests he means to protect her more than anything.

Too bad for him. We've made up our minds.

Everyone readies themselves with torches made of utensils and shields fashioned from Saran wrap and stainless steel cabinet doors. The cart-bearers double check their loads. I accompany Joe and Tremaine, Prairie goes with Ramon and Tomi, and Kirsten and Raina split up across the last two squads.

Joe leans into me while Tremaine pushes our cart. "What do you say we cross over now and hit the info desk first? Might be the best route for cover."

"Well, the play area is right...Uh..." I stop myself, with no fond memories of the play area. It didn't give us good cover before, though it'd be better than crossing the atrium totally exposed.

Joe, on the other hand, doesn't seem interested at all.

"Yeah," I say, "what the hell. Let's do it."

Joe motions for Tremaine to shift his cart to the left and follow.

We creep into the fog, cutting across the J.C. Penney wing. My heart flutters as the walls vanish and our waypoints disappear. I'm in the center of the mall, and I have no clue what's around me.

Only pill bugs' armored backs lumber like coffee stains in the distance. They move away, so I don't ask Tremaine to try out our bait.

We make it probably halfway across the atrium without sighting anything dangerous. The opposite balcony comes into view. Joe steers toward a pillar and peeks around it, as if enemy fire is coming from beyond. What if he *does* get hurt? How ready should I be to step up and take his place?

I go around the pillar and come up on his other side. See? No sniper fire. There's no sense giving ourselves a blind spot.

"Info desk is straight that way." Joe chops the air with his hand.

"And beyond that?"

"The jewelry store, right?"

I shrug. "Yeah. After that it's just...more mall. There are massage chairs and kiosks and more crap to sneak around."

"Okay," he starts, which is when Tremaine hollers.

"Whoa!" Tremaine whips a head of lettuce straight at the dinosaurian shadow of a lizard poking through the fog. He beans it perfectly, and the lizard twitches at the impact.

I press myself against the pillar and lift my shield, separated from the rest of the group. More missiles fly at the lizard—lettuce, meat, carrots, one of Kirsten's perfume bombs.

The lizard tenses again when some make contact and twitches while stuff plops into the water around it. When the barrage is redoubled, it runs into the fog.

Tremaine cheers. He must have the best view of anyone besides me. I'm ready to be back with them, so I slide along the pillar, following the glow of Joe's torch.

Something shatters over my head and sprays my face with stinging liquid.

I squeeze my eyes shut against the burn and struggle to breathe. The astringent scent of perfume overpowers my sinuses and shuts my throat. I cough and blink and swing my arms, hitting something.

Joe asks if I'm okay.

I hit his arm, and a spray of oily flaming droplets falls from his torch's head onto my shoulder, igniting the perfume on my coat. The flames engulf my head. My hair goes up, and my oxygen is stolen.

Screams rise around me. I fan my arms, slapping at flames.

More screams, but not on my account.

"Lizard!"

"Frog!"

"Quinn!" Joe shoves me into the water.

But it doesn't help. Not this fire. All he does is rob me of more air.

I push against him, the flames carbonizing my flesh and searing my skin down to bone. If only the beefcakes had any damn clothes on, they could throw something over me to smother it.

The girls are too busy. An attack comes from all sides.

My face goes numb, and my lungs expand. Shock takes me.

The correct choice was to stick with the girls. Turn to page 252.

The earthquake fades, leaving a cacophony of rattling fixtures and groaning infrastructure to paper over a stunned human silence. I wonder if my glare is what makes the earthquake slink away. Seriously, we're in the middle of a fight here.

The guards leave the store and face the atrium, joined by sales associates from the optometrist next door. One of them makes a yipping sound and backs toward the window when a thick fog rises from the main floor and rolls onto the balcony. Raina walks toward them, and I flinch at her making distance between us during such a strange occurrence.

Kirsten follows, groaning, "What the hell now?"

Whatever fresh attack I had on my lips dies.

A murmur rises from the crowd. Wet splashes, more crashing noises. The earthquake no longer counts as a distraction; something else is happening. It makes me want to yank Kirsten and Raina inside and wait out whatever this is, but a rattle of metal from the deep shadows of the store spikes my adrenaline.

And then I get another idea...

What we could do...We could make a run for it.

Prairie shivers next to me, senseless under our predicament, even more so due to the earthquake. And though Raina would share the blame with Kirsten without complaint, she'll save herself if she can. I can lead them. Now's our only opportunity—while the guards are distracted. If Kirsten can keep up, she can come, but I'm not bringing her in on this.

Prairie leaps when I grip her arm.

"We're getting out of here."

She doesn't indicate comprehension, but she moves with me as I tiptoe to the door and grab my bag.

Screams erupt from the concourse. Devastating cries. Someone sprints past the gawkers, eliciting gasps and more yips. The runner precedes more shoppers fleeing the center of the mall, sloshing through floodwaters, heading the same way I want to go.

Good. More chaos can only help our escape and overshadow the drama with the seniors.

I speed up and lean in next to Raina, whisper for her to come and pull on her jacket.

She spins and throws me off, her earlier fury on full display. When a piercing shriek erupts from the atrium, she turns right back around and runs away.

"H-hey!" shouts the male guard. "What the—!"

He chases after her.

Kirsten wheels on me, but Ponytail is on it. She grabs her and holds her fast.

I take one step forward, instinct telling me to follow Raina, but that's not the way I want to go. It kills me to give Kirsten the slightest apologetic look. Or maybe it just feels like it. Her eyes go wide, and her mouth forms into a sneer. I don't catch the rest of her act before I tug Prairie away and sprint for J.C. Penney.

We make a clean break while Ponytail restrains Kirsten, and we aren't alone. The mall has erupted into chaos, and the screaming grows louder. The horde of running shoppers swells on the main floor. I shove past more rubberneckers, clearing a path for Prairie. People do the same thing on the first floor, barreling into those who are immobilized by fear and confusion. They trip over one another's ankles and send each other sprawling. Popup vendor tables and tents get trashed, and kiosks shake when people smash into them.

I'm hardly worried about security anymore. Who knows what the hell's happening at the center of the mall? I'll take the panicked mob's word for it. We need to get out of here.

I check back every few steps, making sure the pink blur of Prairie's jacket is on my heels. On the escalator, halfway down the concourse, we jump its downward-moving steps.

When my feet hit the main level, two things come to mind. For one, we don't have a ride sorted out. And second, I actually got Prairie to follow me. I swell with pride, flying by the seat of my pants…Getting her to join the spontaneity…Doing right by her…

She's just coming down the final steps when her heel slips out from under her. Her mousy brown hair sweeps forward like a mop over her pink jacket and comes crashing to the floor, leaving her flat on her face.

I run to her, pivoting left and right to dodge sprinters. The fog rolls in. Inside it, strange shapes overtake human shapes. Prairie groans and gets up slowly. When we're another few steps away, someone runs straight into me. I bowl over, pushing Prairie forward.

Before I can get back on my feet, the heavy, chunky tread of a work boot presses down on my hand, like an anvil with a waffle iron for a bottom.

I yelp and try to stand, but a kick to the head floors me again. The person tumbles over in front of me, then another steps on my back and collapses. Within a matter of seconds, we've formed a barrier for everyone behind.

I lose sight of Prairie while more bodies pile around us. Another falls on me—a big one that isn't able to get up. More weight is added after that.

My limbs can't maneuver. I have no leverage in any direction, and my lungs swell with the pressure of carbon dioxide pleading to be released. My head goes big and hot, and I swell like a balloon. My trachea constricts, trying to muscle whatever it can down into my lungs to relieve the bad air stuck inside.

The weight above me shifts. My fingers reach out to Prairie. She can get me out of here. I dream of light coming into my world, of my vision resolving itself and finding her pink jacket.

Only it doesn't come.

The pressure builds until I'm in agony. The alarm bells in my body begin to fade. I black out on the flooded floor of Meadow Spire Mall.

Try again. Turn to page 88.

I watch the abomination one floor below—two unearthly malformations pitted in a life-or-death battle. The frog, with its wide trapper-keeper mouth, gulps down a hulking white centipede twisting back and forth, like one of those segmented snake toys you see at every Old West tourist-trap general store on the drive out to the Rockies. Its rear pincers snap at air it can't grasp.

There's a mechanical viciousness to them, a sad destruction of machinery evolved to serve some highly specific purpose. They're not animals to me, not even aliens, and their fight doesn't feel like a battle more than a mixing together of two things completing the very narrow task they've been designed to do in the bowels of the hellish, toxic, underground swamp they came from.

You know, it makes me think of Skye. He hasn't done anything to deserve it, but he's at the center of every weird thing happening to me. My crush never hurt anybody until it came out yesterday. I had put it behind me. My feelings cooled months ago. It's one of those things I can look back on. Yeah, I'm getting older, and I'm growing up. I can better control how I feel about people and be okay when they feel differently about me. None of it had to get dredged up again.

Did Bridie have anything to do with exposing it? No way. The specificity of it all convinces me. Even I know those two lines by heart. They still float to the forefront of my mind from time to time. There's plenty of stuff in my diaries anyone cruel enough could've used. The poem in that valentine wasn't from my diary. I swear it. And I'll eventually remember where it came from, for all the good it'll do. On one point, I'll agree with Kirsten. It was the seniors on cheer. But why? And how?

Skye is this thing tossed between me and the rest of the girls, preoccupying me even with Prairie and Bridie lost and fending for themselves, a ghost at the center of it all, and I feel sorry for him. I put him there, just as much as the senior cheer girls have. It's all so weird.

A hand falls on my shoulder. I jump.

"Quinn. We gotta go." Kirsten speaks soberly. Nothing like the specter of death to shake you out of your own petty crap.

The battle at the bottom of the escalator reaches its conclusion, with the frog coming out on top. The building groans. More screams emanate from the mall. And where there's a scream, there are more monsters.

"Here." Raina emerges from the children's section carrying one of those steel poles with a two-pronged end, made for retrieving clothes hangers from hooks high on the wall. She tosses it to Kirsten and goes looking for more. "Grab some clothes since you're just standing there."

"What? Why?" Kirsten asks.

"Decoys," I say.

Skittering sounds from nearby force Raina to move more quickly, and she jogs back with another pole while I seek out my own.

"Which way?" I ask, turning to Raina, who's consistently out-captained next year's wannabe presumptive cheer captain.

Raina's suddenly indecisive. More crashing, skittering, and screaming come from the mall concourse, and it seems the second level isn't as safe as we thought.

I look down the escalator. The frog licks its pale chops and turns, looking ready to depart. Raina stares too. I don't question why. She's remembering what happened downstairs, struggling to imagine going back.

Kirsten glances at me over Raina's shoulder and purses her lips.

"Okay," I say, "I vote downstairs. We know what's down there, and that's what the decoys are for. And I don't figure a lot of these things want to drown any more than we do, so as counterintuitive as it sounds, it might be safer taking the flooded route. We're already soaked, so it's not like we'll be any less comfortable."

I wait for an argument, but none comes. Raina's still zoning out, and Kirsten's fixated on snapping her out of it. She rubs Raina's back and pulls her close. A glimmer of annoyance passes through me, watching her manipulation at work.

Only a moment ago, Kirsten tried bullying us into getting her way. Now Raina's down, she's suddenly Miss Sensitive. I'm betting she wants to lift Raina out of her funk so Raina will argue on her behalf. Pit her against me. My annoyance turns to anger, and I want to tell Kirsten to go screw herself. I should be the one comforting Raina, but she got there first, no matter how superficial the reason.

Raina sniffs and nods. She looks at me, her eyes refocusing, though tears fall down her cheeks. "Let's do it," she says. Kirsten keeps rubbing her back, but Raina walks away from her touch.

"All right," I say, "but I'm not fighting an escalator going in the opposite direction again."

"Yup," Raina replies.

We creep back around to the escalator we took to get up here, keeping an eye out for more centipedes or surprises in the appliance section. All of us wield a retriever pole and a bunch of tyke-sized clothes. We load our hooks and get ready to go. Me first, then Kirsten and Raina.

"For every blind corner," I say, "we peek and dangle clothes. Just follow my lead."

"Isn't it kinda sick to be using these clothes?" Kirsten asks. "Like we're teaching them to eat kids?"

"Better them than me."

"Jeez, Carpenter."

I step on the escalator, back hunched, ready to duck for cover. We leave a few steps between ourselves in case we need to retreat, which yeah, would mean another ridiculous scramble against downward-moving stairs. I remind myself never to trust another escalator, if we make it any farther into the mall.

Kirsten exhales, her breath shuddering. "Peek and dangle. Peek and dangle."

We descend to the main floor, which glistens with an inch of water covering the short carpet fibers. Gentle waves flow along the aisles.

A loud pop occurs, and a concussive jolt goes through my body. Kirsten yelps, her decoy clothes drop on me, and I almost fall forward, but I'm crouched and ready for it. The escalator has stopped moving, its power unit blown by the flooding.

I wait a moment for the shock to pass, then start descending— the first of three spear-wielding prehistoric women leaving our cave to traverse an unknown landscape. Kirsten keeps muttering to herself, turning "peek and dangle" into a mantra.

The crashing and buzzing of mosquito beasts comes from the hardware section. When I reach the ground floor and step out into the open, my pole a full four feet ahead of me, nothing happens.

Ahead, the water ripples, signaling the presence of something big. The frog, surely. Or are there two? Is the one that fought the centipede the same one that chased us upstairs? No clue, and what's it matter? There has to be more of everything now, plus creatures we haven't encountered yet.

Ambush predators, as Prairie says.

It seems the monsters we've seen so far are too big to hide among the racks. I shouldn't take it for granted—there are certainly smaller terrors out there—but I keep my eye on the bigger pathways. We stay close to the main aisle's edge, ready to dart into the safety of the racks.

When we reach the T-intersection where the next aisle leads to the jewelry department and the mall beyond, I lean around the near corner. The way is clear. But when I check the other direction, Kirsten gasps, and I push her behind me.

A gelatinous frog is at rest, its knees pointed out and stretching across the whole aisle. It's near the entrance to the sports section, which might have served as another exit for us. It faces the opposite way, but its globular eyes may still sense us. Kirsten tries to stick out her pole, but I stop her.

"We can make it." I point to a customer service counter across the aisle. "Go."

Raina comes up beside Kirsten and, after glancing at the frog, bolts for the counter. I shove Kirsten, she takes off, and I follow.

The frog shifts a quarter turn in our direction, hardly displacing any water, even as we kick up great sloshing splashes of it.

By the time all three of us are behind the counter, the frog has fully turned around. It's still far down the aisle, its tongue out of range, but it would only take one or two bounds to get close enough.

"Let's move."

"Peek and dangle," Kirsten says. "Peek and dangle."

The mall entrance is just ahead on our right. We could run straight, cut right, and be out in seconds. Frog gone. No zigzagging required.

I step out into the aisle, confident in my decision and sure Kirsten and Raina will follow. Kirsten whispers, "Peek and dangle!" with added urgency, as if I'm not heeding my own advice. And I'm not.

I freeze and Kirsten bumps into me. A second frog now sits in the middle of the jewelry department, having appeared with hardly a sound, right where we need to go.

"Back, back," I say.

We retreat to the counter. The first frog takes a leap forward.

"Into the racks!"

We move toward the wall, taking the circuitous route between carousels. There's no room for a frog to catch us in here. Each step takes us into deeper water flowing from the mall. Up ahead, by the entrance, a human body lies on its stomach, the water almost high enough to carry it off.

"Quinn," Raina whispers.

The second frog has leapt toward the first one, closing in on our last hiding spot. As long as it doesn't catch our movement, we should be okay. Still, my heart races.

"Peek and dangle!" Kirsten announces in a victorious high whisper when we make it to the entrance.

To the right, the concourse. To our left, a huge display stand blocks our view of the rest of Sears.

I load my pole with a little blue winter jacket and take my first steps toward the concourse. The jacket is knocked aside, and I'm bowled back into the Kirsten. I splash into water and swing my pole back and forth. Kirsten yelps, but I'm too shocked to say anything.

"Shut up! Hey, stop it!" Raina hisses. She hauls me to my feet, and we retreat along the wall, thrusting our poles forward, dropping clothes when a new set of creatures ambles into Sears.

It's a herd of massive pill bugs, their bodies awkwardly shoveling water aside as they go. Their shielded backs look like layers of freshly lacquered fingernails, shining like an oil streak, almost kind of pretty. They're as big as golden retrievers, and it takes over a full minute for them to pass. When it's done, Raina pushes her way to the front, peeks and dangles, and jumps back when a straggling pill bug enters.

She sighs and reaches for the walkie-talkie. "Prairie, we're inbound on your location. Keep the channel quiet except for emergency. Over." She waves us on, and we leave Sears.

"Copy," Prairie responds, hardly audible since Raina turned down the volume.

The fog is thick. It's virtually impossible to see the far side of the atrium. I can barely make out the Valentine's Day photoshoot area or the fountain, much less the play area, the food court, or the theater, whose marquee lights can't pierce the grayness.

An angry sky scowls down on us from the skylights. In addition to the scrabbling sounds of monsters, remnants of human panic, and groans of a collapsing building, constant sleet scratches against glass. We slosh through water covering the topsides of our boots, making as little noise as possible and sticking to the wall.

Kirsten and I scan the foggy expanse of the open atrium while Raina pauses at the first store entrance. She peeks into the darkened interior, loads a purple jacket on her pole, and dangles it across the opening.

Nothing happens.

She checks again, hangs another decoy, then rushes to the other side before reloading her pole and sticking it out to cover Kirsten's and my passage.

After crossing, I'm stung by a nettle of embarrassment. Is our caution all that necessary?

One look back into the store and my question is answered.

A body floats inside, palms facing up. And are those people peering from behind the checkout counter? I want to tell them to come with us. But we can't delay. I can't endanger Prairie or, for that matter, Kirsten or Raina. We're a unit. And honestly, I can't make promises to anyone. Those people—if that's what I saw—have as little reason to follow me as I do them.

We pass along the edge of the atrium, and the mess caused by the mall's collapse into the swamp becomes clearer. Within our limited view are more bodies—some complete, some dismembered. Patches of water shine red in the dim light. Shopping bags, clothing, products, and packaging litter the floor or float on the scrim of water, if they're light enough. Trash bins have been upended, their contents of wrappers, cups, and napkins bloated and bobbing all over the place.

I spot a stroller tipped on its side. No cries from within. I don't know how good of a sign that is, if the child is safe in its mother's arms, far away from here. Or not.

A shadow in the distance changes shape, perhaps the swiveling of a head, like that of our original lizard friend's. It's far enough away, beyond enough display signs and other mall junk, not to be too concerning. We should be okay, as long as we don't draw attention to ourselves. And the balcony's overhang gives us cover from above.

Raina repeats the peek and dangle at the next couple of stores. We move past them without a problem and reach the wing of the concourse which dead-ends into J.C. Penney. Straight shot to Prairie.

So far, so good. Whatever we're doing is working.

The first burst of mayhem has died down. Maybe the swamp monsters are on break too, taking stock of the situation. Like, how could they not be looking at the mall and wondering, *What the hell is this place?*

This is our habitat, not theirs. We're the ones who should be hunting the concourse, with the nerve and focus of the cavewomen we've been forced to pretend to be.

The three of us get down on our knees and crawl through the dingy water when we reach a big store with shattered windows. Raina looks inside its entrance, hums annoyedly, and loads her pole with a striped sweater. The instant she puts it across the opening, it's gone. Snatched out of sight by...I can't even say what. It sends my pulse racing.

"Shit." Raina scans the concourse, considers how exposed we'd be from the balcony and from creatures in the fog, and grunts. "Same tactic as before. Let me get to the other side and cover."

"Yeah, yeah...Peek and dangle," Kirsten says.

Raina takes a deep breath, loads her pole with another sweater, and gets her feet under her. She thrusts the clothing across the opening. Right as it's snatched, she makes a run for it. But the thing inside takes more than the decoy, getting a grip on her pole too. When it snaps back into the store, Raina's pulled along with it.

"Rain!" I scream, scrambling to the entrance.

She splashes back out and lunges to safety on the other side. Raina leans against the wall, breathing heavily, and nods to signal she's okay. She peeks inside, grimaces, then gestures for Kirsten's pole.

Kirsten tosses her pole, which goes unnoticed by the thing inside, then wads up a pair of snow pants. When she tosses it to

Raina, it's nabbed in midair. I see it this time, or a spiny protuberance from it.

Raina grunts and pulls off her torn puffer jacket. She hooks it onto the pole. "Both of you, at the same time. Dangle and run. Start on 'Go.'"

It's our only option.

She counts us up to three. On 'Go,' she stabs her jacket across the entrance while I stick kids' jeans out with my pole. Both are ripped away into the store's murky, flickering darkness. Kirsten darts ahead of me. My pole is yanked too, but I'm able to keep it and make it across the opening.

We're down to two poles and less than a half dozen pieces of clothes, not that there aren't more strewn everywhere.

Another cluster of pill bugs creeps along the opposite side of the wing. From the second floor, some cumbersome creature tests out its barely used, probably vestigial wings, crashing from one balcony to the other. A slithering insectoid, which we identify as a giant millipede, lumbers from one store to the next. Here and there, I detect sharp, thin limbs sticking out of one hiding place or another, but they disappear into shadow and fog.

Ambush predators.

So far, I don't see the looming forms of amphibious predators too large, too dopey, or too intimidating to hide from everything else.

It's not just creatures either. Splashes from overhead indicate a small crowd making a run for it. At one point, I catch sight of people moving down the opposite side of the wing, trailing the pill bugs. Each person ignores us as much as we do them. We're in the same boat, and outside of each group, there's no trust.

It's everyone for themselves, but I guess that's just how things are. I wonder if I'm supposed to be better than this, then my mind is drawn right back to Prairie and Bridie. And Skye.

More storefronts, some with broken windows. With each one, my heart leaps out of its chest when Raina juts out her pole. We reach the point I can see the outline of the wristwatch kiosk—Prairie's first hiding spot. The three of us pass The Sharper Image without a problem, and soon, Prairie's jewelry kiosk appears out of the fog.

The water is lower here, farther from the atrium, which means we make less noise. It's easier going. We move faster.

Raina presses the speaker. "Prairie, we got eyes on your location. Send final confirmation that you're under the jewelry kiosk outside of Penney's, please. Over."

"Affirmative. I'm inside the jewelry kiosk outside Penney's. Over."

"We're arriving momentarily. Be ready to move. Over."

"Copy."

Raina loads a tiny, multicolored ski jacket on her pole and hangs it across the final storefront standing between us and a short diagonal sprint to Prairie. We'll be vulnerable in the open but so close to escape. Then we can take our pick of two sets of doors at the ends of the hallway running the length of J.C. Penney.

"Here we go," Raina says. She wiggles her jacket. Right when she starts to cross the opening, a barbed leg drops on her pole, slides down its shaft with an earsplitting screech, and hits Raina in the shoulder.

She falls to her feet. Her pole goes flying.

I lunge without thinking, swinging my retriever pole inside the store. A leg lashes out, and I deflect the blow pretty much accidentally.

Kirsten grabs Raina's pole and joins me. I try sidestepping my way past the store entrance, attempting to get through this final leg of the journey. We're practically on top of Prairie. And with her, we're out of here.

Another barbed leg lashes out. The hard clacking sounds they make against the floor suggest they're capable of spearing us or worse. I deflect one more blow. Yet another comes, aiming for my head. I bat it away, but its barbs scrape my arm when it falls, shredding my sleeve. Searing pain goes through my forearm. I cry out and lose my grip on my pole.

Raina is steady on her feet and pulls Kirsten back. I fall on my side and, staring into the darkness, kick myself away from the store entrance.

Raina towers over me, wielding a pole but swinging at nothing. It seems the creature was acting in self-defense. Kirsten helps me to stand, and we retreat from the store.

Without a backward glance, we stumble toward the kiosk.

"Oh no," Kirsten cries, just as we reach it.

The right-side hallway leading to the exit that would get us to Kirsten's Jeep the fastest is blocked by another hulking mosquito. It moves in our direction, alerted by our last clash, its wings raising a feeble chainsaw sound.

"Get inside!" Raina cries.

Kirsten rolls over the counter. I follow, my wounded arm screaming. Raina lands on me right as the mosquito beast knocks against the kiosk and continues down the concourse to the atrium.

We breathe heavily, our bodies tangled together on the wet floor. Kirsten's eyes are wide, and her torso shivers. Raina's stare is distant, her jacket missing, her sweatshirt cut open to reveal a bloody wound comparable to mine. And Prairie cups the radio in her hands, hair soaked and stringy, blood on her face.

"Prairie!" I jump across the other girls' legs and try to wrap her in a hug, hardly getting my hands over her shoulder blades.

She pats my upper arms in return. The others groan in pain. I hiss and recoil from the stinging in my arm.

"Is this it?" Prairie asks. "Where's...uh...?"

I shoot a look at Raina, who's hardly listening. She rotates her shoulder to see how badly she's hurt.

"This is it," I say.

"Where's Warren?"

Kirsten's head whips in her direction. "*Who?*"

I stare hard at Prairie, flick my eyes toward Raina, and shake my head, imbuing my look with meaning.

Prairie squints, then her face falls.

Raina swallows, and I expect Prairie to offer awkward words of comfort.

Instead, Raina interrupts our silence. "Kirsten. You owe her an apology."

Kirsten barely registers the assertion, but once she notices us looking at her, she huffs in disbelief.

"No, it's okay. It's not—" Prairie says.

"No, Prairie. Don't say that. You deserve it."

Kirsten begins. "This is such bullshit, Rain. If you hadn't—"

"*No.*"

We raise our heads in surprise for a second time. Mine and Raina's. Kirsten's.

The sound came from the disheveled girl in pink. Prairie. I've never heard her speak so authoritatively in her life.

"No," she repeats, almost thoughtfully this time. She takes a deep breath and clears her throat. "I don't want an apology. But I do want to say something."

Raina and I turn to Kirsten, who doesn't say a word.

"Kirsten," Prairie starts, muscling out the name, straining to make eye contact with the cheerleader who's been nothing but horrible to her. "I did come here today for Quinn. It was my decision, and she didn't drag me along. I know you don't think much of me, and you never have, and I've never liked you either because of it. But I can make my own decisions, and even though Quinn and I don't really talk a lot..."

She chokes back a sob and collects herself. None of us interrupt.

"...Quinn's my best friend," Prairie says, her eyes watering. "I wanted to protect her from *you*. Because you are bad for her. I've seen you do bad things to her, and she seems to forgive you or forget about it every time, which is supposed to be a good thing, I guess, but I can't do it. I don't know why she's friends with you, but it's her life, and I don't want to judge her because she's never judged me. You must make her happy, and I don't see it. I haven't seen it all day. So today, I wanted to protect her. From you. That's why I came. I am not weak or pathetic, and being a Jesus freak, if that's what you want to call me, that gives me strength. It doesn't make me pathetic. I am nice and I am kind. And you should know the difference between that and...and being a freak."

She rubs her eyes and sniffles, which signals the conclusion of her speech.

We trade looks. Kirsten's jaw is working, and her eyes water. Out of rage, resentment...guilt? Ha. I don't know, but she takes this one on the chin. For once, someone else is a step ahead, and for once, they let her know it.

I only just notice my own eyes tearing up, so I rub them and ready myself to say something stupid. Thanks, or I love you too, Prairie. Something that'll come out weird.

Raina saves me the trouble. "That's cool, Prairie. That's cool."

"Yeah," I stammer, wiping away snot. "I—"

"*Wait*," Prairie says, her eyes fixed on the floor, her voice as powerful as before. She takes another deep breath. "I didn't *just* come here for Quinn. I came because I wanted to too."

"Yeah," Raina says, "we understand."

"No," Prairie replies. "I knew Joe Molson was here today. And I knew he was going to be dressed like Cupid, with hardly any clothes on, and I really wanted to see him because...I think he's the cutest guy I've ever seen in my life, and he's also in really good shape. So...I didn't really come because I felt forced to. I came for that too."

Her admission hangs in the air. She looks up at us defiantly. My eyes instantly dry. Kirsten twists her expression in confusion.

Raina hides her face behind crossed arms and starts shuddering. I lean in closer, wondering if something has triggered her grief. Then I see her dimples and discern the sound she's trying to mask as giggling instead of weeping. She lifts her head and laughs more loudly. It cuts through the fog and echoes off the walls.

"Shh! Shut up!" Kirsten hisses, even as I chortle, even as a smile twists across her lips.

Prairie staves off her own laughter and remains stoic in the face of our breakdown.

Raina passes a loaded look to Kirsten, who sighs and glances at Prairie. "Hey. Hedlund. That's cool. That's...good of you. I didn't mean to be a dick."

It's the most Prairie will get, and she doesn't act like she wants or needs it. "The exit's right over there," she responds. "Let's go."

We tourniquet children's clothes over my forearm and Raina's bicep, then peek over the counter.

"Looks clear," Prairie whispers, though the fog keeps rolling in, obscuring the interior of J.C. Penney.

A mosquito beast made it this far. So did whatever attacked us from that store. We can't even see the exits from where we are, and we won't until we round the final corner and get right up to J.C. Penney.

"Let's go," I say.

We vault the counter and splat onto the wet floor. The four of us are fewer than fifty yards from the doors and safety outside, freezing as it is. Half a football field. One pass to a wide receiver and a crazed sprint to the end zone.

A hissing sound stops me. Not from an animal or insect, not even a mutant one.

It comes from Suncoast, the closest storefront on the opposite side of the concourse.

A person leans out of its entrance, breaking the one rule shared by all people in every other group. He waves a welcoming arm, guiding us to him.

"Psst! Hey!"

♥*♥*♥

Convince these people to follow you. Turn to page 192.

See if Bridie's inside. Turn to page 7.

That glitter sticks out like a sore thumb. Like the chitinous carapace of a mutant bog insect or the vanilla-ice-cream hide of a deformed swamp frog. These new creatures may be bipedal, but they're no friends of mine. How could I argue we had to escape this way when it would bring us straight through a bunch of scumbags?

I mean, I know why. Bridie. I remember who she was with and that we'd be linking up with our enemies if we found her.

To be at their mercy makes it that much worse, so it's fortunate I conjure a way to retake the initiative and keep ourselves from being in another beefcakes-to-the-rescue situation. It's for the best. If we let the seniors take control, we lose it for good. They'll call the shots. The beefcakes will back them up. After all this, yeah...They're not giving us a second chance. We need to drive this thing, and we need Joe above Alex.

Trent and Gabe traffic-control the first elements of our beefcake platoon. I do some counter-corralling of my own. It can't just be us girls who go. I grab one of the boys. Tremaine is closest. He's pale as a ghost, his eyes tired. Any second, he'll collapse to the floor. I wrap my arms around his shoulder and spin him around. Then I go to work on the others.

"Kirsten! Help Brian."

Kirsten glances back and scrunches her face. She's already following the pack. But she guides Brian, who's struggling to keep a bereft Tim from collapsing to the floor.

Gabe's eyes flash on me. He sees what I'm doing, but I owe him nothing. I haven't done anything to him. Alex is right there beside him, and when he notices a hint of disarray, he fixes me with a death glare. I return it.

The nearest storefront is dark. Its windows are shattered. If anything has been hiding inside, it would have made itself known. Another thing I note: the seniors don't direct us upstairs, where Band Avenue is, so their choice of hiding place can't be any better.

"Quinn? Where you going? What's happening?" It's Joe.

Crosstalk rises while Trent joins Gabe, screaming at us to follow. Their voices are bitter, condescending, and make the hair on my neck bristle.

Tremaine goes with me, his arm over my shoulder. The shadows in the fog keep their distance. I just have to get him inside, giving everyone the shorter path. If we split in two, they'll follow me. I know it. They know me, not these seniors.

"Let me help." Prairie approaches and assists me with lugging Tremaine into the store.

He falls against a tilted display rack, and its remaining Valentine's Day knickknacks plop into the water. Poofy red and white linens, pillows, and bean bags litter the store. Prairie holds Tremaine while I turn around to usher in more people.

The sight I'm met with makes me blanch.

The group moves away from us, guided by the seniors. Kirsten and Joe are the only two who hesitate. Raina's busy aiding Omri. She hardly notices what we're doing.

"Guys! Hey!" I shout.

Joe screams the same at me. He must think I'm crazy. There isn't anger in his face, but he's obviously so exhausted, he doesn't want to help with a problem I shouldn't be making. Nevertheless, he breaks into a jog. He's going to drag me back to the group. I'm losing, have only slowed us down and endangered Tremaine and Prairie to boot.

When we get to the senior's safe space, it'll be the icing on the cake. I don't know what I'm doing. And neither does Prairie. We'll have lost whatever authority we gained. If only I didn't have to worry about one last public humiliation. Not after this.

Joe sees it before I do and stops running. He screams my name and breaks into a full run. The stained white beanbag off to my side uncoils from a malformed orb into something like a playground slide covered in painful-looking nodules. Its white, pug-nosed snout sniffs the air. Its blind eyes stare at the ceiling, and a translucent tongue tastes for my scent.

I hardly get a chance to move before the fangs penetrate my skull, right behind my eyes, between my jaw and my cheekbone. The impact nearly snaps my neck, and the injection of venom fills my mouth, burning my gums.

My muscles spasm before I even meet the inside of the thing's mouth, and my last view is of its throat before I succumb to the sweet release of its numbing anesthetic, freeing me from the pain of my entire musculature being acid-washed by poison.

♥*♥*♥

The correct choice was to go with the seniors.
Turn to page 278.

I didn't think my nerves could fray any more. But those screams...I'm a twitching mess, thundering blood pressure in human form. The scent of dead body drapes me like a ghost in a wet bedsheet contest. That pile of human slop could have been me. If that man had pulled me into Suncoast...If I'd stayed in that empty store with security...The rattling in those vents...

"They're inside!" Kirsten shrieks.

Her words untwist the knots in the beefcakes' brainstems. They bolt for the door, Ramon grabbing Tim, Brian grabbing Tremaine, Tomi grabbing Omri. Credit where it's due—they leave no man behind. And I go with them.

This store was the seniors' idea. Crawling into the vents? Their idea. What were we thinking, letting them take the lead? We passed through the gauntlet, through teeth and claws and pincers and tongues. They helped us out in a pinch, sure, but we never should have given them control.

We're rescuing *them*, remember? And by the way, where the hell is Bridie!

Kirsten goes ahead of me. I tug Prairie's sleeve, and she slips and slides on the wet floor before getting her feet under her. Gina and Valerie stumble after me, their screams having reduced into heaving sobs and shallow breaths.

"Wait! What're you doing?" Joe cries.

Skye objects too. As I knew they would, trusting the seniors too easily. Which is why I act so urgently. Which is why I usher Gina and Valerie out the door first.

"Let's move!" I bark.

Now, I'm in control. There's an empty shop across the concourse to hide in. Its windows are shattered. Nothing loomed inside when we passed it. We can take another breather there, then charge for the exit.

Half the beefcakes are out. Trent and Gabe rush past me and reach the girls.

"Over there!" I holler, not caring the monsters can hear.

The beefcakes stumble under the weight of their wounded, unsure of themselves. One direction they know; another they don't. Neither is tempting.

"Straight ahead! To the pillow place!" I shout.

I push Gina, who sneers at me, but my command motivates her, and she rushes into the fogged-out pillow store.

Joe screams at everyone, with Raina by his side. She yells my name.

No one listens.

I move around, sheep-dogging the group toward the store before anyone else intervenes or something leaps out of the fog, which is a surer threat than anything. Another shriek from inside the pillow store reminds me of that.

Omri and Tomi stiffen and plant themselves to the floor. From behind them, Gina backs out of the shop, wagging her hands and signaling her inability to cope with whatever's in there.

In front of her, through the broken window, a bumpy white snake four times the size of an anaconda cavorts in the air, its mouth attached to Valerie's face. Valerie stumbles before she teeters to the floor. The snake thuds down on top of her.

Tomi spins Omri around and runs. Gina rushes to Trent. The rest of the beefcakes split between Macy's, the atrium, and the first store, with Joe and Raina.

I'm left alone on the concourse, abandoned even by Prairie, who never made it beyond the storefront. Her face remains scrunched in consternation. Except when she looks toward me and her eyes go wide.

I don't see it in time to beat a retreat.

It's cleared the fog, up close in its sticky pale glory. Not a lizard, but smoother—too smooth and lower to the ground, like a child's drawing of a lizard.

A salamander.

It leaps on nubby legs ending in milky, bleeding toes, like half-inflated balloons. It latches onto my neck with a flat, froggy mouth and presses down, its upper jaw catching my lower one and pulling it to my chest. Tendons stretch and snap, widening my mouth into a gaping maw. My face erupts in fire.

Its bite crushes my ribs and presses on my heart, my lungs, everything necessary for me to live.

♥*♥*♥

The correct choice was to regroup and stay sheltered.

Turn to page 271.

This is one hell of a Valentine's Day backdrop. Cupid-Joe towers over me, looking like Schwarzenegger at the end of *Predator*—but if Arnie was more of a track and field guy— flanked by idiotic, plastic playground bugs, grinning through a thick fog and holding out his hand for me to grab. Where's the camera? Where do I smile?

"Get up!" he shouts.

My survival instinct cuts through the surrealness. I recognize a non-mutant helper when I see one, so I grab his wrist, and he hauls me up.

"Over there!"

He pushes me away from the girls, toward the food court, basically right where we came from. I'll take all the help I can get, but manhandling isn't something I'm keen on. These are the limits of his wisdom on the field of battle. I wriggle out of his hands and cry Raina's name.

Instead of laying eyes on her, I find another non-mutant helper.

This one sports a bloody bandage over his bicep and not much else. He tries to turn me back around, but I push past him to where Raina and the other girls huddle together. Shadows skitter in close, and flames from torches encircle us. I sense the girls' relief, but we're still hopped up on adrenaline. More guys close in.

A hand falls on my shoulder. Its fingers dig deep, and I lash out, flailing my arm and catching whoever is grabbing me across the chin.

"Agh!" Joe rubs his jaw and reaches for me again. I'm not even sure he recognizes me. "No, this way! Come on!"

"No!"

The guys corral the girls, swinging glances left and right, looking for monsters. They push them toward the food court. None of the guys look like they know what to do.

This might be the first time all day I think I know better than anyone else. I run over to Raina and refocus her from the glistening six-pack abs fencing her in.

"We gotta keep going." I speak only to my own team, locking eyes with each one.

Raina and Prairie break free. Kirsten is fixated on rescue, but I plow through them all and lead the way. I'm the reason we wrenched ourselves away from the promise of J.C. Penney; I'm the reason we're backtracking. And it's almost done.

Once we're on the far side of the atrium, we are charting new terrain. We're going to find Bridie and get out of here. I maintain my momentum and break through the line of scrimmage formed by these guys.

The Abercrombie models from earlier.

I vault the opposite wall of the playground and splash into the atrium's floodwaters. Theater to my right. Info desk to my left. Macy's straight ahead.

"Quinn Carpenter!"

The sound of my name coming from a deep male voice, using every syllable like a new condemnation added to my bill, so close to how my own mother would say it when I was in trouble, puts a stutter in my step.

So, he *does* recognize me.

Instead of stopping me, it urges me on, making me windmill my arm like a soldier in an old propaganda poster, urging my people forward. Joe knows me, and I treat it as a sign of respect. He'll follow someone he knows. The girls will come, and so will he. If he does, so will his boys.

"Joe! Come with me!" I shout, my voice singing with confidence.

Raina pushes past the guys, towing Prairie after her. Kirsten's hair whips back and forth while she struggles to make up her mind. This is how I win her over. Action. Initiative.

A shadow swings through the fog over my head, like a girder on a construction site. The stick bug is back. I sweep my head low and charge, passing between its forelegs. A tug on my shoulder lifts my chest up to the sky, and I slide down on my butt. The stick bug's mouth parts reach for me. It lowers the trunk of its body, but I roll to the side, evading its spindly mouth-fingers.

Raina and a couple of the guys shout behind me. The stick bug shifts its stance, the trunk of its body aiming at them.

I get up on my elbows. A new shadow passes over me—skinnier, faster. I don't grasp what it is before it gains a body and impales my chest right beneath my breast plate, cracking the cartilage between my ribs, crashing through my organs, and pinning my spine to the floor. The second stick bug's pincer-toes spread out when its foot lands, carving through my back and elevating my torso off the floor.

Pain is virtually nonexistent, accompanied by an immediate assumption of my own doom. This sweat-inducing panic that I haven't done everything I've meant to do, seen all the things I want to see...

"Quinn?"

Joe hollers my name, questioningly this time. He can't see me. But he remembers me. Maybe I should have trusted him. Maybe he wasn't leading us back to J.C. Penney.

We can't go backward.

I wish I could go with them, anywhere, even Penney's.

The stick bug struggles to lift its leg through the hole it punched through my chest, wagging its pincers, shaking my body, and I enter a state of shock from which I never recover.

The correct choice was to follow Joe. Turn to page 234.

The lizard thing rears back and plops onto its thick white tail like it's sitting on a stool. Its bleary gaze twitches between Kirsten and me, and its fore-claws hover at the ready, waiting for one of us to make ourselves stand out over the other.

Camaraderie doesn't account for what I do next. The sight of this thing activates my own lizard brain, which is less an organ for decision than an all-encompassing desire to be far away from here. My last passing thought is to assume Kirsten's instinct will take over too and we'll both run like hell.

How many times do you hear that line in the movies: "I thought he was still with me!" Because who else wouldn't run when you are?

My hand slips out from under me when I scramble backward, so I do the next most logical thing. I barrel-roll to my right, making space between Kirsten and me. My toes are planted on the ground.

I get up, shoving power down through my quads and my calves, readying myself to run. Kirsten's with me, I think, not to excuse abandoning her, but to convince myself I'm not alone.

What I don't take into account is the quantity of mouths the lizard thing has at its disposal. It can only pick one target, and my clumsy escape provides one. I give it focus. My form is vital. I'm desirable. And I'm slower than I think.

Its jaws clamp around me. Thin, razor-sharp teeth shred through my jacket and my shirt, snap my bra straps, and slice skin before the pressure of its vise grip tightens and keeps me from slipping.

My chest compresses against my spine. My shoulder blades bend in a direction they weren't designed for. Ribs snap, and my sternum fails. My chest cavity collapses on itself, squishing my lungs and my heart, piercing them with shards of bone.

The lizard-thing picks me up and swings me back and forth, ensuring my death will take. My gradual burning demise from suffocation and internal hemorrhaging is cut short when its aim is accomplished. A swing of its head gets my body in the perfect position for the whiplash to have its effect. My neck snaps.

♥*♥*♥

Try again. Turn to page 251.

"What the hell's this now?" Kirsten asks.

She comes to a stop. Only because I've stopped. Ahead of us, Prairie and Raina skid to a halt too. They urge us to come on.

It's just, these are the first strangers I've encountered who haven't hid in the shadows. So why? What do they want? What do they know? We were in Sears so long, and Prairie's been hunkered down. I wonder if there's something we haven't pieced together. Like, why aren't we hiding like they are?

I'm flooded with the possibility of new insights, but even more than that, I wonder why they haven't just gone out those doors. The mall is going to fall on everyone's heads if they don't. And if *we're* the right ones and are this close to escape, we owe it to these people to tell them they should get out as fast as they can.

There's too much confusion. The person in Suncoast, the other girls, all demanding I do something. But I have to know. Something about helping Bridie storms to the front of my mind. Because I'm not done with the mall yet. Even once we're outside.

I run to the store.

The person's murky silhouette clarifies into an adult man, somewhere in his forties, with a goatee and a paunch. He's covered in sweat, and blood stains his jacket—the day's new uniform.

"Hey—" I start.

He leans out of the entrance and grabs my shoulder, pulling me in.

"Hey!" I scream and throw up my hands to fend him off. Pain shoots through my wounded arm.

A windmill of limbs activates behind me. The girls have closed in.

The man, battered by fists, shrinks back into the store and cries out.

"Hands off, jackweed!" Kirsten roars, putting herself before me.

He holds up his hands to signal a truce, that he meant no harm, but isn't that what they all do?

"Whoa, whoa, whoa! I'm just trying to help! You gotta get in here before any more of those things come around."

His eyes are wild. He checks down the wing and looks past us, at the store where we encountered the last creature. Behind him are a few other adult men and, further inside in the dimness, the huddled forms of several more people—men, women, children. The security gate hangs down, covering the top third of the store entrance. A teenager about our age, someone I don't recognize, has his fingers around its lowest rung, ready to yank it down.

Prairie comes running up to us and, without even assessing the situation, starts shaking her head. "Nuh-uh. Uh-uh. No."

The man's eyes narrow to slits. "Don't listen to this girl. We tried to get her in here, but she wouldn't come. This is the safest spot you're gonna find. Now hurry up before we shut this place up."

The gate makes a rolling sound while the teenager struggles to keep it at the same level.

Prairie tugs at my sleeve. "Quinn, come on. We...Wait. What is everyone doing?"

The metallic slide of a gate comes from behind us. Someone has locked themselves into one of the businesses we passed moments before. People in the one next to this store we're at now do the same. Another across the wing...

The idea spreads like a virus. Some of these people watched us dangle clothes and dart across their entrances like doofuses and never said a thing.

"What are you *doing?*" Prairie questions everyone at large but directs this query to our man.

There's too much noise to cut through, and only I hear her.

Raina and Kirsten join us and tell us to leave. I get it. But these people don't. Evidently, they don't understand the mall is collapsing. Can they not see the water rising every second? Hear the building's death throes?

"Prairie, they need to know what's going on. Hold *on* a sec," I tell her, speaking over Raina and Kirsten. "Look, man! The mall is flooding because it's crumbling to the ground. If you don't get outta here, you're going to be underwater, or the roof's gonna collapse or something."

Spurred on by the people in the other stores, a couple of teenagers rush up to us, leap, and pull down the gate held by the other kid. I yelp and leap back so it doesn't slam down on my toes.

"Open it up! Come on!" the goateed man tells them, pleading on our behalf one last time.

They refuse.

"No! It's not that!" Prairie says. "What are you people doing? Don't shut the doors!"

It's in that second, cut off from these people, I'm struck by an idea, though not what Prairie's worried about.

"Wait a second," I cry. "Who's in there?" I scour the shadows, looking for anything familiar, anyone I'd recognize. Hairstyle, an article of clothing, anything. "Who's in there with you?"

Bridie. I need to find Bridie. Ran this far across the mall. Shocked and terrified, unable to recognize her little sister.

Kirsten and Raina shout at me. I'm holding them up. Too many people are speaking at once. I'm not helping. But I have to see. I call out to the people in the darkness. Heads swivel in confusion and fear, uncomfortable with the further tumult I've brought.

Raina yanks my shoulder. "Get a hold of yourself, Quinn. We gotta go!"

"What if Bridie's in there?"

"She *isn't*. She would've said so if she was. It's the wrong side of the mall. We gotta *move!*"

"Please," Prairie says, shaking the gate. "I warned you! You need to get out of there!"

"Shut this girl up," says one of the teenagers.

"Yeah, beat it, you frickin' morons."

"Get lost."

Prairie stares helplessly, latched onto the gate.

They tell us to take her away. Kirsten obliges. She steps up to the gate, fans out her arms, and ushers us all away. We move back by the kiosk, with her watching our flanks like a hawk. She tells us all to shut up. Drawn out into the open, we obey.

Kirsten sighs and speaks fast. "Quinn, go. What's the problem?"

"What if Bridie's in there? Or someone else we know?"

"Dude, Bridie's not in there. And I know the guy who pulled down the gate."

"What? Who is he?"

"He goes to East. I don't remember his name. He's a dick. Next?"

"What about the mall falling in on itself? None of these people know that."

"What?" Prairie's eyes glaze over when understanding arrives. "Ooh, I see. Oh, no. But that's not what I—"

"Quinn." Kirsten grabs my shoulders, lowers her head, and gives me a shake, rattling my attention directly onto her. "You can't save the whole world. You can't convince a store full of terrified people what to do."

"She's right," Raina agrees.

Kirsten shakes me again. "*Quinn.*"

They're right. I know it. But I couldn't live with myself if I hadn't tried. These people are only doing what feels right, same as us. I think they're wrong, but I remember. We're a team. The four of us have to work together and for ourselves.

Before I know it, I'm nodding. I'm agreeing. We're going to leave these people behind.

In all this time, as exposed as we are, nothing new has come charging down the concourse, from J.C. Penney, or jumped from the balcony. It's only a matter of time. The girls are satisfied they've convinced me, and I move with them. I avoid a backward glance, following Raina and Kirsten, sticking to the plan.

Which leaves it to Prairie to hold us up this time. She goes back to Suncoast.

I call to the others.

"What *now?*" Kirsten whines.

Prairie turns and says, "They have to open those doors! I tried to warn them before."

"Warn them about what?" Kirsten asks. She moves on Prairie and, without hesitation, their confrontation forgotten, starts tugging her away.

Prairie stands her ground, squeaking her boots against the floor and whining at Kirsten to stop.

"This is ridiculous," Raina says.

A loud crack echoes down the wing, followed by a structural groan and screams.

"Don't you get it?" Prairie asks. With her free hand, she claws at Kirsten, who yelps and backs up. "Remember what I said about ambush predators? I watched half the animals in here scrambling around, looking for shelter. They were just as scared as us. Think of what they are. Where they came from. Hot, dark chambers where they could hide wherever they wanted. Where do you think they're going to go?"

I'm surprised by her reasoning. She's put together the creatures' origins almost the same as Raina. Underground swamp monsters.

The mall groans again. Another series of shouts from the atrium.

Prairie's warning comes into focus.

Underground swamp monsters.

Drawn from their holes and crevices...drawn *back* to them.

People inside the store begin to whimper. How many others have holed up in stores like this? People we passed by, too scared to make a peep. Or too dead to make one.

I recall the skittering sounds from the empty storefront where we were held under guard, right when the mall first shuddered.

Prairie continues. "They'll be in the shadows. Using back hallways and heating vents! They broke out of their cozy little ecosystem right as a blizzard has hit. The water flooded them right out of their home! Where else are they going to go?"

"They're trapped."

"Exactly! And now...now, we're making all this noise and..." Prairie goes back and starts rattling the gate. "You need to open this! You need to get out!"

She tries lifting the security barrier herself, but it doesn't move. Besides, the teenagers inside rush to hold it down, so even if they hadn't engaged its lock, she'd lose.

I join her and search for the goateed man, the one person who cared to reach out. It won't help to shout at a store full of people. Kirsten's right. I can't convince everyone. But if one person would listen...

A loud pop goes off at the store's rear. Sparks fly through the dusky air, raising shouts from all inside. The available light decreases by a startling degree.

It's not just this store. Popping sounds go up and down the wing, like shattered bulbs on the red carpet in an old-timey movie. The lights in all the stores have gone out, leaving us in a leaden darkness beneath the bitter hammer blows of a February blizzard. The concourse lights are still on, so we're not plunged into total darkness, but the effect is frightening, nonetheless. The creatures have that much more of their natural gloom.

Prairie's more frantic than I've ever seen her, shedding tears and losing control. We keep rattling the gate-turned-cage for these bewildered, careless people. The teens pry at our fingers, tell us to shut up and to go get killed somewhere else.

Kirsten and Raina don't know what to do except to tell us to stop.

It's getting darker and warmer. And the water is rising. The creatures' world has burst out of the ground somewhere in this mall, and they won't waste any time finding the source of this racket.

The first screams get cut off. They're shocked outbursts, not unlike the surprised cries from when the lights went out. It's only after this initial round that a shriek issues from the darkness, stopping even the teenagers from holding down the gate and taunting us.

One by one, the gated storefronts are turned into mesh speakers for tortured screams and desperate cries, unlike anything I've ever heard in my life.

We're in the middle of a prison, the inmates contending with lions locked up with them. Crashing and yelling and splashing emanate from darkened bunkers, and soon, the mesh security gates, left alone by those sheltered within, are slammed into by people who can't get out. They've activated the locks. They're electric. And the power to them is gone.

Shouts come from the back of Suncoast.

"We have to get them out of there!" Prairie screams. She tries raising the gate.

I help, but it doesn't move.

Raina jumps to my side, and the three of us try lifting, but it won't budge. Not even with our best base to help.

Kirsten rushes over and tells the teenagers to hit the gate's button. One of them is already trying, and it does nothing. We practically froth at the mouth, howling at them to do what they can't do, to rescue themselves from their own mistake. From the shadows, I just about make out the slashing of insectoid limbs, the lunging of monstrous heads housing vicious mouthparts.

Prairie bawls, shaking the gate. The teenage boys, who just a moment before taunted us, now grasp at our fingers, begging us to do something.

But there's nothing we can do.

They've locked themselves in, and the creatures are feasting. Water splashes out from the slaughter inside and covers our boots in an inky red. The teens are smashed against the gate, grimacing, unable to breathe, while the survivors rush forward, looking for escape. The gate bows outward, and I wonder if their combined weight might break it down.

If they do, we'll be right underneath it.

I'm hugged from behind and pulled away before I can move on my own. Kirsten. She has me while Raina picks up Prairie by the waist and pulls her away, screaming.

"*We gotta go!*" Raina shouts.

I'm ripped away from the slaughter inside Suncoast, only to remember how many more threats are out here on the concourse.

When I jostle free from Kirsten, I run. We go as a team toward the freezing cold, the last place anyone from the cheesehead state wants to be in the dead of February.

We round the nearest corner. The fog by the doors is intense, where the mall's heat meets the blizzard. The water's temperature changes as we kick it up and splatter ourselves. And it's getting deeper. It should be shallower. We're nowhere near the center of the mall.

Then I recall how flooded the parking lot was.

I remember, as we come up to the doorframes appearing from the fog, why we had to park on the other side of the mall.

I remember, as we reach the vestibule and find it filled with a floating pile of bloodied, dismembered corpses, why we were forced to park as far away as we had to.

Everything, everywhere, is flooded. And now the wind is freezing it.

"Prairie, what the hell!" Raina cries. "Didn't you notice this happening before?"

Prairie sloshes up beside her. "I kept my head down. It was crazy over here. I...This is—"

"This is impossible," Kirsten says. "This is worse than Sears."

The opposite doors, obscured by mist, look no more promising from here. Then the sounds coming from the concourse shift. Screams die down, replaced by splashing and buzzing—opportunistic predators bound our way. They'll find the only scraps are behind closed doors, and they'll be pissed.

The creatures will keep hunting until they find us.

I move to the inner set of doors and start hauling out bodies. They looked bloated already, but it's just winter clothes, some of them puffed up with trapped air. There are missing limbs, slash marks across faces, chests, and backs. Who's to say how many bodies were dragged away whole, to be digested by a mix of toxic lizard and bug enzymes.

"We have no choice," I tell them.

I hardly have to because, as stunned as they are by the sight before their eyes, they know this is what we came for. Raina joins me, and we continue dragging out the dead, climbing over others, kicking them back with our feet, to Kirsten and Prairie to haul out of the way.

We get inside the vestibule, where the temperature drops a disturbing degree, to the point the surface of my jacket goes crisp and my nostrils dry. The glass door is glazed with a wavy layer of windswept ice, making it look like a blown glass window from a colonial era house.

We'll make it to the Jeep. Then I'll come back. I'll get Bridie. There's no mosquito beast on our tail, though the memory stirs the fear of something perhaps even more plausible happening. I gawk toward the concourse, expecting at any second another human stampede, if any survivors are left. We could end up just like the people underneath us.

Like the people back at Sears.

We keep hauling bodies, Kirsten swapping spots with me inside the vestibule when my arm acts up, until finally Raina says, "This is it." She pulls back the head of a man sitting upright in front of the outer doors, making enough room for us to get right up to it and start hammering away.

"No," Prairie replies. The way she says it makes me stop immediately.

She had stopped helping.

Bridie. I can't hear the word "no." What does "no" mean?

Kirsten and Raina drag one final body out of the water. For the second time since this started, we're inches—millimeters—from escape. It only takes one glance at what Prairie sees to know we're not getting out...again.

The sitting man's body was blocking the crack between the doors. When Raina pulled it back, a small waterfall started spurting through. The body also obscured my view. Outside, the flooding has built up over two feet high. And it wants to get inside.

"We can't get out here," Prairie murmurs.

"Come on. Let's bust it down," Raina says. "Kirsten, find something heavy or...sharp."

"No," Prairie objects. "The water will knock us right back into the mall. We'd have to swim out from the middle all over again."

Kirsten and Raina look at her, then over to the water.

Raina throws up her hands. "I'll take my chances."

This close to escape, I can't blame her. She rifles through random shoppers' bags and comes away with a cordless drill strapped inside its cardboard display box. Raina clamors over the remaining floating bodies and starts bashing it against the glass.

"Stop! You haven't even thought about the cold!"

"What about it?" I ask.

"I mean, we could freeze."

Raina grunts, adjusts her footing, and batters the door again. "We got the Jeep. Just run like hell once we're out, and we'll warm up in there. Now, come on!"

I back up along with Prairie. Kirsten sneaks past us, patting her pants and jacket.

I cringe with every blow to the door. Each brings the prospect of a deluge of water knocking me down into a raft of corpses before floating me into the open maw of a hungry swamp creature.

From amidst the sounds of approaching creatures comes the busted-lawnmower buzz of a mosquito beast. It breaks into view in the concourse and slides into the opening to J.C. Penney, where it raises a storm of shattering glass and clattering plastic and metal.

"Come on! Quick!" Raina urges. "Grab something!"

"I don't like this," I say.

"It doesn't matter if you like it!" Raina replies. "We gotta go!"

"I gotta find Bridie!"

Raina drops her drill from a backswing and snarls. "I have to get back to my mom and little brother. You ever think of that? Who's going to look out for them now, huh? And what about Prairie and her family? Or Kirsten and hers?"

There's hatred in her eyes. Her lips tremble. Every muscle of her face is stretched to a quivering tautness.

She swallows. "Besides." Raina turns back to the door and hauls the packaged drill back like a cumbersome softball. "You can come back in. That's the plan, isn't it?"

It's my turn to feel angry since I know what she's implying. I don't like how it feels, and I don't feel as justified as her, but that just makes me angrier. She bashes the door and inspects the scuff mark at the point of impact. I step up to her.

"You're not coming back with me, are you?"

Raina breathes heavily and looks off to the side, shifting loose my accusation from her shoulders.

My blood boils hotter.

"*Are* you?"

She bashes the door again while Prairie squeaks in protest. "Please. Raina. We have to try another way."

"Let's get to the Jeep," Raina says, leaving it at that.

"Kirsten, don't you have anything to say about this?" I whip around, hoping against hope she'll back me up.

There's really no telling at this point. She wants out more than anyone, and she's not going to help find Bridie.

Kirsten's hardly paying attention. To anything. To us or Prairie or watching out for the mosquito beast. She looks catatonic.

"Kirsten, hello?"

She murmurs like the movie ghost of a murder victim, saying something we're supposed to spend an hour and a half deciphering before we can put her spirit to rest.

"What is it?" I demand.

"My keys," she says.

"What?"

"I don't have my keys."

Prairie makes another, somehow even weaker peep.

Upon her next blow, Raina presses the drill into the door and holds it in place. "Say that again?"

"I don't have my keys. The security guys took my bag. I don't have them."

"Prairie." I turn to her. "You grabbed our bags, didn't you? Kirsten, are they in your purse?"

"I...I did, but no...the lizard," Prairie says.

Raina mutters. "Kirsten, you freaking moron. I can't believe you didn't think of this."

"What about you!" Kirsten explodes. "You didn't grab your dad's keys, did you? You got those on you?"

Raina's eyes flash with murder. She tamps the temptation down deep, somewhere it better stay forever because whoever uncaps that rage when she's not so close to her own death will most definitely feel theirs. "There's bound to be people outside, all right? Like, other survivors or people passing by, or an ambulance or something. How could there not be?"

"Prairie," I say, not ready for Raina to convince me, "what were you saying about freezing?"

"Uh. Hypothermia. If we don't get warm fast enough."

"Yeah."

"Yeah. It's hard to say how bad it'll be. I mean, I think I remember how many minutes it takes for hypothermia to set in when you're in water. But in the air? I don't know. It depends on the temperature. But we're already soaking wet, and...and there's the wind chill to think of. It'll probably be worse. I don't know."

"Bad?" I say.

She shrugs. "Bad."

"There's gotta be people around," Raina mutters.

I watch the water sloshing against the glass, ready to take us out at the knees if Raina's next blow finds the perfect chink in the door's armor.

"Stand in the corner or something!" Raina says, throwing her arms out, her patience run dry. "Just...let the water go by or something!"

"That won't work!" I scream. "And you're not coming back for Bridie."

"We found Prairie! That's who we're here for."

"How are we going to get warm?" Kirsten cries.

"There are *people* out there!" Raina screams.

"*Where?*" I demand. I look out into the darkness.

It's not yet dusk, but it's late enough that February's weak sun is low in the sky, shrouded by a blizzard compounding the ordinary gloominess to bring about a virtual twilight. No one's around out there. No survivors, no gawkers. I can't make out the road from here either, and there are no beams or twinkles to suggest headlights or sirens.

It all happened so fast. Has word even reached the outside world?

Just get me out of here. Please, get me out of here. And Bridie too.

"Hey, what is that?" Prairie asks.

Raina is sputtering on about there being people outside to help us. Kirsten fights her because it's her natural state, but even she can't deny how badly she wants to smash down the door.

Prairie yells. "*Guys, listen!*"

At first, I think it's just the same pop music from before, but we haven't heard it this loud since Sears. And if it wasn't audible on the concourse, then the main sound system short-circuited at some point.

But we do detect music. It has rhythm. It's only one instrument. An electric guitar, grungy as hell and competently played but missing notes in its urgency. It's not a recording. Someone is playing it live, someone here in the mall.

"What is that?" Prairie asks.

"That shit is *blaring*," Kirsten says. "Is it coming from Band Avenue? That's on the other side of the mall."

I almost can't bring myself to tell them I know this song. In fact, I've obsessed over it for over two years.

Before I told myself to cut it out and grow up, when I stopped listening to it...

Stopped fantasizing about being in the front row of a sold-out concert while it played to a raging crowd...

Bouncing along and waiting for the lead guitarist to wink at me, for his hand to reach down and lift me up on the stage...

For him to kiss me in front of everyone as the pyrotechnics exploded...

I sigh and swallow my embarrassment. It's way too coincidental for everything else that's happened today. And it's just so, so utterly stupid.

"Guys..."

The girls turn and wait for me to tell on myself, which I have to do.

"It's Skye."

♥*♥*♥

Leave the doors and reroute through J.C. Penney.
Turn to page 34.

Fight to find Skye—and Bridie since she might be with him.
Turn to page 72.

I'm flush with a feeling of triumph I'm careful to protect. My fights with Kirsten are nothing new. We have our ups and downs, and they follow each other fast. Takedowns like mine always come handcuffed to misgivings and regret because really, besides Kirsten, I don't have many other people I can talk to. If only life was like how I claimed Prairie thought it was—all of us cool kids were tight all the time, holding no grudges, inflicting no slights, and remembering none done to us.

But today? After yesterday? I'm holding strong. And Kirsten has taken off with hardly a public showdown. The shoppers barely noticed a thing. They keep circling carousels, staring at walls of clothes, and scowling at discount tags less generous than they'd like to see. The cashiers people-watch the concourse or sneak peeks at catalogs under the counter. It's as if nothing happened.

My friends, on the other hand...

Prairie appears as troubled as ever, emotionally underequipped to handle a blowup which threatened to be much bigger. Well, she doesn't get to judge, and I know what side she'd be on anyway, so I don't really care.

It's Raina who gets to me. Her apathetic gaze draws the lingering traces of my anger at Kirsten. She thinks she's so above all this. My pride sours, and I sneer at her.

"What is it?"

She shrugs. "I didn't say anything."

"You're not going to tell me that was a low blow?"

Raina shrugs deeper, until she's nothing but a shrug, a big shrug trying to topple me off her. "If you say so. It doesn't really matter to me."

"Dude, what is your deal today?"

Her shoulders drop, and her eyes flash with an anger outmatching mine. It would be lying to say I'm not intimidated, but I'm done with her aloofness. I'm perfectly justified in my annoyance.

"I don't have a *deal*," she snarls.

"Good, because we can leave now, thanks to me. Prairie and I don't want to be here, and it's pretty clear you don't either. And you haven't seen all the crap Kirsten's been doing all day. She's been straight-up subhuman. I'm surprised security hasn't stopped her yet."

"Whatever. You go if you want. I gotta wait on my dad."

I turn to Prairie, who makes a shrill sort of chirp.

"But we don't...He's our only ride too," she murmurs.

The reminder stings. Of course, we could find Kirsten, and I could make enough of an attempt at amends so she'll drive us home. We can recommence our fight at another time, on a leveler playing field, when one of us doesn't depend on the other for something as trivial as a ride home. And yeah, I think pretty highly of Kirsten by making that assumption.

It's enough to cause my misgivings and regret to show up. I should act like an adult and apologize to Kirsten.

Raina sighs. "Look, you can wait for my dad if you want, even though you're the reason we're in this toxic hellhole in the first place. I'm gonna go make sure Kirsten doesn't follow through with whatever prank she has in mind and end up killing Bridie or something."

She moseys away, and my stomach goes into turmoil. Raina is almost past the checkout when I call out, "Wait!"

She stops and turns.

I come up to her, trailing Prairie. "I'll come too. Though honestly, she'll probably end up buying Bridie dinner and a new wardrobe, just to spite me even more."

There's no point in drawing things out. For all her faults and misconceptions, Kirsten knows I'm not in a good spot. We have a saying on the cheer team. Whenever someone screws up, an elbow goes in someone's face, a shoe stomps on someone's toes, a ponytail whips someone across the eyes, or someone gets dropped, the rest of the team enters into a guttural chorus, each member doing their very best—and by best, I mean worst—Stallone impression. The words turn into weights dangling from our tongues, which we struggle to spit out until we're so out of sync we sound insane.

She drew first blood.

Technically, since Kirsten claims everything she's done today has been *for* me, I did it. I drew first blood. And she'll know I was just lashing out because I'm upset. So, I should get my damn penance over with.

I can't stop myself from wondering one thing, though. Before we leave August Max, I blurt out the question to Raina, hoping she doesn't think I'm trying to score more points on Kirsten.

"Were you with her? Did you see if Bridie is actually here or not?"

Raina sighs again. "Yeah, I saw her with Nicole too."

I murmur an okay, and we leave it at that, starting our search for Kirsten.

Not long after we're back on the concourse, Prairie makes her presence known with an outburst that makes me jump.

"Holy smokes!"

Raina and I stop to see her leaning over the railing, looking down the concourse toward J.C. Penney.

We join her, and at first, I don't see what the big deal is. People continue to mill around the main floor, with the densest part of the crowd concentrated in the atrium. Besides the greenhouse-thick fog, nothing seems amiss. Then I notice how many people down the J.C. Penney wing lean over the second-floor balcony like us.

Below them, the first-floor crowd condenses and presses in our direction. And behind the people are a suspiciously high number of workers in orange and yellow vests. At the workers' feet, the mall's polished floor appears to shine more brightly than normal.

"Whoa," Raina says. "Is that all water?"

The first floor glitters with reflections from the mall's overhead lights, from neon displays and storefront names. One worker's boots raise haloes of splashing water when she breaks away from her coworkers to retrieve a mop bucket.

"Holy mackerel. That just goes to show we should've left this land to the waterfowl," says Prairie.

"Why would you want birds living here?" Raina asks. "I wouldn't touch that water with a ten-foot pole."

"What do you mean?"

"This place is a frickin' Superfund site. Or it should've been treated like one anyway."

"What's that mean?"

"It means the army base south of here dumped all sorts of crap that ended up in the swamp and killed off all the wildlife. The only silver lining is that Lake Mendota would be even nastier than it already is if the pollution didn't end up pooling here instead."

Prairie looks wounded. "Why would they build a mall on it, then?"

"What do you think?" Raina counters.

"They must've cleaned it up."

"Doubt it."

I can sense Prairie's injured pride for missing out on such a critical piece of local history. If it makes her feel better, I haven't heard jack about it either.

"Where'd you hear all this stuff?" she asks.

Raina doesn't respond.

The scene darkens, and my gaze is drawn to the skylights running the length of the mall. Angry, navy clouds are closing in, pushing the lighter, dull gray sky ever eastward. The clicking and clacking of sleet, along with the low moan of wind skating across thick glass, are detectable over the music and crowd noise.

The front's no longer approaching. It's here, ready to flash freeze everything right as the melt has reached its worst point.

"I guess it's time to go," Prairie says, making an attempt at sounding casual.

"Yeah," Raina replies grimly. "Let's grab Kirsten and get outta here."

"Yeah..." I echo.

It's no different than our current plan. Only more urgent. I picture Kirsten sliding the Cherokee on black ice, falling into a ditch or nailing a telephone pole, or flooding her engine in a gigantic puddle. However pissed we are, we should all make it home.

I home in on movement down by one of the far skylights. By the size of it, I think I spy a sparrow, a bird of some kind, that got caught inside. Must not have received Raina's memo about the pollution. But the closer I look, the stranger its movements seem. Its wings don't flap like a bird's. In fact, they move so rapidly, the creature–if it's a creature at all– looks like it's being held aloft by nothing at all. It reminds me of the housefly from earlier. An unseasonable appearance. Maybe some balloons got away from a storefront?

I frown and rush to join the other two.

Right as I catch up, Raina points ahead. "First objective complete. She's right there."

In the lounge area by the skywalk connecting the mall's second-floor walkways, Kirsten sits on a puffy black sofa, her blond hair standing out like a lighthouse beacon.

Along the way over, we notice more safety-vested workers on the first floor. Their mops and "Wet Floor" signs are no match for today's conditions. One guy with a new roll of caution tape looks conflicted about unfurling it. They might close the whole place down before he decides where it could possibly do any good.

There's even flood-fighting equipment upstairs with us, hinting at roof leaks or plumbing problems. Next to Kirsten's couch is a rolling bucket with a mop head clasped in its wringer, its handle resting on the floor.

"Kirsten, we need to roll. Mall's closing," Raina claims.

Prairie and I don't contradict her.

Kirsten turns her head and blinks at us with the nonchalance of a laundry-folding mother watching the O.J. trial. The aftermaths of our blowups usually involve this sort of affected casualness— performed far better than Prairie's— as if nothing's happened, or that if something has happened, it doesn't matter.

But today—now? Something else is stirring inside of her...something that stops me from saying anything else.

Raina applies the pressure. "Kirsten. Hey. Quinn says you had your fun, so let's haul ass before you do something royally stupid. The weather's getting bad, and Prairie needs to get home. She's got a family thing. And my mom and brother are waiting on my dad and me."

Kirsten tilts her head at the news. I give Raina a sideways glance, watching how this'll play, but I won't stop her. Prairie proves she won't either. She's smart enough and meek enough to let Raina do her talking for her.

"Royally stupid?" Kirsten asks, a touch of scandal in her voice. Her hands move from her lap to the edge of the cushion, and her eyes well up. "Everything...*everything* I've done today has been royally stupid. I've been doing nothing but a bunch of moronic, idiotic crap, hoping that we could have some fun, hoping that anything might make Quinn feel the tiniest bit better, and none of it's paid off, has it?"

Her chin juts out, and tears spill down her cheeks. She nods menacingly at each of us, one at a time.

"*None* of it," she repeats, looking at me.

"Kirsten," I say, sensing a climactic blowup. "Let's get outta here. We can do a movie night, okay? I'd love that so much more than this. You can stay the night. I doubt my parents will be thinking of church in the morning. Let's just hit the road before everything ices over."

"There's only one thing I wanted to do today, Quinn."

"I know." Since I'm only interested in getting us out of here, I let the next part roll off my tongue. "I'm sorry. And I appreciate—"

I speak too late. Though, honestly, nothing would stop her at this point. Right as I apologize, Kirsten leaps to her feet, propelled by a single-minded conviction—which I never should have doubted—to make today all about my revenge on the world.

We watch in stunned silence while she knocks the mop away from the rolling bucket, then pulls the wringer off the bucket's side and tosses it on the floor. She lifts with her legs like Coach trained us, grabbing the bucket with one hand on the bottom, one on the lip. Then she kneels on the couch and heaves the bucket's gray contents over the railing.

Prairie squeaks, louder than she's done all day, and Raina, more animated than she has been, explodes with an impressive, full-throated, "What the *hell*?"

A slug of opaque mop water slithers from the bucket. It stretches out in obedience to gravity, like a decomposing liver stretched taut. Red streamers and glittery hearts are incorporated into the sludgy mix, along with toilet paper and salty floor grit. The globular mixture disappears over the railing.

I can't stand this part, this split second between witnessing the attack and not seeing its target.

But I'm the only one who makes a move, one that would exonerate me from complicity if it didn't accidentally make Kirsten's action that much worse. Only I have seen the full extent of her devilish streak today. Only *I* know an assault this brazen would have a very specific target in mind.

I bowl into Kirsten's shoulder, twisting with the impact, my ribs smashing into the railing. She pitches forward. The bucket slips from her grip and becomes a second bomb. And it's all my fault.

My torso droops over the railing. I see what Kirsten's done, see her target. The newfound knowledge comes with a fleeting sense of satisfaction, as crazy as that sounds. Kirsten was telling me the truth. And so was Raina.

Bridie is here.

My sister stands at the edge of the first-floor lounge, beneath our own, her eyes bulging, hands frozen in panic, outspread claws wide enough apart to catch a beach ball. The mop bucket wobbles on the floor like a lopsided die. Her friend Nicole writhes on the floor, howling and clutching her shoulder.

Bridie turns her head to her wounded friend, then looks up, tracing the bucket's trajectory right back to my horrified face.

Grimy water and streamers pool at her boots, but despite Nicole's obvious injury, neither of them are soaked. My gaze goes lower.

Directly underneath us comes a mixed chorus of curses and cries. More seniors. Girls and guys. Gina, Valerie, Trent, and Gabe, among others. Several of them drenched and festooned with shiny, slimy Valentine's Day vomit. A shaggy head of hair lowers itself to the floor when one of the seniors crouches and plucks a foil heart out of the dirty water. It glints gold under the reflected mall lights.

Don't, I beg of the shaggy-haired boy. Don't look at me. Don't see me if you do. Don't be the person I know you to be.

He looks from the heart over to Bridie, and then he follows her gaze up to me.

Hey, Skye.

♥*♥*♥

Apologize. Turn to page 61.

Run. Turn to page 80.

Raina pulls hard on my wounded arm, leaning into J.C. Penney. I cry out, shattering through the noise of the incoming water and the buzzing mosquito beast. She lightens her hold, given a split second to realize how she's hurt me, and I wrench my arm out of her grip.

"No!" she cries. Raina recoils after releasing me, eyes wide, falling in the direction she desperately wants to go.

I can't follow. Not with this pain, not when I'm so torn, with no time to make a decision.

So I pull Kirsten with me, away from the throbbing, into the lap of Skye's song. And since Prairie holds Kirsten and Prairie knows where she wants to go, the three of us tumble onto the concourse.

A tide of sludgy, silty water comes for us, bubbling across the surface of the mall floor. Raina slips away, and I cry out her name.

"Go, go, go!" Kirsten yells.

The mosquito beast emerges from a thick hot-shower mist.

The water hits us halfway up our shins, freezing cold. My calves tighten, then my quads, my hamstrings, until I'm tensed all the way, fighting for balance. Nonetheless, our entangled trio of bodies falls to the floor, pushed toward the doors we tried to escape through.

The edge of the wall approaches. Kirsten holds me around the waist. Prairie has her leg. Being the farthest out from the corner, I extend my arms, trying to prevent us from slipping down the hallway. When the wall comes, the other two are unable to grab it. It thuds me in the chest. My fingers scrape across smooth, wet brick. I dig in my fingernails to no avail.

The only thing arresting my movement is Raina's hand on my jacket. She's bounded ahead of us and now slams her side into the brick wall, straining with all her might to keep the water from sweeping us away. With one final exertion, she pulls me up, and I'm able to lever myself around the corner, followed by Kirsten and Prairie, both drowning in the gray-red wave.

The mosquito beast slides past us on its side, legs kicking, wings flapping, spraying us with more water. It collides with a slushy crunch into the piled corpses.

I slip and slide away from the corner, pulling Kirsten along as she spits. Prairie coughs. The water keeps pounding at our feet, now pushing us into the wall, farther down the concourse. Bodies follow the mosquito beast. Some spread out and bonk into the wall by us.

Inside J.C. Penney, another mosquito beast barrels across the jewelry department, drawn by the chaos. A handful of other things are in pursuit.

Low to the ground and spread wide as a merry-go-round, pale arachnid-type water skimmers struggle to skate across the shallow depths of the store, craving an influx of water they're about to get.

We make it past the closed gates and humid raw-steak scent of Suncoast before we take a break, looking back at the incoming water and ensuring the creatures and the errant mosquito beast don't give chase.

Call it a decision made.

Kirsten keeps spitting out water, concerned with nothing else but getting the cocktail of salt-sludgy oily parking lot and blood out of her mouth.

Raina regains her breath and glares at J.C. Penney. She had to have seen what I saw. Creatures we haven't fought, in numbers we couldn't handle. I'm smart enough not to say anything.

But I'm also cowardly enough not to say what we have to do next.

I wait for Prairie to spit out the rest of the water's aftertaste, having scraped her tongue raw with her teeth. By then, the creatures make it known they won't bother us farther down the concourse.

"We better get going," she says.

I nod. The least I can do is take the lead. The rest follow, our team restored.

The mall looks completely different to me now we know the dangers lying in wait. We keep our distance from the gated storefronts, more out of the horrific memory than actual fear. From inside each one comes a doom-laden quietness broken only by the newspaper-folding lap of floodwater nudging broken fixtures, spilled products, shopping bags, and human remains. Deeper inside must be coiled up or resting creatures of unthinkable shapes and sizes, their killing instruments—which made quick work of panicked shoppers—soaked with blood.

The open stores are the worst, though, especially without anything to peek and dangle with. I swear I detect ambient light gleaming off shifting carapaces and slithering wet skin.

The risk doesn't seem worth shouting to get the attention of the people we might know across the mall. Skye's guitar still plays.

Monsters roam out in the open. By now, we all buy Prairie's talk of ambush predators, but they aren't the only things to worry about.

"Look," Prairie whispers when we've snuck past the first un-gated storefront, no peeking or dangling involved, just taking a wide berth.

We stop and squint and see far enough down the concourse to notice the floor is buckling, with peaks and valleys extending into the clapped chalkboard-eraser dust of the fog.

"That explains the groaning," Raina murmurs, shoving past me and taking point. She pats her sweatshirt and her pantlegs, and furrows her brow.

"Radio?" Prairie asks. "Gone?"

Raina grunts. "Let's find some weapons."

I scan the untold amounts of refuse around us for something dangerous-looking to wield. Raina grabs a cane, the kind with four knobs on the bottom, and makes a disappointed face, then decides to keep it.

I don't know what to say to anyone right now. Yes, I got my way, but the victory feels hollow and hurtful. They don't want to be here. We very well might have outrun the mosquito beast the other way, but we may have not. And we could have found ourselves staring at a fish tank of floodwater on the far side of J.C. Penney.

I hope they know I didn't make my decision out of the foolishness and goodness of my heart. Of course, I want to get out too. I do hope we find Bridie, but if we don't, there's no doubling back again. We will bust our way out. I will lead the charge.

And no, I'm not doing this to be selfless. As of this morning, I don't think I had whatever selflessness might've been inside me in the first place. There's not enough now to make me rush into danger, just to rescue someone who only half the time treats me okay. So what if the path to safety leads to Bridie? It's sort of a package deal.

Nearly a third of the way down the wing to the atrium, we huddle next to a fallen wireframe display rack of stationary, stickers, calendars, and planners. Kirsten reaches into the water and retrieves a metal yardstick, handing it to me and getting another she uses to practice-slash through the air.

"Hey, Raina," Prairie says, "I'm sorry about your dad. About how...Well, I just want you to know I'm sorry. I didn't get a chance to say so."

Raina's head jerks at the mention of her dad. She looks over Prairie, less like she's assessing her sincerity and more like she's reminding herself who she's being addressed by. The temper that's been waxing and waning all morning, even before the mop bucket incident, stays cool

"Yeah," she says, making eye contact before staring back down the concourse.

The edge of the atrium is visible. I picture the landmarks beyond, thinking of where we can take cover, breaking the journey into manageable chunks. The information desk straight ahead. The fountain and Cupid photoshoot to the left. Children's play area and food court to the right.

"So, uh, quick question," Kirsten murmurs, her gaze turning to Prairie. "We never got a chance to hear how you were separated from us."

Prairie doesn't answer. Instead, she gazes far away, toward the step beyond the next. Kirsten's words circle her head and slip into her ear. Her brow scrunches, and she asks, "Who? Me?"

"Duh, you. What happened back th—"

"Wait, shush!" Prairie bats down Kirsten's question with her hand.

Her warning sends my heart racing. I squeeze closer to the wireframe rack. The others huddle around the checkout counter.

From the atrium comes a shadow, low to the ground, darkening in the misty firmament. As it closes in, its sides spread out. The shadow grows to the left and right, getting no taller but widening so much, it'll eventually take up the whole floor. Then the first central shadow hardens into a familiar outline. So do the ones flanking it. Then the ones following those.

Individual creatures.

Pill bugs.

A herd of them.

Kirsten sighs with relief, though she doesn't move from her hiding place. "Okay, thank God for that."

"What do you mean?" hisses Prairie.

"Dude, we're good."

The bugs bumble closer to us, walking with a strange bucking lope that's strange to see from things shaped like upside-down bowls. It must be because they can barely keep their faces above the water. They're hunting for someplace dry. I don't think they'll find what they need, and I almost feel bad for them.

"We've seen these before," I tell Prairie. "Just...hold on a second."

"Yeah, and while we're waiting, tell us what happened. After the lizard," Kirsten says.

Prairie studies the pill bugs a moment longer, not taking our word for it. Then she says, "There isn't much to say. I thought you were right behind me. I tried running back up the stairs. But that centipede thing was still up there, and when I turned around, you were already gone, and the lizard was in the way again."

"So you were trapped?"

"No, I was able to get to the main floor again, but I ran in the opposite direction of the lizard. I figured that's where you went too. Same direction as everyone else."

"What happened to that dude who was fighting it?"

"Huh? Oh, I'm not sure. I...just ran. I thought you guys were down here too. Lots of people were." Prairie pauses, her eyes glazing over. Something's stuck in her throat, some memory she can't put into words. Something she's already worked to repress. "I...saw the guy who had that, actually." She points to Raina's cane.

Raina's head twitches when she recognizes us looking at her. She turns over the cane in her hands, inspecting it with mild interest.

"He was struggling to get up, and I ran over to...But...I never made it to him. I just kept moving."

"How'd you end up in the kiosk?" Kirsten asks.

"There was a security guard on top of it, waving people on, trying to make himself big. I was getting bounced around on both sides, so I went straight for him and ran through the little swinging door. Then something flew right through him, and he was gone. He dropped his radio. So that's how I got that."

I ask, "Did you reach anyone besides us?"

Prairie shakes her head. We digest her response. There's more to it than we want to know.

"It's not like we heard anyone else," Kirsten says.

None of us really know what that means, but I think I might. No one's made it. No one's outside, trying to reach us inside. We're the last ones left.

The pill bugs mosey over and overtake our position. Prairie clenches her yardstick, but otherwise acts as unbothered as the rest of us. I'm starting to get antsy.

Skye's stopped playing. No one's mentioned it, but they're all looking at me. They also know better than to state their opinions on the subject.

While the last of the herd passes by, I put my hands on my hips. Something jagged presses into my palm. I pull my hand away, startled, until my memory is jogged. It seems I've found something else to break the awkward silence.

"Prairie..." I pull the CD out of my pocket and give it a wiggle. Nothing rattles. Somehow, it's undamaged. Not a single crack or nick. "Here. Saved it for you."

"Oh...thanks." She accepts it and stares at its spacey cover art.

"That saved our lives, you know, from the lizard. I forgot to thank you for that."

Kirsten harrumphs in what I think is approval, so I don't give her a dirty look.

"I bet it did," Prairie says. "It's Boston."

Kirsten, with a bemused look, turns to Prairie and rests her elbow on the kiosk, placing her chin on her fist.

Prairie notices Kirsten staring and, holding the CD in both hands, like Indiana Jones with a precious idol, looks down and shrugs. "I...didn't buy it for my dad. It's for me."

Kirsten laughs. "*Boston?*"

"I've been wanting this for a long time. They're so big and operatic and...and sentimental. There's so much love in their music."

"I should've known your dad wouldn't touch that." I smile for what feels like the first time in ages. It upsets me that she has to be so sneaky about liking them, but that's another kind of crush, I guess.

Prairie smiles too. "My parents would lose it if they knew I had this."

"You know what, Hedlund?" says Kirsten. "That's what Anti-Valentine's Day is all about. Doing something good for yourself and telling everyone else to go screw themselves."

Raina snorts.

"Literally," Kirsten continues, "telling everyone else to go to hell because they're a bunch of stupid pieces of shit with bad taste who deserve to die miserably while you go and buy whatever—"

"We get it, K," I say.

Kirsten stops, fluttering her eyelashes and shrugging like she doesn't care, then watches with a cocked eyebrow while Prairie admires her recovered copy of *Third Stage*. "My parents have a hell of a sound system at home, and they don't give a crap what I listen to, so when this is all said and done, maybe we can blast that thing at my place."

Stunned, I look to Raina to see if what I heard is real, but she's off in her own world, watching the pill bugs navigate the shredded remains of the lingerie tent.

Prairie's smile fades a little. Kirsten's insults must still be on her mind, but she manages to hang onto this brief spell of happiness. "Yeah, maybe," she says.

Kirsten nods and looks away, having used up all her generosity. "And then there's Raina," she says, "who didn't want anything to do with Anti-Valentine's Day."

"Come on, K. Leave her alone," I say.

"Heck no. She was such a drag this morning. And, I mean, now? Let's appreciate how far we've come. We got Prairie. Now we're on to Bridie and a bunch of dumbasses from school. We're, like, the last people left."

I lean into her and speak quietly. "Kirsten, stop. We haven't accomplished everything, you know what I mean?"

"We have a minute here, okay? Can't I get in some girl talk before we face some lizards and shit again? So, Rain, come on. What's happening?"

"*Kirsten,*" I hiss, "do I have to say it out loud?"

"No, don't worry about it," Raina replies suddenly, having heard it all. She takes a deep breath, stands tall, and stretches her back.

"I'm not worrying, Rain. I'm saying Kirsten is being a jerk."

"No, let her go. It doesn't matter."

"It matters, Rain. Your—"

"My what? My dad? I told you. It doesn't matter. So come on. What are you asking me, Kirsten?"

Kirsten's unfazed. I think maybe her adrenaline is kicking in again. Maybe her kindness to Prairie acted like an extreme sport or something, unlocking a trove of new chemicals in her glands that need exploring. She bypasses the comments on Mr. Harris, pretending none of it happened, treating the whole day—swamp monsters included—like the same high school drama we've been stewing in for three years already.

"I want to know why you were such a bummer this morning."

"Why I was such a bummer this morning..."

"Yeah."

"It's like I said. It doesn't matter."

"What doesn't matter?"

"He's dead, isn't he?"

My jaw drops. Kirsten squints, her smile sketched in place. Her endorphins, or whatever, get caught in a traffic jam of neural cross signals.

Prairie peeks around the wireframe display. "What do you mean?" she asks softly.

Raina presses her lips together and looks away. "I mean, he's dead. If it wasn't today, it'd have been six months. And if not six months, then a month after that."

Kirsten's teasing smile drops.

"And so on, and so on," Raina continues, "until he'd finally be gone."

The news is enough to make our current predicament shrink into the background. But instead of consoling her or asking for more details, what immediately flashes through my mind are my pettiest of problems. The prank, the mop bucket, Bridie and Skye...Even more trivial things still. They come to mind, accompanied by a swell of shame, until I realize my brain's putting things in their proper order, shuffling the unimportant ones to the back of the line so I can grasp what Raina's really saying.

What really draws me in are Kirsten's big emerald eyes, wide open and pleading for me to address Raina. I just look at her sadly, dumbfounded, unable to think of anything. If I say sorry, Raina will brush it off, claim it doesn't matter. Her dad's been spared one kind of death for another. I doubt it's worth comparing. And I don't think she's ready to grieve. Not while we're still in here.

Kirsten keeps her mouth shut, but Prairie doesn't share our little telepathic bond.

"I'm so sorry," she says. "What—"

"Colon. But...it doesn't matter." Raina's tears are close but not near enough to drop.

I can't imagine how strange it must be to anticipate some limited time left, to find you have none at all.

My priorities in order, silly issues pushed to the back, and my guilt somewhat assuaged, a fresh wave of it passes over me for being such a jerk to her before.

"I'm sorry," I say, blaming myself for making it sound so general-purpose.

Raina shrugs. "You didn't know."

I think about specifying, about apologizing again, for more and more of the things I've done. But it'd only lead to a fight. Her resolve has been blasted to pieces since I forced her to come this way. She had a mission before. Raina was driven. I've robbed her of it, but her pride won't let her admit that. This is her resigned to being resigned, so it's not just Bridie I feel responsible for now. It's, well, everyone at this point.

"What's this?" Raina points a lazy finger at the pill bugs, whose progress has stopped on the far end of the lingerie tent.

We watch the ones in the rear probe their comrades' shells with feelers and attempt to climb up their hindquarters to no avail. Ahead of them, the leaders bump into one another, refusing to go forward another inch. The water's too deep. They'd drown if they went any farther. Eventually, they decide on a direction and start taking the herd back toward us.

Kirsten clenches her fists. "Come on, you freakin' snails."

"They're not snails," I say.

"Yeah, I'm not an idiot. They just move like them."

"Give it a minute." Raina leans against the kiosk, looking bored, before doing a double take and standing up straight.

My eyes are already tracking what she sees.

A new shadow blots the foggy canvas in the atrium. Something with a craning neck and a twitchy energy, something an awful lot like our old friend, the lizard thing.

"God dang it," Prairie says.

"Are we backing up?" I ask. "We should back up. Get back to another kiosk or into a store or…"

Raina hands off the cane to Kirsten, who fumbles with her yard stick, and goes in search of more weapons. I do the same, using my peripheral vision to the max, looking for monsters, for anything long and heavy, swingy and bludgeony.

Finally, I end up pulling a downed diner table umbrella from the nearby kiosk, which sold suntan lotion and other summer stuff for the Spring Break crowd. I'm pretty sure Kirsten pocketed a small bottle of oil from there before. Sliding the top of the umbrella pole out of the bottom portion, I unscrew the base, giving myself a nice steel rod for doing some damage.

We line up four abreast, armed with our play swords. The shadow lizard tastes its surroundings and watches for prey while the pill bugs pass us by. The leaders enter the fog, and the shadow lizard twitches its head but does nothing. The bugs go right around it, passing it on all sides in their futile quest for drier ground.

Prairie groans. She points at the lizard, whose neck looks like it's sprouted another snout. "There's two of them."

The first one skitters forward, almost out of the fog now.

Kirsten clears her throat. "Guys, you know how I said I'm not an idiot?"

"Still trying to believe it, K."

"Try a little harder 'cause I have a pretty stupid idea."

"Is it the same one I'm having?" Prairie asks. With all eyes on her, she points at the pill bugs. "The lizards don't seem to care. What do you think of…you know?"

"Can we crouch that low?" I ask.

"We might have to crawl."

"If we can keep up by crawling," says Kirsten.

"Screw it." With that, Raina scuttles forward, staying low, heading straight for the back of the herd before it's out of range and no longer gives us any cover.

For Bridie, I remind myself. Screw it.

The three of us follow Raina, who lunges forward, splashing into the water and startling a pill bug. It moves to the side, and she scrambles on all fours next to it. We approach, just feet behind her.

The lizards keep periscoping, using whatever method they have to hunt for prey. Their prominent nostrils, beady black eyes, little earholes—I don't know. How do these lizards work? Everything about us might signal our presence to them.

Except our smell. Between the bloodbath behind us and the mosquito slime coating our jackets, that should be okay.

I'm also glad these armored goofballs aren't too disgusting, if you don't look closely. And they're shy. I crouch, trying to walk on the balls of my feet, my back hunched up just past the height of theirs. My boots keep sliding, so I have to get down to my knees. The water covers my lower legs, and half my forearm disappears into the murky water as we crawl. My wrapped arm aches from the added strain.

I think this is going to work until the edge of a pill bug's armor plate catches on my jacket and tears through to my skin, just above my wound.

"Yow!" I yelp.

"Yeah, watch out," Kirsten says.

The lizards' heads tilt this way and that, more rapidly than before. Their slimy whiteness stands out at this distance. We'll be clearer to them too. If their pattern detection is that good and they're hungry enough, they might just charge into the herd and take the soft treats hiding inside. Something about them just tells me they know what's up.

One foot at a time, we pass the final couple of stores before we hit the atrium. The pill bugs continue to give us cover. Is anyone alive inside these stores, watching us scuttle like fools across the floor?

An optimistic thrill flows through me. We're almost there.

The plan doesn't entirely go how we like, though, when the pill bugs pivot to the left and start making for the fountain. Inch by inch, foot by foot, the info desk grows more distant. The far end of the atrium as well.

Raina keeps following, head down. We all stick with it, hoping to find cover at the fountain. Who knows, maybe the pill bugs will bumble all the way down the next wing, just like we hoped for, simply taking a more circuitous route. But with every new vista opening in the fog, we encounter more horrific remains, floating bodies, and viscera. And with them, the possibility of some new monster whose hiding place we haven't guessed.

It's not just Raina making the decisions either.

Prairie calls to us, wondering what we're doing.

"Just keep going," I say.

"The lizards are moving," she responds.

I risk a look back. The lizards have turned to follow the herd. Both look as clueless as before but still as menacing.

They totally know we're here.

I fall on my butt, then get back to my knees, finding the pill bugs have turned again. The herd is breaking in two to go around the fountain. The ones on either side of me peel away, leaving me exposed.

Raina crouches by the fountain, watching the pill bugs split like a zipper. I scramble up next to her. Kirsten and Prairie join us, and we start creeping along the edge.

The lizards move closer, heads high, still gathering intel.

"Keep moving?" Prairie half asks, half tells.

There won't be any more cover past the fountain, except for the now randomly scattering pill bugs.

Raina looks ahead and quietly swears.

"Info desk." She gets up and starts running, kicking up water.

"Wait. Rain!" I hiss, but we've already given chase.

Raina leads us to the far end of the info desk, staying hunched. We keep our heads lower than the counter. It's a straight shot down the atrium to the Macy's wing.

Another silhouette appears ahead of us. Taller than the pill bugs, shorter and squatter than the lizards. Another frog. And we don't have any shields with us.

"The front way's blocked," Raina says.

"I see that," replies Kirsten. "Options?"

The pill bugs are nearly fully dispersed and begin the slow process of reorienting by clustering in small groups. The frog leaps off to our right, further blocking the way down the Macy's wing. The lizards, still trailing us and looking for more hints of prey, briefly catch on its movement.

Raina makes the call. "Screw it again. Break for the food court. We need to get away from the big boys."

I say, "Wait, what if—"

Kirsten blurts, "Yeah, Rain, what the—"

Without further warning, she's off again, tempting danger by sprinting in the open, her four-pronged cane swinging like a ridiculous Olympic torch. The three of us run after her, dodging the odd pill bug here and there.

The fog is intense. It should give us cover from behind, but we can't see what's ahead. With her lead, Raina very nearly disappears. We kick up a racket, splashing through ankle-high water but going slower than I like.

Prairie at my side, Kirsten just ahead, we rush into a waist-high wall. We've reached the children's play area—a little jungle gym with plastic bug-themed obstacles for kids to climb on. Fitting. Ladybugs and caterpillars and butterflies grin at us with rosy-red dimples and vacant dewy eyes. We slosh our way past it, coming to its far end and finding Raina inside, crouching behind the wall.

"What is it?" I ask.

She gestures for us to get down.

I gasp when a battering ram escapes the fog, swinging toward us. It's the size of a telephone pole—a grayish twiggy insectoid with wide-set, shaky limbs that stab the floor with tile-chipping strength. Nothing here gives us real cover. The creature trips over the half-wall, and it catches itself by placing a foot directly at Raina's. Raina huddles into herself.

I don't think twice when I swing my umbrella rod.

It connects with the gummy forelimb, which recoils in surprise and scrapes Raina's shoulder, then comes back, instantly and assertively, for me. I take another whack and connect again, but I can't keep up this fight. This thing won't be defeated by a rod alone.

Raina rolls out of the way and comes back to our side of the wall.

Kirsten screams next. I can already guess. The lizards. Sloshing through water, knocking aside pill bugs with their wobbling gait.

"Back! I mean, forward!" Prairie shouts, bounding over the wall into the play area.

Is she talking to me? The lizards? She swings her yardstick in the air, giving us cover from the lizards while Raina, Kirsten, and I hop the wall again. We deflect the lumbering stick bug's awkward steps, hoping to divert its course. I couldn't say if it wants to eat us or not, but it's pushing us toward some things that do. Kirsten slashes a leg out of the air. Her yardstick rebounds and lodges in the eye of a smiling ladybug.

I back into Kirsten. Prairie and Raina link up, and the four of us swing and swing. The lizards close in, keeping a safe distance, heads bobbing and tongues flicking. One rears on its hind legs and lets out a deep-throated hiss, experimenting with our reaction. But our reserves are depleted.

The stick bug has stopped stabbing. Instead, it sweeps its forelimbs through the air, more curious than wounded by our blows. One swipe makes Raina lose her balance. I get in front of her and dodge another.

"You good?" I call.

Raina scrambles backward, slipping in the water, and cries out a warning.

The stick bug's backswing catches my shoulder and knocks me over. I groan, more pain going through my wounded arm, and lose hold of my weapon. The monster looms over me, and a vague but all-encompassing fear goes through my body.

Like this is it.

Like I know it's going to hurt like hell, however it plays out, but because I can't entirely process what's happening to me, I can't tell how it's going to go.

Kirsten and Prairie pant from the exertion of repelling the lizards. Now their backs are exposed. Raina and I scramble backward and hit the backs of their legs.

The stick bug swings another leg over us, hitting nothing. It steps forward and lands a pincered claw next to me. From the trunk of its body—until now as solid as a log—two multi-segmented appendages emerge. A mouth opens and closes like a fish's. It reaches forward, its claws looking for purchase on my jacket. I have nowhere left to go.

A slash of yellow light and a brief burst of heat pass over my head. The appendages retract with the light swinging back and forth, and a body moves in front of me. A human body holding fire, stabbing forward, illuminating the stick bug's blunted face and causing it to retreat clumsily over the play area half-wall. The flame comes back toward me, reeled like a hatchet, and spills liquid fire onto my jacket. I smell burning oil and feel it eating down to the skin.

"*Ah!*" I scream, batting at the tongue of flame, putting it out at the expense of another burn to the palm of my hand.

The fire loop-the-loops through the air, catching the stick bug's trunk and causing it to leave us faster.

Another human shadow slips to the side, flame held high and burning through the fog. A few more arrive, invading the kid's play area. They stand over me and Raina and put themselves between Prairie and Kirsten and the lizards.

The person standing over me roars. That's when I notice how incredibly stylish his jeans are, how low slung over his hips, exposing a full three inches of plaid boxers underneath.

We're surrounded by another herd.

Not pill bugs. Not some pasty, soft, cuticle-looking mutants from the underworld. These are bronzed and toned, and their shells only encompass their lower abdomens in the form of six-packs honed by countless sit-ups.

One of them towers over me, his torch held high, scanning the horizon for threats. No jeans on this one. Is that...linen? Yeah. I guess that's right. Cupid doesn't do denim.

He reaches down with his free hand.

"Follow me!"

Follow Cupid. Or I mean, yeah... Joe. Turn to page 234.

Stand and fight with the girls. Turn to page 188.

The last tremor fades away, and the heat rises in me. A flutter of surprised voices comes from outside the store, security guards included. Raina has turned serious, Prairie looks petrified, and Kirsten's tears dry to salt before my eyes.

How dare the mall fall apart when I'm just warming up? For the first time in my life, I have the upper hand on Kirsten. I'm saying everything I've ever wanted to say, and it'll stick because I'm not going back. We're far enough into high school, I can afford to let her go. No one else has done more to screw up my life, and I'm happy to call this situation the cherry on top of her shit sundae.

If I'm going to claw my way back from my Kirsten-induced social ostracism, it's not going to be with her help. I'm resolved on the matter.

"What the hell now?" Kirsten complains.

Raina goes out to join the guards on the concourse, so with our chief mediator—at least on a good day—out of the way, I move in for the kill.

"Here's what's *now*," I say, going toe to toe with Kirsten. "We're done with each other."

"What?" she asks, returning to being embittered, just like that.

"I said we're done. And the funny thing is, you're right about me. I do always come back to you. I do always let you boss me around. I admit that I've been a coward. Okay? It's true. And what else is true is, it ends today."

"Dude, what are you—"

"Quinn," interrupts Prairie.

I steamroll past them both. "So, you can tell people whatever you want, which you will. And I choose not to care because whatever you say, I'll just prove wrong. You're going to keep bitching about me until the day you die because you can't stand it. You can't exist without me to boss around."

"Quinn, seriously, don't you want to see what's going on?" Kirsten tries to nudge past me.

I grab her shoulders and push her into the store's dank darkness.

"What the hell, Quinn!" She shoves me back.

Outside, people run along the concourse, though I couldn't say what direction they're going in. Prairie calls to Raina and is ignored. One of the security guard's radios lights up with staticky screaming.

"You're a bitch, Kirsten." I say calmly. I push her again, and she stumbles into the darkness. My insult connects, and she lowers her brow.

That old Kirsten anger is back. No longer playing the victim.

I expect her to charge past me, pretending like none of this is happening, ready to use the earthquake as an excuse to forget I worked up the nerve to confront her. Instead, she shakes her head and turns into the dark.

"Brother," Kirsten mutters, whisking stray hair from her face and kicking over a broom left leaning against the wall.

The exposed ductwork ahead of her shudders, which I assume to be an aftereffect of the earthquake. I wonder if it'll fall. Hope it will. Scare her. Hurt her.

I follow. We're not calling this a draw. She's not getting away from me. A sliver of rationality tells me to leave her alone, that the best way to prove my point is to turn my back and never acknowledge her again. But seeing her walking away, even in mock defeat, makes me recommit.

"Did you hear what I said?" I demand.

She spins lazily and meets my eye for a second before gazing at the concourse. Kirsten doesn't say anything. She doesn't move.

I step closer. Her face is scrunched, and she's paying me zero attention.

"Rain?" Kirsten murmurs, leaning forward and squinting.

I look back. People are sprinting away from the atrium. Only one guard is out there with Prairie. Raina is gone.

Kirsten gasps, spinning me back around and quickly disabusing me of the idea she's surprised by Raina's disappearance. Her stare goes a thousand yards, through glass and walls, beyond the spot where Raina last stood. Kirsten flinches and wheezes, and then she's wrenched backward onto the bare floor. A storm of shadows convenes over her, inky black limbs stabbing into her chest and stomach.

Before I can scream, more shadows appear behind Kirsten. They're low to the floor, nearly scraping the cement with every movement. They make no sense. But they don't need to for them to launch themselves at me, climb my legs, and plunge sharp fangs into my chest.

There is heat at first, followed by a numbness. More shadows leap and take me down. I can't move, my vocal cords constrict, and I suffocate as my lungs cease to operate. All the pain happens in my head. The alarm bell goes off, telling me this is the end.

I fade to black.

♥*♥*♥

Try again. Turn to page 88.

Clamped between the frog's binder-clip mouth, the centipede writhes and bends back on itself, unable to gain an advantage. I turn away from its foregone demise, unable to stomach the sight. To watch them turn on one another makes me see another side of their terribleness, an instinctual desire to fight, consume, and survive, which reminds me these are animals and not just murderers of humans, killers of my friend's dad.

I don't want to feel sorry for them. It's too weird, too...inappropriate. I look over Raina and Kirsten for injuries. Besides their dazed expressions, they seem okay. But what about Prairie? Or Bridie? Or Skye? These creatures may not be target-oriented SCUD missiles, but they're dangerous all the same, pouncing at anything that looks like prey, lashing out at whatever comes across as a threat.

I try to scrub from my mind all the baggage I've brought with me today. I can't keep lugging it around, wondering if Bridie had a hand in the prank or if Skye holds it against me. Those are shed easily enough, but Prairie's being here because of me? That ball and chain isn't going anywhere.

I jump when something brushes my shoulder. Kirsten looms over me.

"Quinn. We gotta go," she says, no longer Little Miss Sarcastic.

I lean forward, avoiding her touch. More screams issue from the floor below. People running for their lives, panicked, not taking stock. I want to avoid them more than I do the monsters.

Look at the mob in the hardware section, Warren the security guard...Pretty much everyone who ran like psychos at the first hint of danger...They've put us in this situation more than the monsters themselves.

Suddenly, the hope everyone we know is being helped by others dies. I don't want Bridie or Prairie to be with anyone else. Either they've made it outside or they're hiding, waiting for us.

Raina is hunting through the children's section.

"Rain, what're you doing?"

"I'm looking for something."

"We're getting out of here. Out this way." I gesture to the mall entrance beyond the appliance section. "If that thing came barging in here, it's gotta be the worst thing up here. Otherwise, it'd have picked a fight with something else."

And it would've sent a mob of shoppers running ahead of it, so we're good. No one's left up here.

Raina says, "Yeah, but—"

"No buts. If we want an eagle-eye view, we need to stay up here."

I almost tell her I want to avoid people, but I don't know if she'd agree.

Luckily, siding with Warren must have taught Kirsten a lesson. She says, "Rain, let's get outta here," before hazarding a look down the escalator and wrinkling her nose.

"Guys, come on. We should have some weapons ready or something. Hold on," Raina complains.

"To do what?" Kirsten counters. "What could you find up here that could do the same damage as anything in the hardware department?"

"Rain, let's just get out of here first and figure it out."

Kirsten adds, "Yeah, and if it's bad, we'll just...come back in here. The frog's got us covered from below."

Raina pauses, and from behind a clothes carousel, she frowns at something in her hand and drops it to the carpet with a thud. She trudges along and joins us by the washers and dryers.

"Thanks," I say, my feeble way of smoothing things over. "Let's see what we can see."

"Aaand, holy shit," Kirsten mutters, karate-chopping her arm across my chest and stopping me in my tracks. She backs away from the store entrance, pulling me with her.

A new set of pincers hovers by the mall entrance, bobbing to the beat of the Cars song playing overhead.

"Centipede?" Raina asks.

"Wait!" I knock down Kirsten's arm and inspect the thing more closely.

Another round of human screams and crashes comes at us from behind this new creature, so while I'm trying to take the initiative, I'm suddenly unconvinced the second floor will be everything I hoped it to be. I squint, trying to peer more beyond the tips of the pincers.

"That's not a centipede. It's a...It's a giant-ass earwig?"

"If you're trying to make me ralph, you're succeeding," Kirsten says.

"I don't know how that's better than a centipede," Raina mumbles.

"No, hold on." I move toward the thing.

A normal-sized earwig is ralph-worthy, sure, but on a scale of fluffy bunnies to spiders, they're not spiders. They run away from you. Their pincers are there for protection, not hunting.

"I bet we could make it," I say, honestly trying not to puke from its gooey, glistening, Crisco-colored shell and cancerous growths.

The girls don't get a chance to object.

A meaty thwack issues from outside the store, making the earwig's pincers flare up and out. Scuffling footsteps and hurried breathing accompany more thuds. Something is attacking it.

The earwig retreats and spins, swinging its pincers toward its aggressor.

Only, its attacker has already jumped and slid across its back, stumbling to his feet as he enters Sears. It's a teenager—someone I've never seen, but someone our age. He wields a metal pole with a little two-pronged knob on its end, like what store associates use to hang clothes on hangers way up on the wall.

The boy gets up, takes a wild swing at the earwig, and runs toward us, eyes bulging, covered head to toe in blood. One shoe is missing, and one hand is so bloody, a finger or two might be gone.

Something else is absent too, which I realize when he takes up his pole like a spear and shoves it straight into my throat.

I fall back and hit the open door of a dryer, knocking it shut before the back of my head cracks against it. The pole digs into my skin, cutting two small holes and shoving tissue into my esophagus. It pushes against my trachea, cutting off my breathing. The insane teen twists and thrusts again.

Raina and Kirsten scream and clobber him. He falls over, kicking, clawing, his mind gone. I pry at the pole, but the prongs don't align with their entry holes, and I tug at skin, trying to extricate it. My breathing weakens, my throat muscles unable to control the flow of air. Hot blood pours down my neck.

The teen scrambles backward into the earwig's pincers, which clamp around his waist. He hardly seems to realize it's killing him. Blood pours down his sides.

The shock comes for me. As Raina and Kirsten drag me away, the pole dangling from my neck, my mind goes blank.

The correct choice was to take the downstairs path.
Turn to page 169.

"Come on!" Cupid—er, uh, Joe, I guess—shouts, shaking his hand.

What's he think I'm going to do?

My arm stings, my chest throbs with the recent blow, and I'm bruised all to hell. My whole body flares with agony. But I still take a second to be amazed by his hand's smoothness and how the cords of his tendons flex like steel wires when he wraps it around my thin wrist. His fingers meet his thumb, and he pulls me up. Joe does it so fast, I nearly fall forward, but he catches me and sets me upright before helping Raina.

Something lands on my shoulder. I scream, spinning and slapping at whatever's snuck up on me, only to find another guy about Joe's age. His head is bandaged, and one bicep has been wrapped with bloody gauze, but he's otherwise free from manufactured clothing above his hips. He carries a torch in one hand, and after rubbing his jaw and groaning, he holds out his hand. I take it, my smaller one gobbled up by it.

We scramble over the half-wall, and he pushes me forward.

"Go! That way!" He swings his torch left and right, hollering as he goes.

More shapes loom in the fog, familiar ones, welcome ones that don't make me hesitate. One after another, spaced every ten yards or so, are chest-baring, torch-bearing Abercrombie models roaring like lions and beating their chests. Makeshift torches spew flaming fuel that fizzles in the floodwater. They become a line of beacons leading to the food court.

I make it to the seating area and snake my way past tables, hopping over floating bodies.

One glance backward shows the girls are following, their energy restored for one final sprint to safety. How much farther are we supposed to go?

My bodyguard pulls at my arm. I run, or rather trip over myself, until we get all the way to the Calgary Kitchen counter. Standing behind it, holding open a swinging employees-only door, is another model with buzzed black hair and a chunky metal necklace. He waves me in. I collapse under the smoothie machine, fully out of breath, when my bodyguard yanks me up by my jacket.

"Not yet," he scolds. He pushes me through the flapping door, inside the kitchen, and into the smell of damp baking bread mixed with swamp degradation.

Dew drips off pebbly cream-colored walls, and steel tables take up most of the space beside the massive ovens, with exhaust fans climbing into the ceiling. At the very back, a door leading to an access corridor is blocked off by a shifted stove with a wheeled prep cart stacked on top of it. Bloody handprints are streaked across the cart's steel structure. The door shows signs of splintering.

I turn around and clutch my bodyguard's shoulder. "Wh-where—"

"Hold on!" he screams. He slaps the door open as the others rush in.

First a model. Then Kirsten. Another model, Raina, then one more model. The last one skids to a stop and looks outside, his head turning side to side while he tries to cut through the fog.

"Prairie!" I say breathlessly.

Kirsten and Raina join me when I rush the kitchen entrance, and we fall backward together when Prairie bowls into us. On top of her falls another body. My breath leaves me, and I groan in pain and frustration as we extricate ourselves from the dogpile. A hand presses into my shoulder to balance itself.

Cupid. Joe Molson. The one to guide in Prairie.

No one notices I'm crying, but no one would mention if they did. Everyone breathes heavily, red in the face. Dripping with sweat, swamp water, and blood. The models have carried in their torches, which appear to be cobbled together from various kitchen utensils— ladles, spoons—with dishrags knotted around their heads. They make the heat inside the kitchen unbearable, even if they provide the only light, aside from the meager gray shaft of outside illumination coming through the swinging door's porthole. Before I know it, two of the models stuff their torches in a filled sink to extinguish the flames.

I look over our saviors, half marveling at their physiques, entirely grateful for their intervention, idiotically wondering why I'm worried about playing it cool in front of them. They must think we're idiots. Damsels in distress, for sure. But I shouldn't care about social graces, and I don't. More than anything, I'm impressed by how put-together they are. From what I can tell, they know what they're doing, and I'm suddenly more embarrassed.

Joe runs his hands through his hair and shakes his head, sprinkling his model-friend with water. I briefly replay it in my head, shot in slow motion, in black and white, with sensual pop music in the background.

Man, I have to start thinking of him as Joe. Good ole Joe Molson from church. Star of the football team. Not Cupid, the hunky stranger.

He speaks first, this hero among heroes. "Well, that was frickin' wild."

A model says, "Yeah, Jesus. Can we not do that again?"

"Seriously. I'm not leaving this kitchen. We need the frickin' cops."

"More like the SWAT team."

"Yeah, like they have a SWAT team in Madi-shit. Make me laugh some more."

"My dad would kill me if he saw me do that."

"Dude, your girlfriend would kill you."

"Yeah, that's what I'm saying."

"I shoulda stayed home today, man. I shoulda stayed home. I knew this job wasn't worth it. Anything farther than Aurora, I've always said is total shit. I tell all the guys not to do it. Not worth it."

"Am I bleeding? I think I'm bleeding."

"You were bleeding before."

"But, like, worse. Is there blood here?"

"Where?"

"On my back. It stings like crazy back there."

"Oh, whoa, yeah!"

"What do you mean, *whoa?* How bad is it?"

"Dang, how'd that *happen?*"

Joe speaks up. "Okay, guys. Take it to the back. Napkins and vinegar and...bandage him up." He rubs the bridge of his nose like he's fighting a killer headache, then leans on a counter and exhales.

Two of his Abercrombie models usher the wounded one to a sink while he complains, trying to glimpse the shallow gash weeping an admittedly dramatic curtain of blood down his right shoulder blade.

There are nine of them in total, counting Joe, whose placement at the front of the kitchen, paired with the direction of everyone's haggard, pleading expressions, suggests he's the rightful leader. Each of the models is in the same alluring stage of undress they'd been in for their job, all soaked through. Most of them are wrapped in an array of red-and-brown-stained bandages, freely bleeding from smaller cuts and scrapes. As fit as they are, sporting the sort of obsessively pursued BMI required for someone to bother paying you to take your photo, they're beat to crap, their spirits showing the cost of the day's battles.

They mutter some more about the stupidity of the rescue operation, utterly aloof to our presence. With every new complaint, my gaze wanders a little closer to the girls, to see if they're getting a load of the same thing. Raina shies away, pushes past a model to go across the kitchen, and starts redoing her braid. Kirsten pesters Prairie to check her for injuries too—which none seem to have been incurred.

I feel like I'm back in school. We haven't come through all this insanity, taken all these risks, fought off all those creatures, only to see ourselves dismissed so casually.

"Um, thanks for your help?" I say, letting my sarcasm sizzle like the oil fire from their torches.

Joe, as preoccupied as he appears, may not deserve it as much as the others. The sound of my voice makes him stand up taller, focus his eyes more, and nod, still looking like he's not ready for a conversation yet.

"Yeah...yeah," he says. "You're welcome." He pushes off from the counter and looks through the porthole.

"No, thank *you*," calls the model who's getting his back bandaged up. He looks over his shoulder at us. "For sabotaging our escape. *Gah!*"

His co-model pours vinegar over his wound.

Kirsten spins, knocking away Prairie, who's looking through rips in Kirsten's jacket for blood. "Escape? What do you mean?"

"We were getting out of here before you showed up. Man, I am so done trying to help people today."

"Where were you going?"

I prick my ears. News of a plan? Yes. Please. These guys can't have wandered far from the atrium. They've had a front-row seat to the mayhem.

The model sneers. "Away from those things, dumbass!"

Joe smacks his hand on the door, causing it to swing open. I jump at the noise and the sight of the open food court air, where the monsters are.

"Alex, chill. They didn't know what we were doing."

"Then we should've left 'em and gone our own way."

"Dude, *enough*." Joe's words thunder, not bouncing off the kitchen steel, but denting it deeply.

Alex is left shaking his head and wincing, with his two buddies dabbing at his back. The other guys look at their feet and chew the insides of their cheeks, seemingly despondent and disappointed but unable to really pinpoint what they want to say.

"Sorry about that," Joe goes on. "Where'd you come from anyway?"

I'm ready to answer, but Kirsten gives me the eye. While I don't get it at first, I see her kick Prairie's foot.

Prairie clears her throat and brushes her hair behind her ear. She stammers, "Uh, we came from J.C. Penney. Back that way."

Joe frowns. "Penney's? The east wing? You're sure?"

The models look at each other. Their muscles tense as they shift, holding themselves like they're getting ready for something.

Kirsten snorts. "What'd she say, man? Yeah, we came from Penney's."

"That's where we were going."

"No!" Prairie says. "You can't go there."

"Yeah, ix-nay on the enney's-pay," Kirsten says. "There's nothing but flooding, monsters, and floating bodies. We went up and down that wing just to find her, and both ways were nuts. Monsters jumping out of stores, blocking the exits, creeping overhead and crap..."

"There were a ton of people hiding down there less than half an hour ago," I say, "but not anymore. You might've heard. We...saw it happen."

Joe's eyes drop to the floor, and it's like his pupils expand to encompass his irises. His eyes turn dark and foreboding. Some models part their lips. Their shoulders sag and arms drop. They look to Joe, who does a better job hiding how stricken he must feel.

"But you made it down there and back. That means we can do it. We have the numbers. And weapons."

The models perk up, then they look at Kirsten, like they're tracking the ball at a tennis match. I'm already disappointed. Their plan is revealed to be worthless. We're back to fighting to push forward to Macy's.

Kirsten defers again to Prairie.

"That might be true, but...the exits are blocked. I don't think any exit down there will be open."

"What do you mean?"

"Yeah, why didn't you get out if you were down there?" asks the buzzcut model.

"It's all flooded." Prairie looks back and forth, waiting for someone to object.

We girls don't. Even if we're wrong about the hypothermia bit or the fact emergency services aren't waiting on the far side of the flooded pond of the parking lot, it's too late to go back. I've crossed it off my list of possibilities. Backtracking a second time feels too close to tempting fate. There are creatures in J.C. Penney too. And who knows how many sets of compound eyes and sniffing noses got a good look at us two times through, only waiting for us to wander around a third time to mount their attack?

The guys talk over one another, saying the same things we've already argued about. Our testimony doesn't matter. They haven't seen it with their own eyes. Only once they start pointing out that we're *girls*, that we couldn't bust our way out but *they* could, do I intervene.

"Shut the hell up!"

They stop talking. But the way they look at me suggests they're just waiting to pounce on my counterarguments and tell me I'm wrong.

"Listen to Prairie," I insist. "She got down there and survived all on her own, and we went after her. She's seen it all. Then *we* saw it all. There is no getting out from there. That's why we're heading to Macy's."

Joe, who watched his models bicker with crossed arms, refusing to interfere, points across the atrium. "That way?"

"That's our best bet. We started at Sears, made it to the doors, and it was the same story there. Frozen shut. Creatures everywhere."

I keep Bridie to myself. These guys aren't interested in another impromptu rescue op. Their only desire is to escape. Maybe they do stand a better chance going another way. Maybe we all do, if we stick together. I don't know. But Bridie's still out there, and I feel like as long as I push to find her, I'm being as brave as I'm supposed to be.

Joe's mouth becomes a thin line, and he passes a look to the other guys, communicating something I don't know. But they know something. He nods at the swinging door and tells us to follow. I subdue a thrill of terror at going back outside and join him behind the bakery counter. Prairie and Kirsten follow me, along with two shaggy-haired models who look like they could be brothers. Raina comes after them.

"Is it safe out here?" I ask.

"Don't worry about it. It's been quiet right around here." Joe leans his hip against the counter and jabs his thumb in the direction of Macy's. "That's where you're going?"

"Yes."

"No," he says. "You can't."

"Why not?"

"If you're saying the Penney's wing is full of monsters, it's worse over there. You can't see it now, but right on the edge of that wing, by Manz Jewelers, where it meets up with the center of the mall, is a big crack in the ground. That's where all the water and the steam has been coming from. That's where *they* came from, and most of them ran that way."

He lowers his hand and hangs his head. I glance at the others, who all appear just as defeated.

"But...Bridie, my sister, is over there."

Joe frowns, and he does me the courtesy of looking me in the eye. "I'm sorry."

"How can you say it's full of creatures? How do you know?"

He gestures at himself. "I was working when the crack formed. It didn't leave us any time to react. Steam started blasting out, then water, and the creatures came right along with it. It was like a zit popped. Everything came out at once. I fought my way to the middle of the mall, joined up with these guys at Abercrombie, and made it over here. We watched more and more of those things crawl out of the ground and go down that way. And if they went in another direction, more often than not, they came back.

"Then the fog got too heavy, and we weren't able to see much more. We wouldn't have found you girls if we hadn't already started scouting our way out of here. Even if we'd heard you but were still hiding in here, there's no guarantee we would've...*could've*..."

"But you must've heard the guitar playing over there, right? There are people over there."

Joe shrugs and ruffles his hair. "I can't explain that. There's gotta be some survivors. I don't know how. We're not in the best shape to go looking for them. It's like Alex said. We were just trying to get out.

"Look, I want to trust what you're telling me. If it's bad down that way, it's bad. I get it. I don't think there's any place in here that's safe. But trust me on this too. It's bad down *that* way. We saw what went down there, and we haven't seen anything come back, human or otherwise. We don't expect any route is going to be monster-free. We know we have to fight. Our best bet now is on Penney's."

"No," Prairie says. "There's the flooding, for one thing. And you may have seen a lot of creatures in the open, but there are tons that are laying in wait. That's what got all those people before. They tried hiding in the stores, and the creatures came in through the back. They like the darkness and the warmth. In fact, I don't think a kitchen is the best place to be hiding..."

"Oh, we know that, believe me. Haven't you noticed there aren't any bakers or burger flippers around? We busted in here to find most of the staff carved up and the last one cut in...well, still alive while this thing was...What matters is, we fought it off, got it out the back door, and sealed the place up. Like I said, we're willing to fight. So if you tell us what you saw back there, it'll help us prepare. You can come with us too. We'll protect you."

Kirsten rolls her eyes. "He's not listeninnng."

Joe sighs. "What is it?"

"You're only hearing what you want to hear."

"Which is?"

"That there are fewer monsters to fight. You're ignoring what we said about the flooding and the frozen doors. Oh, and the mountains of dead bodies in the way. And jeez, some of those doors are probably locked too. Security guards were sealing off flooded entrances way before all this happened. So, listen. You can beat up as many of those things as you want, but it's only to get you to a door that won't open for you. And if it does, you're going to be a bunch of beefcake popsicles because it's subzero degrees outside and windier than the inside of a tornado."

"She's not lying," Raina says, looking more worn-out than before.

I've never seen her features so hollow, hopeless, but I'm kind of glad she speaks up. Joe might take her more seriously, given how much more like hell she appears than the rest of us.

"And it's the same at Sears."

"Yeah, we kept our eyes on Sears. Bad stuff through there too. That's why we haven't considered it."

Raina nods to indicate behind her. "What about the theater? No one's—"

"No." It's not just Joe who says it. The model-brothers, until now silent and attentive, speak with him, more loudly and desperately.

Joe clears his throat and averts his gaze. "Stay away from the theater," he says. "We saw what went in there."

I've never seen circles actually forming under someone's eyes, but all three guys look depleted, like they're hearing some ancient evil voice speaking inside their heads. The theater is just off to our right, on the north side of the atrium. Its still-lit ticket booths stand out in the cottony fog. On a day like this, tons of people went to catch a movie. We almost did too. Now the guys are telling us there's nothing left inside besides something far worse than can be put to words.

"It makes sense the creatures would go to Macy's, if it's less flooded," says Prairie. "If they're trying to avoid the water, it makes sense."

"So, we're down to two options. Macy's in one direction, with more creatures but presumably better conditions at the doors. Or Penney's in the other direction, with fewer creatures but worse flooding." Joe looks out into the gray, pondering.

"My sister is down by Macy's," I say, not actually knowing it, only assuming that's where Skye's guitar solo came from.

"You told me, and I'm sorry. But we're not making a decision based on that alone. There are eight guys here who are all from out of town. Their families have no idea what's happening to them. I'm only thinking through the risks."

Prairie says, "Don't assume you know how many creatures are down the Penney's wing. And besides, the water is only rising higher every minute. The mall is sinking. Everything is going to fall down into that crack soon."

"We know. We've felt it."

"Right. So, the less water around us, the better. Less risk of collapse."

I go up to Joe. It feels weird. I've never talked to him before, outside of shaking his hand at church, exchanging a shy "Peace be with you." But it takes the mop-haired guys out of the equation. It puts Prairie's arguments behind me. I need to make an impression, need him to see who I am, to remember my face and Bridie's name.

"Joe."

He flinches at my show of familiarity.

"Bridie and her friends are down there. And as of a few minutes ago, they were still alive. You heard the guitar. If they can make it, so can we. There's no one left down by Penney's. They're...slaughtered. So if you want strength in numbers, if you want to rescue all these guys, please, *please,* come with us."

He looks at me with regret. With remorse. I've cornered him. He doesn't want to have to say it again, that he's not willing to help. I wish I could be angry enough with him to scream, and I almost am. Maybe I'm trying to build up to it, but I've fought with so many people today, and none of them have been interested in anything other than saving themselves.

"I'm sorry, but there isn't a lot of time to make up your mind," Prairie says.

Your mind, she said. It might just be the Quinn and Prairie Show from here on out. And like every other time someone has noted the mall's failing structural integrity, it groans like a victim pinned under a crashed vehicle. The high-pitched grumbling descends into an unnerving, heavy clunk.

The day is darker, and pretty soon, it won't matter that there's fog in here. Even with the available light, which will probably fail at some point anyway, we'll be left in the dark with creatures that lived in it for decades.

Joe runs his tongue over his teeth and turns away. "We won't stop you, but I need to think of the guys first. They came to me."

"*Please*," I beg. "Please, come with us and you'll see it's the right way."

"Quinn, I'm—"

"Shut up," Kirsten says. She's holding up her hand and staring into the fog, her eyes locked on something I can't make out yet.

We position ourselves around her, and she points toward the food court's containment wall, to a shadowed form low to the floor. It moves in our direction and resolves into a pill bug. A number of its legs are missing or mangled. There's also a crescent-shaped bite mark etched into its armored plates, which leads me to think it was attacked by a lizard during our last escape.

"All those things have been down there for years without us humans, right?" Kirsten asks. "Everyone's gotta eat something."

"What are you getting at?" asks a mop-haired brother-model.

She looks past everyone, right at me, her hair somehow bouncing playfully off her shoulder. Her devious grin, the one she makes when she thinks of dumping filthy mop water on people's heads, is back.

"Quinn? Idea?"

Give up and go it alone. You won't win over these guys.
Turn to page 128.

Try to convince Joe with Kirsten's crazy idea.
Turn to page 89.

A last tremor passes through my legs. The echoes of the earthquake shrink into nothing.

So, what's this? Telekinesis? Will I get blamed for this now too? That would add a whole new layer of absurdity to this day, but I kind of wish it was true. I wish I caused an earthquake, if only to freak out Kirsten once and for all.

The male security guard lets go of the store's doorframe. He steps carefully onto the concourse, as if the floor will drop out from under him. Ponytail follows. Employees file out of the optometrist's next door, and some shoppers stop outside our dormant storefront, all looking where the boom came from, which is now the source of a loud hissing sound.

A thicker fog rises from the first floor, like some roadies broke in and turned on a bunch of smoke machines. It spills over the balcony and creeps across the gawking people's feet. It comes to the windows, climbs up the glass, and crawls through the entrance, which, paired with the darkening skylights, only obscures our view even more.

Raina is the first to regain her senses and leave the store. She squints in the same direction as everyone else. Kirsten goes next, getting outside and throwing up her hands.

"What the hell now?" she mutters.

Following the hissing comes a new sound, like breaking waves or a washing machine with its agitator going—something watery that's definitely not the fountain.

Then the screaming starts. Nothing like the kind a cheerleader like me is used to. Not the screams of a crowd braying for a penalty flag or applauding the football team's appearance from the locker room. There's no control of any kind. The screaming isn't part of a show. It's spontaneous and desperate.

They must be screams for help.

I mean, there's just been an earthquake in the middle of Wisconsin. You tell me where the nearest fault line is, and I'll tell you why that's so crazy. So, should we help? Is anyone going to? I know CPR, thanks to health class and a strict coach. But who needs CPR after an earthquake?

The people outside our store, Raina and Kirsten included, crane their necks and look over the railing, tracking something on the first floor.

"What's he doing?" asks someone.

They turn back toward the atrium. Kirsten yelps, and Ponytail grips the pepper spray on her belt. The group breaks apart when someone sprints through them, past our store, and away from the atrium. He shoves one of the shoppers in the arm, and they holler at him, but he doesn't break his pace.

Next comes a woman with a double stroller, her face more drawn than a melted candle. The group makes room for her, and more of them question the woman, who says nothing while making a hasty retreat.

The screams keep coming. Short, loud, gasping ones. Interrupted ones. Ones without any hope of rescue, that don't ask for help or plead for anything at all. Just...screams. There are no anguished cries, like cries of grief. The earthquake's done. What else is there to be afraid of?

Sloshing water too. The sounds of people running through floodwaters. More people start pushing past our group of gawkers, and one or two at a time, our group starts retreating too, wearing worried, uncomprehending looks on their faces. Raina, Kirsten, and the two security guards maintain their positions, all bent forward, searching the fog.

"Can you see anything?" asks Ponytail.

"Nothing," her partner responds.

"What's going on?" I ask, needing to hear something, *anything*, other than the screams. My heart pounds. I kind of don't want to know, hoping to keep this at a distance, whatever's happening.

But within a matter of seconds, whatever's happening closes in on me. It's heralded by shocked gasps from the people who remain outside the store with Kirsten and Raina. An optometrist's assistant blubbers and covers her mouth.

"Kirsten?" I say.

The sounds of splashing feet increase, coming closer. A horde of people run down the first-floor concourse toward J.C. Penney.

"'Kirsten...Raina." My voice trembles.

Ponytail jumps when her radio explodes with noise, bringing the distant sound of screams closer, made ghastlier by the crackly static. A shiver runs down my back. Prairie makes the first peep I've heard since we got here, and I move to her side without thinking.

Ponytail unclips her radio and holds it to her mouth, waiting for a break in the screaming. She's on the verge of tears, visibly struggling between cutting off the desperate call and asking for clarity. There's someone on the other side after all. Someone in a predicament so dire, they can't speak its nature.

With a final shocked cry, the last of the group in front of our store leaves, joining the growing number of people running away from the atrium. We're down to ourselves and the security guards. Instead of retreating, the latter two creep toward the action, drawn by whatever sense of professionalism they have to earn their paychecks.

One man running away is covered in red and white. I mistake the colors for some kind of Valentine's Day costume. The white is fluffy and the red shiny. A performer maybe? An angel to Joe Molson's Cupid? But that's not what I see.

The man's appearance sticks in my brain even after he's long gone. His matted hair, the hitch in his step, his trailing arm...What I took to be fluffy white angel's wings was the down stuffing spilling out of the back of his shredded puffer jacket. The scarlet I took to be some kind of vinyl or other shiny fabric was actually blood covering his head and torso, and the white halo—a glistening combination of red and white—a sliver of hard bone. An exposed section of his skull.

"Kirsten! Raina!" I shout, suddenly lightheaded, feeling like they're a million miles away. We need to stick together. That's become the most important thing. I step falteringly to the store entrance. Kirsten's closer, and I reach out to pull her back in.

She flinches and jerks away, but her face is full of alarm. Kirsten sees what I'm trying to do. Stick together, work as a team. She turns around and extends a hand toward Raina.

But Raina's already running. She goes toward the atrium, against the tide of terrified people.

And suddenly, everything feels a thousand times worse.

"Raina!" I shout at the same time as Kirsten. I exit the store and stand next to her.

The distance is blurred by a wall of fog. All the lights in the mall—the overhead lamps, the shop fronts, the neon signs—swim inside a cloud, looking like a Ferris wheel has sunken into a bog. The skylights do next to nothing to counter the gloom. There's no natural daylight left.

More people stream out of the fog on both levels. Their feet throw up a symphony, sloshing in the ankle-deep water. They bump into one another, push each other to the side, throw looks backward as they go. They smash into obstacles like signs, kiosks, furniture, and other people downstairs.

She isn't coming back. And we can't wait for her.

Raina's gone.

Kirsten looks at me. We know where she's going. And wouldn't you know it? It's the same plan as before. Get to Sears. Get out. It's just that there's apparently something worse than a bunch of mall cops in our way.

Kirsten's mouth sets into a grim line. Her nostrils flare. Maybe we are telekinetic because we don't need to discuss it. I dig in my toes and get ready to run, when suddenly I remember.

"Prairie!" I shout.

She stands in the store's entrance, her shopping bag clutched to her chest, our purses dangling from her arm. I nod at her, and she stares back, wide-eyed.

Before I give the nod to Kirsten, a sound emanates from the dark bowels of the store—a metallic skittering, like an animal is loose in the vents. But it's more than just one animal. It's like a basketball team running sprints. Another shiver runs up my spine, and before one more second can pass for us to decipher what the hell is going on, I push Kirsten and start running after Raina.

More people come racing toward us. A hand slaps my face. I ricochet off someone's chest, sending them flying into a store window. The smell of copper fills my nostrils when a bloodied woman collapses in front of me, streaking my jacket with blood.

We barrel through the fog, getting better at dodging bodies, sprinting through openings, and shouldering our way through others. The athletic ones have already gotten away. Men and women holding kids, older folks, and nonathletic people, one of whom I topple into a cafe table set outside a makeup shop when he doesn't look up from his jogging, still litter our path.

I keep Kirsten's bouncing blond hair in front of me. Just follow the plan.

The fog gets worse. The swampy odor has reached a never-before-smelled level of disgustingness. I almost lose track of the mall's geography, which is ridiculous. It's practically a straight line. We'll run straight through, I tell myself. Whatever's in the way, we're just passing through. Raina and her dad and Kirsten's Cherokee are mere minutes away.

We get close to the atrium, close to where the fog blooms from out of the floor. Not so normal for an earthquake, I think, but nothing about today *is* normal.

Those escaping the atrium thin out, but we haven't gotten away from all people. We've only shifted from the ones who made a clean break to those who are actively fighting for their lives, at least according to the silhouettes and sounds of combat we hear from all around us.

Desperate screams surround us. I try to focus on our mission, but the shadow plays going on in front of me, off to the sides, are too alarming to ignore. Shapes larger and faster than men loom through the fog, flitting through it with ease. Lightning-flash slashes of dark swords cut through human-shaped blobs. Other inhuman forms make buzzing noises, wet sounds, hissing sounds. They meet in the fog and tussle and collapse to the floor before disappearing in opposite directions.

This is a terrible mistake. What are we thinking? Why are we following Raina? What's the point of rescuing someone who's rescuing someone else, when no one knows what's happening?

We get to a semicircular section of railing by the skywalk and run ourselves into it. The atrium is right below us. Carnivalesque lights pierce the gloom. Glimpses of shiny shield-like bodies, knobby appendages, and glistening flesh come from the fog. We don't have time to take any more of it in.

"First floor or second?" Kirsten asks.

"First!"

Where it's flooded? That's where Raina will be, where her dad will be, in the tool section. That's where the car is. Am I answering her correctly? I don't know. We just need to keep moving. Kirsten starts running again, following the railing, coming to the stairwell, and heading down.

Caution tape is ripped from this stairwell too, in everyone's haste to get away. Some haven't made it. We have to jump over bodies on the stairs, reaching the epicenter of the crisis, the belly of the beast.

We just have to keep running and go straight through. Sears. Raina and her dad. Kirsten's Cherokee.

Blood pools on the landing. I flinch away from an arm still clutching the railing, the rest of its body gone.

Just a little farther. That's all I'm thinking, when an image flashes in front of me. Skye's eyes, looking at me from the first floor, surrounded by raging seniors. My sister's eyes, gazing in disbelief while her friend, Nicole, cries out in pain.

Oh my God.

Where is Bridie?

We're past the landing, close to the first floor, where water laps at the top of the bottom step.

I almost say something to Kirsten, knowing deep down it doesn't change the fact I want to get the hell out of here. But I have to tell her. She's not thinking of Bridie at all. None of us were. I take a deep breath, look up into the fog between me and my sister, and only scream. When I see what's standing in our way, I can't get the words out.

It's shaped like a lizard, its skin whitish and glossy, like a waterlogged worm. Almost foamy too, like it's swollen from the fog. It raises itself on hind legs to reach the height of a man, its gnarled forelegs scooping at the air with batwing claws.

Kirsten looks up and screams too. We reel backward. Our feet slip out from under us. Our butts land hard, and we slide down the last few steps to the first floor.

The thing looms over us.

It's a day just for us, Kirsten said.

No boys allowed.

No girls that suck either, for that matter.

I'm taking my girl shopping, Maura!

Better get started on that new closet for her, Mr. Carpenter!

You just see. We'll make her dreams come true!

It unleashes a hoarse song from a throat hidden behind a wide, flat mouth, with rows of teensy tiny razor teeth.

Yeah.

Happy Anti-Valentine's Day, Kirsten.

♥*♥*♥

Run for the food court. Turn to page 191.

Retreat upstairs. Turn to page 103.

Attack. Turn to page 293.

We're a team, and despite the advantage of all this added brawn, none of us think for a second about splitting up. The guys agree and organize themselves into the same trios they had during their last escape attempt and unplanned rescue of us.

Joe insists on breaking things up, however. He plans on going first, with Prairie. I may have picked the direction, Kirsten might have spearheaded the food chain strategy, and Prairie laid out the details, but Joe's Napoleon complex is unrivaled, apparently.

"It's not rocket science," Prairie tells him. "Veggies, salt, sugar, and flour to the non-scary ones. Meat for the predators."

The grave look on Joe's face tells me not to press the issue. Maybe he thinks the boys need to see we have some skin in the game.

Before Prairie tries again, I tell her she'll be safe with him and that I'm right behind her—one last push past her inhibitions, even if I don't like it.

Prairie takes a deep breath and agrees. She'll accompany Joe and Tremaine. Raina, Kirsten, and I make up the second team. Behind us are Ramon, Tomi, and Omri. Alex guards our back with Brian and the mop-haired brothers Sam and Tim.

One person from each team, me included, pushes a cart full of foodstuffs. Another carries a single lit torch, with others ready to go, and the remaining members wield newly cobbled-together weapons. Everyone wears a shield fashioned from a sliding stainless steel door ripped from the Calgary Kitchen cabinets, wrapped in a band of Saran wrap to give it something of a handle.

We roll out of the food court and into the fog, ten paces between teams, our cavewoman quartet turned into a quadruple-sized caveperson clan.

Outside the food court, pill bugs mill about like lost cattle. They're joined by some new arthropod-like things. Not the full-sized water skimmers we glimpsed in J.C. Penney, but smaller and skinnier, skating along the water's surface with a surprising degree of grace.

Joe's team halts when they appear. A bug like this should be smaller than a fingernail clipping. Magnified to this size, every appendage, each segment, is designed to terrify. Yet they wander around as blithely as the pill bugs.

Prairie taps Joe's shoulder. As the cart pusher, she rips open a bag of iceberg lettuce and throws a torn-off clump of it at one of the mini water skimmers. She hits its antennae, but the bug hardly notices. Prairie shakes the rest of the lettuce out of the bag and tosses it. The bug ignores it and glides off into the fog.

She frowns. Joe and Tremaine scowl but don't say anything. At least, not yet.

Prairie motions for Joe to keep going and pushes her cart again. After a few steps, Joe puts up his hand. We stop, not even halfway to the play area.

I leave my cart and grip my shield. Joe rotates his wrist and beckons for Prairie. Another mini water skimmer appears, moving faster and nearer than the first. Its antennae probe the surface of the water.

Prairie rips open a flour bag, coating the front of her jacket with its contents, then heaves half of it in the bug's direction. A hardened plop of flour lands in front of the mini water skimmer. It gets a thick dusting along the top of its body but keeps moving.

Joe's shoulders drop. The guys will start losing faith. Alex's rebellion might start anew.

The water skimmer approaches me. We need to give it another shot. None of the guys will try. I drop my shield and grab a pack of sugar. Stepping away from my cart, I rip the bag open and dump all its contents in the bug's path.

The sugar dissolves in a silty clump, and my retreat helps swirl it around. The bug barrels into it, its antennae going clear overhead, sensing nothing. Then its face hits the sugar clump, and the bug comes to a screeching halt. For a few seconds, it does nothing. Then, little face appendages shovel sugary water into its mouth. It drinks as much as it can, swinging its head in an ever-wider circle, looking for more.

A wave of sighs and quietly uttered exclamations pass through the group. Prairie relaxes.

"Idea," Kirsten whispers. "Mix it with the flour. Make sugar bombs so it'll stick to whatever we throw them at."

After giving it a thought, Prairie agrees. I tear open one bag each of sugar and flour, wet my hands, and make sugar/flour snowballs for Raina and Kirsten to lob in all directions. Prairie, Joe, and Tremaine do the same, as do the rest of the beefcakes. Soon enough, the group is hurling sugar bombs out in a wide fan before us, throwing far into the fog. The bombs splash into water and smack against walls and windows, where we hope, with some confidence, they'll attract some sweet-toothed swamp monsters.

We eventually pass the play area. I notice for the first time how much blood stains the plastic bug fixtures while a child-sized shoe spins slowly in an eddy. Joe doesn't give it more than a cursory glance. He has to keep his eye on the prize and keep leading the group.

I wonder if the other guys know what he saw or how he reacted. It's just the kind of thing a guy like Alex could use to take Joe down a notch. I'm grateful that doesn't seem to be the case.

We're in open terrain now, heading for the info desk. Overhead, metal beams creak and groan. Loud cracks signal tormented skylight glass, which I'm surprised hasn't shattered and fallen on us yet. Outside, the blizzard maintains its attack, pelting the windows with snow and wind. I can hardly see outside without any discernible natural light.

The info desk comes into view, its counter splattered with sugar bombs, a couple of which have attracted some arthropods. We catch up to Joe's team just as they crouch by the wall and he waves for us to hide.

Ahead of us, the ghostly form of a giant frog hops into view, going to the other side of the desk. We hold up our shields far from our bodies and listen to its splashes continuing down the length of the info area. Once it seems safe, like the frog is well behind us, Joe inches away from the counter. The fountain is our next stop before hitting the Macy's wing.

Before Joe can build momentum, Alex urges him to move. His team, closest to the frog, clatters its shields against the desk, throwing pleading looks forward.

Joe nods, but he freezes again. The beefcakes are already bunching up, leaving Kirsten, Raina, and I nowhere to go. I catch a glimpse of what Joe sees: the statuesque form of a lizard's head protruding from the fog.

"Get your shields up," Raina says, turning to the beefcakes in the back. When I do as she commands, she stops me. "No! Not for us."

Raina hands me a spear and pushes me to join Joe's team. She instructs us to hold out our weapons, and we turn ourselves into a spiny bush facing out to the lizard.

"What are we doing?" Kirsten asks.

"Hush."

Everyone's about to lose it. The beefcakes in the back are quaking, and we're stuck in the middle, with a lizard in front of us.

A loud slap turns me around. The beefcakes yelp and swing their shields, cracking them against the counter and smashing them in the water.

The frog has emerged from the other side of the info desk.

The beefcakes are only further provoking a hungry predator. I can barely move and can't think how to help, wondering if the frog's already nabbed one of their shields.

It throws back its head, revealing a wide mouth full of wiggling appendages.

It's swallowing one of our sweet-toothed arthropods whole.

The beefcakes continue panicking and keep pushing into us.

"Wait!" Joe hisses. "The lizard!"

It only takes another moment for the lizard to advance. We put up our spears. The beefcakes haphazardly reassemble their shield wall while the frog gulps down its meal. The lizard's head tilts one way, then another. With spring-loaded efficiency, it pounces into the fog and reemerges with an arthropod, its wriggling thorax caught in a lipless mouth.

We keep our spears trained on the lizard as it swallows, tilts its head again, and observes us with a plastic-black eye. It skitters to the other side of the info desk, tracing the frog's path and startling it into retreating too.

After a stunned moment, Joe leads on, reminding us to keep our distance.

We reach the fountain amid a crowd of pill bugs, arthropods, and water skimmers, which I think we've drawn out with the sugar bombs. Once we crouch by the fountain for another breather, we make another stockpile for the final push forward.

"The crack will be right ahead of us," Joe says, nodding toward Manz Jewelers. He tests the sharpened point of his spear against his thumbnail, shaving off a little white curlicue. "Where they came from.

And we need to make sure we don't fall in. It's their front door, so let's assume it's going to get nasty."

Once every cart's top level is piled with sugar bombs, we move. If our other foodstuffs on the bottom levels get washed away, that might be okay. Sugar bombs have proved effective so far.

Joe breathes deep and grabs a bomb. "Start chucking."

He tosses it, and a few seconds later, it makes a plunk. Everyone joins in, seeding our path with dissolving sugar—tempting out hapless prey from the shadows and hungry predators to the feast.

We throw twice as many bombs as we did on our way to the info desk. It's all about getting past the crack, but are we overdoing it? Sounds come from all sides and above—skittering noises from creatures that seem to move without exhausting themselves, unlike us.

Joe makes straight for Manz Jewelers, and I shoot a look at Kirsten. "Is he serious? Didn't we warn him about stores?"

I call to Prairie. She looks back at me while Tremaine helps push their cart against the water. Prairie nods and reminds Joe.

"The crack is right ahead," he says, speaking up for all our benefit. "We have to keep from falling in. It's just these couple stores on our left."

He keeps us on the same path, and we pass under the gleaming letters of Manz. Inside, its display cases are all smashed, coated in blood and gore. Granted, there are no good hiding places in here for any creature. Joe goes inside first, approaches a pillar, and peeks out on the Macy's wing. The rest of the group piles in behind us.

"We're down to the last of the sugar," I warn.

"Yeah, well, we chucked a ton of it past the crack, so we should be good. Make the rest into bombs now. Let the bugs start eating what we chucked."

We roll together a last batch of sugar/flour snowballs. Then I rip open my bags of hamburger patties, chicken nuggets, and Chinese chicken, just in case. I chuck the last of the empty bags into the water and throw the rest of the vegetables off the cart.

Kirsten fishes through the water for some jewelry. "Anyone want some souvenirs, now's your chance," she says.

The beefcakes regard her with annoyance. They must not have their own version of her in their group. Tomi might have the same spark of mischievousness in his eye, if he weren't under such immense stress. As if Kirsten isn't stressed herself.

"Guys, this is when it gets messy," Joe announces. "Keep your shields out and torches up. Hold your weapons tight. Throw the last of the bait as soon as we're past the crack." Quietly, Joe speaks to me and Prairie. "Bridie next. Then Macy's, and we're outta here."

I say, "If she's in Band Avenue, that's on the second floor. We gotta let them know we're here."

"We'll call to them when we get there. Nothing before," Joe says. "Let's do this thing."

He waves on the beefcakes, and we leave Manz.

At the first storefront, a skinny new age shop, Tremaine and Joe push together with their shields and peer inside. Tremaine lobs a few sugar bombs and two handfuls of burger patties around the entrance. Joe takes a perfume-soaked towel from Prairie and whips it across their path, spreading its scent like lamb's blood to keep away whatever death may lurk within. He crosses the threshold, and the two of them stand guard as our team moves past. When the last two groups cross, Joe and Tremaine take back their original spots.

At this point, everyone checks overhead. We're just passing under the atrium skywalk, where shredded Valentines Day streamers and bunting hang. On our right is the seating area where I last saw Bridie—the scene of Kirsten's prank. For all this talk of a crack forming around here, I wonder if I know *how* it began. A mop bucket cracking the foundation, unleashing Mother Nature's mistakes to do the rest. It can't be true, but I hate to think it's possible.

We get to the next store, and Joe and Tremaine take up guard duty again.

"There it is," Joe whispers.

He points to a spot just on the verge of where the fog takes over. The floor is buckled, sloping into a thin, jagged chasm, like the mouth of a rotten jack-o'-lantern. The near part of the floor is caved in. The other side almost looks level. The crack goes from one side of the concourse to the other, running to the shattered windows of the next store we have to pass, right on the other side of its entrance.

This is it. The door to the underworld.

The water laps inside its cavernous opening, making a guttural echo, and when the waves recede, foggy fumes belch forth before being snuffed by incoming surf. The fog emits an odor mixing putrescence and chemical artificiality, like a bathroom full of sweaty workout clothes and an unflushed toilet.

Where are the creatures? We couldn't be closer to the monsters' lair unless we put on scuba suits and dove in. I get they're flooded out, but wouldn't they stick close by, waiting to go back home? They were forced to escape into our world, which is now a frozen, desolate place. I wince at the thought.

After today, none of these creatures will be left alive. Without their home, they'll freeze if they make it out into the open. Or eventually, someone will come and kill them all.

Joe peers inside the store, tossing in bait and smearing perfume before crossing and signaling for us to follow.

Prairie's up next, but she can't move. Her cart's stuck in the deeper water, its chintzy rotating casters unable to stay straight. She turns it around and starts to pull. Kirsten moves to help, but I need her assistance with my cart too. So do the guys behind us. Ramon raises a bow wave with his cart, really putting his back into it.

"C'mon," Joe hisses.

He passes a nervous glance inside the store, then rushes across its threshold, pulling Prairie's cart before remembering the plan. "Why are we doing this? Just chuck the rest of the bombs and—"

Joe stops at a loud clap.

Kirsten gasps, and I look up to Prairie and Joe.

Tremaine isn't standing guard anymore. He's suspended in the air, legs wriggling, his shield slamming against the wall. A hairy, spidery arm, hidden among fallen bunting, pulls him up by the wrist.

Joe ditches his spear and jumps for Tremaine's legs, wrapping them in a hug and yanking the model down a few feet. Tremaine screams. Raina lunges and folds herself around Joe, breaking the creature's grip and bringing them all down to the floor.

I watch it all from behind my cart, holding a suddenly useless sugar bomb. The other beefcakes scramble past me to mob Tremaine. They wave torches in the air and brandish their spears.

Kirsten looks back and mutters, "Oh, shit."

I turn. None of the beefcakes are left behind us, and the last two carts have been knocked over, their sugar bombs dissolving in the water. Coming in, close to Manz, are statuesque forms. Arcing necks.

The lizards are back.

"We gotta go!" I holler, throwing the rest of my sugar bombs as far as I can. Then I go to the cart behind me.

"What are you doing?" Kirsten cries.

I don't answer, just scooping up as many melting sugar bombs as I can and lobbing them in front of us, behind us, in the direction of the lizards, toward whatever. And because we haven't tried it yet, I pitch the meat directly at the lizards, in the wild hope they'll pluck it up and leave us alone.

I'm not counting on it, though. All we have is speed now.

"Well, that lasted long," says Kirsten when I rejoin her.

The beefcakes let us into their shield wall—or more like a shield and spear igloo—which covers Tremaine.

Prairie hunches down next to him, examining a hand mangled beyond repair.

Just as she gets Tremaine to his feet, one of the beefcakes utters, "Uh, guys?"

The whole group is punched apart.

A pale blue pincer as big as a toboggan propels from the store entrance. It's followed by the antennaed head of an enormous, multi-eyed crawfish.

The beefcakes fall in all directions, and left in the middle, as Prairie drags Tremaine away, is Ramon, his shield caught in the pincer's pebbled teeth. His arm is trapped in the Saran wrap of his shield. The pincer squeezes and metal bends, threatening to crush his arm.

Joe leads a charge with Brian and Tomi, stabbing at the crawfish's face. Raina goes wide, thrusting around its legs to get its sensitive underside.

The shield collapses on itself, and the Saran wrap loosens. Ramon slips his arm free just before the shield crunches in half. The crawfish, attacked from all sides and having captured no prey, opens its pincer and swings it back and forth, looking to grab something. It catches Omri in the chest. He bawls and falls into me. I catch him, feeling the deep hot groove slashed across his pecs.

Half of the group is past the crawfish, Prairie and Kirsten included. Raina and I are stuck on the other side, with the lizards closing in.

Kirsten asks what we should do.

This crawfish has lain in wait long enough, and even though it has our measure, it's not put off. It'll keep fighting until someone gets dragged inside.

"What about the cart?" I ask, looking around to the beefcakes with us.

Alex keys in on my meaning. He tells us and Tim to keep fighting. We maintain a wide berth and swing our spears, allowing Sam and him time to retrieve my cart and haul it up in front of the crawfish. When its pincer sweeps outward, they lunge into its path. On the appendage's inward swing, its pincer catches on the cart's top level and clamps shut.

"Go!" Alex screams.

I bolt across the crawfish's front with Kirsten, followed by Alex. Sam and Tim come behind us, and they're the ones caught unawares by the other pincer. It swings for us, and after it goes past my face, I hear the distinct sound of someone's wind getting knocked out of them. Then there's bellowing, and the half-naked spearmen of the Abercrombie tribe go in for the kill.

They don't just stab. The models hack away at the thing, going for its eyes, its sensitive mouth bits, the joints of its armor. I turn to join them, but by the time I do, one of them has slapped a perfume-drenched towel across the crawfish's eyes. It slides with disturbing speed back into its store, and our group is left with one less mop-haired Milwaukeean. Alex and Brian drag Tim, kicking and screaming, from the entryway. If only there was a place to drag him to.

We cluster together, exactly as we planned *not* to do, our shields high, spears bristling, and torches waving. In the immediate aftermath of the fight, our baiting plan is working. Odd creatures with ungainly abdomens and fragile translucent body parts linger, all of them looking mutated or diseased, with unusual growths dangling as lifelessly as the vestigial wings and eyes serving other creatures no good in the underworld. They slurp up the sugar water, and following them come spindly shadows of predators.

It's the culmination of our plan, and we're only a third of the way down the wing.

"We have to run," Prairie tells Joe. "Down the middle."

"We can make it to the last staircase," Kirsten continues.

Raina and I sign off on the idea.

Joe, having lost one of his own to the crawfish, nearly another to the second-floor monsters, agrees.

We high step through the water and away from the wall, keeping our formation tight and watching our sides. With every foot, we pass some new distracted, sugar-devouring creature.

When a frog's tongue shoots out and grabs the little beetle closest to me, I don't do anything but run. A centipede skitters between stores, nabbing a beetle on the way, and some sort of tube worm coils around a pill bug. I run.

We keep going until the staircase appears in the fog, just beyond the point where our sugar trap ends. Nothing feeds out here. We haven't thrown anything this far. But still, drawn by the commotion, coming from stores and peeking from the balcony, sneak more shadows, none of which want sugar.

We're surrounded, but they don't seem to want to start a fight over us—the last thing going right for our group.

"Shields! Spears!" Joe cries.

Just a few of us can act: Tremaine nurses an obliterated hand, Brian hangs onto Tim, and Ramon tries to keep Omri from collapsing.

Alex rushes forward to join Joe. He chucks his torch ahead, causing a pale salamander to flinch away. He roars and mock-lunges, making himself big. I have to admit, it's the only thing we have left. How quickly this all fell apart.

Creatures prowl, waiting to jump out of the gray. We work our way back to the wall. I don't know why. Maybe so we're not surrounded.

Alex keeps leaping, keeps roaring, despite Joe pulling on his waistband. A crawfish squirts out of the storefront across the wing, and Alex goes for one last big lunge, one more howl.

As his breath leaves his lungs and his cries die out, its spirit grows in the form of an earsplitting shriek, causing us as a group to wince and cower. It's the sound of feedback coming through a microphone, loud enough to pop a speaker.

The crawfish darts inside. The rest of the creatures, frightened and confused, move away, back to the darkness they came from. I look more closely at a couple of shadows forming on the balcony.

They have two arms, and they're throwing things at the last of the monsters, which skitter away into the fog.

The feedback gives way to an overly distorted guitar playing the grungy chorus of a Temple of the Dog song. When the last of the creatures disappear, a cluster of filthy humans in stained winter wear rushes down the stairs. There's still glitter on some of their coats.

Take shelter in the nearest store. Turn to page 182.

Go with the seniors. Turn to page 278.

To drive home Prairie's point, the mall finally breaks.

A snap and the smacks of thick glass plating hitting water travel down the concourse. Replacing the water-swirling and groaning white noise of the sinking mall is an unearthly howl of diverted wind. Time is up.

With the group stunned into inaction, Prairie says, "That's cold air pouring in now. It'll disperse monsters all over the place, including straight for us."

For once, Kirsten looks wounded. Maybe she's finally realized her beloved mall, her court of intrigues over the past few years, is well and truly dead. Raina rakes an angry gaze over the group, urging them to see the light. If we wait any longer, we're done for. The atrium will crumble, the monsters will flee, and we'll be killed clawing at the frozen doors.

We can't keep waiting on these people, but we can't do it without them. Everyone needs to help, and they need focus.

And I'm fed up. Prairie waits too long. Joe doesn't say anything.

I've been letting others call the shots long enough. We never came this way because of Bridie. The monsters and flooding forced us to. This was always the only way.

I spent yesterday in humiliation. The beefcakes doubted us. The seniors didn't trust us. Kirsten has bullied me all day. All my life. It's now or never. It's my time.

Joe clears his throat. "Guys, I think she's—"

"All right," I interrupt. "We're splitting into groups. We have three things to do. First, distract the monsters. Second, break a ton of glass. Third, get through those doors."

Broken down that way, it doesn't sound so bad. I point to Skye and stutter once, but I push through.

"You said the music kept them at bay, right?"

"Uh, yeah, it seemed—"

"We're doing it again. Would anything make it work better?"

Prairie's eyes light up. "More bass. Make them feel it. That should keep them startled and from sensing our movement. There's still electricity on the second floor, right?"

"As far as we can tell," Skye replies.

Alex crosses his arms, and I turn to him—ambassador for the toughest crowd.

"You, beefcakes," I say, to which Alex cocks an eyebrow. "You're on window-smashing duty. Get whatever you need to go up against that glass. It's going to be thick. Throw things at it. Hit it. Whatever."

"I did track and field. Hammer toss...shot put..." Ramon says.

"Javelin," Tremaine chimes in, lifting a useful finger.

"Kickoff Pro Shop. Two stores down. There'll be lots of stuff in there," Joe says.

"Okay, good. Now—"

"Hold on," Kirsten says. She wears a smug smile, like I've missed the most obvious thing in the world. And it drives me nuts when she points out that, actually, I have. "The chandelier."

"Oh!" Joe blurts. "Yes!"

My mind flashes to the crystal chandelier hanging above the lounge, just inside the doors—Meadow Spire's flourish for the upper-crust shoppers avoiding the atrium-area gaggle. I picture how low it hangs and wonder if it's heavy enough to shatter the massive west-facing windows above the doors.

"We need rope," Joe says, preempting my instruction. "Kickoff too. They do hiking stuff."

"If there isn't, would a ton of electrical cords work?" Skye asks.

"Should do." Joe turns to the beefcakes. "The balcony runs almost the full length of the mall, just past Macy's. We can lasso the chandelier up there and drop the rope to swing on the first floor."

Alex, until this point switching between grimaces and spiteful smirks, nods.

"Who's on door duty?" Raina asks.

I point to the seniors beside Skye. "You guys. And us. Prairie, Kirsten, Raina, and me."

Alex scoffs, and I realize my mistake. I've volunteered the Madisonites to take up positions closest to escape. But I only meant to let our groups work with their own people, as everyone's comfortable doing.

Raina jumps in and recovers my fumble. "No, *not* us. I'll stick with the models and smash windows. If I can throw Kirsten through the air, I think I'm qualified."

"What's *that* supposed to—"

"And someone has to stay with Skye," Prairie proposes. "He shouldn't be left alone, playing guitar. It might help to have two instruments actually."

Joe frowns. "You sure?"

"We have enough people for everything else."

"I could use the company," Skye agrees.

I stand beside Alex, turning our opposing battle lines into something of a huddle. The beefcakes converge on one side of the circle. The seniors close the other end, staying silent and attentive.

"Okay," I say. "Skye and Prairie on distraction duties. They go first, before *any* of us move, to freak out the monsters. Then the beefcakes and Raina are on window-smashing and chandelier-lassoing. Once we make some headway, we'll shout, 'Olly olly oxen free.' Got it? Then, the guys and girls are on door duty while the rest provide security, if we need it."

"We're supposed to hear you over my guitar?" asks Skye.

"Play in thirty-second bursts. Stop and listen."

"I'd prefer something visual, just to be sure," Prairie suggests.

"Okay...we'll yell and throw tennis balls. They'll have those at the store."

Trent lifts his hand. "And what about us? You think we're just going to move some bodies for the girls?"

"Absolutely. But more than that, you need to provide security. There's no guarantee what's going to happen."

Skye makes a strained, mumbling sound. "Not to sound selfish or anything, but what's the signal for when the doors are open? Prairie and I will be way back here, and the second-floor guys will need to backtrack to get to the ground floor too. Unless they plan on rappelling down or something."

To this, Alex makes a curiously satisfied smile, pouting his lips and nodding. "Not a bad idea," he says.

"So? What's the signal, then?"

After a few seconds of vacant stares and scrunched brows, Kirsten answers, without a hint of irony or snark. "Go Bobcats."

It's simple, the first thing that comes to mind, an automatic chant to spur us on to victory.

"Band Avenue and Kickoff. Back here in ten?" Joe asks.

Our mission stands before us. We disperse. Joe leads the beefcakes, Raina, Trent, and Gabe to Kickoff. The rest of us—Kirsten, Prairie, Skye, Gina, Valerie, and me—climb to the second story and make it into Band Avenue.

The store's windows are blown out, and we crinkle over broken glass when we enter—a preview of things to come. Sheet music is spilled all over the floor, along with guitars, benches, and amps. Splashes of blood shine across black vinyl surfaces and carpeted walls. In the back drum room, the overhead lights flicker.

Skye wastes no time giving orders. "Let's be quick. Don't go anywhere near the back. Gina, Val, you see those thick cords on the wall, with the big silver connections? Grab as many as you can, with some extension cords. Prairie and Quinn, grab a guitar each and bring them to the front. Kirsten, help me with the amps."

"If we're picking axes, I'm not missing out," Kirsten says. "Quinn? You want to help him out?" She pushes Prairie ahead and leaves me with Skye, who doesn't notice her little ploy.

He crouches to grab an amp the size of a steamer trunk, unplugging the guitar he used before with a wrinkled nose. We need it on the concourse, where he can maximize the impact. I grab the other end, and we baby-step it out the entrance.

Skye goes back in and wanders the main sales floor, stepping over microphone stands, speakers, and pedals.

"You want more?" I ask.

"Heck yeah. As much as we can give them. Oh, right there." He points at a beast of an amp that rises to my waist from the floor. Skye shifts a bench out of the way, and I move some smaller amps stacked in front of it.

"So, how'd you girls link up with golden boy Joe Molson?" he asks while we assess how to transport the beast.

We move to either side of it, searching around its soft-molded edges for a handhold.

"It's not a long story. Somehow, he made it through with those Abercrombie guys, and they saved us down by the play area."

"Huh."

We both find a grip and start dragging the beast out from its nestled home among the other amps.

"Too heavy?" he asks. "Just keep dragging it."

So we do, pausing only to kick things out of our way.

"You know," I say, breathing hard and navigating the messy landscape of the sales floor. "I should be asking you the same thing."

"What's that?"

"How did *you* end up with these guys?"

"Ah, yeah," Skye mutters.

I've touched on a sore subject.

"Longer story there. Trent and I go way back. We stopped hanging out freshman year, when he joined JV football, but then last year, we started hanging out again. Or it's more like he started talking to me again. He was always making fun of me for not playing ball before and for getting into choir and music. Then out of nowhere, it's like he was okay with it. Like he didn't think it was wimpy or embarrassing anymore."

Yeah, when playing guitar made girls like you...

"If I told you something, will you...Well, can I just tell you since this might be my last chance to say it?" he asks.

I stop dragging, and he goes one step ahead of me. The amp skews forward on his side.

Gina and Valerie come from behind. He tells them to start connecting the amp to the power inside the store, then to knot extension cords, in case the beefcakes need them for the chandelier.

When they're gone, he continues. "I became good friends with Eric Messier freshman year. He knew every instrument. Everything but guitar. You know him, right? Total nerd." Skye smirks and blushes, ashamed even at his gentle jibe. "We started a band, saw each other every day, played a bunch of shows, but then last year, it just stopped. *I* stopped. I didn't return his calls. Came up with excuses to miss practice. And I mean, I dunno. Was I just tired of him? Or like, did I really want to hang with Trent more? 'Cause, like, Eric was always a snob about everything. He'd mock everyone all the time, and he was, like, always talking about Ralph Nader, you know? But he was cool. And then we just...drifted apart. He doesn't have a band anymore, and I do, and...it feels wrong. It's been bothering me all year."

Skye drifts off, only snapping to when Prairie and Kirsten coming jogging. Prairie totes a classic Fender Stratocaster in white and eggshell blue, and Kirsten grips the necks of a matte black barbed death metal bass guitar and a ruby red Flying V like a pair of dead geese.

"Know your way around these babies?" Kirsten asks.

Skye laughs. "Yeah, those are good."

Prairie and Kirsten run out to set them up.

Skye focuses on the amp again, but before we start dragging, he adds, "I think deep down I just regret abandoning him and, like, our friendship. I just had to tell someone. So...thanks."

"Yeah." I don't know what else to say. Really, I'm just thinking how his situation sounds like Kirsten, Prairie, and me, turned into boys and shaken in a bottle. I guess it's nice to know the person I idolized for so long has a screwed-up life too.

We move the amp another few feet, when the urge to share hits me. Skye stands up when I stop dragging.

"What is it?"

The words come out of nowhere, tumbling from some precarious perch at the top of my head and out of my mouth. I don't try to stop them because, like he said, I might not have another chance.

"I did have a crush on you."

He glazes over, then squints a little. "Huh."

"Keyword: *did*," I add quickly. "I don't anymore. And no offense. But yeah, I had a crush on you freshman year, and that's why they pulled that prank on you—or I mean...on me. I'm sorry you got dragged into it. I just figure, if you know, it'd help you make sense of it."

"Oh," he says. "Yeah, it does. That makes sense. It's just...I never figured anyone had a crush on me before."

"Well, you're looking at one."

He sharpens up. "Was it because I was in a band?"

"It didn't hurt."

He smiles, and I wonder how much of it comes from the flattery and how much comes from memories of jamming with Eric Messier.

"So, we're even, if you're okay with that," I say. "One confession for another."

A cymbal crashes to the floor in the drum room. Accessories and gear rattle where they hang on the wall.

"Even," he says. "Guys! We need some help back here while we get this amp out!"

Kirsten comes running and starts whipping random merchandise into the drum room, startling something into retreating farther back.

"Move your butts!" she says.

We get the amp onto the concourse, where Gina hooks it up and runs in to give it power. Kirsten continues to provide cover.

Skye observes his setup, then says, "Hey, Quinn."

"Yeah?"

"Don't be sorry, okay? It's not your fault. And break a leg out there."

"You too."

He goes to turn on the first amp, hands the gnarly black bass to Prairie, then straps on the Flying V.

Kirsten comes behind me and puts her hands on my shoulders. "Sorry about what, lovebird?"

Just like a moment ago, the words come spilling out of me, and they resemble nothing like an accusation. I confess, for the second time today, something I think I've known since Skye finished reading that poem to a guffawing audience yesterday morning. I heard it spoken out loud once before, with an audience I once believed to be safe. There's no better time to say it. After all, I might not get another chance.

"I know it was you," I tell her.

Kirsten cocks her head. Her grin falters.

"The poem in the valentine. I didn't write that in my diary. I said it out loud at one of our sleepovers. It came from a line I wrote in a poetry assignment for Ms. Warczyk's class that I crumpled up and threw away. Bridie never saw it. The seniors never heard it from her."

"What?" She scrunches her forehead and drops her mic stand to the floor, ready for some classic Kirsten verbal diarrhea.

"It was you. I don't know why. Maybe you wanted Gina to endorse your captaincy to Coach for next year. Or maybe they had something worse on you, and this was your only way out. I don't know. Whatever it was, I know it was you."

"No! It's...Valerie likes Skye! And she overheard me say something, like I don't even know what, and I walked it back. She wanted to let you know—"

"Just stop. I told you, I already know. And I'm done with it. I'm not doing anything else about it, and neither are you. It doesn't go any farther than this. We just need to get the hell out of this mall. And then we're done."

I push past her to head for the stairs. The mall groans. Wind howls. Monsters lurk in the fog. And Kirsten calls after me.

"Quinn, what does that mean? What do you mean, we're done?"

Stick close to Skye and make sure everything's working.
Turn to page 112.

Rejoin the beefcakes. Turn to page 286.

"They're inside!" Kirsten shrieks.

The words send a shockwave through the group. We saw what happened behind locked gates before—people torn apart by monsters from the dark recesses of stores.

The seniors don't get the message right away. They're stricken, covered in gore, frozen in place. The girls make the most harrowing sounds I've ever heard. The guys don't utter a peep, only hold out their arms and pucker their lips, letting the remnants of their former comrade drizzle off them.

The beefcakes, though? They weren't there to see the monsters feed on those locked-in people, but they know what an eviscerated body means.

"Come on!" Ramon yells, rushing to pick up Tim.

Brian puts Tremaine's arm over his shoulder. Tomi goes for Omri. Joe and Alex watch them with looks of betrayal.

"Where are you going?" Joe yells.

"They're inside! We gotta go!"

The rest of us play a round of *Who's got the answer?* We exchange glances to no avail until Gina and Valerie make a break for it, slipping on viscera and falling over themselves.

I wonder if that's the right idea. We're in the least flooded section of the mall. The doors to the outside are within reach. The beefcakes have the momentum.

But something about this is wrong. We can't be panicking; we don't have a reason to. Nothing is inside the store. Not yet. Before I say anything, Skye joins the rush for the concourse with Trent and Gabe.

"Wait! You can't!" he screams.

Brian leads the pack onto the concourse, holding Tremaine. He's ready to bolt, not even waiting for the rest of the models.

I join the dash, and it's not until I reach the entryway that I decide whether I want to leave or stop the others from trying. The answer comes easily once I'm exposed to the mall. We can't keep rushing into things. It's brought us nothing but grief.

Skye's cries for everyone to stop are echoed by Joe, then Prairie.

The beefcakes hesitate outside the store, maybe recalling what we just went through, maybe realizing they practically all count as walking wounded at this point.

Gina and Valerie, followed by Trent and Gabe, blow past them and run into the open. They make it almost five or six paces beyond Brian and Tremaine before freezing, remembering what they've done. They pivot toward the middle of the mall, hunting for a new hiding spot with what's left of their panicked minds.

I rush out and grab Gina's arm. She's a classmate after all. I can't help but try.

"Get off!" She flashes me a vicious look and pulls away.

I hold on, but she's bigger than I am. Gina starts prying at my fingers and batting my head.

"You can't go!" I cry from under a new wave of blows.

The splashes of a bounding predator approach from the fog. Valerie yells while Gina pummels me. Then she gets the bright idea to squeeze my bandage.

I scream and drop her arm.

The water sounds come closer, and someone else takes my other arm. I'm pulled back into the store by Raina, and once inside, I watch Alex and Joe on the concourse, waving spears at a salamander-like monster to cover the others' retreat.

Skye pushes everyone back to the checkout counter. He huffs and puffs, speaking the same mantra as me: "You can't...You can't..."

"Can't what?" Kirsten asks, her tone prim and super annoyed at once.

After taking a gulping breath and hawking a loogie, Skye points feebly toward Macy's, where Brian threatened to run off to. "You guys can't get out that way."

Prairie spins away from watching Alex and Joe fend off the salamander. "Why not?"

"Yeah," I say, "because you can't—"

"We tried already," he continues over me. "We had a group of four check it out, and only one came back." He tilts his head to the mess on the floor—the remains of the expedition's sole survivor.

"The song you were playing. Was that a distraction?" I ask.

"Yeah."

"Did it work?" Prairie adds.

Skye sighs. He picks up a sweater from a nearby table and wipes the gore from his face and hair before starting on his arms. "I think so...at first. Brett said they got all the way down the hall before anything came after them. Brett's the guy who, uh...He worked in here actually, and...that's him over there. He said the doors were blocked by a pile of bodies. Like, a frickin' Holocaust pile of bodies. They tried moving them to get someone out, but the monsters came and took out half the group. He said their guy got all the way to the door while he was fighting these things off, but, uh..."

Skye trails off, drawing Prairie and me in closer, farther from the rest of the groups' sobs and groans of pain.

"They were frozen shut," Prairie finishes for him.

Skye looks up, but he stares straight through the walls. "Yup."

Joe leans in, half paying attention, half trying to help the beefcakes settle down. A parallel discussion is happening. I catch details of Skye's report getting repeated, along with insistences to go back down the mall where we came from. All junk. We haven't been in a messier situation all day. And that's saying a lot.

Prairie wanders away to the store entrance.

"Prairie," I warn her, but she doesn't listen and leans outside.

Skye continues: "I wasn't there, so I don't know how bad it really was. But...bad enough that Brett didn't want to try again. He had three guys with him. That's why he wanted to try the vents."

"We know how that turned out," Kirsten says.

Her light tone gives me a touch of indignation, but, you know, it's been a day for picking battles. What's there to say when she has no other way to cope?

Our little group goes quiet, defeated by the tragic tale of Brett. Joe joins the larger group, who are still going full steam. He suddenly shouts, making me leap.

"You can't go there! We just came down that way, first off, and the exits are blocked."

"Based on their word," says Alex. He points not at us, but at Prairie exclusively, standing alone by the entrance.

The rest of the beefcakes nod, along with Gabe and Trent.

"We're going," Alex announces. "We should've tried Penney's all along."

"The doors are frozen shut," Joe protests.

"Flooded, actually," Raina says.

"We'll take our chances."

"So, you believe that exit *right over here* is too hard to deal with, but the one all the way across the mall isn't?" Joe asks.

"They might not've been strong enough," Alex replies.

"Oh, I see how it is, Superman," Kirsten says.

"And not the point, numb nuts. It's *flooded*," I say, invigorated to trash-talk the guy whose face just asks for it.

"We weren't there to see, were we?"

Raina simply steps next to Joe and crosses her arms, her shoulders as high and as wide as his.

"It's a slaughterhouse through there," Joe says, sticking to the main point. "You won't make it past the atrium, if you even get that far."

"Her fault again," Alex says. "She convinced us to come this way for nothing."

Joe steps up on Alex. "It's *not* for nothing. We're here. We're alive. We wouldn't have made it this far if it wasn't for their strategy. If you go to Penney's, you're going to your deaths."

Alex picks up his weapon. "It's not an argument. We're not a team. Every one of us can go our own way. What do you guys say, huh?"

Joe scans the nearly nude followers whom he's treated as his charges since the monsters broke free. This may be the moment they break free from him.

It must be a new sensation for Joe. But I've seen this sort of thing before, in something as pointless as a group project at school. You've taken charge and think things are going swimmingly, only to find the people around you abandoning your ideas and doing it their own way. You go from team leader to outcast in an instant, and as you try to assert some control, you see there's no point. The desire to break away has been in everyone's heads all along. They never had faith in you in the first place.

They never saw you as a leader. They never saw you as a teammate.

Our alliance with the beefcakes is at an end.

"Skye, you coming?" Trent asks.

"I don't know, man." Skye shakes his head, exasperated by the sudden decision to join a mutiny or not.

"Sayonara," Kirsten mutters. Mingled within her resentment is some satisfaction.

A full two-thirds of the group assembles themselves. Only Joe argues against it.

"Guys, we can figure this out. We're safe in here. And we have an exit that isn't flooded *right here.*"

"We're good, man," Alex tells him. Then to the group, "Let's do this."

They gather a smattering of leftover weapons. As beleaguered as they have been this whole time, they start to leave, with a dash of new fire in their eyes.

They nudge past Prairie, who's never left the entrance. Her eyes boggle. This whole time, she hasn't heard a single word anyone's been saying.

"What are you doing?" she cries, earning herself some sneering and condescending looks from Alex, Tremaine, and the seniors. "What's going on?"

"Shut up," Alex calls over his shoulder. "You're not blowing it for us this time."

"But I have it!" she shouts.

Gabe tells her to shut up, too, whereas my ears perk up. I take an interest in how suddenly Prairie's ruined pink jacket strains to contain her energy.

"What's she saying?" Skye asks.

"I think..." I start, but I have to see it play out.

Joe and Raina run onto the concourse to cut off the group.

"Stop!" they both shout, loud enough to bring every monster down on top of them.

"I think she knows what to do," I say.

"I have it!" Prairie says again, but she doesn't continue without looking to Joe for permission.

Before he can give it, Alex marches up to him, fists clenched. He pulls back his right arm and swings a wild haymaker for Joe's head. Joe ducks and counters with an uppercut to the half-nude upstart's chin. Then he gets Alex in a slippery armlock and nods at Prairie. The beefcakes gawk, and the seniors complain.

"Everyone, shut up and listen!" Raina roars.

The seniors stop.

Prairie checks that the chaos is contained, then she smiles nervously. "I have it."

"What's that meeeaan, Hedlund?" Kirsten drones.

"*Listen.*" Prairie steps onto the concourse and points to the skylights.

Aside from swirling water and the mall's groans, the storm is in full swing, as it's supposed to be until morning. A howling wind sweeps the skylights, sanding the glass with hard, stinging snow.

"This exit faces west," Prairie says. "It faces *west*. It faces the *wind*. That's why it froze so easily."

"No shit, it's frozen." Alex spits blood.

The rest of the group grows wary, standing in the open.

"We can use that," Prairie says.

"Use what?" Joe prompts.

"The storm. This is where the chandelier and floor-to-ceiling windows are. The doors are frozen shut, but we can give ourselves time to get through if we use the wind. We just have to break a bunch of windows first. Like, a ton of them. Let the wind come in, and it'll drive every one of those things away."

"How do you know?" Kirsten asks, her prompt actually well-meaning, like Joe's.

"Virtually every one of these things is cold-blooded. Or I mean, they gotta be. It's a bunch of insects, amphibians, and reptiles, right? They're exothermic, which means they can't regulate their own body temperatures, so they have to rely on their environments being amenable to them. They can't stand extreme temperatures, and they *especially* can't stand the cold. They might be giant, mutant killer...mutants, but...look, they're going to hate it. It's not just regular cold outside. The weather report from yesterday said it's subzero with the windchill, with gusts over sixty miles per hour."

Joe releases Alex, whose rapid humiliation has lost him his swiftly gained support. I liked him better when he was bullying Trent.

"So, we break the windows..." Joe says.

"And it doesn't matter how long it takes to break down the doors. The monsters will all be gone. All that's left to worry about is frostbite."

The idea works its way across the group. They start trading looks. A couple of beefcakes stare forlornly at their crotches at the mention of frostbite.

They've all heard Joe's arguments against going backward, and it didn't work. He didn't give them a new way forward. Prairie has.

Joe grins. He starts laughing and shaking Alex by the shoulders, overjoyed and hellbent once again at the prospect of saving his beefcakes.

"I'll take it," Raina says.

Kirsten nods and smirks.

Our group has our way out. We just have to run the play.

And yet, I still can't help worrying where the hell my sister is.

Back up Prairie. Take the lead. Turn to page 263.

Let Joe speak up for Prairie. Turn to page 145.

"Go!" shout our rescuers.

They shove us into a department store as dark as any we've passed, though this time, its entrance is flanked by a couple of teenagers windmilling their arms for us to come in. Alarms go off in my head, but I'm willing to take a chance. We all are. Besides, I recognize these people. Their faces. The glitter.

Once inside, our beefcakes tend to their wounds. Omri collapses onto a low display of sweaters, struggling to breathe. Ramon grows pale, surveying the damage to his chest. Tremaine goes weak, looking at his ruined hand, and is kept from falling by Joe and Brian, the latter of whom drops a sobbing Tim to help.

And yet I don't do a thing.

Glitter. Our rescuers. I know this group.

The last people with Bridie.

As everyone pants and wipes their brows, muttering complaints, I move around and call her name. For each new girl's face that isn't Bridie's, my hope fades and my embarrassment builds. Until finally...the reckoning.

"Look who it is. The frickin' little Carpenter girl," says Gina, as glittery as they come.

With way more energy than she should have, she shoves me in the chest, then rains down a hail of wildly placed full-arm slaps on me. I cower, too exhausted to fight back, accepting the blows.

Actually, it's not so bad to just get it out of the way. Give me this over the slow-motion poisoning of my self-esteem via the school rumor mill.

But then she adds kicking. Gina catches me right below the kneecap, sending a sharp, debilitating tremor up my leg. That's enough. I drive into her while she pummels my back and tries to knee me in the chest.

The other seniors go after Kirsten, leaving it to Raina, Joe, and Alex to squeeze between bodies, yell for the fighting to stop, and pry us apart, at the risk of sharp nails and errant limbs to the crotch.

I've forced Gina into the display rack serving as Omri's hospital bed when someone comes between us. The person pulls me back, and Gina's last kick narrowly misses my chin. I spin, ready to punch, and Skye backs away, hands up in surrender, with Joe coming up behind him.

Skye's hair hangs in his face. His cheekbones push against ivory skin smudged with blood. His coat has been slashed, and some of its stuffing is gone. His guitar-strumming hands shine bone-white. He looks like winter in hell, but it suits him.

"Are you all right?" he asks.

"Don't you see who it is?" Gina complains. "Your frickin' stalker girl? Why'd we risk our lives on her?"

"Go to hell, Gina," spits Kirsten, trying to get in a swipe at Valerie, who's held in check by Alex.

"You're dead, Fortner. I swear to God, you're dead."

"A mall full of swamp monsters tried and failed, so give it a try, skank."

A fresh burst of fighting threatens to break out. A piercing whistle puts a stop to it.

Joe removes his pinky fingers from the corners of his mouth and raises his arms, shepherd-on-the-mount style. "Knock it off! I don't know what any of this is about, but let's focus. Thank you for helping us. Okay? Can I say that first?"

"Yeah, helping a stalker freak! She was probably obsessed with hunting him down to die in each other's arms!"

Joe fumbles his words. "Okay...Wh-what?"

"What'd they do to you guys?" Gina asks. "Steal your frickin' clothes, march you through the death pit?"

"Uhh, they came like that, dipwad," Kirsten says. "We didn't have to do anything."

Another commotion arises. Skye puts his arm around my shoulder, sending a trill through my heart, and ushers me away.

Quietly, where the others can't hear us, he mutters, "Hey, look. I know that thing yesterday was a prank. I don't actually think you're a stalker. That's just them saying that, okay?"

I'm dough in his hands, this long-overdue fantasy of close contact short-circuiting my brain. With a nod, I slur an affirmative answer of sorts, probably sounding tired and confused. Which is fine because I haven't *not* been tired and confused since yesterday morning.

I wouldn't mind explaining a little more, though, maybe more coherently. He has a right to know why he's been dragged into this soap opera. And I want to get it off my chest. The crush. I never thought I'd have to confess it out loud like this, but it feels like the right thing to do. If only I knew how to bring it up, where to start, how to end, without cycling through explanations on top of explanations, without coming off obsessive.

All my worrying circles me back to the one thing I really *have* had on my mind, which drove us to this part of the mall.

"You sure you're okay?" he asks.

I clear my throat, and I sort of say what I need to. "Are you really friends with Bridie?"

"Huh?" Skye wrinkles his brow. "Oh. Sure. We had some classes together and joke around sometimes. Not really...close, though. Uh..."

He looks nervous, as if I'm about to go into a jealous rage for his affection, and it makes me like him a little less. I get he's concerned about a confession of love from a girl who'd apparently tell him, *Yes, it was a prank, but I do love you so!* but it still hits like a dagger to the heart.

I start up, and I'm surprised that what I say next doesn't come out as a question, but an assertion of the truth. "Bridie didn't help plan it."

Skye's face can't settle on an expression, but his eyes widen. "The prank? No way. Total opposite. As far as I know, the only reason she came out today was to scream at Gina and Valerie for doing it. Honestly...it was pretty awesome."

A grin comes on fast. I knew it. Deep down. Because if I'm honest with myself—honest enough to accept what happened to me yesterday was total crap—I know she had nothing to do with it. Bridie and I fight like real sisters. Privately, where no one can see. Besides the fact we're not feuding right now, she wouldn't put it out in the open, where people can take sides and make things even worse. If she did or I did, well, we might as well be swamp monsters too.

...how I love you, oh sky...

It wasn't from any of my diaries. Not even Kirsten could have dug into them. I'd written the poem at the height of my crush. Maybe from an English assignment? Something I turned in, knowing the teacher would have been none the wiser, and tore up without another classmate laying eyes on it. But I was in love. I memorized it. I might've said something out loud...

The group is about to lose it again. Kirsten won't quit with the insults. The guys try to shush her and keep everyone apart. Skye turns to join the fray, but I grip his arm to stop him.

"Bridie...We came all this way. Where is she? Is she here?"

Skye's face finally settles on an expression. And the dagger digs deeper into my heart, spilling icy blood through me.

"She isn't here."

The iciness goes down to the bottoms of my boots. My vision swims.

Bridie isn't here. Where else would she be? Hadn't it all happened so fast? There's nowhere else she *could* be. There's nowhere left where anyone's alive.

I feel her death already, this vacuum, this thing I'll have to tell my parents. The horror on their faces, the years of life it'll rip away from them.

I stammer and look into Skye's eyes. He softens at my pleading look.

"You guys hurt Nicole pretty bad with that mop bucket. Once everyone started chasing you, Bridie stayed with her. So...I don't know. Maybe they got out or got her someplace safer in the mall for help."

There's no safer place in Meadow Spire Mall. It's not even worth saying so.

"But...you didn't see her go? You didn't..."

His mouth is working, but the words won't come. He manages to say he's sorry and that he didn't wait around long enough to see what happened.

"I had to stop Gina and Valerie from killing you guys, so I followed them. After security caught you and told us to piss off, we started back here, but the ground practically broke apart under our feet. We've been in survival mode ever since."

"She was already gone by then? By the time you made it over the crack? You didn't see her at all, even from, like, a distance?"

Skye squints, thinking hard or pretending to. If it's not easy to remember, it's not hopeful.

"I'm sorry," he says again. He's holding my arm and supporting my weight.

There's nothing else to say, nowhere left to hunt for Bridie, and no one who would join me if I tried. The sky is fully dark, and we should expect the rest of the power to cut out any minute. The mall's imminent collapse is coming too. Too slow for the naked eye, but once it happens, it'll happen all at once.

My thoughts are interrupted when Kirsten yells my name.

"Don't listen to these dillholes, Quinn," she says.

Valerie draws confused looks from the poor beefcakes, whose day has only grown stranger. She sweeps a chipped red fingernail at Kirsten. "C'mon, Quinn. Let's ask Kirsten who helped with the valentine. You think we came up with that on our own?"

"Oh! See that?" says Kirsten triumphantly. "The pricks finally admit it. All it took was a little sludgy convincing."

"Seriously, are you *demented*, Fortner? What is your *problem*?" Gina says. "You want to turn around and play with us? Because that's not gonna fly. Wait till Monday, girl. You're dead meat."

Valerie looks at me. "She told us exactly what to write in there. And seriously, we wouldn't have even known you had a crush on Skye in the first place if it wasn't for her."

Kirsten laughs. "Like you wrote anything in that valentine that a million girls haven't said about a million boys. And dude, everyone knows everyone's crush. It's high school. You're just trying to screw with us because you failed to dodge a mop bucket."

"And then you sic your stupid *sister* on us?" Valerie continues, turning on me. "Tell that idiot to go after Kirsten, if she doesn't like how pranks work."

Joe steps up to her. "Knock it off. She's worried sick about Bridie. Isn't she with you guys?"

Valerie glares at him, her eyes unfailingly flitting to Joe's exposed pecs.

One of the senior boys gets in Joe's face—Trent, a third-stringer who's started and ended every football season riding the bench, with a splint on his forearm from summer training. "Don't tell my girlfriend to knock it off, Molson. You got a problem, you bring it to me."

"Okay, squirt. What'd you do with Quinn's sister?"

"Why don't you and your fairy friends go look for her?" He shoves Joe's chest. His hands slip on sweat, making him wince when his wrist bends.

Skye mutters, "Guys, do we really need to—"

Raina jumps between Trent and Joe. Alex leaps in front of her and, wasting not a second, grabs a fistful of Trent's varsity jacket. He rabbit-punches Trent in the nose, releasing him immediately so he stumbles and falls into a rack.

The able-bodied beefcakes line up with Joe—Madison's star running back, its own Cupid, their chosen leader. The seniors form a battle line. Prairie, looking by turns fascinated and devastated by this latest development, is pulled into formation by Kirsten.

Joe clenches his jaw and stares at the floor, making no move to retaliate. He holds up a hand and turns it over, inspecting the blood and grime. The beefcakes look to him, having found their new cause in the wake of Trent's disrespect. All this nonsense—and it's nothing but nonsense—about crushes and pranks is lost on them, but they stand to fight.

"Enough," Joe says. "I don't care what this is about. I care about these guys and girls. And now Sam is dead."

"And I don't care who *Sam* is," Trent whines. "He's not the only one who's gone."

Skye expels a shocked breath. "*Trent*. Guys, we gotta—"

"He's my *brother!*" Tim screams. He's sitting up now on the pile of ruined clothes, snot running from his nose and tears smearing his face. His eyes are barely open.

Ramon gathers him in his arms and hugs him.

"And now we have a missing sister," Joe says. "You tell us she isn't here? Then we'll go find her. If you want to join us—"

"Like hell we're going with you. They're the reason we're here in the first place. We'd have got out of here if they hadn't dumped that shit on us," Valerie snarls.

"No one told you to chase us," Kirsten says.

"No one told you to—"

"Guys! *Stop!*" Skye shouts.

He grips my arm tighter, like he's not just supporting me, but wants me to stay as still as possible. At first, I think he's as sick of this crap as me, but there's something else. He looks to the back of the store, pauses, and listens.

Joe starts to ask what's going on and gets shushed by the seniors, who've latched onto whatever Skye's noticed. It sounds to me like our shaking kitchen-cabinet shields. Wobbling sheet metal or...something sneaking through vents.

I rip my arm away from Skye and back up. Everyone in our group nears the door. We should've known better. No store is safe.

Skye, instead of following, runs to the dark back of the store, followed by the senior boys, then the girls.

"No!" Joe and Prairie cry.

Joe hesitates to leave his beefcakes but ends up running too. I follow.

Something else is happening. The seniors have their own thing going on here. They group around a stepladder set up just past the checkout counter, next to the impulse-buy displays. A thick yellow rope dangles from an open panel in the ceiling that feeds into a square metal vent.

"Come on, help me!" Skye yells. He's three steps up on the ladder, and it teeters until the girls grab its legs, holding it steady.

Trent grips the trailing rope, and with Skye, they flex their arms and lean back, letting gravity help.

There's someone in there. They sent someone *into* the vents, maybe thinking that was their ticket out of here.

"Come on! Pull!"

Skye's and Trent's hands climb the rope while they pull it out. With their last yank, we hear the person's body coming close. Trent ends up crouching by the floor. His feet slip, and he splashes into the water. Alex runs up and climbs the other side of the ladder. He takes the rope, just beneath where it rubs against the edge of the vent, then he hops off, twisting to Skye's side of the ladder. Skye holds fast and jumps too. They both float to the floor.

The instant Alex's toes touch, the seniors' duct-crawling adventurer appears in the vent's opening. Or what's left of him anyway.

A thick red wave of blood splatters Skye in the face. Then the solid remains that squeegeed the blood come, one piece at a time. Strings and globules of soft flesh and hard bone splash down on

Skye's head and shoulders and land around Trent, whose eyes boggle at every recognizable piece of human surrounding him. The glitter sticking to their clothes is coated under a fatty layer of gore.

My first instinct is to sigh at the disappointment. And then I wonder how many times these seniors have actually left this store and seen what's happened today because Gina and Valerie scream.

They scream and scream.

Regroup and stay sheltered. Turn to page 271.

Get the hell out of there. Turn to page 185.

Skye hooks up the bass guitar to the beast amp with a loud pop. Then there's a desperate shout from the bottom of the stairs. Our mission is underway.

I rush across the skywalk and start down the stairs before the fog clears enough to see the beefcakes beneath me. Some of them wear overstuffed backpacks, a couple others with rope draped over their shoulders. Most of them swing hockey sticks or baseball bats.

But when I reach the landing halfway down, I realize I've misidentified some of the weapons. A few of them are legs—hairy ones telescoping from an arachnid's bulbous body—surrounding Brian.

I have no weapon, but one look at the creature shows me fragile limbs and a thorax even smaller than my torso. I can help.

Joe spots me and swings at the creature's hind section. He tells me not to do it, but I've already climbed the guardrail. Digging in my heels so I don't slip, I leap and land on the creature's back. The beefcakes recoil when it crashes to the floor under my weight. Its body has no give, though, and pain punches into my stomach. I slip off its abdomen and land next to its scrambling legs.

Brian breaks free from the creature, and while I scrabble backward, the beefcakes renew their assault, beating the thing until it retreats down the concourse.

Raina, with a fresh coat of sweat, helps me to my feet.

"More coming."

"Lots more." Joe wheels his arm, ushering us upstairs. "We need music, stat."

"Someone's gotta be down here to catch that rope," Raina warns.

"I know, but Skye needs to get going."

"He's working on it," I say.

Joe keeps corralling us, so Raina and I lead the pack upstairs. When we reach the middle of the skywalk, a thumping and buzzing commotion rises above the howling wind from the atrium. We know what it signals—a mosquito beast on the prowl.

"Come on!" I shout, pushing Raina.

We reach the others and watch while Skye checks the settings on his amp.

"Come on, Clapton. Get it going!" Alex shouts.

Skye strums once, making no noise besides the fine twang of its strings under his fingers.

Prairie crouches. "The switch is on, but the little green light's not showing."

Everyone swivels to look inside Band Avenue, which has gone fully dark, without even the flicker of illumination from the drum room. The lights in every store on this side of the mall have blinked out, leaving only the dim overhead ones and a gloomy sky to give us anything to see by.

"Simple enough problem..." Skye mutters.

"There." Prairie points across the way, where the lights are still on, powered by a different breaker.

"Let's move!" I say.

For once, no one argues. Planning only gets you as far as your first improvisation.

Skye unplugs both guitars, Brian and Ramon hoist the beast amp, and Kirsten rushes into the store to retrieve the cords. I take the smaller amp with Prairie, and we move at full speed. The rest of the group forms a protective shell around us. Kirsten calls from behind. The creature inside Band Avenue is a centipede. All the better to leave.

We pass over the skywalk just as the mosquito beast plows through the cluster of massage chairs below, bouncing around like a panicked turkey. It gains elevation and crashes into the bottom of the skywalk, making it shudder under our feet.

Joe, Alex, and Tim sprint ahead before we reach the other side of the mall.

A tube worm rears up from Afterthoughts, the store we were aiming for, and the boys slash it like mad. We move to Fashion Bug next door. Trent, Gabe, and Raina rush inside, weapons raised, ready to take on whatever might be within. Skye dashes in next, cords in hand. Seconds later, the amp pops to life and lets out a rumble from the guitar bouncing against his stomach. The second cord goes in and immediately subjects us to the blast of a poorly played bass riff. Prairie's wasted no time playing.

I almost recognize it, and while everyone gets situated, I shout, "What's that?"

Prairie turns red. Her fingers strain to press chords on the awkwardly huge guitar dangling from her neck. "'Foreplay/Long time'! Boston! Skye showed me!"

Skye joins in on guitar, playing something else and stomping on a pedal to unleash a wall of distortion. Together, they sound atrocious, but I guess that's the point.

Joe and Alex come back to the group, having slashed the worm to ribbons, and we lean over the balcony to see what sort of effect the music is having. The way toward the doors reveals nothing but fog and a deceptive veneer of calm. We'll only tell how bad it is once our bait-train goes down there.

On the other side of the concourse, the vague outlines of creatures appear to act strange, either frozen in place or bobbing heads back and forth, putting more consideration into coming forward.

A gust of air billows over my face when a dark shape flies in front of me, its wings blathering like an old prop plane. I scramble away from the guardrail and end up in a pile with the rest of the group. The mosquito beast has vaulted the walkway, putting a hitch in Skye's and Prairie's playing. They pick it up again, but it seems the mosquito isn't troubled much by it.

"Guys!" Tim shouts back at the guardrail, looking down the concourse. "Frogs!"

We might've scared some things away, but the apex predators only seem to be drawn in.

Raina grabs two Valentine's Day floor banners from either side of a nearby storefront. "Here!" she shouts at Gina and Trent, handing them over. "Wave them around!"

"Are you crazy?" Trent yells.

Gina looks at what she's holding in horror.

But then Valerie and Gabe join them.

"It's okay," Gabe shouts. He takes Gina's flag and joins Trent. "We're okay up here, okay? We just need to provide cover."

The girls are reluctant to move, so Gabe tells them to stand guard nearby, protecting the senior boys with Skye and Prairie. No one presses the issue. We're down four people on the door team, but there's new business to attend to, and it comes at a cost.

With banners waving across the skywalk, frogs spying and a mosquito beast bumbling close by, Alex stops us at the top of the stairs and motions for Kirsten and I to go down.

"Are you nuts?" Kirsten shouts.

"They got you covered," he insists.

I should've been ready for something like this. "We're going with you. We need to see what the door looks like."

Joe comes up behind us. "What's the holdup?"

Gina and Valerie scream. The mosquito beast has bounced into Trent and Gabe like a gigantic beach ball, sending them to the floor. The mosquito fumbles over the far ledge. Trent gets to his feet. Along with Gina, Valerie, and the beefcakes, they clobber the mosquito with hockey sticks. Gabe crawls away, cringing and cradling a hurt arm. Under intense assault, the mosquito beast drops and lands on the first floor with a shudder.

Alex wipes his brow, points back at us, and whines to Joe. "They want to follow us to see what the doors look like."

Without missing a beat, Joe says, "Let them." He moves ahead of Alex, leading us across the skywalk and down the concourse to Macy's.

We don't slow down, no matter how big of a store we pass, no matter how terrible a mess spills from their doors. Our group keeps close to the railing, jumping over shopping bags and baskets, bodies, an overturned stroller, and every other piece of detritus today's catastrophe has thrown in our way. Whatever may lurk in the shadows stays put, and we place our faith in speed and disorientation.

The chandelier appears out of the fog. Bereft of electricity, it looks like it belongs in the foyer of a haunted mansion—this brittle, ornate snowflake signifying the tenuousness of life, its shattering death imminent. I detect its cable swaying in response to the mall's death spasms.

The music goes quieter when we reach Macy's. The light slightly increases, courtesy of the huge array of windows and the still-lit department store, showing off its sleeping wares as if it continues to be the most extraordinary thing around.

The balcony ends just past the Macy's entrance, leaving about twenty yards between us and the west-facing windows.

Joe skids like a slapstick comedian into the guardrail and slips a loop of climbing rope from his shoulders.

Kirsten and I lean over the balcony to check out the doors.

"Ho-ly," Kirsten says.

The floor is littered with bodies. And I don't just mean the floor in front of the doors, where they're piled higher than the exit near J.C. Penney, despite the apparent efforts of the late Brett's squad. The guy didn't lie. It's political mass-murder bad. A full-blown massacre occurred here. Limbs and torsos bob in the rising red water.

Our afternoon was mostly defined by a peculiar lack of humans, but here, they're everywhere. All shapes and sizes and ages. All dead. The doorway pileup contains the largest amount of whole bodies, where death probably came in the form of crushing. On top of the pile and around it, bodies are slashed and half-consumed, with guts spilling onto the floor. It's a veritable mountain of corpses to shovel out of the way.

"Yeah. Crap."

Not even the windows to the sides of the doors offer much of an option. They begin at chest height above a brick wall, and we'd still have to move bodies splayed across them before we could lift our wounded and climb out ourselves.

"Alex," says Joe, while he and Bryan work on knotting their ropes. "Do the honors."

Alex's backpack lands with a loud thud. From it he pulls a five-pound rubberized dumbbell and a coil of climbing rope.

"That's what you got?" Kirsten cries.

"There was a mud puppy or something in there. Don't ask," Raina answers.

After Alex loops the rope around the handle and ties a simple knot, he leans back, swinging the rope like a sling before releasing it and sending the weight directly at the glass. I hold my breath and watch the window—the final barrier between us and freedom.

The weight hits the window with a loud clack, sending a sharp reverberation through it but leaving nothing more than a scuff. No one reacts. Tomi, Ramon, and Raina knot their own weights. Tremaine and Omri stand guard. Alex remains undeterred. He hauls the weight back up by its rope and hurls it, hitting nearly the same spot, chipping off pieces of glass this time.

Raina starts chucking too, aiming for the same spot. Soon, she, Alex, Ramon, and Tomi are timing their throws, and eventually, a crack forms in the glass. We keep watching, eager to see progress after the musical distraction got off to such a slow start.

With one more timed volley, Raina and the beefcakes breach the window. The entire pane doesn't break, but a triangular shard as tall as me falls to the floor. A whistling gust of wind bursts inside and peppers our faces with stinging snow. The group cheers. My skin tightens immediately at the dryness. I inhale the fresh air like I'll never exhale again.

It's our signal.

I look at Kirsten, and though we have a job to do, I see the hurt in her eyes, the itch to talk to me.

"We need to get down there," I say, "and we need help."

Kirsten catches my eye and nods, her hair waving in the wind. "Fine."

"Joe! We need someone else with us."

He looks down at the bodies and frowns. "Tremaine and Omri," Joe says. "Head back with them now. They should feel the wind soon, so they can stop playing."

"Got it," I say, but when I reach the wounded pair with Tim, standing on guard duty, they're staring down shadows in the fog.

At first, I think it's the seniors or Prairie maybe, but the closer they come, the less human they appear. Then a feeler slips out of Macy's. Tim rushes ahead and crashes a baseball bat down on it, causing the creature to retreat inside.

If we go all the way back, it'll be a battle. If we try going through Macy's, it could be Sears all over again.

"Uh, Joe!" I cry, turning back to him.

He's finishing tying his lasso. Joe shouts for the weight-chuckers to make room, and when they pause from chipping away at more windows, Joe whirls the rope over his head. With the easy confidence of a rodeo champion, he throws its noose so it spins in a wobbly open circle, letting the rope stream from his other hand like a snake. The noose drapes around a number of upturned tines on the chandelier, and he pulls the rope tight, cinching the lasso. One try, and he's hooked the chandelier.

The beefcakes cheer. Alex, Raina, Ramon, and Tomi go back to throwing weights. Joe, Brian, and Tim line up with the lasso rope, while Joe singles out the side south-facing window as their target.

Kirsten and I stand there with nothing to do and nowhere to go. Omri and Tremaine stay vigilant, maintaining the rear guard in case any shadows decide to manifest into a real threat.

If we go that way, they certainly will. If we try Macy's, who knows?

I'd chuck some weights myself. They have extra ones with rope. But I don't have the muscle mass, and they're crowding out the end of the balcony anyway. There's only one place where Kirsten and I will be of any use—clearing bodies. It's just a matter of getting there.

Another giant window shard falls to the floor. Screaming wind blasts us, muffling the atrocious mixture of Prairie's and Skye's music. They'll quit as soon as the wind chills them. And we won't have started on the doors yet.

I look back at the extra rope at Brian's feet, struck with an idea. There's no need to take the stairs or an escalator and risk the monsters. Not when we can rappel.

Rappel to the first floor. Turn to page 298.

Get downstairs through Macy's. Turn to page 160.

The lizard thing marvels at our appearance. It almost falls backward, if its dinosaur-sized tail were not there to prop it up. Its astonished gaze flits from Kirsten to me, a slightly gaping mouth suggesting confusion rather than aggression.

It's that split second of mutual surprise that gives us the advantage.

Kirsten's terror projects the same indetermination as the lizard. I'm the only one with my thinking cap on, and it says this thing has us right where it wants us. Move in any direction and it'll spring on us like a jack-in-the-box.

You don't know it until you're backed into a corner, but the only way out is forward. No matter what stands in front of you, that thing is softer than the wall, and if your life matters that much, you'll gnaw through it like a rat through bone.

Our greatest disadvantage is a lack of weaponry. The lizard's are on naked display. Its massive, knobby fore-claws...Its mousetrap mouth...All powered by a spring-loaded torso. Killing this thing is out of the question. Distraction is our only weapon. Escape is our only objective.

"Rahhh!" I flail my arms, stealing the lizard thing's gaze and making it rear its head and drop its jaw.

It loses its confusion for all-out aggression.

My zipper growls when I rip my jacket off. I roll on my side to free my arm.

"Kirsten! Get up!"

From my other side, I sweep my jacket into the lizard thing's snout and scramble to my knees. I flick my jacket again and get to my feet, nearly being taken out by the wet floor.

Kirsten has the cover to rise, but she only scuttles away.

"Get up!"

We have to act as a team. There's no time to explain. We're not a hive mind; we're not trained for something like this. Still, I don't know how she can't see what she has to do.

The trailing sleeve of my jacket slaps the thing's snout. It shakes its head and snorts, standing higher on its tail. I move to backhand its nose, confident in ruining its balance and making it retreat, if only far enough away for us to make our next move.

"Raahhhh!" I send my jacket into its face.

Its claws lash out at me. I catch its snout full-on, and it snuffles, annoyed, when the fabric catches its nostril.

A claw hits my stomach, but it catches on nothing. Three serrated blades travel through flesh and bowels like garden shears through a hose. I double over, collecting my stomach contents into my arms like I'm trying to hold together water. My skin goes clammy, and I grow cold all over.

I fall, cracking my head against the floor. The lizard thing has recovered from my slap. It gapes down at me with its stupid, angry gaze, like I should be fine for another round. Still in its fighting stance, too stupid to know it's won.

My guts press outward, refusing to be wrangled by my hands. The pain turns into a conveyor belt to eternity.

Try again. Turn to page 251.

The bed set showroom surrounds me with the plush, poofy whiteness of a dream. The last time I was here, I was about ten and came to get new sheets because I refused Bridie's hideous Rainbow Brite hand-me-downs. It's not a good memory.

We jumped on the beds. We got grounded. Mom made me feel like I was a baby again, immature, and I was like nine. So as cushy as it is, I'd rather not be here.

Bad memories aren't the only things that will be creeping up on me. I lean onto the first bed by the escalator and hawk a thick exertion-induced loogie onto the floor. Manners be damned, Mom.

Kirsten skitters around, looking for monsters behind bedroom sets here, appliances over there. Raina plops on the bed next to me. She holds the walkie-talkie to her mouth like she's struggling with its weight. Her eyes are sunken. This must be the first she's allowed herself to rest since leaving her dad.

"Raina, we gotta go. Two jumps and that thing'll be right on top of us. Kirsten! Come on, let's go."

"Yeah. Totally," says Kirsten, distracted by guard duty.

Raina didn't get a taste of the frog's abilities. Not like Kirsten and I.

I watched that tongue fire across my path like a battering ram, punch my best friend to the floor, and convince me she'd been killed. The frog's assault left Kirsten rattled, so much that she's hardly nursing her bruised side from where its tongue smashed into her. We need to trust our instinct to run, need to unlearn what we've taken for granted, and that means running farther away than just out of the monsters' reach.

I lift Raina. She doesn't fight me.

Raina sends one update over the radio: "Prairie. We're getting to a safer place on the second floor. Stay tuned. Over."

Kirsten claps her hands and hurries to the washers and dryers.

"C'mon, Carpenter. Get her moving."

"She's moving, K. Why don't you grab some, like, weapons or something?"

Kirsten sputters some whiny response, then yells, "Whoop!" She disappears with a crash behind the first row of ivory appliance sets, her arms flailing like a ref calling a touchdown before slipping in mud.

"Kirsten!" Raina regains her energy and blows past me. She rounds the appliances and stops.

I expect her to start whaling on some other creature, but she bends out of view, then straightens, helping Kirsten to her feet.

"Ow." Kirsten grimaces, rubbing her thigh.

"Maybe don't give us a heart attack right now?" I say.

"Not like I'm trying."

"Well, going forward—" I stop.

A fleshy feeler the color of a frozen corpse slips into view behind the washers. I grip Kirsten and spin her around. The three of us watch the feeler probe the washers, then move forward, revealing itself to be attached to the head of a giant centipede, with wet pincers and gauzy eyes.

The thing skitters past us, its legs clacking against the tile like a playing card hitting the spokes of a bike tire. It's nearly the length of a bus, and when it eventually runs out of legs and segments, its rear pincers bob against the floor before it disappears.

Okay, I mouth to the others. *Let's go.*

They nod. And since it's my idea, they let me take the lead. I tiptoe to the aisle and check on the centipede, which is exploring the bedroom area. We have a clear path to the mall. I wave them on.

Take nothing for granted. The outside of Sears won't be far enough away. Not that I know what awaits us in the mall, but even after everything we've seen, I'm not sure what could surprise me anymore. We're going into the belly of the beast to make it out of here. Not what I had in mind, but I didn't expect to lose Prairie or to see Bridie here, or, you know, find a ton of slimy mutants springing out of nowhere.

I come to a screeching halt when a pair of pincers appears on the concourse right outside Sears, but I don't get time to alert the girls. Kirsten yelps and shoves into me. I look behind us.

The centipede has had enough of bedroom sets. It follows the path it took to get in there, which we're on.

"No, but...Wait!" I cry.

The girls run past me, freezing only when they spot the new set of pincers.

The centipede is drawn to us, our vibrations—or noise—making it scurry faster. I race after the other two. Kirsten jumps over the new pincers instead of running in the opposite direction from them. Once I'm there, I know why.

It's not another centipede; it's a giant malformed earwig with cancerous growths and a sickly pallor, whose mouth poses no threat. Putting it between us and the centipede is almost a stroke of genius from Kirsten, if that's what she had in mind.

So, I jump the earwig right after Raina, who loses her footing and lands on the thing's shielded back. She slides to the floor and causes its pincers to fan out defensively, showing off its bony inside edges. One of the pincers catches my thigh, and I fall on the thing's abdomen, sliding down between them.

They collapse around my chest.

I fight, clawing and rolling back and forth, forcing it to loosen, twisting me further down until the pincers tighten again and close around my neck. Its grip isn't that strong, but a barb catches me, stinging my throat. Hot blood pours from my skin.

I try putting my hand to the wound, but the pincers keep opening and closing, its barbs puncturing and scratching my face.

By the time the centipede comes closer and takes an interest in my legs, laying its feelers around me before nibbling at my boots, I'm already losing it.

I think of the shame that drove me out of that showroom. If only we had taken a minute to reset. If only I didn't hate that place...

Raina and Kirsten scream my name, but they sound a thousand miles away. Then I don't hear them at all.

The correct choice was to take a breather. Turn to page 148.

With half of the beefcakes working the rope, the chandelier swings with an ever-increasing arc after an achingly slow start. Every heave brings it closer to the balcony, then closer to the window.

I upturn Joe's backpack. Another coil of climbing rope spills out, and I unravel it. I rush to the edge of the balcony, where I tie the bulkiest, tightest knot I can around the guardrail.

Kirsten hooks her hand around my arm. "Quinn, the windows—"

"There's no time!" I shake her off. "Omri, Tremaine!"

The storm has a noticeable effect on the fog, which swirls like a breath blown over a boiling kettle's steam. It makes it easier to see what teems below. Our pill bug herd has ventured this way, and it's brought company, which, so far, seems untroubled by the dropping temperature.

The music falters. They can't feel the cold, can they? And yet they need to make a break for it.

My stomach clenches, seeing how we've done everything wrong, waited too long. The best thing would've been for everyone to bum-rush the doors. But it's too late for that. The music got us here. Arctic air blasts through an ever-widening keyhole. I'm sitting on the most important task. The doors need clearing now.

After tugging the knot a final time, I drop its length over the guardrail, along with a couple of aluminum baseball bats. The bats clang and bounce, and the rope makes a terse wet slap.

I don my winter gloves and lift one leg over the guardrail, then the other, taking the rope. Wrapping it once around a leg, I squeeze it between my calves and slide. It burns through my gloves. I drop fast. My feet slam tiles, my knees buckle, and my hip crashes into the floor.

I get up and back away from the Macy's main entrance, scooping up a bat. The storm dips down this low, licking at my face, but not enough to turn away the fleeing creatures.

Omri takes the rope next, using a backpack to protect his hands, inspiring me to throw my gloves to Kirsten. When Omri has slid down to five feet above the floor, he whimpers, his wounded chest grated by the rope. He drops to the floor, buckling his legs and rolling. Omri winces when he rises, favoring his left foot, and I hand him a bat.

Up top, Tim takes Tremaine's place. He rappels gloveless, hand over hand, touching the floor slowly but safely. Kirsten slides down next, practically floating, her drop fast and landing smooth.

Tim takes my bat, and Kirsten and I go to work. The chandelier above and behind us swings back and forth, and our beefcakes menace the approaching crowd of creatures. We grab limbs from the closest bodies and drag, sometimes stumbling, having grabbed something semi-detached.

"Heads up!" Raina yells.

A giant glass panel crumbles apart at spiderwebbed seams and shatters to the floor, spraying us with shards and water. I protect my face, then get back to work.

When we reach the bodies piled up in the doorway to the vestibule, Kirsten peels away to mutter something.

"Kirsten, what is it? Get back here!"

"It's not working!" she shouts. "Look!"

I haul a body back to her and glance at the chandelier, where's she pointing. With the beefcakes pulling at full strength, the peak of its arc just barely brings it to the window. Its jingling ornaments only brush the glass.

"They need to try *this* one," she says, pointing to the west-facing window above the doors. "I *thought* that was the plan in the first place!"

I quickly judge the chandelier to be mounted closer to the doors than the south wall. Barely, but worth a shot. If we smash the west window, we wouldn't even need to chuck more weights.

Kirsten shouts her idea to Joe while I wave to get his attention. He looks down at us, red-faced, muscles close to spasming.

"It's too hard for you!" he cries. "We can barely do it ourselves."

"Then *you* get down here and do it!" Kirsten shouts.

Joe looks to Brian, who nods and says something. He responds and backs his team away from the balcony.

"Heads up!" Joe calls, coiling the rope and throwing it over.

The chandelier's pendulum swing shortens when they line up to climb down.

Omri and Tim have taken to throwing shards of glass and other scraps of junk at the approaching creatures, bopping things off pill bugs and lizard snouts. When I spot a frog coming close, I strip coats from bodies and give them to the boys to use as tongue magnets.

We have to keep working on moving the corpses. Kirsten and I haul them down and through the doors, crumbling the hill one dead person at a time. Their shoulders catch in the frames, slowing us down, and once we reach the bodies on the downhill slope into the vestibule, it's too hard to lever them out on our own. I stumble backward, huffing and puffing.

Omri screams when he's stripped of his blue waterproof jacket by a giant pink tongue. He grabs for another. Tim dangles a red coat like a bullfighter, before dodging behind upturned cafe tables for cover.

"Well?" Kirsten asks, dragging a body from the edge of the pile. An easy picking. "Are you helping, or aren't you?"

It's been a long day. But I've had it with her attitude.

"Am *I* helping? Am *I*?"

I yank the body from her and throw its legs to the side. The next one she pulls I steal from her too. She throws up her hands in disgust, then stomps over a field of corpses, into the vestibule, where she starts pulling from the bottom of the pile. I'm fascinated by what's become of her—Kirsten Fortner, prissy cheerleader, who's never looked out for anyone but herself. It doesn't make a difference that we made it this far as a team. She's a survivor. Kirsten's going to do what she must to get out alive. Part of me admires it. But the other part of me is sickened by it.

Joe makes it down the rope, plants his feet gracefully, and watches Brian start over the balcony, when a new wrinkle ruins our plan. The creatures inside Macy's, undeterred by the cold, decide it's time to pounce.

The weight-chuckers abandon their work and start hacking away with hockey sticks and bats. Ramon falls, his leg caught by a pincer. Brian swings his legs back over the balcony and joins a tug-of-war for him.

There's another scream when Tim's arm is caught in his decoy jacket, a frog tongue stuck to the other side. He clings to a cafe table as he's pulled away, scraping it through the water. Omri leaps for his legs, ignoring the gash to his chest.

Joe jumps too, keeping the frog's tongue from pulling Tim any more. He screams for Kirsten and me to keep working.

What else is there to do? I jog for the vestibule, but before I take two strides, I notice the lasso rope dangling off to my side. Its motion has been reduced to a gentle swaying. We have a job to do. The beefcakes are smashing windows and providing security. Prairie, Skye, and the seniors ensured us safe passage. Our one job is to open the doors. We're almost there. Just a few more bodies in the vestibule and we can bash our way out.

But ours is the only job that's going well. It's the sole one without a big question mark hanging over it. The music has stopped. The weights haven't broken enough glass. Everyone is tied up, unable to continue, and the monsters aren't stopping.

Kirsten notices I've paused and screams, telling me we're almost there.

I can picture us on the other side of the doors in the freezing cold, free at last. But it won't be everyone else. They might make a run for it, and they might make it. But only the storm will ensure they do. It's the surest path to our salvation. We need to take out this swamp once and for all.

The mall is ours. It's *always* been ours. And if speeding up its ruin means we stay in control, so be it.

I grab the rope and step back until it goes taut, a diagonal line connecting me to the chandelier.

"Are you insane?" Kirsten shouts.

"We need the storm! We need these monsters off our backs!"

"No, we don't!"

"We need them off *theirs*!"

I pull on the rope, but that only makes me slide forward on the wet floor. The rope's angle grows closer to ninety degrees, and then I fall on my butt. I scramble to my feet and try again. The dangling crystals indicate I had a minuscule impact. But it *is* an impact.

Kirsten becomes stuck watching me, hands around a corpse's ankles. I bring the rope taut again and pull, anchoring myself, bending my knees, and digging in my toes. It's almost to no avail. But almost means more than nothing. The chandelier's crystals hang straight down, gravity tilting its body toward me. I slide forward, but this time, I don't fall.

I check behind me.

The boys have won back Omri, but they're fending off another centipede while a frog waits for a clear shot at them. I could help. But I can't. I shouldn't. This is how I need to help.

When I turn back around, I'm suddenly face-to-face with Kirsten. She's red with rage—the face that says she didn't get her way, not yet anyway. Her revenge face. She grabs the length of rope between my hands. I let Kirsten have it and pick up the slack behind her.

"On three," she commands. Kirsten counts us off rapidly.

We heave in unison, and we slide, but we don't fall. The chandelier swings for the first time, showing us its underside, reversing toward the west-facing window.

She counts us down again.

"Three!"

We heave. I can tell by the weight, this thing is a wrecking ball in disguise. We just need to get it going.

When it reaches its farthest point, we pull again. My wounded arm complains, my feet start slipping, and every cut and bruise wakes up, reminding me what I've been through. The chandelier swings a couple of inches closer.

From the balcony comes a hoarse, gravelly cheer. I glance over.

Two new figures emerge from the fog and race up behind the Macy's creatures. One swings a guitar down on a monster's back, and the beefcakes renew their push. Skye is here, and with him is Prairie, looking like a chewed-up piece of gum on the bottom of a shoe with that jacket on. Bright scarlet blood cascades down her face. The sight freezes me, and I hold the rope longer than I'm supposed to.

"Let go!" Kirsten shouts.

The rope pulls me forward. I release it and fall into Kirsten. She lets the rope go and stumbles too.

"What the hell, Quinn!"

I scramble for the retreating rope, loping over Kirsten, when a new pair of hands appear and stop me in my tracks. Raina lets the trailing rope slither through her hand. The chandelier moves to the window. She hands me the end of the rope.

"Behind me, okay?" Raina says.

I stumble backward with it, making room for Kirsten in the middle. Even though I can hardly stand any longer, there are three of us now. When the rope reaches the end of its arc, we pull. This time, we keep our feet under us.

A guttural scream makes us turn. I expect the worst. Joe or Tim or Omri have been killed, eaten by a frog. I'm so convinced, I don't believe when I see them still standing, still fighting. But bearing down on them now is the mosquito beast, bouncing off the floor like an untied party balloon. It launches itself over the phalanx of creatures, startling the frog and lizards into darting for the sides of the concourse.

We pull again, but Raina doesn't take her eyes off the mosquito. When we release, she drops the rope and steps out of line. Kirsten shouts at her, but just as soon as Raina leaves, Alex takes her spot. His appearance startles me as much as Raina's did. I check the balcony. Gabe and Valerie have arrived. Gina and Trent are still missing.

With reinforcements, the beefcakes get back to smashing windows. Tomi instructs Gabe and Valerie to watch their backs, but they're not paying attention. Valerie is bawling. Gabe stares into nothingness. Prairie moves Ramon closer to the balcony and eventually collapses. She caves to her knees, out of sight too. Skye leaps to her aid.

Alex screams to them for more help, seeing how they have a surplus of bodies now. Skye's head pokes up, but just as quickly, his focus goes back to Prairie.

Behind us, Raina wields a hockey stick and forms ranks with Tim, Omri, and Joe. The mosquito beast bears down on them.

The balcony victory is promising, but the cost has been high. Two of our beefcakes wince as they chuck weights. Prairie and Ramon are seriously wounded, and two seniors are gone. And now a mosquito beast is coming for Raina, same as the one that nearly wiped her out before. Everyone seems so far away, and I feel like I'm doing nothing to help. The last of my strength bleeds out of me.

Alex's shoulder smashes into mine. "Pull, dammit!" he yells.

I falter and stumble to the floor, splashing into the warm flood waters.

"Oh, screw this!" Kirsten yells. She drops the rope and rushes for the doors.

Alex shouts and swipes one hand out to stop her, but she makes it to the vestibule and begins pulling bodies.

The mosquito beast barrels into our security squad, and all but Raina tumble to the floor, defending against its charge and making it bounce off the windows.

The beefcakes up top have bulked up their numbers, but even so, half of them are out of commission, either wounded or too stunned to help.

Alex doesn't waste a second breath on Kirsten. He turns around and pulls me to my feet. I burn at his touch. He's bothered me this whole time, and I don't think I'd like him on a good day, but he gets me to my feet, puts the rope in my hands, and with a coach's stern bark tells me, "You can do this!"

The chandelier is swinging back at us. We've already missed one revolution. It's slowing down. A whimper burbles from the depths of my throat. Alex double-takes and swats my shoulder.

"Come on! You can do this!" He turns back around and watches the chandelier return to the window one more time, waiting for it to reach the extent of its arc before pulling.

The whimper bursts past my lips. It feels like the mall caves in around us. The monsters bear down on the group. The storm blankets our remains.

"On three!" Alex shouts.

Raina swings her hockey stick at the mosquito beast's proboscis. Omri, bent over, drags an aluminum baseball bat behind him. Tim pushes over Joe, saving him from a frog's tongue that snaps the air like a whip.

"One!"

Beefcakes chuck weights, sending small glass shards into a pile on the floor. Sleet shoots through the broken windows, assaulting their bare skin. Half of them spin, and Tomi loses his weight over the edge. They raise weapons to fight some new creature skittering out of Macy's.

"Two!"

Kirsten rolls a corpse over the stack of bodies in the vestibule. She hunches, out of my sight, looking for another and working like a madwoman, as if she's stolen my last bit of energy. The chandelier approaches the end of its arc above her. It's time to reclaim my strength, whatever's left of it. I can't help all my friends at once. This is all I can do. The chandelier's weight pushes against gravity for one last instant before coming to a standstill.

"*Three!*"

Alex pulls, his muscles tensing, his feet sticking to the floor. I tug, the cords of my tendons tightening until everything wants to snap. My feet give out, and I slide into Alex's heels. But I don't keep falling until I hit the floor. There's another body behind us. I keep my feet under me. The weight of the rope in my hands...I'm still pulling.

The chandelier swings toward us, showing us its bottom, the entirety of its crystal-encrusted rim, as if we're standing right under it. In that moment, I look back and see Skye holding the rope, having come from upstairs to help.

He sees me gawk at him with my despairing, weak eyes, telling him I can't do this. *I'll try*, they tell him. Yes, I'll try, but I don't expect us to win.

There's no strength in him either. No encouragement or hope or even any desperation to win. His eyes are tired and sallow. His mouth hangs open, and his chest heaves with labored breaths. When the chandelier swings back toward the windows and above Kirsten, he nods. Skye can't hide the resignation in the gesture, but he repeats aloud, for his sake. And maybe for mine.

"We can do this. We can do this."

Alex counts to three. We pull, and this time, all of us keep our feet under us. The three of us step back, bringing the chandelier closer.

We pull again and step back, letting more of the rope slide through our hands, allowing it to travel farther. Its glass baubles bat the window, sending a shiver down my back.

"More! Come on!" Alex screams, his voice breaking. "On three!"

"We can do this..." Skye says. "...We can *do* this!"

On the balcony, the beefcakes are back on the defensive. Behind us, Raina rejoins the boys, fighting off the mosquito beast. Omri is spent, weakly lobbing things at an approaching crawfish and lizard.

"*Three!*"

We pull.

The chandelier hits the window.

"*Three!*"

We pull.

The chandelier's baubles fan out when it smashes into the glass. Some of the crystals crash to the floor, hitting corpses and shattering on the tiles around Kirsten. She covers her neck, hauling a body over the pile from inside the vestibule.

I scream at her to move, but she won't listen to me. And I have to stay where I am.

"Kirsten, get out of there!" Skye screams.

"We're not stopping, dammit!" Alex yells. Is he talking to Kirsten? To us?

It doesn't matter. We can't stop.

The chandelier hits the window again, dropping more baubles and making the pane shudder.

"*Three!*"

We pull.

"Kirsten, stay in there!" I scream when the chandelier swings toward her.

She's probably moved another half dozen bodies this whole time—enough to high step our way to the outer door, where a few more corpses lean against the glass. Kirsten rushes into the mall in a frenzy, looking for something.

More baubles shatter. The chandelier's central mass hits the window that much harder.

We pull.

"Kirsten!"

She doesn't listen. When she spots Tomi's dropped dumbbell, she bolts for it, then returns to the doors. She's making a break for it.

I look back at Raina, who throws a broken hockey stick like a battle ax at the mosquito beast, bursting a compound eye with its broken end. A crawfish moves in, and Joe wedges a baseball bat into its pincers. No one's paying attention to Kirsten.

The chandelier flies over our heads, hitting the end of its arc and going temporarily weightless at the limit of its cable. This is it. The one. It swings back for the window, like a hot rod off the starting line.

"*Kirsten!*"

She hears me and looks, dumbbell in hand, a sad expression on her face. From right outside the vestibule, she can view all the devastation at once. There's a near-apology in her eyes, as if she'll regret this someday and she knows it. She'll have to bury this memory forever.

The chandelier smashes into the window. Undercutting the shattering of baubles and stems is a loud snap. Three cracks spread like etched lightning in the window, as if they'd always been there. It becomes several sharp panes, their color changing shades of silver as they fall from their setting. They drop heavily, crashing with rumbling shocks to the floor amid explosions of crystal.

Kirsten disappears in a shower of deadly splinters and splashing water. A black line—the edge of a pane—cuts through the air past her, and she drops from view.

Skye and Alex pull the chandelier one more time, instinctively, disbelieving of our success.

The mangled chandelier passes over our heads, dropping little glass grenades, accompanied by a blistering wall of wind. It burns my face and freezes my sweat, cutting down to the bone through my soaked clothes. The fog instantly swirls and eddies around the balcony's uprights, getting battered back down the concourse by the storm.

The creatures don't immediately retreat, but the glacial wind gives them pause. Feelers go out of control. Pill bugs start bumping into each other. The lizards and salamanders seem to shrivel into themselves. When the wind hits the mosquito beast, it bumbles forward, then stops flapping its wings, going nearly catatonic. Raina is there with a baseball bat, to finish it off with a fatal blow to the head.

I turn away from it all and sprint to the doors, rained on by chandelier crystal and window fragments. Tramping through the corpses, I reach the vestibule, finding a thick, wide shard lying atop a few bodies.

Next to the shard is Kirsten, moving as lazily as a half-frozen fly. Blond hair covers her face. Her designer jacket is well and truly ruined. Its sleeve goes beneath the glass shard, and where it should connect to her shoulder, the arm doesn't meet the body.

Her limb has been severed clean off.

I scream for help.

♥*♥*♥

Get help. Turn to page 131.

Get Kirsten out of here. Turn to page 321.

"Found'em," says Mr. Harris, who pulls his daughter, Raina, under his arm and jostles her until her face goes as dark as mine.

The implication of their sudden appearance sinks in, and my stomach backflips. I'm supposed to put on a happy face? Swallow this food and go along with whatever nonsense Kirsten has planned? Pretend I'm as pleased as everyone else that Raina came to the one place she hates the most, all on my account?

Not a chance.

"Doing okay, Quinn?" Mr. Harris asks.

"'Thcuse-mmeh," I mumble before speed-walking past them, without any heed to etiquette.

They can gossip about me all they want. Join the rest of Madison. I'm still in no state to meet it head-on. I'll be back at home, stretching the weekend into an eternity and hoping for the sweet release of death once again.

"Dude, where you going?" Kirsten calls.

Away, you brat. I'm going away from *you*.

Prairie calls my name, ending it with an uneasy lilt. "Qu-*inn?*"

Not to worry, Prairie. You can come too.

The pay phone bank is right across the atrium, in full view of the food court. As long as I'm in sight, Kirsten will see me as fair game to pester and cajole. So I go back where we came from—back to Sears, so Kirsten thinks this is all she gets, that she's stepped too far. She'll catch up to make sure I don't do anything crazy, and that's when I'll make my stand. I'm ready to pay whatever cost to win this battle, even if it means weeks of her passive-aggression.

With my head down to avoid detection, I chew at the wad of breakfast crammed in my mouth. I'm forced to navigate groups of shoppers and go around maintenance workers pointing at the bathrooms and talking to security.

My backtracking brings me to the heart decals stuck to the floor. I follow the direction of their ballooning lobes instead of their points, making my way out of this sea of commerce and romance, risking a final glance at the line of shoppers waiting for pictures with Cupid.

A cluster of grins arrests my attention. Six or seven of them. Sophomores. Fellow Bobcats. A mix of boys and girls I've seen in the halls and turned my nose up at. They seemed like little shits their freshman year, and nothing has changed. The group watches me intently for what feels like far longer than I've noticed them.

Two of the sophomores burst into laughter and point.

"Write me a poem for a buck?" asks one of the boys.

"You bring Skye with ya?" jeers the girl next to him.

"What is *wrong* with her face?"

Bobcat Cheerleader Dead at 17. Classmates Blamed!

Freaking *sophomores*.

I pick up the pace, acting like I know nothing about what they're saying, but before I turn away, one of the girls lifts the velvet rope and ducks under it.

"Hey, Carpenter!" she calls, all giggly. "C'mon! Come with us! We want a picture!"

I enter the Sears wing and veer to the left side of the concourse, going against traffic and hoping to drop my tail. But her cackling is joined by one or two more, punch-drunk on their luck at spotting me. I cut between shoppers, focused on getting out of here. My chewing slows. I could use Kirsten right now to put those sophomores in their place. Actually, I can most likely count on that, but until it happens, I'm on my own.

"Hey, watch it!" scolds a man not far behind me.

"Quinn, we want a picture with Cupid!"

My blood freezes and my cool breaks, right outside the harem tent. I can't keep scurrying away with these morons making a scene. The tent flap is open, and I dart under it, finding myself alone and ensconced in the pop-up shop's red-lit interior. I move in deeper and monitor the flap. My heart races when the giggling comes closer, but then it passes. It recedes. I sigh and start chewing again.

The inside of the tent is rather disappointing, given the allure of its outer facade. Wire racks line its walls. Two smaller racks bisect its middle. Hanging from wobbly hooks are all manner of nylon and pleather lingerie, fishnets and frills, with accessories glowing like rubies under the light. I spot whips and handcuffs and blindfolds and all sorts of things I suspect are meant to be scandalous but which would only make Kirsten and me roar with laughter.

Before I can look closer at the things protruding from the back corner, the tent darkens. A man blocks the open flap.

"Hey, you can't be in here without ID," he says.

"Oh..." I mumble.

He enters, a brick of a man, and grabs my arm, clearly used to doing this at bars or clubs. If someone were to lay hands on me under any other circumstances, I'd scream bloody murder. Despite the situation, I almost do but only manage a gasp, which sucks the amalgamated remains of hash brown and cinnamon roll into the top of my trachea and seals it shut.

He hauls me into the light of the concourse.

"C'mon, girl. Get outta here."

I can't speak. When I attempt to rip my arm away, he hangs on by instinct, as if he's got a brawler on his hands.

"What's the matter?" someone asks. A woman.

"Nothing, she's—"

"What the hell, you idiot! What's wrong with her?" the woman cries.

My face heats up, and my chest swells. A breath tries to press through the obstruction, and I bring my free hand to my throat. The bouncer lets me go, and I fall to my knees.

"She's...she's choking! Help! Someone help! She's choking!" yells the woman, who I suspect to be the store owner. She towers over me, fishnets climbing legs like the Sears Tower, up to a skirt that practically winks as if to say, "Ha! Caught ya lookin!" Her platinum blond hair swishes while she screams.

One man drops his wife's hand and rushes over. He wraps his arms around my waist and pushes me forward, his fists clasped beneath my sternum.

The woman keeps begging for help despite his presence. She stumbles on her three-inch heels and falls, landing on the rear of her teensy tiny skirt.

The points of her heels rise, accusing me of causing this emergency, just as I'm pitched forward. That's when the giggling returns.

"Oooh my God, what!" screams a sophomore, stuck between hilarity and horror as she witnesses the pinnacle of my degradation.

In their excitement, the sophomores barge into my helpful stranger, and he falls on me with a small cry.

My gaze descends, and my left eye is greeted by the sharp finger of a stiletto still pointing at me, telling everyone who I am and what I've done.

My eye bursts, which is an interesting sensation I can't explore for long before my brain is punctured and I lose my capacity to describe it.

The correct choice was to make small talk with Mr. Harris.
Turn to page 40.

"Yeah..." I begin. "We totally talked about doing homework, didn't we?"

I give Prairie a rescue-me stare, but simply by being here, Kirsten's already turned the screws. Prairie shrinks away, unable to back up my claim.

Dad blurts, "Homework? On Anti-Valentine's Day?"

Prairie stammers, "Oh, no, I was just dropping off—"

"Quinn, you can stand to take a Saturday off. I've never known you to be *that* good of a student."

Kirsten chuckles on Dad's cue.

"I didn't mean to ruin any plans," says Prairie. "And I have to—"

"Nonsense! It sounds like you girls got your wires crossed. I think you're all going to the mall today. Homework can wait."

"No, Prairie's here to help me study, Dad. I wasn't feeling good yesterday, and I need to catch up on stuff."

"You're not feeling good?"

"Well, after yesterday..." Kirsten starts.

"What happened yesterday?" Dad asks.

"That's why we talked about going to Meadow Spire."

"Oh, not feeling good like...lady stuff?" Dad becomes grave.

"*Dad!* You...Yes, you're exactly right. That's it. And Prairie and I talked about doing homework today."

"Do you need a Tylenol?"

"No, no! You can go to the mall!" Prairie declares. She drops her backpack, shaking the house, before crouching over it. It's the only way she can zip it back up. "I didn't mean to interfere. I was just dropping stuff off."

"Does anyone else need a Tylenol?"

"I'd rather have a quiet day inside. It's supposed to be terrible out anyway," I say.

There can't be any mistaking my honesty. Why can't they all just *leave*?

Dad pouts, Kirsten smirks, and Prairie looks mortified.

Bridie enters the room.

"Sup, Prairie," she says.

"Hey, Bridie."

Bridie surveys the scene. "They're not trying to ditch you, are they?"

"Shut *up*, Bridie," I say.

She glowers at Kirsten, then back at me.

Kirsten claps her hands. "I know what an adult would do in this situation. They would compromise, right, Mr. Carpenter? We got our wires crossed. I thought we were going out, Quinn wants to stay in, and Prairie found the perfect thing to keep us busy. Now, it might not be true for Quinn or Prairie, but I could stand to spend a Saturday morning focused on my studies for once."

Oh, don't do this, you brat.

"Someone's thinking." The relief on Dad's face is obvious after Bridie pushes past us, diminishing the risk of any teenage sniping.

"Study 'til noon, okay?" Kirsten suggests. "We'll avoid the early rush to the mall, then we'll check the weather and see how we feel. I need to you two to teach me trig anyway."

"You're not in trig."

"I might be someday."

No. We're not going to do this. Kirsten will see my room. She might even be looking for a way into it, hunting for clues to explain yesterday. Prairie will see too. Someone will spill to my parents. It's a miracle Bridie's kept her mouth shut this long. There's only one more thing to try, and it's crappiest toward Prairie.

"Okay, but I'm not making any promises. I may just crash after we study."

Kirsten shrugs. "Works for me. I know how to spend my daddy's money on my own." She winks at Dad.

"But can we get out of this house? I was cooped up all night."

Kirsten eyes me, sensing what I'm getting at. I turn to Prairie to throw my Hail Mary.

"Can we head to your place?"

Prairie's eyes take an excruciating moment to shrink to normal size, but she nods vigorously. "Yes...Yeah, we can...I mean, I have to...Yeah."

Do you get that you're rescuing me yet?

"That'd be awesome." I let my words drift off into a feigned sigh of exhaustion.

Really, I should be exhausted, but Kirsten has me wired. I already felt guilty when Prairie showed up. Now a broadsword twists in my gut. I'm using her so bad. It makes me feel even worse when I wonder how long it'll take to get over my guilt.

It's my only option, though. I don't want to go to the mall, and I don't want Kirsten in the house. She'll never follow me to—

"Great! Let's go. I'll drive us back to your place, Hedlund. I can't believe you took more than ten steps out there."

My mouth hangs open, but I stop myself from uttering a single syllable. My bluff's been called. Kirsten gets her keys out and tilts her head. Dad sips his coffee, nodding in approval. Prairie is drained of color, but she mouths an *okay*.

Dad retires to his easy chair. "Prairie, say hi to the missus, why don't'cha? Tell her how your folks are doing."

Prairie speed-walks down the hall to the kitchen, leaving her marble block of a backpack by the door.

"You gonna get ready?" Kirsten asks.

There's no way out of this. Not without causing a scene. Like, a bigger one.

"Fine." I will my stare to wither her into a prune.

Intent on getting this over with as soon as possible, for everyone's sake, I march upstairs. Once I'm in the bathroom, an impulse to stall grips me, and I take my time putting up my hair and washing my face, keeping the water running to drown out my lack of activity. Bridie enters after a moment with her toothbrush and spits into the sink.

"You okay?" she asks.

I dab my cheeks with the towel and look at her reflection in the mirror, wondering what I might see there. How much does she really know? Or...did she have anything to do with it?

"Yeah. Fine."

"Mmm," she grunts as I leave.

Kirsten insists Prairie ride shotgun. I slide onto the jeep's back seat and clap the slush from my boots—a result of our recent spate of bizarre weather. A thick blanket of snow, a super-fast thaw, now a cold front swooping in like the next horseman of the apocalypse. My teeth chatter against the freezing wind.

Prairie's backpack sits next to me. It's so full, the corner of a book sticks out from between the zippers at the top like an iceberg. She glances at it and frowns like she doesn't recognize it, then offers me a smile.

Put a stop to this. Do it now. Apologize later.

Kirsten drives us two blocks over, splashing slush and kicking up a wake the whole way. I can't imagine going as far as Meadow Spire. And with the freeze coming in? Yeesh. I also can't believe what I'm doing this very second. Going to Prairie's? With Kirsten Fortner? All I wanted was to stay in bed all day. Now, I'm in a new freaking dimension.

We get inside, greeted by that good old casserole smell and two-degrees-too-warm temperature of the Hedlund homestead. Hasn't changed in years.

Prairie's anxiety is off the charts. "Wait right here? I need to clean my room up a bit." She's off to hide some cutesy, churchy things from Kirsten's piercing gaze, dragging her bag up the stairs.

It won't make a difference.

She doesn't know the extent of Kirsten's gossip-making abilities. Prairie's room could be an empty cell, and Kirsten would still find something to tease her about. It makes me feel so much worse. Worlds are colliding. I'm literally smashing planets together.

When Prairie reaches the second floor, I whisper, "Behave, please."

Kirsten scoffs, plucking a ceramic angel from a bureau in the hallway to examine it. "What's the matter with you? I'm a perfect gentlewoman. And you did this to yourself, by the way."

"I wanted to stay home."

"You need to get out, is what you need. Show people you're not embarrassed."

"I *am* embarrassed."

"Hey, guys?"

Prairie's voice makes me look up. She's stopped in the hallway just past the staircase, her backpack balanced on the balustrade above our heads.

"Is this one of yours?" she asks.

The thin balusters give out from under the weight, and the top rail bows forward. The backpack slides into space directly over me. In her hand is one of my diaries.

And troubled earth tumbles down, far too shy...

Kirsten.

She thought she'd find the poem in one of my diaries, which I'd kicked under my bed just before I went downstairs to greet her. She snuck into my room anyway. She slipped it into Prairie's bag. She just had to see for herself.

Prairie drops it when she sees her bag has slipped. The diary tumbles through the air, riding the invisible coattails of her AP- and Honors-curricula-laden backpack.

Kirsten gasps. Prairie's backpack hits my face.

My vision goes black, stars burst out into the blackness, but it's my diary, which definitely did not contain the poem, that makes up my final thought.

The correct choice was to invite Prairie to Meadow Spire Mall.
Turn to page 25.

"No." I punch the power button, ending the call over Kirsten's barrage of objections and insistences that I come out with her. The phone slides from my hand and slips off the side of the bed, landing with a papery thud on the diaries I searched last night for the offending verses. Came up nada, as I thought I would, but leave no stone unturned...

And troubled earth tumbles down, far too shy

Nope, not touching that.

The real problem, though, is Kirsten's coming over, no matter what. I don't want company today, much less care to exist, but there's no stopping her. And despite the fact she's spent countless hours watching TV or jabbering with Mom and Dad while I showered or crammed for a test, I can't leave Kirsten alone with them today. They already know something's up. And now I'm getting calls at weird hours? And Kirsten will be pounding on our door?

When she barges in, she'll put on some extra cheer, which should be impossible but isn't. Nothing's out of the question for Kirsten, and it'll only make my parents more suspicious. There's never any winning with her. It's her train, her tracks. I'm just waiting to get my ticket punched.

So, I might as well beat her to it. Put on a smile, answer the door before anyone else can, guide her upstairs or to the basement, and have it out where no one can hear. Maybe she'll drop the whole thing. And if not, as a last resort, I'm good for a massive tantrum to win myself the rest of the day.

That makes me feel better—taking control, changing tracks. What's there to lose when Dad will start asking questions by nightfall and Monday's right around the corner? I was never going to do this in my own time. Kirsten has only sped it up and cut into my wallowing. I might look at it as a favor, if I don't want to stay mad at her for another week or two.

I kick the comforter to the foot of my bed and sit up. Across the room, my broken mirror shows my pajamas, but the reflection cuts off at my neckline. Its missing top section leans against the wall by my bed, where I placed it during a tiny window of cautious sensibility.

I adjust to the chill in the air, force my spine to stay straight, resist flopping back down. Kirsten's up and moving, probably pulling out of her road right now. Fifteen minutes, tops, 'til she's here.

I got this.

Tidying my room takes priority. No primping, no breakfast. Hide the evidence of last night's tornado. The bigger the mess, the harder it'll be to get rid of her.

Diaries first. Kirsten will key in on them, and good Lord, she can't be allowed to see what else is written inside. She already likes to pretend she can read my mind. If I gave her the actual radiographs, my life would be chaos. I can't undo all the wreckage from my freakout, but the diaries have to go.

I sweep my legs off the edge of the bed—the side I don't normally use, where I dropped the phone, which I better put on my dresser in case Kirsten calls back. Or someone else. Raina, maybe? Hopefully? Raina has been acting weird, but she knows what happened. She has to. Raina would have seen how miserable I was. Wouldn't she? Why couldn't she have called instead?

The diaries I'll slip between my mattress and the box spring. Kirsten may be a princess in most people's eyes, but if I keep the sheets rumpled, she won't feel those precious peas under her butt when she flops down and makes my bed her own.

And troubled earth tumbles down, far too shy
To stop its flight and cry, how I love you, oh—

Stop. Enough of that.

But should I check them again? I wonder...They're full of random stuff, rhymes and random poems weaving in and out of streams of conscious angst. Some scribbled out, others abandoned, some embroidered with hearts and bubbles and other strange things, like daggers and pointy suns and crescent moons and bows and arrows.

I was nearly out of my mind yesterday. Maybe I missed something. Maybe I convinced myself the verses weren't here and they really did find their way into that valentine the way Kirsten says they did...

No. I don't have time, so I shake the impulse away. Hide them. Deal with Kirsten.

I slide off the bed, robbed of my endless night, of an early death. Monday will be here before I know it. That's when I'll really die, I guess. Slowly, then all at once. That's my prize for having a crush a long time ago. How fair life is...

My foot lands on something slick—a magazine. I continue to stand, thinking nothing of it. The place is a mess. There's less carpet visible than crap on the floor. Except the magazine is on top of another.

My leg slides out from under me, kicking the upper magazine away. I lean forward to regain balance, stomping to complete the maneuver. But I land on another magazine, and my foot slips backward this time, forcing my ankle into the bed frame. Pain balloons from the point of contact, and I yelp. My arms arc out in front of me.

I pitch forward, diagonally, into the wall. A triangular reflection of my billowing hair and shocked face comes closer the lower I go. My forearm rides the upward angle of the mirror's shard and pushes it away from where it's leaning. Right before I hit the floor, its accusatory point enters my neck. A sharp, hot sting accompanies it— a perfect contrast to the throbbing in my battered ankle.

I open my mouth to scream for help, but moving my jaw makes my neck burn more. My pulse grows more apparent, pumping blood into the open air like a shipwreck survivor bailing water from a lifeboat.

From the cover of *Details*, Skeet Ulrich wears a disheveled suit, sporting a devilish goatee. His nose is crinkled from where I stepped on him. Such a betrayal. He isn't even the crush who made me want to die.

I can picture the headlines.
See What You Did?
Shouldn't Have Laughed, Folks.
Madison Mourns Teen Beauty. Whole School Arrested.
They'll find me amidst my chaos. It's what I wished for.
The light fades around Skeet. He's the last thing I see...

♥*♥*♥

The correct choice was to get out of bed and deal with Kirsten.
Turn to page 11.

Kirsten's lips move, giving shape to words as vague and airy as her voice. Her arm, under the thick shard, lies palm facing up, its dirty manicured nails curling gently inward. She's as pale as every mutant swamp creature we've encountered. Blood covers the corpse she lies on and wells in the cruddy water.

"Raina! Joe! Anybody!"

I rip the jacket off another corpse to try to stanch the flow, pressing with what remains of my energy into her side. Her body slides away from me. Her head bumps up against another piece of glass, and she stirs.

Her eyes squint open, and her expression changes from dazed to quizzical. "Quinn?" she wheezes.

Raina lands near me, rips off her puffer jacket, and pushes me out of the way. Skye arrives, too, and helps compress the wound.

"Belt!" Raina shouts, pointing at Alex.

He rips his off and throws it over.

"Where's Prairie?" I demand. "She can help."

"No, she can't," Skye says.

I look at the balcony and spot Prairie being led to the rope. No point backtracking away from the storm now. She covers her face with a bone-white hand. Her jacket is stained in blood.

"Quinn?" Kirsten stirs more, asking what's happening.

I scan the corpses for her dumbbell, finding it under the shard covering her severed limb. When I lift it, I avoid stepping on her arm, retrieve the dumbbell, and let the shard fall, pressing her fingers into a fist.

I scramble over bodies, into the vestibule, and kick away the rest of the corpses leaning against the outer door. Stuffing my hand into my jacket, I grip the dumbbell through my sleeve.

Its first impact makes the window shudder. I pull back and punch again. The dumbbell hits, and a crack forms in the glass. I pull back, punch. The crack spiders out.

I'm getting out, and I'm taking Kirsten with me, dammit. But I'll never owe her anything ever again, and I'll never ask her for anything. We'll be even for the rest of our lives.

I punch, and the storm comes inside. Wind whistles through the shattered door. Snow batters my face like tiny razor blades. I kick loose the jagged remains from the frame and stumble backward over bodies, judging the fruit of my work—the pitch-black portal of our deliverance.

When I go back inside, I'm in time to witness Brian tumble down the rope from ten feet up. He lands with a snap and clutches his ankle, screaming in pain. More crashes and rumbling masonry sound from far down the concourse.

Kirsten's sitting up, batting away Skye, who tries to pitch her onto her side to raise her wound. I take her one good arm and drape it over my shoulder, then hold my palm up and paw my finger at Skye and Raina.

"Keys!"

Raina and Skye blanche.

"*Keys, goddammit!*"

Joe spins away from a fading Omri, rifles through his loincloth, and throws a set at me. "Red Crown Vic! Parked right under a light by Sears!"

An outburst from the balcony startles us.

A creature keeps venturing out from the Macy's entrance while Tomi tries to guide Gabe and Valerie to the rope. Raina rises, unsure what to do.

"*Go,*" I tell her.

"What're you..." Kirsten wriggles, trying to free herself.

I take her through the bodies and plod into the vestibule.

Skye follows, stammering how he wants to be of assistance.

"Help *them,*" I command. "I got this."

I can picture ambulances on the other side of the mall, clustered close to the least un-flooded entrance by Sears. We can take a quick walk over there. It's nothing.

There are enough cries from inside to make Skye hesitate, and before he can waste another precious second, I execute my first step outside. My heel lands on a sloping hill of ice-glazed snow, sliding my leg out in front of me and dropping me on my butt. Kirsten falls into me and groans. I glide us farther out onto a veritable skating rink, only to find the upper layer is iced over. My foot crunches through into several inches of freezing water. Around the mall, snowdrifts pile up higher than me.

"J-jeez, it's cold," Kirsten complains.

"It's...gonna get worse," I say.

Not the most inspirational, but if there's anything to keep Kirsten going, it's something to complain about. She dragged me here against my will. I'm dragging her out. At this point, I refuse to let her be the death of me or to let her death be on my conscience. This day was supposed to be all about me. Right, Kirsten?

Snow stings my face and pelts my jacket, the storm wrapping me in its hug. An unrelenting wind darts this way and that, its intensity never decreasing, its howl tumbling over the flat ice-encrusted floodwaters. An all-consuming cold, like a giant bucket of crumbled dry ice, sears my skin. My sweat forms a shell on my face and my hands. My hair solidifies into a rigid weighty chunk. My thighs tighten, and my shoulders lock up.

It's so cold, my feet feel better dipped underwater, away from the lashing wind attacking them anew with every step. I push forward, like the prow of a ship through an ice sheet, with Kirsten doing nothing to help.

"It's my day, K-Kirsten. You hear me? This is m-my day." My words are close to babbling.

Step by plodding step, we get closer to Sears. There has to be something around the corner. Ambulances, fire trucks, police cruisers. Concerned citizens. Uniformed helpers with shiny foil blankets and heated vehicles. If they aren't, Joe's car will do.

"We're gonna make it, K," I say.

"Y-yeah, j-jeez."

We're fifty yards out from the Macy's exit, rounding the corner to Sears, and no flashing red, blue, or yellow lights reflect on the snow. The overhead lamps illuminate the lot, making all the parked, snow-encrusted cars shine a nearly uniform yellowish-white.

That's okay. Joe said he parked right under a light. Easy enough.

A rumble underfoot stops me in my tracks. Out here, nothing else would stop me. Plummeting into a toxic underground swamp is now my greatest fear. I turn to look at Meadow Spire Mall.

The outer brickwork, where the Sears store meets the mall's central structure, cracks. Sears tips down toward the atrium, and the whole building sinks lower. Glass shatters, and the skylights bulging higher than the roof collapse. The spire tilts next, its unlit silveriness disappearing into the atrium like the fall of a saluting arm, putting an official stamp on the fact that Meadow Spire Mall is dead.

I wait for the inevitable to happen, for the cracks to spread under my feet and take me with the mall, but it doesn't go that far. Out in the parking lot, we're still safe. I have to imagine the irradiated under-swamp, home to such varied mutations, still lies beneath us, stretching an unthinkable vastness across the land.

We keep moving. There are still no flashing emergency lights, no people. If they're here, they're not close. Joe's car it is.

"R-right, K-K-K? Today was all about me."

But it wasn't *just*. It was about her too. All about her, this friend I hate so much, who I'm dragging across a barren plain teetering on the edge of the netherworld. A plain we've crossed many, many times, having driven store associates and fast-food workers to madness. Gone to the movies, just to spy on the latest odd-couple dates from school, played pranks that wouldn't be discovered for hours, giggling like lunatics. Stuck together like conjoined twins, our heads bowed into each other, our hair flapping together as a single curtain.

It's exactly like that all over again. Going to the car after a day at the mall. So what if our hair is a little matted, our skin a little blotchy, our jackets torn, bodies clawed, and we're short an arm? We've done this walk before, hugging all the while.

I stumble and fall. My hands break through to water. Back up, in the air, the pain scorches my skin, then burns out like a matchstick, taking my hand with it. It's so cold, it's like having ghost-limb syndrome.

Another twenty yards, and there's still no sign of life. We're almost out of the flood, close to the parked cars of countless dead shoppers, getting to the cutoff point. Here, snow drifts in odd clumps along outcroppings of frozen slush and wheel ruts. I scan for the Crown Vic, even though I'm not close enough to distinguish colors. Instead, I focus on its body style, its blocky front end, the particular curve of its frame.

Kirsten mumbles. I hold her tighter and check her face. Her eyes are closed, and she's not shivering. I wonder if the cold helps, slowing her circulation, like being pre-hypothermic helps keep her from bleeding out. It feels insane, feels wrong. But I stick to it.

I get us past the nearly buried traffic cones blocking off the flooded lot and into the first row of cars, walking with someone else's legs at this point, unsure how my nerves are functioning enough to keep me upright. Like I'm in an arcade game shooter, powered by unseen ghost legs across a devastated landscape.

Ahead of us, the back corner of J.C. Penney just barely sticks out from beyond our view of Sears. And that's when I see it.

Flashing lights.

All the colors of the Fourth of July—red, white, blue, yellow—like they've pinned down an everlasting firework fountain.

"K-K-Kirsten. Look!"

"Uh?" She jolts in my arms.

"Th-there!"

I can't point. We have to keep moving. Help is still far away, and we need to find Joe's car, warm ourselves, and get Kirsten there fast. I can barely speak, but I have to make her stay awake.

"A-almost th-there. Hey, K-Kirsten, remember the...the..."

"Whuh?"

I shuffle us down the first full row of cars, seeing no Crown Vic under the nearest light. Nothing to the left, nothing promising to the right. Onto the next row.

"Re-remember when...the moms...c-caught the kids...eating the floor candy...?"

No Crown Vics in the second row.

"And you p-p-put the f-f-foam f-from your coffee on that guy's hand and t-t-tickled his ear?" I think of the look on the guy's face and snort out snot. It freezes on my lips.

I check the cars under all the lights in the third row. No Crown Vic.

"And...and the kid that s-started crying at the m-murdered teddy bear? A-and wh-when we went past the signs you v-vandalized and...th-they were all taken down? And there was some soccer m-mom yelling at the worker?"

"Heh."

No Crown Vics. My body heat is migrating to my chest. I recognize the onset of the slow descent into death, the false comfort of going to sleep in an inhospitable world.

We pass down more rows, and I still don't see Joe's car. Kirsten and I might have to make straight for an ambulance.

I can run it if I have to, can't I? Can I bring her with me?

We're past the Sears entrance when I see it. Joe's car under a light. Crown Vic body style. Cop car. Seen it millions of times on TV, on the road. He wasn't full of it after all. It's a good spot, closest to the handicap section. Makes sense for a Molson. He probably arrived at six a.m., just to stretch and hold the doors for mall walkers.

The Vic's red, right? It looks red, even under the orange glow of the light and crusty glaze of snow.

"K-Kirsten!"

Her feet barely lift off the ground. I drag her to the car, trying to get the keys out of my pocket. Eventually, I jam my fist inside, commanding my fingers to spread and re-close. I set Kirsten down next to the driver's-side rear door and fall to my knees.

Fumbling with the keys, I press them between my palms and wriggle my fingers until the right key sticks out from its random partners on the chain. After carving up a mess around the keyhole, I get the tip inside, ram it home, and twist.

Except the key *doesn't* twist. I take a breath, pull it halfway out, jam it in, and twist again. Lefty-loosey, right? No? I try to twist to the right. Nothing. The key stays where it is.

So maybe it's not a red Crown Vic. I back away and squint at the nameplate on the door.

Caprice.

It's not the right car. A cop car. But the wrong kind of cop car.

"K-Kirsten, it's..."

No.

We'll get up and keep going.

The wind whips my face. My eyes sting. Everything else is numb.

The car has to be here. Maybe Joe didn't mean he was right under a light?

As I wonder this, a stream of smoke rises between cars, which I think of as a gust of drifting snow. I blink and look in the same place. The smoke licks the air again before dissipating into the air, instead of turning into a finer dust scouring the ground. I should know what this means, but I need to get us moving.

Leaving the keys in the car door, I turn around and crouch in front of Kirsten. Her head lulls. I grip her shoulder and cradle her neck.

"K-Kirsten."

"Uh..."

I'm not sure if I can lift her. She needs to help herself. I slide down next to her and pat her cheek. Kirsten stirs, and drool from her open mouth freezes to her face.

Just give us a minute. It's my day. It's going to end how I say it ends.

It's an epic day that will fade to black, stamp itself into history, and live on for eternity. Even if we don't. And if so, we went out with a bang. All those pranks. All that mayhem. Fighting the battle of our lives.

"K-K-Kirsten...r-remember the look on their faces? Wh-when you...dumped the water on them?"

"Heh-heh."

Coming from the same spot where I spotted that smoke, a bright light ignites the gloomy orange glow of the overhead lamps. I know what the smoke is. And the lights.

Car exhaust.

And headlights.

It's a running car, which noses out from its parking spot and turns toward us, blinding me from where I kneel on the ground. The car races in our direction, sending a shiver of terror through me and using up the dregs of my adrenaline. It's too much like the things that came after us all afternoon.

"K-Kirsten..." I turn to my friend. The bane of my existence. "S-s-sometimes...I...j-just...really...hate you."

"Heh-heh...H-h—huh..."

"K-K-Kirsten?" I hold her cheek, put my nose to hers, and cover her with my warm exhalations, feeling the teensiest bit of her breath on my chin. The last she has to give.

"H-hah..."

Tires skid on ice. One of the car's doors swings open, and boots crunch onto snow. A person's body falls hard and gets back up.

"*Quinn!*"

"Hah-hap..."

"K-Kirsten? Wh-what is it?"

My friend's eyes open, barely, creased at the edges. Her pupils align with mine as I hold her close.

"H-H-Happy...Anti...V-V-Valentine's...Day. S-s-s...s-s-slut."

Hands reach under my elbows and pull me up. Kirsten's head lulls to the side, but someone slides into my place to keep her from falling. They gasp when they see what's happened to her arm.

I'm dragged to the car and dumped in the backseat. The heat inside is overpowering. It probes the turtle shell of frigid armor I'm wearing, looking for a path to my skin. Kirsten is thrown onto the backseat from the other side, and we lean into each other—me shivering and sniffling and chattering, her not moving one bit.

Bridie gets behind the wheel and guns it.

October 10, 1998—Eight Months Later

It's third and long. Ten seconds to halftime. We're just past Saint Mary's High School's forty-five-yard line. The clock drops to nine seconds.

Eight...

Going to keep dropping to zero.

We're kicking off in the third and down by eleven. Not the best situation, and not the worst either, especially against Saint Mary's. But they don't need to take tonight from us. They won their Homecoming game last week. I could care less about the standings. They just can't have tonight too.

It's almost dusk. A crimson horizon bleeds to lavender, then black, where stars peek out between the shredded remnants of a passing storm. The lights have been on for half an hour, reflecting the rainwater pooled on the track, gleaming off players' helmets.

Steam billows through their face guards, enveloping the line of scrimmage in a cloud. Lance Molkowski's helmet pivots left and right, and he calls out the play, probably a Hail Mary to Charlie Sink. Nate Butcher stands with his hands stuck in his armpits and sneers, believing he could have got us an easy three—which yeah right. And anyway, Charlie's got hands like Venus flytraps. Doesn't matter if he's covered. If he makes it past the ten-yard line and the ball is on target, he'll get it over the line and pick the turf from his teeth if he has to.

The stands are impossibly loud. My ears already ring, and my voice is hoarse. My calves are killing me, but the girls keep cheering, so I do too. I arc my pom-poms high in the sky with every leap. Our squad joins the frenzy of the crowd, abandoning any pretense of coordination. Our mascot jumps so high, I fear he'll hurt an ankle on landing.

The snap comes. Helmets crash, and a swell of green uniforms rushes to the outside of our line. Lance sees the blitz, drops his throwing arm, and skitters out of the pocket. Our linesmen break the attack, but their linebacker makes it past our tight end, skidding on mud but keeping his feet.

Downfield, Charlie hits the thirty, the twenty-five. He's double-guarded.

The Saint Mary's linebacker knocks our halfback off his feet and opens the way to our quarterback.

Lance runs, stealing inches from the linebacker and closing in on the line of scrimmage. An opposing tackle, held in check by ours, lashes out and catches jersey. Lance pivots, his arm pulling back, long fingers pressed between the grass-stained lacing on the pigskin.

I jump higher and stomp into puddles on the track. And I scream, killing the other girls' ears, but their screams kill mine too.

The linebacker dives.

Lance is in mid-stride when his arm levers forward, sending the ball soaring on a clean trajectory, just as the linebacker's shoulder makes impact with his hip.

Charlie is past the twenty, watching the ball. The defenders clock it, too, fingers splayed, testing the bounds of passer interference.

Charlie puts up his hands, showing-off-a-baby style, waiting for the delivery. He's beyond the ten when he drops his hands and his leading foot presses hard into the turf, signaling a change of course. The defenders collide with him.

The crowd's pitch rises.

The angle of the ball's descent doesn't align with Charlie's position. His head turns. It's clear the ball is aiming for Danny Molson, younger brother to star alumnus Joe Molson, up-jumped sophomore and varsity debutante. His hands are out. He's only got one man tailing him. Danny has left his side of the field for the surprise play. We're putting all our eggs in one basket. One ball for four receivers.

But Danny's not his older brother. He's not even Charlie Sink. He's only on varsity because our upperclassman receivers were...Well, they were at the mall in February. The crowd's bellowing transforms jarringly into a terrified intake of breath.

The ball passes between Danny's hands and hits him in the chest. He claps his arms closed like alligator jaws, and the ball rebounds off them, going up in his face. His hands find the ball's contours, press into them, and hold it against his face guard. He's at the five-yard line.

Defenders lunge from front and back, and Danny can't see a damn thing. He's speared in the thighs, his legs taken out from under him. Danny spins midair, chest up, crossing the thick white line before his shoulders hit the torn blue-sprayed turf. He skids farther into the end zone, trailing three defenders.

The ball protrudes like a growth from his head. It never touches the ground.

The ref's arms go up. His whistle pierces the crowd's roar.

Then everyone really ruins their vocal cords.

We jump and hug while the players on the field jostle the dazed younger Molson, who nearly walks off with the ball before the ref tugs it away. Nathan gets his moment and kicks an easy one between the uprights, raising another swell from the crowd before halftime.

The team leaves the field under a final volley of cheers, clapping pom-poms, and a sideshow from our mascot. When they've passed into the tunnel under the bleachers, the mascot follows, and I rest my voice with the rest of the squad. It's only minutes now until the big show.

I scan the crowd, looking for a face I know to be stationed off to the side of the blue-and-white-bedecked student section. When I spot him, I shake my pom-poms and shout his name.

Joe Molson notices and waves back. I point to the tunnel his brother just stumbled down. He laughs, shrugs disbelievingly, and keeps clapping, grinning from ear to ear. Behind him, Alex shakes him by the shoulders, making him crack up even more. Then Alex gives him a noogie.

Next to them, Prairie leans away from the horseplay, smiling uneasily. This isn't her scene at all, not one bit, but we wouldn't take no for an answer. Joe finally convinced her to come. She brushes stray brown hairs behind her ear, tucking them under the band of a dark purple eyepatch that matches her jacket.

The patch grew on her, or so she told me. By the time she was ready for a false eye, she told the doctors no way. The patch felt more honest or something. Nothing would bring back the vision a centipede's pincers had ripped away from her. A false eye would only make people stare harder, trying to figure out what was off, until her impatience forced her to explain.

As if you couldn't already tell something bad happened to her. The centipede left a scar from her hairline to her chin, cutting her lips in two and forcing her to part her hair on the opposite side.

I've never told her, but Prairie could march straight into the middle of the student section and be crowd-surfed for the rest of the game if she wanted. From our classmates' point of view, she's not the same Prairie who walked into the mall that day. And it's the same with her parents.

They haven't been on good terms since her lie to end all lies, which ended with her critically wounded, traumatized for life, and worse yet, at a mall. Somehow, my name was left out of the story.

I'm guessing she said the ruse started with her claim of going to my house that morning, so she gets away with spending most of her afternoons in my room, cramming for AP exams and forcing my own grades up in the process—thanks very much, Prairie. And God help me, I can sing all of *Third Stage* from memory. But I know I'll miss the jam sessions when she's gone to whatever school I surely can't follow her to next year, so I put up with it.

She winces when I bark her name and flicks her wrist, giving a weak wave. Then the horseplay comes for her. Omri shakes her shoulders. He isn't the only beefcake who came with Alex. I wave to them all: Alex, Omri, Ramon, Brian, and Tremaine, who waves his silver hook.

"Line it up, girls," Raina says. "Shake those pom-poms."

Our squad forms a tunnel, twelve girls to a side, reaching from the tunnel to the field while the Homecoming court members mingle and laugh in the tunnel, awaiting their cue to process.

Principal Marini walks past us, tiptoes through the mud, and takes a microphone from the AV club president. She thanks everyone for coming, gives a brief spiel about the school's history and heritage, how we're all doing such a great job of upholding—blah, blah, blah— then announces the court. Nine couples total, including the king and queen. whose coronation is usually saved for this moment.

But this year's was announced at yesterday's pep rally. Not even they could upstage the big show.

We wear our cheer smiles the whole time, and thankfully, Marini sticks to the script. She makes no mention of the Valentine's Day massacre.

There was talk of a vigil or a moment of silence or something. No one wanted it. Not for Homecoming. Having survived the incident myself, I agree with the decision. We've already had a moment of silence at prom, a slideshow at graduation, a beginning-of-the-year memorial service, and more than enough candlelight vigils, school prayer assemblies, and church petitions on top of all the private funerals and civic services.

Now it's time for a party, a rebirth, a look to the future.

Let the conspiracy theories fade into the background and the legal challenges enter the long tedious phases of review and appeal before what I assume will be an overall patchwork of disappointing conclusions. Let the surveyors figure out how extensive the underground network is. Let the environmentalists protest the government. Let those battles happen on their own fields.

Tonight, it's Holy Trinity versus Saint Mary's, and the only fight is on the gridiron. We both lost people that day, and we want to move on.

Not that everyone won't be getting a big reminder any minute now.

Bridie's the one person I feel is missing tonight. It's strange not to have her at home anymore, not to mention school too.

After Valentine's Day, there wasn't much said between us. She got me to the emergency crews, who'd only showed up moments before I busted down that door. We kept on being sisters, but when she left for Loyola, she actually told me to visit whenever I wanted, without making it sound like a false promise. I've already taken her up on it a couple of times.

Once because I insisted she come watch Skye perform on Navy Pier. He was talking it up since the beginning of the school year. Skye and I have a couple of classes together now. We talk, and by that I mean, like, normal talk. We joke around. We're...buddies. On the pier, Bridie listened for one song and told me to gag her with a spoon.

The court passes through our gauntlet of fluttering blue-white pom-poms. I look across at Raina. She has bags under her eyes, and when she isn't waving pom-poms or performing, her posture droops under the weight of her increased responsibilities.

Raina took a job at her father's garage, worked all summer, and still picks up afternoons and weekends when she isn't cheering. I only really see her at practice and in the cafeteria, but she doesn't talk much. She's too damn tired.

I never ask why she tries to do it all. I think I already know. All it takes is remembering how her father's face lit up for us, how much he liked the idea of his daughter having good friends, doing well in school, and having options. Mr. Harris broke his back keeping a roof over his family's head, and once he was gone, Raina stepped up to make sure it stayed there. As for the rest of it—her teenage years, leading cheer, occasionally getting into trouble...The usual hijinks aside, I've seen her face a couple of times in the paper on articles covering the local army base protests. I think she does that for him, too, even if it drains her to do it.

Raina catches my eye, and I just cheer-smile because I don't really know how to look at her. I think there's something about me that disappoints her.

Once last month, before a prayer assembly, she sighed and muttered, "I'm just here for the weighted GPA," and I didn't know what to say.

I want to ask her how she's doing, but I feel like I'd be plunging the handle on a TNT detonator, so I let it lie and tell myself I'll work up the nerve someday.

She cheer-smiles back, but her face is weary. Not even the paw prints on her cheeks add much joy. Still, she tilts her head toward the court as if to say, *These frickin' chumps?*

The crowd claps and hoots its approval as the king and queen receive their crowns and scepters. When they leave, the marching band assembles at midfield. Our mascot re-emerges from the tunnel and runs the gauntlet up and down, high-fiving us all.

"Ready?" Raina calls.

We robotically respond, "Yes, Captain."

The band launches into its performance, beginning with some big brass number. We don't have to do anything for a few more minutes.

Raina comes up beside me. "I can't believe we're doing this."

"*We're* not doing anything, technically."

"We're enabling. Look it up."

"I don't know," I tell her, gazing at the crowd still geared up from the Hail Mary touchdown, watching out of the corner of my eye while the mascot jumps and waves. "I got a good feeling about it, whether I like it or not."

I honestly don't know if I do. It's just something to say to Raina, to get her on my side, which is where I truly wish for her to be.

The band concludes its first number. Fans start to rise, stretching their backs and legs and turning to leave for the restrooms and concessions, but everyone in the student section stays put. They start hooting, expecting something to happen. The band's bass line starts a drum roll. They've been told this halftime will be special, besides the presentation of the Homecoming court. They just don't know why.

The conductor throws his baton two stories high in the air and roars at the crowd.

"Are you there, Bobcats?"

He catches the baton. The drum line builds onto the roll, cymbals shivering, snares rattling. Then come the deep brasses, the trumpets, cornets, flutes, and piccolos, belting out the opening of the school fight song. It stuns just about everyone into watching. Led by the students, the whole crowd roars the response.

"Bobcats here! Bobcats ready!"

Our squad lines up on the track, hands on hips, cheer smiles on.

Our mascot skips in front of us, waving on the crowd, pointedly using only their left arm.

We start our cheer, the most rote one we have, waving pom-poms, kicking up our knees, chanting to the music. The crowd matches us word for word.

One by one, pair by pair, our squad members sprint past the mascot standing center front. They somersault or reverse-somersault, nail their landings, cheer-smile, and punch the air.

Halfway through the chant, two members—both sophomores because no way any of us older girls wanted to do it—land somersaults on either side of the mascot.

The chant goes on. "Foes retreat and Bobcats roar! That's the fight we have in store!"

The sophomores lift off the mascot's head, revealing the person inside, sporting a perfect blond ponytail held in place by shining blue and white ribbons.

The crowd nearly doesn't finish its chant.

One of the sophomores undoes the mascot suit's back zipper. The student section erupts in chaos, jumping up and down, throwing into the air their beanies, scarves, and gloves, popcorn, candy, noisemakers, literally everything they have.

The suit slips down to the ground, revealing Kirsten's slender figure, hip cocked saucily to the side. Her remaining arm is held high, the nub of her other one noticeably pointed up too. She's sleeveless in her uniform and in a skirt without leggings. Goosebumps stick out the instant the cold air hits.

Everyone loses it. Even the adults in the crowd. Everyone this side of the Mississippi and a little beyond knows the tragedy of poor Kirsten Fortner.

She steps out from the suit and joins the cheer, starting small.

We're the only ones who knew about this, and we still don't know everything Kirsten has in mind. She disappeared all summer. From what we heard, she was working with Coach on something, but then, apparently—according to Raina—she dismissed Coach.

No one was allowed to see her practice. Not until it was perfect. Our instructions were to perform the fight song like normal, besides the mascot unmasking, and let her do her thing. I mean, after all, can't we trust little ole Kirsten Fortner?

As if.

She skips along the track, pumping her fist in the air, getting everyone on their feet and leaning in, to the point of falling over the guardrails. The whole crowd is into it. Students. Old folks. Little kids. The random geeks and dorks dragged against their will. The visiting stands cheer, knowing what they're watching. Kirsten turns and waves to them, raising another cheer all around.

"Stout of heart and strong of will! Bobcats always fit the bill!"

She reaches the end of the stands, turns, and sprints down the track. The crowd goes wild, anticipating what's to come. Kirsten reaches midfield and dips forward, planting her arm on the track. She cartwheels once, twice, and keeps going all the way down. Kirsten plants her feet one last time and performs a backflip, executes a perfect landing, back arched, smiling to the heavens, arm held high.

The stands enter riot mode, the stomping and cheering overcoming the fight song's melody. The band drowns out as the stadium is filled with the unadulterated joy of witnessing a phoenix's rebirth. Tonight, all of Madison cheers for Kirsten Fortner.

She goes the opposite way, sprints, cartwheels, and ends on a back flip. She skips back to midfield, pumping her arm.

We set up for our pyramid for the closing verses, but Kirsten bumps our normal top flyer out of the way. The bases grab her, readying for the toss.

"For real?" Raina gasps, but it's too late.

She's taken her place at the base of the pyramid and springs me up onto her shoulders. Then the bases toss Kirsten up over my head. She sits on my shoulders.

"Bobcats roar! Fight and roar!" the crowd hollers.

I pitch my neck forward, and Kirsten somersaults down into our bases' waiting arms. She bounces to her feet and performs a final single-arm cartwheel and backflip, ending right in front of the bleachers.

The Homecoming court and the football team watches from the tunnel as the crowd loses its mind. Fans throw more things on the track. Streamers, ribbons, confetti. School-branded hats and scarves and sweatshirts. The court members shower her with their corsages and boutonnieres. Kirsten picks up the gaudiest of them all, slips it over her wrist, and blows kisses to the crowd. The bandleader offers her his baton. The Homecoming queen crowns her and hugs her.

Kirsten breaks into tears now, making the glitter on her cheeks shine brighter. Joe and the beefcakes jump up and down like madmen, and Prairie laughs disbelievingly, without a shred of irony.

Kirsten turns to us, and the squad forms a group hug, with her at the center. Raina makes her way inside, rocks Kirsten inside a bear hug, and slaps her back, then passes her to me. Kirsten looks at me with her green, green eyes, cheer smile on for the crowd, our pupils locking onto each other's. Neither of us blink. We don't hug right away. We just look at each other.

"You brat," I say, which she could only tell if she read my lips.

Kirsten comes in for a hug. I squeeze her tight, and her nub presses into my shoulder.

"Freaking love you."

The words echo back so swiftly, I can't tell if it's me saying it or her.

We release and she turns around, belonging to the crowd once again.

Raina comes back and puts her arm around my shoulder. She's warm, and I don't want her to move. She shakes her head and mutters, "Fortner," before sighing and slapping my back. "Let's clean this crap up," she says, stooping to retrieve apparel thrown onto the track.

I join her, picking up a beanie and scrunching up a scarf.

There's a particularly deep puddle where there's a rut in the track, and despite the crowd, the water's surface is still. I squat next to it and drop the things I've picked up into a little pile. I spread my fingers. Taking a deep breath, my heart racing, I press my hand down to the pavement.

The puddle barely covers my fingers. It's cold. Not warm at all. Not rising.

I exhale. My heart slows down.

I remind myself it rained this afternoon. It'll be dry by tomorrow, when the crowds are gone, this game is in the bag, and the stadium goes quiet for another week. It'll be dry by the time we get dressed up for Homecoming, go out for dinner, and dance until midnight. It'll be dry by the time we head to class Monday morning, full of new memories and gossip and plans on making more of them both.

The water doesn't rise. The ground doesn't cave in.

We're safe here. We're alive. And we're living.

THE END

How Did You Do?

We hope you enjoyed the book and wouldn't mind giving us a little feedback. Thank you so much for your support.

Please scan the QR code to answer a few questions about your reading experience.

For more fun-filled deaths, please check out the TNTD series.
Available on Amazon: <u>The Try Not to Die Collection</u>

About the Author

P.W. Feutz is the author of *The Sun Is a Circle Meant for Serving* and co-author of *Try Not to Die: Back at Grandma's House*. He lives in Michigan with his wife and two rabbits, Shirley and Watson.

Visit https://pwfeutzauthor.wixsite.com/p-w--feutz for more.

https://www.facebook.com/pwfeutz

https://www.instagram.com/pwfeutz/

https://www.threads.net/@pwfeutz

Acknowledgements

I owe special thanks to Mark Tullius, who has championed my work with a pedal-to-the-metal intensity since we first met. The very idea of this book wouldn't exist without your gracious invitation to join the TNTD family and pitch a number of my own ideas, the winner of which developed into this book. Presented with such an opportunity, I've written what is probably my most fun story yet.

My thanks is also due to Lyndsey Smith for your editorial wisdom. You've elevated this simple tale of frenemies and foes into the polished story that it is now. The final version of this novel bites harder, roars louder, and lurks more unnervingly in the shadows thanks to your meticulous work.

Thanks also to the myriad authors, instructors, artists, and fellow scribblers I've either pestered or associated with over the years, whose tidbits of wisdom, criticism, enthusiasm, and camaraderie live long in the folds of my gray matter, even if you don't remember anything about what you said or how we met. Believe me: I remember, and it helps me every day.

Thanks as well to Mom and Dad. You always had books in the house, you always encouraged my creativity, and you had perfect taste when choosing '90s-era blockbusters to bring me to. No, I wasn't too scared to keep watching *Jurassic Park*, and yes, I know what the middle finger in *Mrs. Doubtfire* means now.

Lastly, thanks to my lovely wife, who continues to encourage my writing after years of toil and doubt (all mine). You bring that Lewis Hamilton-let's-keep-pushing mentality I need to get across the finish line. And I absolutely have to credit you with the beefcakes' existence. Joe Molson would've been far lonelier without their company, and the book would've been far poorer without them.

Download Your Free Copy

Includes the first two chapters and one death scene
from each of the first seven books in the Try Not to Die series.
Also look for Volume II which contains books 8-14.

<u>Download for free.</u>

Made in the USA
Columbia, SC
06 January 2025

49194168R00191